ONE OFF

One Off

Mark Kestigian

RED ALL OVER

Published by Red All Over Publishing 2012

Red All Over Publishing is a division of Ground Floor Media Group

www.redallover.com.au

A CIP catalogue record for this book is available from the National Library of Australia

ISBN 978-0-9873915-0-6 (pbk)

Cover design by Ground Floor Media Group

To my parents, Mike and Jean Kestigian
There are not enough words in all the world's dictionaries to capture all that
you are — and have been to me — from Willimantic, Connecticut to Kallista,
Victoria — and everywhere in between.

To Leo and Esther French and Vartan and Vartanoush Kestigian
The best grandparents ever.

To the 'kids in fur'
Socrates, Lord Beazley, Plato, Duke Ellington and Princess Tara.

And most especially to my dear wife Karen
For her endless love and unconditional support.

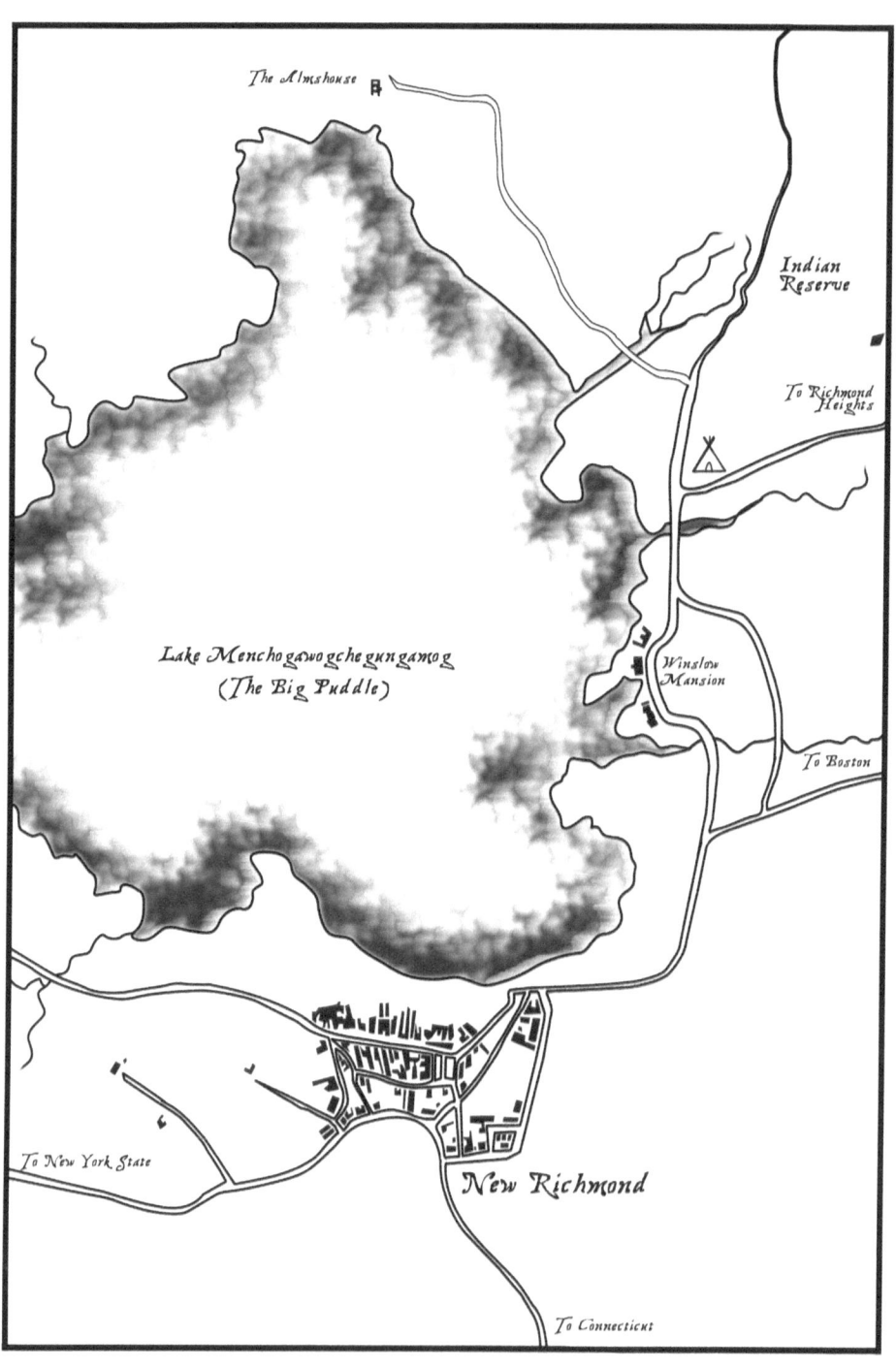

The Almshouse

Indian Reserve

To Richmond Heights

Lake Menchogawogchegungamog
(The Big Puddle)

Winslow Mansion

To Boston

To New York State

New Richmond

To Connecticut

PROLOGUE

Call me Walt – or Walter if you must. Anything's better than Howard, which is my real first name. It's not that I don't like that name. It's what comes after it that pisses me off. Would you want to be called Howard Johnson? I kid you not and no, I'm not descended from the mega food chain that lit up highways between Montpelier and Miami long before the Golden Arches littered up the landscape.

I'm descended from a rather congested – some might say dyslexic gene pool - that contains connections with world leaders and red-blooded bluebloods as well as with a small, nomadic tribe who became inexorably intertwined with this aforementioned famous food group before getting fed up and fending for itself.

Actually, my real name isn't Howard Johnson. Well, it is and it isn't. I preferred being called by my middle name – Walter – just to keep kids and other n'er do wells from laying one after another tired, old references to HoJo's on me. So the full handle is Howard Walter Johnson II. The 'official' name is Howard Walter Johnson's II, but let's keep it to Walt for now, and I'll explain more about this later.

I have a big story to tell. It includes tales of murder and other mayhems; misappropriations of Native Americans' lands; dastardly business dealings; ribald sex romps and other feckless acts of daring doo-doo fuelled by the two substances of choice by hopeless wanderers – booze and more booze.

Have I missed any hot spots? I trust not, but no matter if I have. At least this gives you some idea of what to expect in this tale that opened with the rather obvious reference to a supposed American masterpiece.

I never thought much of that book. I couldn't even figure out what was so great about the opening, other than the fact that the name

Ishmael sounds like something you'd find on the end of a fishhook, which sits well with a mariner's tale.

I'm not boasting, but this book will cover a lot more ground than detailing 150 ways to tenderize whale blubber or how to sail up wind at night. I am, however, a novice novelist so it might take me a while to hit my straps. That's why I've highlighted several titillating topics that will figure prominently throughout this wondrous journey.

While some of you might like the sections dealing with death, destruction and other misdeeds, there are also plenty of bits bound to cover the full spectrum of emotions between laughing and crying. It will cover all these things, not because I'm some hero of heroic proportions. Quite the contrary. I'm just an ordinary guy whose life (after the boring bits are edited out) contains more extraordinary and bizarre tales than all of TV's mid-afternoon soap operas combined.

That's enough of the hard sell for those of you still deciding if this book's worth buying. I've got lots of ground to cover so you might as well pay the fare and come along for the ride.

Chapter One

My father's father was a murderer. But he never did any time. He never got sent away, unless you consider leaving your homeland and every living soul you knew since childbirth, for an unknown country half-way around the world, being sent away. He wasn't a soldier or any other occupation that might have made this heinous act 'legitimate'. He was just a young man, very young, perhaps no more than 14, who killed another human being and got away with it.

Not that I know very much about this heinous act. I didn't even hear about it from him or any other member of my family. It was dropped on me one night by a very drunken pal of his from the old country - Armenia. I don't know why he felt the need to share this diabolical info with me, but he did and I've hated both of them – scratch that – most old Armenian men ever since. This might seem like a harsh judgement, but not to me. My grandfather and his old cronies were very hard to get to know in large part because they spoke a language that sounded like something Venusians would parlez. Forget about getting to know them and why they might have done any number of misdeeds in some misbegotten and forgotten land. Everything – even the simplest sign of civility – saying 'hello' was hard work. So as soon as I could afford a set of car keys, I said 'goodbye', because I could no longer live under the same roof as a murderer.

That was then. And now, I am back, still unable to live with the stain of being related to a killer, but unable to move on until I can reach some sort of closure on this sad family secret.

My paternal grandfather's name is Sarkis Bedrosian and as you've already learned, he used to call Armenia home. For those in need of a geography lesson, Armenia sits on a small spit of land between the Black and Caspian seas, surrounded by Georgia and Azerbaijan to its north and east; Iran and Turkey to its southeastern and southwestern flanks respectively. About the same size as Belgium, Armenia contains a range of mountains, rivers and fertile yet rocky landscapes. It sounds like a great place if you dig stone walls.

Recognized as the first country to adopt Christianity, no doubt because its humble inhabitants needed all the divine guidance they could muster given that their homes were located on one of the world's great freeways for world conquerors. If there were roadside plaques noting the big names that plundered their way through Armenia's steep steppes, they would include none other than Alexander the Great. Sooner or later, Big Al and the assorted other highly-skilled practitioners in the fine arts of Rape and Pillaging 101, wound up trespassing through Armenia and ravaging the noblest of the Near East's savage lands.

It would seem some of these skills rubbed off on the locals who were fortunate, or unfortunate enough, to have passed on these primordial skills to the likes of dear old granddad. Now, you may think it odd that I never asked him about his murderous past. But just how do you broach this subject? And when? Do you do it while sipping a cup of tea at breakfast? Or perhaps wait until he's got a carving knife in his hand about to slice into the Thanksgiving Day turkey?

I did ask my father a couple of times, but got nowhere there. In fact, I never could get close to mentioning the word 'murder' or even 'kill' anywhere near my granddad's name. While such foul deeds often motivate many others to up and move their families, my Dad decided this was far too drastic and opted instead to simply shift a few vowels and consonants around until he'd changed his birth name of Torkum Bedrosian into Howard Johnson's. No big deal. Actors have been doing that for years. When Marion Morrison went looking for a new name, he didn't go for Kentucky Fried, did he? No, he settled for John Wayne. When Archie Leach wanted to come up with something that exuded more cool than a polar ice cap, he chose Cary Grant, not McDonald's Fucking Hamburgers! But oh no, not my Dad. Torkum Bedrosian probably is a suck-face name in Armenia, let alone in the United States. So what does he do? He swaps it for one of the daggiest, most uncool and sorriest names imaginable and in so doing, irrevocably changed mine as well. Still, in retrospect, the name change was not high on my list of pet family hates. To be honest, I'd long since gotten over that problem.

Changing one's name is easy. What hasn't changed lo the many years that have passed, however, is the knowledge that swishing around in my gene pool is a globule with a big red stain attached to it – indelibly perhaps unless I can come up with some way to remove it.

The best anyone was able to offer me about the murder, was that it had something to do with the attempts by the then Turkish rulers to overrun Armenia while most other countries were getting ready for, or were already deeply embroiled in The War to End All Wars. There have been many books and articles published about various attempts by supposedly bloodthirsty Turkish regimes committing genocide on the Armenians, but I'm not so sure. While both my father's parents spoke from time to time about horrible goings-on in the old country, none of their siblings ever suffered from the supposed uncivil actions taken by the Turks against the Armenians. I never met any of their brothers and sisters, but I was assured many times they not only survived, but either stayed on in Armenia or moved to other parts of the globe, including Lebanon, France, South Africa and Australia.

It was rare when my grandfather would talk about the old country, but when he did, it was usually about his run-ins with mythical-sounding beasts like the tur, (a native wild goat), the mouflon (wild sheep) and the chamois, which was a cross between a goat and an antelope. I don't know whether these beasts really existed or whether it was all part of some one-man crusade to cover up the real past with flowery, bright tales of Camelot-like proportion.

I wasn't looking for much from my father's father. Sometimes I could almost overlook his murderous past. That was part of his story; his journey. Mine was much simpler. It was just about trying to fit in with my all American friends whose grandfathers had no such stains on their genetic fibres. There wasn't a lot of ethnic diversity in the town where I grew up. Most people's backgrounds were so English, French fries were considered ethnic cuisine. My friends and their relatives differed from my Dad's Dad in another way, too. They didn't massacre the English language every time they opened their mouths and even understood the importance of all things Massachusetts Bay Colony - including baked beans, steamed clams and Yaz.

Which brings me to my mother's side of the familial foliage. While my father's parents arrived in America via boat, my mother's forebears did so as well – only their boat was a lot older and much more famous. It was called the Mayflower and therein lies another huge tale that I will get to shortly. While America is filled with great stories about how people from different backgrounds came together to form millions of new cross breeds, my particular genetic pairing never clicked. I was neither Armenian nor American as the azure-tinged blood that flowed through my mother's veins meant she craved all things English, boasting a direct genealogical tie to Edward Winslow, who soon became one of the fledgling Plymouth Colony's first governors. Just how the great great great great great granddaughter of America's First Fleet wound up with the one and only son of an uneducated immigrant from Nowheresville, Near East is indeed another story I hope to learn more about as I try, after unsuccessfully spending the first 33 years of my wretched existence, running from all and sundry family members in hopes of hatching a new identity; a new beginning.

It was not going to be easy. While moving away helped wipe away any thoughts about the ancient actions of my grandfather in his hilly-billy homeland, try and come up with an answer to the following genetic riddle: What do you get when you mix a Third-World country bumpkin with a First World wondrous woman? Answer: a surefire Second-Class citizen – pure and simple.

Suffering from dual-familial identity crises were just two of my problems. It didn't help that I hailed from a town that would have made a bombed out Beirut suburb look glamorous. What's New Richmond, Massachusetts really like? Imagine you're driving along a pleasant-enough-looking country road that you've never seen before. A sign in the distance appears out of nowhere and before long – you are right beside it. It reads: Welcome to 'Cholera, Colorado' or 'Bubonic Plague, Pennsylvania' or 'Shithole, Idaho'. None of these places is likely to figure high on anyone's list of 'must-sees'.

So let's get this straight: I'm not returning home because I want to. Rather, I am like a reluctant salmon that fights its way up river to where it all began so others may begat, if you get my drift. There's one big difference between me and the salmon and I'm not talking about which one has bigger gills. The salmon knows it's a fucking salmon. They belong to a recognizable tribe that come hell or high water – swim, eat, breathe, spawn and yes, die, knowing where they belong. Me, I got no idea of where I fit in due in large part to the fact that the bonds attached to my tribe; my nuclear family were detonated in less time than it took the Enola Gay's uranium-enriched cargo to go splat all over Hiroshima. No, I envy the hell out of the salmon. I didn't want to come back to where it all began, but something way down deep inside kept telling me that I must go back before I can ever contemplate moving forward.

There's one more interesting little piece of the aquatic equation that I might as well bring up before we really start humming along: The obtuse reference to 'Moby Dick' was not coincidental. I've read and re-read that book without knowing why exactly – until now. You see, there are a couple of similarities between that tale and this one that could best be described as 'spooky'.

The most obvious one is the overriding role played by water. My forebears floated ashore to the New World in search of new beginnings while Melville's characters hit the high seas in search of one very old foe. And while I would never characterize myself as an Ahab-like figure, we do share an interesting physical feature or should I say disfigurement? We both have only one of something most people claim in pairs. And while his leg was chewed off by an obviously inflamed marine mammal, my physical impairment carried no epic tale around it. I was graced at birth with only one ear. On its own, it doesn't sound like much of a problem. When someone loses an arm in a sawmill accident or in a car smash, they undergo monumental amounts of pain, great losses of plasma followed by blood-curdling screams. Long after the pain and anguish has expired, these sorts of one-offs at least leave the victim with a story to tell. Because I was born with the impairment, there was no pain; no anguish; no story to tell. But that's not quite right. It's not right at all. I'd give anything to experience the pain that goes through anyone injured in a serious accident, because at least I could then feel something. How am I to feel or even make sense of all the stares I've gotten over the years from people who showed more compassion for the Elephant Man than they did for me? Even my mate Ahab and his impairment differ

7

from me and mine in that he *asked* for his impairment. He poked the bloody harpoons one too many times at the Leviathan and it struck back. I didn't ask to be born this way and I certainly didn't ask to be greeted by enough stares of fear and loathing to fill the earth's oceans. That's enough about me. For now, anyway.

For the sake of this story though, it could be argued that I am some sort of modern-day Captain Ahab – not roaming the high seas in search of the white whale, but rather the hills and dales of New England in an attempt to bring some order to the chaotic pathos abounding around me and my unkind kin(d).

ↄ

"Hey, Johnson – where's the 'Road Kill' piece?"

This is probably as good a time as any to fill you in on how I earn a living. You don't have to be Sherlock Holmes to figure out I'm in the news business. What you wouldn't know is the particular newspaper I work for. It's called *'The Record'* and is the oldest paper of its kind in all 50 states. What kind? That's another story in itself. It used to come out daily but for reasons known only to one deranged past publisher, now hits the streets twice a week – Wednesdays and Saturdays. *'The Record'* has been owned by the same family – the James' since its inception in 1799. Coincidentally, John Adams, (another relative on my mother's side), was just the young country's second president when *'The Record'* started, while in France, a young upstart named Napoleon Bonaparte assumed power.

It's got quite a history. It's also much more colorful than my own newspaper record which consists of three different daily rags in various parts of the country in eight years. Even in my own humble experience, *'The Record'* stands well and truly in a league of its own. Apart from the supermarket tabloids, it's probably the country's most famous – or infamous newspaper – which will become apparent shortly.

Few people would know anything about the town where *'The Record'* is printed, apart from its 10,000 or so inhabitants. Located on the southern shore of a near Great Lake-sized body of water with an Indian name that's longer than the alphabet, sits New Richmond, (originally

Richmond Plantation), a quiet town directly due west from the Bay Colony's original settlement in Plymouth, Massachusetts, nestled neatly near the borders of neighboring New York State and Connecticut.

New Richmond is shaped like a horseshoe caressing Lake Menchogawogchegungamog's southern shoreline. It was, and effectively still is, the center of power for this tri-state region, which, to be honest, is no great claim to fame. And while readership numbers have been in steady decline in more recent times, the paper has picked up a cult following around the country – mostly because of its all-too-colorful mistakes rather than for any good deeds.

I know a bit about New Richmond in general and 'The Record' in particular, because I spent the better part of my youth delivering its contents to the good townspeople of neighboring Richmond Heights, which might best be described as the area's food bowl, housing much of the region's larger farms. In fact, the residents of Richmond Heights would've been easily outnumbered by the number of cows, sheep, pigs, geese and other assorted creatures running amok. The two toughest things about having the only newspaper round in Richmond Heights were the vast distances between mailboxes and the near-constant smell of fresh cow, pig and horse shit wafting in the breeze. The only good thing about having the newspaper round was that it got me away from my own personal piles of cow and pig shit that piled up at a monotonous rate at my grandfather's mini-farm.

New Richmond had changed quite a bit since I last saw it, though. As a boy, it was a big deal to leave the farm and go downtown to do some shopping and grab a meal with my father. It seemed to me some of the old shops had given way to vacant lots catering to daytrippers and other interlopers, which seemed odd because few locals ventured downtown anymore, preferring the air-conditioned and banal safety of strip malls.

I was venturing down these mean streets for the first time in over 15 years for one not so good reason: I needed a job. And word around the traps was if you were semi-illiterate and enjoyed a social drink or three, you could score a reporting round at 'The Record'. The main drag seemed much narrower than I'd remembered it. Then again, the shops likewise looked different – and not in a good way. Many of them dated back to the late 1800s. Some old buildings look historic when they're that old. These just looked like they needed a good lie down. Most of the town pre-dating this period had long since been destroyed by fire, time or unscrupulous property developers. The first building one sees is an old folks home. Next to it – a funeral parlor with the slogan, "We Never Rest." I was soon at the other end of the village where the faded red bricks of the police station and equally-jaded city hall stood side by side. Strange place: death and dying at one end and theft and lying at the other.

I got out and walked back along the street toward the newspaper – a typical 150-year-old, two-story brick building. Much of it was taken up by a huge printing press that I couldn't see, but certainly could hear chugging away. I figured they'd given me the wrong street number, but as I entered the doorway, I remembered from my boyhood days that the newspaper's center of gravity was not the press building itself, but a rather non-descript, two-story building directly across from '*The Record*'.

My job interview was to take place in a bar located across the street known as the 'Final Edition'. The place was still in disrepair from the last night's and/or last year's revelry. There were chairs in various states of distress both on top of the bar and loosely allied with small square tables. Any clean air in the room had long since given up and been smothered by several clouds of smoke and the stench of stale ale.

I no sooner opened the door when this voice bellowed out over the sounds of the Allman Brothers' *'Blue Sky'* blasting from a neon-lit jukebox: "What'll it be?"

"Excuse me, I'm lookin—"

"For *'The Record'* I know. Well this is the interview suite so take a seat and have a drink on me," the bartender said as she skirted around the chairs and tables to turn down the jukebox.

"Can I get an Irish coffee?" I asked, not knowing if that was a bit bold, given it was only 10.30 in the morning.

"You passed the first test. We only like drinkers here. My name's Melinda but everyone calls me 'Mel'," said this woman whose black, fluffy hair was piled up on top of her head seemingly about to scrape the derelict ceiling fans.

"Walt," I replied. "Nice to meet you."

Mel took a second look at me and realized we'd met before. "Walter. Walter Johnson, isn't it?"

"Guilty," I replied.

"Whose grilling ya?" Mel asked.

"Ah, I believe it's Martin."

"Shame."

"Excuse me?"

"Shame it's not the old lady. She's the only one knows what going on," Mel said obviously referring to the paper's notorious Publisher – Mrs. Constance Wheeler-James. "But I don't have to tell you that, Walt."

Before I could answer, the door opened and a younger, male version of Mel walked in – minus the ceiling-height hairdo. He strode in the door as if he were entering his office, which it would soon become apparent, he was.

"Hi, Walter. Sorry I'm late. Glad you found our 'office' okay," he said. "Can I get a drink, Mel?"

"You payin?"

Martin's reply was returned with a one-finger salute.

It became clear that this was not 'The New York Times'. Or any other newspaper for that matter. The seeming lack of professional journalistic qualities didn't bother me. It was rather refreshing. What did worry me though was that the woman behind the bar seemed more civilized and rational than the one running one of America's most notorious tabloids.

Martin was just about to start the interview when another regular – certainly of the bar if not the paper – stumbled in the door. Neither member of the James Gang looked up.

"You're late," Martin said to the chap without turning around. The man, aged somewhere between 40 and 59, had long black hair streaked with gray and bundled into an attempt at a ponytail. The only thing more wrinkled than his rugged face was his attire – which consisted of a faded blue blazer (with no buttons on either the sleeves or breast), a white shirt with enough spots and blotches to resemble a Jackson Pollack drip painting and torn blue jeans.

"Aaarrhgghgm," came the reply as Mel placed a glass of local beer and a shot on the bar.

"I'll talk to you later about that story for Saturday. I need to conduct an interview right now," Martin said turning to me with a Cheshire-cat sized grin. "Sorry about this, Walter. We're not usually this disorganized. It's been busier than usual with some special investigative pieces we've been working on."

"No problem," I said.

"I don't remember you, but I believe you used to live around here?" Martin said.

"Yeah. I grew up in Richmond Heights."

"Of course," Martin said. Though class lines had long since blurred, New Richmond still had a solid black stripe, delineating the HAVEs from the HAVENOTs that would've made Mason and Dixon proud. And Richmond Heights was certainly the address for practically every HAVENOT since the town was founded.

"Anyway, I saw on your resume that you'd worked in Cincinnati – at *The Post*."

"Yeah, that's right."

"Why'd you leave?"

That was a tricky question so early in the interview. Did I tell him the truth that I hated covering town council meetings and sewer line disputes so much that I slugged the regional/county editor in the mush or did I lie? "Couldn't forgive the Reds for beating the Sox in '75," I said.

Martin James' eyes lit up as if on fire before exclaiming – "Good answer. You're hired. Drinks all around!"

With that, a loud groan broke up the room's stale air. It seemed to emanate from the jukebox which was now jiving along to Fleetwood Mac's *'Go Your Own Way'*.

"For Christ's sake, Leo, go home already," Mel said to whoever Leo was behind the record machine.

"He can't cuz he's coming in to help edit copy later on," Martin said.

"Leo's editing?" Mel asked with a tone that said 'Leo' and 'editing' did not make for a perfect match.

"Ohh, yeah, good point, Mel," Martin said to his elder sister all the while staring at me. "Well, Walt, how'd you like to take a look at your new 'old' home?"

"Ahh, yeah, sure," I replied.

With that, Martin jumped out of his chair as if it were alight, gently slapped the chap holding up the bar and made his way for the door. I decided to let my colleague go first. I didn't have a lot of choice in the matter as it turned out, because he needed me to help steer him through the doorway.

"You'll see we're a bit cramped, but I'm sure we can squeeze you in," Martin said talking to me, (at least I think he was), as we crossed the town's only main drag. We entered the newspaper and headed up a narrow flight of stairs. It was quite dark, even in broad daylight, and the only sound was the ever-present chug-chug-chug of the printing press.

At the top of the stairs, Martin opened a door and a cacophony of voices greeted my one good ear.

"Hey, Marty, where's that op-ed piece for Saturday?"

Martin ignored the inquisitor and stepped around my as yet, unintroduced colleague, to show me the newsroom. It looked like the bar across the street except decaying bits of wooden furniture were replaced by rusting, squeaky metallic chairs and desks that were piled with paper and toilet-paper-sized rolls of Associated Press wire copy long enough to cover the Great Wall of China. Computers, which had quickly swept through many newsrooms over the past year or so, had not yet reached 'The Record'. Rather, antique quality Royal typewriters sat proudly amid the mess on each and every desk. Martin introduced me to about five staff members, though I couldn't hear anyone's name due to the collateral noise. My nameless and hung over comrade hovered behind me as if he too was meeting everyone for the first time. Perhaps he was.

Martin then began looking around the newsroom, I suspect for some place to seat me and/or my talkative mate. "There doesn't seem to be any empty spaces right now," Martin said cautiously.

As if on cue, the pony-tailed barfly leaned between Martin and me and proceeded to throw up everything that he had digested for the past three weeks. The end result wound up splattering all over the better part of the desk and typewriter immediately in front of us.

"What luck," Martin said without missing a beat. "A seat has just become available."

Chapter Two

Given what faced me that first day at '*The Record*', it was most appropriate that my initial piece of reporting involve a gruesome traffic accident. One of '*The Record*'s specialties was to take every day, ordinary occurrences and blow them up into tabloid-like extravaganzas. It was a technique that rarely reared its head during my stays in such Mideastern hot-spots as Cincinnati, Champagne and Indianapolis. Because in each of these cases, I was the more-or-less new kid on the block and shoved down the back of the news beats, getting stuck covering late night council sessions that inevitably involved little more than stupid property disputes and blocked septic tanks. Despite getting stuck with the most improbable events required to make 'news', my editors invariably commented on how dry and pedestrian my copy was. Try as I might, it just didn't seem possible to make some poor schmuck's backed-up sewer system sizzle – news wise that is.

And while this might sound cold and callous, I jumped at the chance to get out to the scene of this accident where there was bound to be blood, bone and god knows what else all over the road. This particular case involved a local junior high school boy who had been accidentally mowed down by an elderly driver who either had been blinded by the bright sun or blacked out for a moment or two.

Most papers would have given it a few lines at best. Not '*The Record*'. We went in for the kill, blowing it up to a half-page, including extensive interviews with the elderly driver, who it turns out had been a POW during WWII, and with the family of the deceased who had now lost both children in less than a year – the other through drowning in a neighbor's pool just four months earlier. Talk about bad luck.

For me though, it was pure magic, earning me a front page credit with my first effort. To be fair, my story's placement on the outside was due as much to the accompanying photo as to any great message contained in my humble scribbling. The photo showed the remains of the kid's bike crumpled under the front right tire of the killer vehicle.

Meanwhile, three cats were huddled around something in the middle of the street in the photo's background. It turns out they were licking what was left of the poor boy's intestines that had not yet been cleaned up. "*ROAD KILL*" screamed the front-page headline.

Welcome to '*The Record*'. In just one day and one article I drew more hate mail and vicious phone calls than in all my other work combined. That earned me much respect among my colleagues, many of whom I still hadn't met but of the ones I had, fit in one of two journalistic categories: those who were on their way down and others who were already out of the business. Way out. Not sure what that said about my own career prospects, but I didn't give a shit. Truly. Funnily enough, one of the only positive messages I got was from the father of the dead kid. He called to thank me for taking so much time to talk to them and to give their son, and I quote, "something to remember him by." I kid you not.

'YOU ARE BECOMING BLINDED BY THE MOMENT. YOU MUST OPEN YOUR INNER EAR AND LISTEN TO YOUR HEART'.

Damn, I knew there was something else I'd forgotten to mention. I swear readers, it wasn't on purpose. Doesn't everyone hear voices? Or should I say 'Voice?' I have for some time now, at least since puberty, been visited from time to time by this singular, same monotonous voice that offers the sorts of New Age mumbo-jumbo proffered above. And yes, I do get the irony in this situation – me, a one-eared freak hearing voices from beyond. To be honest, I'd become accustomed to the Voice, which I remember quite distinctly coming to me the very first night I stayed at my grandfather's farm. I was wiped out from moving stuff all day with my Dad to the farm and then having to help grandpa milk cows and feed other assorted no-hope animals before collapsing in bed.

'IT IS GOOD OF YOU TO COME. DO NOT BE AFRAID OF MY PRESENCE. I SHALL ONLY SERVE TO GUIDE YOU ON YOUR CHOSEN PATH'.

How's that for an opening line? Oddly enough, I wasn't then, nor am I now afraid of the Voice, who I refer to as Vartan, after Armenia's favorite son – Vartan Mamikonian – or just plain St. Vartan. You may have guessed from his Sainthood status that he's been gone awhile. What you may not have guessed is that he goes back – way back to 450 A.D.

and in true Armenian style, became famous for losing. Vartan and his followers had just gotten used to accepting Jesus Christ when a not so friendly neighbor in Persia told them that it was either move over to Zoroastrianism or die. They chose the latter course with many of the Armenians, including Vartan, departing this life in the process. Enough of the history lesson. If it was St. Vartan who was talking to me, I must confess that I missed him while I was doing my time in the Mideast. It was during this dry spell that I'd figured it must be the long-lost ancestor of my father's Armenian forebears, perhaps even the great man himself trying to compensate for their descendant's heinous crime. Perhaps because they were bored tending sheep in heaven or wherever the heck they were stationed. I did think it odd though that this voice, which if indeed it was from some ancient Armenian dialect, spoke fluent American English – a trait not even remotely found in my grandfather, grandmother, or any other Armenian American immigrant over the age of 60. I attributed the perfect American English to the garbled-like static sounds that occurred before Vartan 'arrived'. It was like whatever radio frequency the voice did originate from went through some sort of American dialectic mixer before reaching me.

Just what this latest visit's message meant I could only guess, but to be fair, the big V did help sway me into returning home, rather than heading farther west to try and find a whole new beginning. I opted instead for a whole new old beginning. More on this matter later. Trust me, you're going to love some of his comments.

I did get one other nice phone call following my first big '*Record*' byline – from my favorite relative – Uncle J.R. He was the black sheep of my mother's family, which was probably why we got along so well. His real name was Josiah Ross Winslow IV, but preferred to be known as J.R. – long before Larry Hagman stole the moniker in his one-dimensional portrait of a down-and-dirty, Dallas oil baron.

"Hey kid, when did you get back?" J.R. asked.

"A couple of weeks ago. You well?"

"Never better and looking forward to catching up. Still having your way with the ladies?"

"Oh yeah, New Richmond is filled with beauties so long as you don't mind 'em missing a few molars."

"You devil. Well, hang in there and pop by when you can. Got a special one for you!"

J.R. always had a 'special one' for me and to be fair, they were usually better than the ones I'd pick out for myself. Then again, he'd had a bit more practice, having been in the Navy and running riot in every seaside port from Port of Spain to Perth, Western Australia. I always found it interesting that he gravitated toward the water in much the same way as did his illustrious ancestors aboard the Mayflower. Whenever I broached this topic with him, however, he usually became uncharacteristically morose and/or violent and declared that any family matter reliant solely on some concoction of flesh and blood, was pure bullshit. 'Never met a relative I didn't dislike', was one of his favorite sayings. Though he'd left the Navy some years ago, he still enjoyed hanging around seaport towns and currently lived on the water in a dilapidated house boat in the quaint southeastern Connecticut village of Victoria – some three hours by car from New Richmond along small, windy back roads. He was only in his early 40s when he left the Navy. It was unlikely whatever pay-out he got from Uncle Sam supported him and his vices. It sure was very unlikely that any pension from being in the submarine service kept him totally afloat. Still, he was happy and living a good life. What was not to like?

"Say 'Hi' to your mother for me. See you soon, yeah?"

"Ahh, yeah. You bet," I replied. No sooner had the phone hit the cradle than it rang again.

"Hello son."

Speak of the she-devil. "Hi, Mom, how ya goin?" While the names on the male side of the family paid homage to the Mayflower connection, her own clan preferred the monikers of their most famous forebear – John Adams. She inherited the name of Elizabeth Quincy Adams (John's wife's mother's name). When combined with the Winslow name, it became quite a potent combination, though any pretense of maintaining blue blood lines was certainly smudged when the marriage to one Torkum Bedrosian-Johnson took place. I wasn't even sure if she still used my Dad's names or reverted to her earlier incarnations.

"Like you care. How long have you been home and still haven't called or come by the house?"

"Been busy and besides – what do you care?"

"Now Walter, don't be like that. Do drop by – there's much to talk about."

That sounded ominous. "Yeah, sure. Gotta go right now. Got another story to do. Oh yeah, J.R. says 'Hi'."

CLICK. The ties that bind. Some families were known for their closeness. Not us Johnsons. We were world beaters for not keeping in touch – and meaning it. There was Johnson & Johnson. And there was our clan – Johnson & not Johnson. The ties that bind, indeed.

Chapter Three

"Shoulda led with the cats."

"What?"

"THE CATS! THE CATS! They're the story, you fuckin' ass-wipe."

I was celebrating the success of my first by-line at the bar with a few other '*Record*' inmates when my esteemed puking colleague with the ponytail bumped into me. He was passing his own editorial judgement on my story and obviously felt the lead had been buried too far down.

"Jeez, are you blessed," commented my drinking partner – Lou Cassals – another journeyman journalist who'd found refuge at '*The Record*' some time back.

"How do you figure?"

"Ol' Hugh don't get worked up like that unless he likes you," Lou said.

"And just who the frack is Hugh, anyway?"

"You don't know?"

"I truly do not."

"The one and only Hugh Jackson, one of the Bay Colony's all-time great reporters, best known for unravelling the 'Great Peters Scandal' of 1968 in Boston." (Editor's Note: Gordon Peters had been one of Massachusetts' longest-serving politicians when it was discovered he'd been taking bribes from every over and underworld figure of any size or description for years).

"He did that?"

"All on his lonesome. Along with many other journalistic gems."

"Okay, so what happened?"

"Huh?"

"How'd he wind up in this cesspool?"

"Oh, that. Well, his first wife was killed in a horror road smash; his father took his own life by stringing himself up with fishing line in Hugh's garage; and his one and only near-finished novel was lost in a house fire caused by a cigarette that probably fell out of his snoring mouth and onto the floor."

"Is that all? And now he goes around throwing his guts up whenever he likes and castigating colleagues like moi."

"You could do worse than working with him."

"You're serious?"

"Abso-FUCKING-lutely."

"Why don't you work with him then?"

"Cuz I got no interest in bettering myself. I am what I ain't and I'll live with that. For now, anyway," Lou said. "And you?"

"And me, what?"

"Why are you lowering any sense of journalistic decency you ever had by joining this elite band of no-hopers?" Lou asked.

"Just lucky, I guess. That and the fact that the last newspaper I worked for practically escorted me to the city limits and threatened legal action if I ever returned."

"C'mon, really?"

"Just about. And all because of the way I covered a simple wet t-shirt contest."

The look on Lou's face indicated he was none the wiser so I tried to enlighten him.

"I was working for a weekly out of Indianapolis called the *Indy News*. After weeks and weeks of covering nothing more interesting than a supermarket opening, I got wind that this fairly new-type of contest was brewing at an Indiana University campus bar. I travelled down to Bloomington to cover it and decided rather than writing it as a typical news story, opted instead to write it from the viewpoint of one of the contestants."

"Sounds logical so far," Lou said.

"You'd think so. Only Indiana U happened to be hosting the world's largest 'Women in Newspapers' Conference at the same time, which included a guest list of such luminaries as *Today Show* hostess Jane Pauley and '*The Washington Post's*' Katherine Graham.

"I don't think either of them ever saw the piece, but the paper got picketed by every women's group from Chicago to New Orleans. I even got picketed by gay women's groups, calling for my head which sounded rather ominous – or unlikely, depending on your sexual preferences."

"Why didn't the editor of the paper get flogged? Why pick on you?"

"Hey, go figure. Mostly because my name happened to be plastered all over the copy and the photos. They protect their own out there and I was the only staffer who came from anywhere east of the Ohio River. It was much simpler cutting me loose, though the editor applauded my effort in private, especially the part about me telling the eventual winner what it would take to claim the booty."

Lou's face again gave me the 'I don't follow' look, so I continued: "There were only four contestants, each of which had to perform three times while a barman bathed them in pitchers of beer. The first three women were well into their 30s and had lost most of their feminine curves. The last contestant was a local co-ed, not blessed with the biggest brain in town, but with a body that would have made Marilyn Monroe look positively second rate. I could sense as the evening wore on that the crowd wanted to see some flesh other than the bits being flaunted by the first three contestants. I took the last girl aside and told her to slowly work her t-shirt up during Rounds 1 & 2 before whipping it off on the last dance so everyone could get a good look at her high beams."

"And?"

"She won by unanimous vote and gave me the wettest, wildest tongue job I'd ever had, along with her phone number."

"And?"

"Nah, never saw her again. I did try the number but got what sounded to be a very pissed off father who said he'd 'beat me silly' if I ever came around 'thar', wherever thar was."

"Maybe we should organize a wet t-shirt contest for this place?" Lou suggested. One look at the crowd, which consisted almost totally of middle-aged men convinced us that this was probably not a good idea. Then again, anything would have been better than listening to Hugh Jackson bitching and moaning about 'THE CATS!' 'THE CATS!' to anyone who'd listen, which didn't include yours truly, preferring instead to concentrate on the row of shot glasses in front of me. What a place. Where else could you get quality reviews of your work while you drank? Maybe Lou was right. Maybe ol' Hugh could teach me a thing or three about reporting, but then again – maybe he was just barking mad.

Much later that night, long after my powers of observation had shut down – I apparently confronted Hugh Jackson and told him where to stick the cats. I didn't mind him critiquing my journalistic judgement, it was just his repeated 'meow, meows' from the back of the bar that got the better of me. Before long, we were flailing away at each other on the sticky wooden barroom floor like a couple of upside down turtles. It was, by all accounts, a pathetic attempt at a fight, inflicting more damage on the reputations of the participants than anything else, but the outcomes weren't all bad.

Most of my colleagues were so surprised that anyone actually confronted the living legend of New England journalism that they figured I was either a genius or a raving lunatic, which as far as I could tell from the little time I'd spent at '*The Record*', were one and the same thing.

Indeed, later that morning, while still ensconced at the bar, Martin James, who also had spent the better part of the evening at his real 'office', offered me one of the paper's pet beats – Eastern Connecticut. While most daily newspaper rounds focused on professions like cops, courts and sports, '*The Record*', due to its unique publishing arrangement, emphasized stories grounded in particular parts of the country. And not just any parts of the US of A, but parts that had developed a strong affinity with the paper over many, many years. Not sure what it says for these places, but we had reporters responsible for generating stories in such hot spots as central Vermont, southern Indiana and northern New Mexico, (Taos and Santa Fe but not Albuquerque).

Other go zones included southern Maryland, North Carolina, (but not South Carolina) and northern parts of Florida.

I'd never heard of any newspaper operating like this. Obviously, over the years of its peculiar evolution, the powers that be and had been, discovered geographical pockets of interest in non-breaking news stories. It was so different that we didn't even necessarily look for second or third day leads to stories, either.

Of course, this may have been due to the fact that we didn't publish every day – or every other day for that matter. We came out twice each week – Wednesdays and Saturdays, which was yet another peculiarity about this very strange newspaper.

This meant that most stories, like the 'ROAD KILL' piece, had to be kept timeless. It would have meant just as much – or as little – no matter when it saw the light of day.

I was ecstatic to be covering Eastern Connecticut, which meant I had first crack at any story east of the Connecticut River. Prior to heading west, I'd enjoyed many a fine escapade in this region, usually in the company of Uncle J.R. The other advantage, of course, was this region's proximity. It was literally just around the corner from the paper. Lou Cassals, on the other hand, was responsible for developing stories out of Western New York State and Northern Ohio. Not that Lou got to travel to these places. Instead, you were expected to generate stories based on ones taken from the Associated Press or United Press International wire services. It was someone's job, though I'd yet to figure out whose, to sift through the roll after roll of wire stories and literally cut out any that were datelined New Mexico, Vermont, Ohio, etc, and put them on the appropriate reporter's desk. Often, the stories were left on your desk in neat little bundles like so many rolls of one-ply toilet paper. Those deemed 'important' were usually stuffed inside the typewriter or some other place the reporter was bound to see it like under the desk or next to the coffee machine.

While much of the newspaper was dedicated to different parts of the country, we also had specialty pages that focused on conventional news sections like business, sports and politics. These sections relied mostly on stories from the Greater New Richmond area, and often were difficult to figure out whether they were primarily a story about a court or a cop case with a dash of sports thrown in or vice versa.

There was yet another oddity about '*The Record*'. It not only featured the likes of Hugh Jackson and other burnt-out stars from American journalism days gone by, but a bunch of foreigners from such exotic ports as Glasgow, Manchester, Dublin and Sydney. Most of them were older guys who rarely left the horseshoe-shaped editor's corral, delicately balanced in the center of the newsroom. While these guys obviously had many more years experience in the business than most of the reporters, (indeed, apart from myself and Lou, I don't think any of the other reporters had ever worked for a newspaper before), they still preferred such Anglicized-style favorites as sticking the letter 'u' in words like "favourite" and "colour" and 'Ss' instead of 'Zs' or what they called 'Zeds' damn near anywhere they liked. These guys also were responsible for many of the headlines – which accounts for the one accompanying my next story about a guy in Groton, Connecticut who created monumental sculptures out of supermarket carts. "HELLO TROLLEY" yelled the headline, which probably meant little or nothing to most of our readers, but would have gone down a treat in East Bumfuck, Ireland, to be sure, to be sure.

We'd been 'tipped off' on the story from a small piece that first ran in the '*New London Day*', the daily rag of record in southeastern Connecticut. As usual, the local hack missed the 'real' story, preferring to regale the reader with such corny turns of phrases as "Tom Keenan's supermarket cart works bring new meaning to 'Shop till you drop' and other such winners.

Rather than interview the sculptor, I called up a couple of local supermarkets and asked the managers what they thought about the creations – some of which stood 20 feet high and were meant to resemble such international attractions as the Eiffel Tower and Sydney's Harbor Bridge. One guy said he'd "hang the bastard" if he ever walked near his store again. (He didn't really say 'bastard' but I added it in figuring it gave the quote a bit more punch). Another store manager seemed more reluctant to comment until I told him that the amateur sculptor said his carts were inferior to the other chains. "Yeah? Well we'll see how inferior they are the next time he comes around here! We'll take a cart and shove…" You get the idea. Neighbors of the unique craftsman also were less than impressed with his efforts. One neighbor said her show-quality Persian cat had gotten its coat singed from welding sparks while another said it often looked like "frickin' 4th of July fireworks" with this idiot working on pieces late into the night for much of the year.

Hugh Jackson didn't say anything to me about this story. I did get a couple of nasty calls from the sculptor in question who offered to shave my face with his blowtorch.

That was nothing compared to the crap I got from some of my work mates when Hugh threw me another story that had – in his colorful slang – 'read like yesterday's road kill'. The New Richmond town fathers had decided to lob a huge statue of its favorite son – our nineteenth-century answer to Henry David Thoreau - at one end of Main Street. It pretty much stopped traffic for the better part of yesterday, not including all the speeches and school group ceremonies, etc, etc. Anyway, Hugh had sent our intrepid police reporter – a surly chap by the name of Jim Benton, to cover the event. Hugh had been put in charge of the New Richmond pages, which Martin James felt needed 'more spice'.

Jim Benton was not exactly the guy you'd send to any story you were trying to juice up. Most of his career had been spent as a cop which somehow went south when he was caught sleeping off a late-night booze-up in his cruiser. Sleeping in cop cars was not an unusual offence – particularly for members of the police force in New Richmond. The only problem was when and where the infringement occurred. Would you believe at 11.30 a.m. while stopped at a red light on Main Street? Despite getting dropped from the thin blue line, Martin James figured he'd make the perfect cop reporter, capable of bringing all sorts of new insight into the paper's police beat. That was the theory. In reality, the police beat guys rarely got any scoops, because that would have meant turning on some ex pal or making them look bad. Instead, crime beat guys like Benton would roll over whenever the police told them not to report something that would make them look bad, giving us instead 'exclusives' to stories that were boring as batshit. Things like 'Major

Breakthrough in String of Car Break-Ins' or 'Undercover Sting Operation Nets Three Shoplifters'.

It was always going to be interesting how any staff member would react when asked to do something by Hugh Jackson. To give him his due, though, he gave everyone a chance to shine. He usually handed the reporter a decent-sized sheet of paper or roll of copy off the wire that gave them some insight into the background of the story. It was then up to the reporter to figure out how to freshen it up from there.

Oh yeah, there was one more thing: He always wanted to know if you'd attended J-school. The 'J' stood for "Journalism" School, but it may as well stood for 'S' as in "Shithole" School as far as Hugh was concerned. Leave it to me to find out why when he recently asked moi about my educational training. After clearing through the first few queries, his eyes turned ice cold as he asked me whether "I'd ever attended any J-School?"

"No, why?" I replied.

"Why? Because if you had, I'd have spent the next six months beating that 'two sides to every story' crap out of ya," he said.

"I'm not following," I said.

"Good. Don't," he returned.

"Okay, but doesn't every story have two sides?" I asked.

"Never," he began. "Every story has as many sides as it does people who read the fucking story in the paper. It could have 100, 1000, 100,000 – but you know what? It don't matter," he says.

"Why?"

"Because at the end of the day, there's only one side that counts – yours. Make the story your own and we'll get along fine," my mental-as-anything mentor said.

I wanted to argue the point with him, but decided against it. I'd already ended up on a smelly, dirty barroom floor with this guy once over something as stupid as the opening line of a story. I wasn't about to go back there again for the sake of some seemingly even more bizarre version of journalism that had never been practiced, at least to my recollection, in the so-called civilized world.

For now though, all eyes were on Benton, who as luck would have it, was well beyond the 'freshening-up' stage. I doubted he ever went to J-School, but that was the least of his worries. He always looked like he was half asleep, which he probably was, when he wasn't sucking up to some local or state cop. Of course, that happened to many beat reporters. They didn't just get close to their sources; they were married to them and unable to ever write anything remotely critical for fear of reprisal or worse – no invitation to regular booze-ups.

I entered the news room just about the same time that Big Jim received the news that his copy was crap by Mr. Jackson. Though everyone knew the guy's work was crap, Jackson was obviously the first one bold enough to tell him. It made for quite a scene because Hugh was not the tallest of men, perhaps five foot, five or six inches while Jim Benton was probably close to a foot taller, even in his bare feet. Jackson had no sooner placed the copy back on his desk and told him to 'rewrite it', when Benton had picked up his squeaky desk chair and began to hurl it across the room toward Jackson. A two-man brawl ensued, which by all accounts, was yet another tame affair by 'Record' standards. Once the two had been pried apart by myself, Lou Cassals and a couple of other reporters, a sense of composure came over Hugh who now turned his gaze toward my good self.

"Get me a story," he said and walked away. It occurred to me that the reason I got stuck with it is because I was closest to Hugh when the fight stopped. I noticed that everyone else had long since pulled away, knowing what was coming next. I figured it couldn't be any worse than the shit I used to have to write in Ohio, Illinois and Indiana. And besides, Hugh and I had already met, so what could go wrong? Martin James came over and handed me a copy of Benton's article. It opened with "Thomas Jason Marsden would've loved all the attention as politicians from near and far paid their respects during the unveiling of a huge statue dedicated in his honor yesterday."

It wasn't bad. It was after all, a statue unveiling, not a 10-car pile-up on the main drag. "Got any ideas?" Martin asked.

"About what?"

"About making it better. Hugh's right. It sucks," Martin said.

"Christ, writing about historical stuff is never easy," I said. At this point, the copy was ripped out of my hand from behind by Hugh Jackson.

"Give it some juice, for Christ's sake," Hugh said.

"Like how? I wasn't there," I said.

"For Christ's sake – you got a mind, don't ya? This story isn't about Marsden. He's been cold for over 100 years. And even when he was here, he was dull as dishwater. We don't write about history – history is what the stories become," Hugh said before walking away. Martin and I looked at one another not sure what to make of the great one's last comment. We didn't have much time to mull it over, though, as Hugh happened by Big Jim's desk and mumbled something that sounded a lot like "piss weak."

The next thing I knew, the two were stuck together in a wild wrestling move that spilled over onto Benton's desk. I ignored the combatants this time, preferring instead to think about what an outsider would make of this warm working environment. Interestingly, few people even bothered getting up from their desks for the second round. Lou, for instance, was chatting to someone on the phone – no doubt taking odds on who would win. Martin finally stepped in and broke the two up. Like him or loathe him, you had to give Hugh Jackson credit for one thing – he certainly was passionate about his work.

I took the story away and picked up the prepared speeches from the Mayor and other dignitaries. Nothing noteworthy there. I decided instead to focus on the subject's rather unusual place in history as a watered-down Thoreau living on the banks of the Big Puddle some 100 years earlier.

From my own reading of his work, Thomas Jason Marsden had done little more than plagiarize Thoreau's stuff. When he wasn't coming up with his own supposed pearls of wisdom like: "Time does not run out; life does," and "Take chances, life is too short to wait for wondrous moments," he was seeking intervention from external sources – most notably the region's Native American Indian tribes. He once spent two whole years supposedly living among the Indians in the surrounding forests. When he 'returned', he spoke with a decidedly local Indian clip in his voice. I say 'returned' rather guardedly, because the word was that he often sneaked back into town by the cover of darkness and wolfed down platters of meat and potatoes at the homes of friends and lovers sworn to secrecy.

When he was seen by woodsmen or people out on the Big Puddle, they said his hair was kept in tightly-woven braids and he preferred the simple deerskin clothing of his pond-front neighbors to the finely-starched white, puffy shirts and tight breeches worn by the townsmen. He later gave lectures on his time in the woods and cited all these supposed wise old Indian sayings, but often sounded like little more than direct rip-offs from translations of great Indian chiefs of the Plains and Southwestern states.

I walked outside and sidled up to the statue where a group of visitors were having their photograph taken in front of it.

"Know who the guy is?" I asked pointing to the monumental-sized statue of our favorite son.

"Some local writer, wasn't he?" came the reply from one of the women in the threesome. "No, he was a poet," said the other lady while the lone gentleman in the crowd came out with: "He was a bum."

Bingo. Story time.

```
While local dignitaries came to praise New
Richmond's favorite son during a brief
statue dedication at the top of Main Street
yesterday, other visitors were not sure
whether Thomas Jason Marsden was a writer,
a poet or a bum.
```

I had a bit more fun with the comments from the three interlopers who hailed from Boston, before turning it back over to the Mayor who was certain that Marsden's place in New Richmond's history would remain as "firm and towering as the statue we dedicate to him on this day," before closing with:

```
He may not have been the literary
powerhouse of his Walden Pond-based
predecessor, but intrepid wanderer and
semi-deep thinker Thomas Jason Marsden's
place in local history is now forever
anchored firmly in New Richmond's bosom.
This hulking piece of granite carved in his
image is perhaps more than he deserved -
many statues of George Washington and
Napoleon took up less space - but as Dave
Edwards of Boston noted following the
unveiling ceremony: "I hope the birds don't
even leave their droppings behind, because
he wasn't worth a shit."
```

I didn't make many friends with that one, either. Especially the 'Friends of Thomas Jason Marsden Society" who said I belittled his 'grand reputation as one of the last century's great post-Transcendental thinkers'.

Ooohh, that hurt, but not as bad as the crap I got from Jim Benton the next day. He was still fuming over having the story taken away from him by Jackson. Don't think he had any problem over the punch-up, just the ignominy of having his story pulled. I assured him I thought his story was fine and that mine didn't add anything he hadn't already done.

I was still talking with Big Jim when my phone rang. It was yet another family member – dear old Dad – who was currently assistant night manager at a Howard Johnson's in New London, Connecticut, and who confronted me with another issue surrounding the earlier story on the shopping trolleys.

"Hey, son, whaddya doin?"

"Hi, Dad, good to hear from you."

"I'll give ya 'good to hear from ya'. What are you – tryin to get me killed or somethin?

"What are you talking about?"

"That story – the one about the shopping carts."

"Yeah, what about it?"

"I work with his frickin wife and she knows you're my son."

"Yeah, so?"

"Yeah, so she wants to kill me right about now."

"So long as she doesn't have a blowtorch, you'll be fine. Anyway, how ya been?"

"Okay, just okay, so when you comin down?"

"Soon, pop. Real soon."

"It's been a while. Too long."

"Oh yeah, spoke to Mom the other day, she…"

CLICK.

Johnson & not Johnson strikes again.

Chapter Four

I'd been working at 'The Record' for nearly two weeks non-stop and realized I hadn't had a day where some portion of it wasn't spent in either office – the one with the typewriters or the one with the beer bottles.

I vowed today would be different. There seemed little point in hanging around my corner, three-room luxury suite at the fleabag boarding house I called home, despite the fact that there was a great story to tell about it. For starters, this multi-level rooming house, situated along the town's main drag, separated two of the town's quietest buildings from one another - the town's library on one side and a funeral parlor on the other. While I greatly enjoyed rummaging through the old book stacks in the library in search of clues regarding the Winslow/Adams side of my own genetical equation, the placement of the town's only boarding house next to a funeral home was nothing short of pure serendipity. The boarding house was called The Lincoln – named after the President, not the car. It was said that the Great Emancipator himself once stayed there, and judging by the state of the place and the foul smell that had permanently seeped into the walls, I would not have been surprised if some enterprising urban archaeologist one day discovered the remains of Lincoln, his cabinet and John Wilkes Booth stuffed beneath the floor boards.

Still, it beat the alternative. Actually, it beat either alternative facing me: Namely, moving in with my mother in her hotel-sized house off the not-so-great lakefront or hunkering down again with my grandpa at the ramshackle ranch house in Richmond Heights.

Besides, where would I find a neighbor like the one at The Lincoln? Because I was lucky enough to score a corner apartment, (complete with my own bedroom, kitchenette, bathroom and broom-closet-sized balcony overlooking the town's not-so-main drag), I only had one immediate neighbor. But what a neighbor she was – and is. She was probably middle-aged but could have been anywhere between 55-75 due to the amount of white make-up she pounded onto her facial pores. She was a cross between '*Streetcar's*' Blanche DuBois and Gloria Swanson's '*Sunset Boulevard*' faded film star. Rarely a night went by when she didn't come banging at the door for something or other. Her name was Louisa May Alcott May, I kid you not. It wasn't bad enough that some guy named Alcott and his wife were crazy enough to name their only daughter Louisa May, but then she probably spent the better part of her adult life looking for a guy named 'May' just to top it off. Apart from the mysterious gaps in her smile and the pounds of pancake make-up, she was notable for one other thing: A penchant for perfume that was strong enough to strip paint off walls or in her case perhaps, the enamel off teeth.

I learned to move quietly in and out of my penthouse pad, or as quietly as the creaky floorboards would allow me so as not to awaken Louisa May or her constant companion – a stocky dog with a longish coat and a blue-black tongue that never barked, but was always ready to bowl you over with affection. Pets were not allowed in the building, but few boarders seemed to take heed of this regulation. I'd lost count of the number of dogs, cats, birds, snakes and other assorted animals that called The Lincoln home. As one other tenant noted when asked about the 'No Pet' rule, he replied: "The sign says they're not allowed in the building; it doesn't say anything about living in the building." I found out later he used to be an editor at '*The Record*' and with his keen sense of wordplay, failed to see why he no longer worked there.

The other interesting fact about The Lincoln was that apart from me, most other tenants recalled hearing FDR's "Day of Infamy – December 7" speech – the first time around.

Still, it was a bright, sunny day in late fall and perfect for a jaunt to the country – or at least to Richmond Heights to see if the place as still as disgusting as I'd remembered it. I hadn't had to use my car much since moving to New Richmond, which was good. It was in need of a serious rest – or burial which apparently could be provided by the building on the other side of The Lincoln if need be.

Once out of town, though, the 1970 four-door, beige Toyota Corona perked up and headed – as if by remote control – toward Chez

Bedrosian. And it was not an easy ride, either. First, it required negotiating a series of sharp, hairpin turns out of New Richmond along the Big Puddle's southeastern shoreline, before heading up, up up onto a relatively high plateau. Once on top, the road wound through verdant fields of green on either side. These were the remnants of some of the area's biggest farms – long since having reached their use-by dates and now being turned slowly if not relentlessly – into more and more one-acre square blocks with even squarer boxed homes placed right in the middle.

This plateau ran for about four miles before descending quickly down into Richmond Heights' solar plexus – an atypical New England village featuring a library/schoolhouse, a police/fire department and an Italian restaurant on one side of its central common and a small cemetery, town hall and bank on the other. Richmond Heights gave its citizenry the four pillars of society: Learning, sustenance, security and wealth, not necessarily in that or any other order. Weren't these four items the staples of any good, respectable existence? And when you'd attained the pinnacle of each of these goals, (with the proper mix of how much of each ingredient up solely to the discretion of the individual), what remained? Why, to die, of course. And make way for the next generation; the next wave; well, the next whatever. What more could any Richmond Heights' resident require? What more, indeed?

The town's fathers obviously felt proud enough of their little hamlet that they slow the traffic down from 55 m.p.h. to 25 m.p.h. as they drive through its 'center' like some sort of daily funeral cortege. This may seem like a quaint country ritual, except for the one other deviation (branch) that proves so critical in the town's familial tree.

To reach whichever one of the four pillars you were after – you had to cross a particularly busy four-way intersection, cut in half by the state's most notorious highway – and sight of innumerable serious injuries (see deaths) over the years. To get to my granddad's farm, for instance, you had to cross this busy thoroughfare, and like so many helpless young sea turtles trying to reach the surf before getting picked off by mangy seagulls and other desperate birds of prey, pray to god your vehicle of choice had enough chutzpah to huff and puff its way across the death strip. Do 25 m.p.h. across this suicide strip like you're asked to when driving into the town's center, and you're just as likely to wind up being a hood ornament on some truck either heading east to Boston or west into the Adirondacks.

The beauty of this neat cultural equation had never added up to me before. There was a sort of natural justice to the situation. Regardless of whether you made it (see Four Pillars) across the highway or not (cue the gravediggers), you couldn't miss. You were always going to wind up in the bosom of the Richmond Heights family album – no matter what.

Perhaps this busy roadway shouldn't have been called Route 41. It could have been called Darwinian Highway in which only the fittest survived. The intersection was quite quiet on this Saturday morning, giving me the closest thing possible to a free pass. What awaited me at the end of the trip was far less predictable.

Then again, I wasn't sure what to expect. I hadn't been here in over 15 years. Frankly, I didn't much care, either. In this respect, I was very much my father's man, because I, like him, had so little time or respect for the aged farmer's welfare. In fact, the only memories I had were all downers. There was this cow that fell down a small hillside and got its head and horns perfectly lodged between a large V in a tree. The cow, helplessly stretched on its back with legs flailing wildly, looked like something out of a child's nightmare. It became mine, as they almost inevitably all did, at this infernal farm, because my father had long since left the scene and the old man was too infirmed to even get to this part of his fiefdom, let alone do anything about it. My mind recoils at the very thought of how that situation ended—namely with this unfortunate creature making one last attempt at breaking free, managing only to break its neck from the natural stanchion fashioned by the tree's twisted trunk. Like all too many others, I was left to put the poor dumb beast down. Just one more mess for me to clean up and perhaps an image to accompany a Freddy Krueger-inspired Hallmark greeting card: "Hi everyone, hope you had a great year! Me, I had a bumper crop what with one disease or another spoiling all the veggies to murdering three cows, two sheep and a rather un-game hen! Happy New Year!"

But this was all part of my attempt to well and truly put the past behind me. For better or worse, my only understanding of how the farm had been faring was passed down second hand via my father, who rarely visited; or other relatives like Uncle J.R. They were never long on detail. "Everything's fine/not so good/shithouse;" "The fields are green/brown/covered in snow/mown/not mown;" the farmhouse is fine/falling down/hot/cold;" "the cows are fine/sick/shitty;" "the chickens are fine/sick/shitty;" et cetera, in ad nauseum.

Asking any of these well-meaning people about the state of the farmhouse could just as easily have been plotted on one of those Clue board games where someone/anyone could have taken this blunt object/that sharp instrument and killed someone in particular/no one in general, in the living room/bedroom/kitchen.

Why didn't I talk to my grandfather about it? My grandfather's comprehension of the English language was rudimentary at best and his familiarity with modern technological gear like telephones was even worse. How the frack he kept this farm going was anyone's guess, as his only son had long since departed and found himself running a HoJo's in another state. I know my grandfather never learned how to drive. I know he'd never seen a baseball game or been to a hospital. In fact, the last time he'd left the farm was to bury his wife some 12 years ago in a neighboring village. If he'd had his way, she never would've left the farm. He'd have buried her in back of the farmhouse next to his favorite workhorse, milking cow and sheep dog. He'd never voted, hell, he never would have known who the president was or even what the presidency was, let alone much about the country as a whole or any of its parts, for that matter. If it couldn't be grown, picked, milked, harvested or slaughtered on his 80-acre farm, it didn't exist.

And now, for the first time, I was coming to realize why I'd spent so much time blocking him and his animal farm out of my head. I not only despised him for what he'd done in the old country, but hated him just as much if not more, for not embracing the new country. Hell, even Dad did his bit by changing his name. That was the least he did, but it was something at least.

\#\#\#\#+++SDGHDGKHDHDJ*\#\#\#\#\#**((^^%$$#^^&**(*(()H/\#\#
\#\#\#.

Guess who?

"YOU MUSTN'T JUDGE OTHERS BY THE WAY THEY SPEAK OR THE CLOTHES THEY WEAR. YOU ARE ALL FROM THE SAME TREE OF LIFE," called out Vartan.

'Yeah, yeah', I thought to myself. Just what I needed, my own Kahlil Gibran prosaic prose provider on tap. I wish to heck this fricking voice would go bug someone else's spirit. That was another thing about dear ol' Vartan. He could strike anywhere, at any time. He could alight while in the bath, in the middle of the night or even while on the job.

For many, this farm represented, appropriately enough, the ass-end of Richmond Heights, situated precariously at its far southwestern boundary, surrounded mostly by a long-since-forgotten Native American reserve that bordered on the Big Puddle. It was located at the bottom of a long and winding, one-lane dirt road that featured a few houses and an inane asylum (no sic). How the old man found this piece of land will forever remain a mystery, but then again, anything would have been better than the dirt and rubble he endured in his native homeland. As the Toyota turned off the black top and onto the rocky road, my mind drifted back again. This time it conjured up visions of his prized milker – Molly – who was allowed Brahmin Indian-like entry anywhere, anytime – even into the house – if so desired. This gave the house, my grandfather and practically everything else inside, a decidedly barnyard odor. Why Home Beautiful or some other upmarket homey magazine hadn't discovered Chez Bedrosian yet was a mystery. Who wouldn't have revelled in the prospect of inviting their best mates around for a spot of tea and crumpets amid all the earthy aromas that had saturated every floorboard, inch of wallpaper and human being residing within 10 miles of the place?

The house had been built by my grandfather from rocks collected in the neighboring fields. It obviously was a skill he'd picked up in the old country. Some of the rocks reminded me of the meatballs that my grandmother made for Sunday afternoon dinners. They were small, hard and dry, not unlike the sort of small stones you would see in many New

England rock walls. My theory on the meatballs' hardness was that they probably had to be made that way so they wouldn't spoil while the boys were out and about in the desert herding sheep or whatever else took their fancy. Then again, they'd come in handy as ammo if any unfriendly Bedouins passed by or if in need of felling some Near Eastern four-footed delicacy at 50 yards. In the new country, however, the meatball's range of usages diminished somewhat. I used to say five meatballs made a meal; 500,000 built a house.

In addition to the ramshackle shack, which came complete with a wrap-around, partially closed-in and falling down verandah, was a barn, capable of handling 40 milking head uncomfortably; but more typically packed with closer to 60 in every imaginable position; a small chicken coop; detached garage (which contained no cars, only rusty farming equipment) on its ground floor and a primitive carpenter's workshop on its second story.

Grandfather rarely spent any time in the house. He was either in the barn, atop a stone wall replacing various bits and pieces or high atop his garage gouging some unsuspecting piece of wood into some makeshift bench, chair or chest of drawers.

I did a 360 degree turn around the property's circular drive before cutting the engine right in front of the house. Despite more than 5,500 days having passed since I last saw the place, (but whose counting?), little seemingly had changed. There were chickens still challenging cars for the driveway. A cow's plaintive bellow could be heard (herd?) in the distance. grandpa was nowhere to be seen. The front door was open, but it always was since the only one that had been there, was knocked off its hinges when his prized, pregnant cow got wedged in it many years ago. Destroying the animal was not an option; better to destroy the door which he did and never replaced for fear of such an incident occurring again. (The only time the front door was covered over was during winter when the old man boarded it up good and proper with old planks and barn nails). He didn't receive many visitors.

I didn't bother wasting my time calling out. I knew he wouldn't be inside. Instead, an unfamiliar voice assaulted me from behind.

"What do you want?"

I turned to see a solidly-built young man, with longish hair and facial stubble, heading toward me from the barn.

"What?"

"You heard me – what do you want?" the kid repeated.

"I'm not sure that's any of your business, but since you asked, I'm looking for my grandfather."

With that, the kid stopped cold in his tracks. His head was obviously quickly doing some genealogical arithmetic before another voice, a much higher one, called out: "Walter, is that you?"

"Tis I, indeed," I replied to my as yet, unknown assailants.

"You don't remember me, do ya? That'd figure, you being a big star now and all," the woman said.

I took a chance. "Jenny? Is that you?"

The smile coming over the woman's face confirmed my educated guess. It was indeed, one Jenny Lawton, whose family lived at the other end of the rocky road and who always seemed to be hanging around during my tenure at the homestead some years back. As it turned out, she had a schoolgirl crush on moi, which led to me eventually christening her full, sweet lips out back of the animal pens one hot August night. At least she told me it was her first kiss, though judging by what she could do with those two lips and tongue, always made me question that claim.

"Good to see you, Jenny. And don't tell me this guy is your little brother Ethan?"

It was indeed, her little brother Ethan, who since the last time I'd seen him, had grown more than two feet and gained about 200 pounds. Of course, the last time I'd seen him, he wasn't long out of diapers. Ethan came over and shook my hand. Jenny just stood there with a malicious grin, complete with permanent pouty, lower lip; the kind sported by many angel figures in old-time paintings. At first blush, these figures strike you as being purely angelic. Take a closer look though and it ain't long before they're pulling you behind the barn for some far less angelic action.

"Yeah, and he's supposed to finish cleaning up in the barn," she said turning to her little bro. Ethan turns and heads back toward the barn.

"How you been, Jen?"

This question was greeted by a look that would and probably had – killed. "What? You go away for 15 years without a word and show up out of the blue and ask, 'How ya been, Jen?'"

"Excuse me, did we get married somewhere along the line I forgot about?"

"You fuckin' bastard," she replied and turned to go toward the barn.

"Hey, wait – did I miss something?"

"Yeah, you did. And believe it or not, it's got nothing to do with you. It's got to do with your grandfather who right now is in the barn trying to find his cow so he can milk her."

"What? What are you saying?"

"Hey, you're the genius, Einstein. Go figure it out – I've got other places to be anyway," Jenny said heading for her own beat-up Toyota next to the barn door.

Welcome back. I headed toward the barn and was met by Ethan trying to talk over the roar of his sister's muffler-less car taking off up the hill. "Hey man, don't worry about her. She's got man problems," he said.

"Really?"

"Yeah, she got married a while back and it didn't work out."

"I wonder why. Where's my grandfather?"

Ethan pointed into the barn.

It was quite dark, even in broad daylight but one thing was clear: There no longer was a herd of cows; more like a herdette of two. And there, seated at his man-made milking stool beneath the larger of the two pale brown and white Guernseys was my grandfather – the old gray fox himself.

"Hey, grandpa, it's me, Torkum," I said.

He either didn't hear me or chose to ignore my greeting. The only sound was the slow and steady sound of milk hitting a pail – rat a tat; rat a tat; rat a tat tat.

I walked up from behind and tapped him on the shoulder.

"BASTARD! What for you do this?!" he yelled in the direction of the cow's back end, which is never a good move at the best of times.

"Hey, it's me, your grandson – Torkum."

Slowly he turned but it was obvious he couldn't see me. I knelt over and grabbed his face in my hands. "It's me, Torkum."

"Woooo-hooooo, woooo-hoooo, my boy!" he said, kicking the stool over and most of the pail of milk he'd been collecting.

"Yeah, it's me, granddad. How are ya?"

"Gotta make something go," he said. Like many of his sayings, it sounded more like some code Russian spies gave to one another while infiltrating national security office buildings in Washington in the 1960s. It could have meant a lot of things. In fact, it must have because he used it all the time. At least when I was around. I promised to one day sit him down and get the full translation, but for now, I think it was just his way of encouraging someone in general, and more precisely, me in particular, to do something – probably anything – with my life. And practically anything would have been better than how his had ended up.

"Yeah, I'm making something go. How are you?"

It was hard to see how he looked in the barn's dim light. What was clear was that his glasses – which were always thick as coke bottles – now had a permanent layer of sludge over them that would've given him few advantages over Ray Charles' or Stevie Wonder's eyewear.

"I'm ulll-right," he said. "Good to see you." And with that, he started for the barn door, semi-empty milk bucket in hand. And then, as if on cue, he turned one last time and dropped on me his most famous line/word of advice: "No Back Look."

There was never a lot of conversation with him that didn't include some variation on his two main themes: "Make Something Go" and "No Back Look." It was hardly the range of vocabulary that was going to get

Noah Webster quaking in his Quaker-style boots. It wasn't much, but then again, who among you wouldn't like having their very own dizzy, dyslexic dialect?

THE TRUTH REQUIRES FEW WORDS, I seem to recall ol' Vartan telling me more than once. May be he was right, but it did help to get the words, no matter how few, in the right fricking order once and a while.

"How's the old man doin?" I asked Ethan.

"Okay sometimes, not so good others. We come down a couple days a week to help with the two cows, collect the eggs and move the sheep," he said.

"That's real kind, I'm sure he appreciates it."

"Least we can do for him. I mean, well, he hasn't got anyone else," Ethan said, though not meaning to offend me.

"Yeah, thanks," I said though wondering how the heck he was keeping up with the bills and taxes based on the mass production of two lame cows, a few dud chickens and three dumb sheep.

"Old Man Tomkins comes by on the other days to help and look in on his beefies," Ethan then offered.

"Stinky comes here?" I asked.

"Yeah, though no one calls him that much any more," Ethan said, implying that the events surrounding a very bad – and very public – case of diarrhea had followed John Tomkins around for much of his adult life.

"He's renting our fields for grazing?"

"Yeah, and he cuts the rest of the fields," Ethan added.

That would help pay some bills, but it still ain't covering land taxes. Just another one of my granddad's many mysteries. I made a note to ask my father next time he and I caught up.

"I gotta go," Ethan said. "Walt, can I ask you something?"

"Yeah, sure, you need a lift?"

"Nah, nothing like that. So why don't you have an ear?"

There it was. The sort of question I hadn't been hit with for a while now. And yet, hit me it did – right in the gut. Just like old times. "I don't know. Why don't you mind your fucking business?"

With that, Ethan turned and headed up the road without looking back. Or should I say – 'No Back Look?'

Chapter Five

I don't know whether I was more stunned by Ethan's question or my blunt answer, but it didn't really matter. All I knew was try as I might, I couldn't get away from the one thing I had no control over – a bizarre birth defect. It was probably just as well that my grandfather's phone rang just about the time I walked in the door to make him a cup of tea. It was someone from the newsroom calling to see if I could help out with a story for Wednesday's paper. It seemed some twit had up and quit before even starting the piece and now they had a major hole for the next edition. Actually, they also had a major hole in the front window where this supposed ace reporter threw his typewriter through before leaving.

I bade the old man goodbye and told him I'd be back soon, though I wasn't really sure about that. I didn't even feel bad about leaving this time – in spite of the fact that I could plainly see how poorly he was doing – but figured he'd muttle through until our next visit. And, even though I hadn't seen the place in a long while, it still pulled me. I knew not why, but then again, why should my feelings about the farm be any different to the mixed sentiments I had about New Richmond in general and/or Richmond Heights in particular? Perhaps that was a topic I could raise with my inner spirit the next time he dropped in. The drive back to town gave me time to think about how my life – or more specifically ME – brought out the worst in ordinary people. I'd lost count of the number of idiots like Ethan who felt compelled to march up to me, staring at my deformed hearing vessel, and without any sense of dignity or class – blurt out 'Oyyy, where's your ear, you loser?" My favorites were the little kids who followed me around supermarkets or department stores, pointing and staring; staring and pointing as if I was some sideshow freak.

Those who are born imperfect are perfectly blessed, St. Vartan whispered to me from time to time. It was a great line, but coming from some guy who died more than thousand years ago took some of the shine off. It also didn't help a lot for those of us in the trenches on a near-daily basis. Even the experts treated me with an odd sort of freak celebrity status. One Eye, Ear, Nose and Throat guy in Chicago said it was a miracle I wasn't born with a cleft palette: Translation, you should be in a home or at the very least, tucked away in some insane asylum like Meadlowlands just up the road from granddad's ranch. Another doctor, who preferred to go by the tongue-twisting name of Otolaryngologist Specialist, couldn't figure out how I kept my balance – let alone heard anything or spoke properly while yet another one, whose specialty sounded more like something you'd expect from a porn producer (indeed, his trade was known as video swallowing), gave me several tasteless treats ranging in textures from stale yoghurt through to raw oats. The plan was that by filming each of these unusual items going down my gullet, they could better understand just what may have gone wrong, because, as I soon learned, there's an eerie connection between one's eyes, ears, nose and throat. This last guy loved seeing me because "my problem is so unique." He thought that would make me feel good. It made me feel about as special as the gal with the full beard at the circus. I reckon he got off on watching people gulp down raw oats and yoghurt. Whatever gets you through the night, doc.

In the end, there was no solution; only more questions and requests from quacks the world over, keen to meet the man who defied the odds. It gave me some rare insight into the human condition. And not much of it was good. Most people, or even most societies, depended on having a majority of individuals who liked keeping things in order. Defy the status quo – either consciously or in my case unconsciously – and you were in for some rough treatment. Think I'm nuts? Okay, take a look at any so-called minority group. Everyone one of them has a label to hang on what ails them. Everyone knows about racism, sexism, even ageism, but what did I have? Earism? Wasn't much chance of drawing any attention to my plight with that moniker.

There was one time when being one-eared came in handy. It kept me from receiving a one-way ticket to Hanoi. There I was, flying through my military induction physical with about 50 other poor slobs in 1970 when this one bright spark noticed something odd about the right side of my head. I figured it just might freak them out, but for whatever reason, it was hard getting this guy to look up from his clipboard. (Unlike most of my compatriots who wore shoulder-length hair, I shaved my head so everyone could see just how deformed I was). Finally, he saw the missing bit and whipped me out of line and into another office toute de suite. There, a middle-aged woman, also in khakis, took over. Now, some of my high school compatriots had warned me about her. They said she had a nose for sniffing out loafers, fakes and frauds. She was like the world's best ice hockey goalie, rejecting any and all comers. Word was that no one – *not one* – potential boot camp recruit got rejected by her. I smiled inwardly as I entered her office which, appropriately enough, was about the same size as an ice hockey goalie's domain. She made not a sound as I entered. Her head was buried in a report in front of her – no doubt the results of my earlier medical review by her colleagues.

"So, I believe you have a hearing difficulty," she finally offered in a rather discourteous, almost mocking tone, all the while rising from behind her desk to confront me directly.

I simply turned my head to the left so she could view the world's ugliest un-ear – full blast!

She took a good look and then returned to her desk and once again buried her head in my as yet unfinished physical report. The silence was, well, deafening. I decided to go for the kill. "Is there a problem?" I asked.

"Ahh, well, yes. It would seem you're missing…"

"An ear. It's called an ear and I'm well aware of this fact."

"How shall we record this on your record?" the woman asked, her voice no longer recording any hint of disdain or mockery, not even realizing the marvelous word play she'd just managed.

I decided to make her squirm a bit by not answering right away. Finally, I offered: "Why don't we say, 'One ear'."

"Yes," she said. "Yes, that's great," as if we'd just solved the riddle of the sphinx.

"What next?" I asked.

"You may go," she replied.

"Go where?"

"Why home. You won't be required for any further duty here."

"What?" I asked in an effort to drive home my hearing disadvantage.

She politely got up from behind her desk and ushered me to the door as if I was some sort of cripple.

And with that, I was politely struck off any and all military hit lists.

❧

My day wasn't getting any better as I arrived back in New Richmond. I walked into the newsroom which was unusually busy for that time of day. I collected a cup of piping lukewarm coffee from the machine in the 'employees lounge' area and tried to find an empty spot among the piles on my desk for the drink. A young reporter named Gail Gerard who was fresh from some hot-shot journalism school, took up residence beside me. She thought she was better than everyone else at 'The Record'. Not that that was laying claim to too much, but from what I'd seen of her work, I didn't think Woodward and Bernstein had any cause for worry.

Next to her sat another wannabe star. His name was Mason James – Martin's younger brother who held a record of sorts – even for 'The Record'. Mason had apparently worked six days a week for eight months and still had not published anything. I'd engaged him in conversation a few times – more out of curiosity than anything else. What could be that interesting and still not get you a by-line? He seemed nice enough and never ever made a deal out of his connection to management. If anything, he divorced himself from it by claiming no one would give his ideas any merit. Just what were his ideas? Conspiracy theories mostly. Wild, wacky conspiracy theories that ranged from Elvis still being alive and well and going underground so he could live out his new life as a Jewish mystic to some Loch Ness-type monster living in The Big Puddle, though I'm not sure of the conspiracy behind that one yet.

It was all crazy stuff but he didn't strike you as being nutty. Quite the opposite. In fact, he often seemed more sensible than his older brother who when he wasn't trying to get you to take some bizarre angle on a fairly straightforward story, was questioning your commitment to the paper or at least to its dismal leader. "Are you questioning my integrity?" was one of Martin's favorite lines and one I was dying for him to ask me.

Neither Gail nor Mason was ruining my day. In fact, since the Marsden statue piece, no one had been ruining my days in the newsroom. I noted that rarely did any of the foreign editors ask me for any clarifications or extra words. Even Martin James went out of his way to say how good I was. It was the sight of my pukey, pugilistic sparring partner – Hugh Jackson – heading toward me that got me to wishing I'd not left the old man's phone number at the editor's desk.

Jackson carried with him several pieces of paper which he proceeded to place down in front of me. "What's this?" he said.

Before I could answer, the newsroom's numbers swelled up as if on cue. My desk was placed against a back wall, facing the crescent-shaped editors' tables where three copy editing/headline writers sat in the middle with an assignment editor hanging off each end.

"Why those look like some of my stories from last week," I said confidently. Much of my time as one of the newer members of the newsroom was to take stories from the wire services and stick local content on the top of them. It was known as 'localizing' a story and represented the simplest, cheapest way to get good copy quickly. These stories could be 5 inches long or 5 feet, depending on the amount of local content available – and the size of the news hole.

"It's crap," Jackson said nodding at the pieces of paper now on my desk.

"Sorry?"

"You heard me. It's shit, you know what shit is, don't you?" he said.

At this point, it was as if the power had gone off in the greater New Richmond area. All members of the editors' desk put down pens and pencils or stopped tapping on typewriters. Ditto for the reporters. I could feel every eye in the room boring into me.

"I do as a matter of fact. I certainly do do," I replied, raising a low chuckle around the newsroom.

Jackson's response was far less appreciative of my word play. He gathered up the papers on my desk, crumpled them into a ball and whipped them against the wall behind my head and then walked away.

Again, all eyes turned back to me. I didn't have a snappy comeback for this development. I didn't do anything. Fortunately, my phone rang which gave me some time to think about how to respond to this frontal assault. By the time I got off the phone, the crisis had subsided. For now. But it certainly gave me something to think about that night over a round of drinks at the bar.

I knew those stories weren't Pulitzer Prize entries, but they were decently crafted pieces of journalism, or so I thought. I asked Lou and a couple others what they thought and all agreed. So what was eating Jackson? I decided to confront him the next day and call his bluff.

Jackson sat apart from the rest of the editorial staff. He was housed in a little room down the back called 'The Morgue'. Every newspaper had one. Some were quite useful as repositories of past stories on any and all topics covered by the paper since its earliest days. *The Record's* Morgue was not only in hopeless disarray, but doubled as a mausoleum for reporters who were well and truly surpassed their use-by date. The current living dead consisted of one Wallace 'Wall' Edwards who had covered cops and courts for the paper since returning from Germany at the close of WWII, till some time in the early 1970s. Wall had been known for his no-nonsense approach to journalism. He took no prisoners and more than once received death threats for his work. It was said that if you pricked his skin, black, as in black ink, would ooze out of his pores. His last job, like so many reporters who work beyond their use-by date, was as a columnist. It was cleverly called '*Wall's Street*' but there was little that could be called clever about its contents. It was mostly vague memories of old faces and places that appealed only to those whose minds similarly rambled from one thought to another in less time than it took to sneeze. Wall's time now was spent with a pair of dull scissors, clipping articles out from the previous day's paper and placing them (hopefully) into their proper envelope.

Wall was hard at this task as I entered the door-less repository. Jackson sat opposite him, typing madly all the while sucking on a cigarette.

"Got a minute?" I asked.

Jackson continued to type, not even looking up to acknowledge my presence. Wall likewise ignored me but not for the same reason as Jackson. He wasn't hard of hearing; he just could hardly hear. Another reason they kept him apart from the rest of the newsroom was that he whistled incessantly. And due to his deafness, the tunes were not only incoherent, but often reached notes that could break bullet-proof glass. I stood there in the doorway for a few more seconds and then turned to walk away. A second dose of public humiliation in less than 24 hours did not seem like a wise career move.

"Come here," Jackson yelled, though it sounded more like 'Comeah'.

"What?" I said, turning to face him once more.

"Take a look at this," he said, handing me the fresh piece of copy he'd been pecking out with his two index fingers. It was a revised version of the last piece I'd done earlier in the week. It was a very straightforward story about a community garage sale that raised money for some kid dying of cancer. I'd made a couple of calls and gotten the pertinent stuff like when it started, what was sold, how much they raised, blah, blah, blah. It made for a touching community bulletin board item – nothing more, everything less. It read somewhat differently after Hugh Jackson got done with it.

```
Laurie Taylor kicked and screamed as her
mother took her favorite doll away and
handed it over to a stranger for 5 bucks.

Laurie's tears, along with those of many
other local children, have not been spilled
in vain. The proceeds from sales of
hundreds of items like her precious Barbie,
will go toward helping another neighborhood
kid named Johnny Robbins, overcome his
life-threatening bout with leukemia...
```

The story left me speechless. It was the best piece of news writing I'd ever seen. It was all the more remarkable given that any other reporter, including me, saw it as little more than a community filler requiring little or no extra effort. In Jackson's fingertips, the story became a front page feature, demanding to be read.

"Hey, Johnson, you done reading yet?" Jackson asked.

"Yeah, it's great," I replied.

"Forget about it. I need you to get me a story for Wednesday," he said.

"Me?"

"Yeah, you. You are here to write stories, right?"

"Ahh, yeah. I guess I am," I replied and with that came the first hint of a smile that I'd ever seen grace Hugh Jackson's face.

"We gotta hole in the 'High Society' page. You read it?"

"Ah, not really."

"It's where we take a long look at some local event, place or attraction," he said, emphasizing the word 'long' so I knew this was to be an in-depth, new wrinkle on some old spot. "This week marks the start of 'Living Museum Month' so I want you to take a crack at Olde Richmond Plantation."

Olde Richmond Plantation was located about three miles from the newspaper, nestled quietly along the Lake's southeastern shore. It was meant to represent life in New Richmond, Massachusetts, circa 1765-1790, but always looked like just a bunch of local yocals pretending to be behind the times. Come to think of it, that description sounded a lot like the New-look New Richmond of 1979.

"How much time I got?"

"Plenty. Till tomorrow night," Hugh replied, handing me a series of scribbled notes and background sheets no doubt collected by the guy who decided he'd rather deposit his typewriter onto the pavement below than take on this assignment.

"You're kidding, right?"

"I don't kid," he said.

I took the notes from Hugh and headed back to my desk. He well and truly had laid down the gauntlet now. I don't think he'd given me his version to make me look bad. I think it was his way of instructing; sharing the inner secrets of the journalistic fraternity with another member – hopefully anyway.

I was both honored and scared shitless of trying to match his effort, though. Particularly given the nature of the story on offer: Writing about the country's worst living museum which just happened to be New Richmond's biggest (and only?) tourist attraction.

Despite its failings, Olde Richmond Plantation held some sway in the local community. Any business that lasted for more than 10 years and at one time or another, provided employment for hundreds of residents, is bound to endear itself to the community – at least a little. And while it may not have been a sacred cow, it certainly was a feted calf.

So when my story ran with the headline 'Presenting Past Imperfectly', it wouldn't be long before the lynch mob gathered outside the newsroom. Hell, I thought the story was rather tame, compared to what it could have been if I'd had a few more days and/or Hugh had had a few more beers, before it ran.

It was not an easy story to write, given that I started it late Sunday afternoon and the place didn't open again until the next morning. With no local spokespeople available from the museum, I relied on a wire report from the National Organisation for Living Museums which each year provided a rating on the country's finest and worst examples. Olde Richmond Plantation, or 'ORP' as it's known to locals, always figured high up on the low side. It achieved these poor ratings for all sorts of reasons, including having its 'early settlers' wearing incomplete mid-eighteenth-century costumes. When I asked the National Organisation's leader in a phone interview at his home in Canton, Ohio, just what that meant he replied: "Have you ever seen any mid-eighteenth century soldiers wearing Keds sneakers?"

ORP also let the living museum side down by lack of staff training. When asked what that meant, the fearless leader said: "I overheard a supposed 'farmer' calling one female visitor a "stupid cow" for not knowing the difference between a steer and a bull.

The coup de grace occurred when I showed up with a photographer on Tuesday to get some pictures to go with the story. We'd no sooner stepped back in time when we were accosted by a very large security guard. He told us to get out and that we had no right to take pictures. We assured him that we did given that as far as we knew, ORP had not become a police state.

With that, this goon grabbed me by the arm and started ushering me for the phoney wooden turnstile. The quick-thinking photographer started shooting and the results were absolutely hilarious. Rather than the alleged criminal (see me) shielding his face from the camera, the stupid security guard is grabbing me with one hand while covering his face with a large-rimmed hat to avoid detection.

This picture graced the paper's front page with the heading: "ORP Guard Goes Ape!"

Truth be told, the guard wasn't the only one going bananas. The article that appeared in the story had my by-line, but very few of the words that I'd handed over to Hugh Jackson. And as usual, what had been rather mundane word play turned into something almost magical in his hands.

```
When John Blair isn't pumping gas at his
uncle's Texaco station on Route 41, he
makes a living by lying to people. Every
Tuesday and Thursday he puts on old clothes
and tells people he's never met, what it
was like living more than 100 years ago in
a New England village.
```

Hugh's, or should I say, my story, continued:

```
The only problem is that John Blair, and
every other person who works at Olde
Richmond Plantation, has no idea what it
was like living 100 years ago. To a
generation that's grown up on television
where truth and fiction blur – Olde
Richmond Plantation is just another stage
set where 'Leave it to Beaver' meets
'Bonanza' meets 'Gunsmoke'. It doesn't
really matter what they're wearing or what
they're doing. It's all some silly mirage
```

```
that adds nothing to the visitor's
understanding of anything - past or
present. Only another shilling or three to
a business that trades on passing off
hysterical fiction as historical fact.
```

My far-less colorful copy took over from there, featuring the quotes from the National Organisation's fearless leader; citing less-than-flattering comments from recent visitors; and graphic images of badly done displays like a bunch of old books gathered on a shelf in the corner of the local 'doctor's surgery. The only attempt at deciphering their contents was a three-word sign plastered to the wall next to the bookshelf that read: "Doctor's Old Books."

The story was hailed wildly by my colleagues, though the James' family seemed especially quiet, due to the fact that the museum was run by one of their old pals. The phone rang off the hook for days from people, most of whom disagreed violently with the story and threatened to show me what they did know about life in the mid-eighteenth century – particularly as it related to handling criminals (see draw and quartering, placing in stockades, burning at the stake, etc).

I'm getting ahead of myself, though. That all started after Wednesday and it was still only late Tuesday afternoon. I was just about to hand my story over to Hugh who was keen to grab hold of it so he could weave his particular brand of black magic, when the phone on my desk rang.

"Hey, boy, what ya doin?"

"J.R. – that you?"

"None other and I'm over at The Lincoln sharing a drink or three with a most delightful lady by the name of Louisa May."

Oh, shit. "Oh, really?"

"Great gal. Speaks highly of you, too. See you soon, eh?"

"Yeah, real soon."

"Love to get your opinion of her pad. It's a real museum piece," J.R. said.

"Is it a living one?" I asked jokingly.

"Christ, kid, how the frack should I know. We only just met."

With that the connection went dead. The day was about to end in much the same way it began: Only this time, the museum 'piece' was going to take a bite out of me – big time – rather than the other way around.

Chapter Six

I had no sooner entered my apartment when dear ol' Uncle J.R. was on to me. "Hey, kid, spot me a Kiner."

A 'Kiner' referred to Ralph Kiner, a powerful right-handed hitter who won seven straight home run titles before he turned 30 for the Pittsburgh Pirates in the late 1940s and early 1950s. He also was one of my uncle's favorite players and even more favorite baseball card subjects. My uncle had collected baseball cards – mostly ones of guys from the turn of the century through to the 1950s for many years.

I remember thinking what an odd way to spend Sunday afternoons, rummaging through pile after pile of faded old baseball cards at various shows and old sporting goods stores with a bunch of wannabe baseball players. Every so often I can remember him telling me what a 'steal' he made, picking up such and such a card from such and such a series for such and such a low price. It was quite an art form – collecting baseball cards. There were so many things you had to take into consideration beyond just the obvious point about collecting big names like Ruth, Dimaggio (Joe not Dom) and Mantle: What was the card's condition, (which went from mint to poor with about seven other grades in between); which series was it from and how rare was it; who was likely to gain in value over time versus just collecting players you liked, etc.

It seemed like far too much time spent with lonely old men to me, but if you played your cards right, it had become clear there was mucho money to be made from these four-cornered bits of colored paper. Indeed, cards he might have spent 50 cents, $1 or $2 on, could now be worth hundreds, even thousands, depending on their quality and rareness. Hell, some cards of Babe Ruth and Lou Gehrig had already sold in the five-figure range while the collector's Holy Grail – a 1909-11T206 Honus Wagner was reportedly fetching nearly $1 million! Not bad for something that you could have picked up in their day for the price of a cigar or bubble gum pack, depending on your poison.

Now that J.R. was nearing – or just beyond retirement age – he started trading them in for many times the value he originally paid. It was perhaps the most unique retirement plan anyone had ever dreamed of. Everyone knew about collecting antique furniture, stocks, bonds, old cars, even vintage bottles of red wine, but tiny cards with funny looking men in even funnier poses holding a stick of wood or under-sized leather mitt? I never asked how many he had or even who he kept under his bed in a huge locked box, but there probably would have been enough players to line up on every team that ever suited up from Boston to Los Angeles from the 1890s till the present day - and then some.

"Good to see you, too J.R.," I replied, ignoring his request. It was good to see him, even if he did look as though the good life had gone bad. Though he was only my height, about 5 foot, 8 inches, he always looked larger than life. Much of it had to do with his Easter Island-sized head. It gave every one of his expressions – of which there were too many to name – a sense of urgency/joy/sadness/etc. Once you'd gazed into J.R.'s baby blues, you were hooked – man or woman. Though he featured more than his fair share of bulging muscles along his stalky arms and legs, everyone always commented on his looks. He did a Cagney to die for; ditto for Bogart and John Wayne. It didn't matter. But they were all way past their primes and now, so too was J.R. He seemed less imposing. Perhaps it was the way that time had chucked splotches of gray and white through his wavy hair. Or maybe it was the lines on his forehead and the slight left-hand lean of his upper torso.

"Yeah, you too, kid, but hey, can I borrow 20 bucks?"

"Geez, does ol' Ralph know he's only worth that much? I thought he was worth at least $50?"

"Quit messing with me, kid. I ain't got time for this right now. Just want to take the lady out for a drink or three and see what gives."

"What gives will be—"

"Hey, c'mon, sport. Don't you remember that last time you dropped by and what I did for you?"

"Oh, yeah, I remember. You introduced me to a total frickin' fruitcake who tried to stab me through the heart with a steak knife."

"Hey, she missed, right?"

At this point, my dear neighbor's pet beast bowled through the doorway as if to announce the pending presence of its owner.

"Why, Walter, what a pleasure to see you?" Louisa May said strolling into my penthouse like she was waltzing down the Palace of Versailles' Hall of Mirrors.

"Likewise, Mrs. May, but really can we do this another time? I'm a bit tired."

"You poor boy. You look hungry. Can I fix you an omelette, dear?"

This offer was met by a rather strange gaze from my uncle that suggested any egg-based offering – or any other source of sustenance for that matter – would not be a wise move for me right now. It was quite a look. You should have seen it. Vintage George Raft perhaps?

"Ahh, no thanks, Mrs. May. I think I'll just turn in. Why don't you kids go on without me?"

With that, Louisa May and her trusty four-legged companion retreated to their own lair while J.R. treated himself to $30 from my wallet.

"Just in case," he says explaining the need for the extra sawbuck.

"Jeez, what would that be – a Feller?" I said referring to the money's value in card terms. Bob Feller was a a star Cleveland Indians ace pitcher of the 1950s.

"Nah, way to low for that. More like a Parnell," he replied, (referring to Mel Parnell, another 1950s pitcher, albeit for the Yankees). "But only in very good condition – a mint one be worth five times that," he added.

"Just love it when you talk dirty, J.R. Speaking of mint condition, you better get going or you'll miss out on Mrs. May."

With that, my dear ol' uncle turned and headed for the door, but not before I called out: "Swing for the fences." I was still chuckling to myself about the thought of J.R. hitting a home run with Louisa May Alcott's older sister when the phone rang.

"Hello, Walter. Gee, you're difficult to catch." It was spooky how many times she called me just before or after a visit from her younger brother.

"Ah, hi Mom. Yeah, it's been a bit busy at work lately."

"Been hearing some good things about your work. Love to see you. How about coming by for dinner tomorrow night?"

"Ah, yeah, that sounds great, Mom."

"You remember how to get here?" she said in her most sarcastic tone.

"I'll figure it out."

"See you at 7," she said just before the line went dead.

Chapter Seven

I didn't get much sleep that night. Not sure whether I was more worried about my upcoming dinner with dear ol' Mom or J.R.'s romantic interlude with the living mummy next door. I got a call from J.R. the next day to say it had been a bit of a bust and that he'd dropped Louisa May off at The Lincoln before heading back to Connecticut. I didn't ask why it didn't work out. Finding the right chemistry with an ordinary woman near the same age is hard enough. Finding it with someone whose birthdate pre-dated carbon dating is much harder. He promised to make it up to me by splurging on a 'Paul Waner' the next time I dropped by. No prizes for guessing that he was referring to a baseball player, but if my own baseball card price guide was anything to go by, I could expect a meal worth $100 or $200! You see, Waner was quite a player in his time. He was a big shot in the 1930s, about the time Louisa May started dating. Hell, she probably went out with Waner.

I spent most of the afternoon at the 'Final Edition' hoping that something really juicy like a multi-car pile-up would take place in the center of the village and I'd be called out to cover it. Sadly, no one died or even got severely maimed that afternoon. I did see my new mentor Hugh who dropped by for a top up before heading over to the office. He nodded to me and even asked how I thought the Patriots would go this year, which was something of a breakthrough. He left just before Martin James and his sidekick, a goofy looking middle-aged guy named Jack Saunders, stopped by. They didn't see me at first, probably because I was hiding down back with my face stuck behind the latest edition of '*The Record*'. They were talking about some story to run in tomorrow's paper and from what I could gather, it had something to do with the local living museum.

Martin didn't seem all too happy about the piece. Saunders agreed. No surprises there. Saunders would've agreed with Martin if he'd said the Red Sox would win the pennant in 1980. For those of you who are not baseball nuts, let me explain that the likelihood of this happening was very remote. The last time they had won, the headlines had more to do with World War I than the World Series. I wasn't sure what his journalistic credentials were, but as far as I could tell, they were either slim or none. His big claim to fame was going around the newsroom fronting up to anyone he didn't like and yelling out: "ARE YOU QUESTIONING MY INTEGRITY?" If that piece of repartee sounds familiar, go to the head of the class. Yes, it was indeed the same line favored by his boss, Martin, giving you some idea of the amount of imagination that Saunders' pea-sized brain contained.

Just what querying someone's 'integrity' had to do with writing or editing copy was anyone's guess, but that's the best either one of the non-Dynamic Duo could offer. Someone told me that Saunders had been a small-time politician. His stature in the community was now positively microscopic given *The Record*'s standing in the news fraternity. He was quite tall with a large beer gut that provided ample shade for his smallish feet. His face was overshadowed by a head of hair that only grew on the sides like Larry of the Three Stooges or Bozo the Clown. Take your pick. He also had a huge moustache no doubt trying to cover up his teeth which were stained dark yellow from chain smoking. When he yelled, which was quite often, his shortish arms flailed all over the place like some sort of short-circuited walrus' flippers.

Martin was saying something about having to front up to the old lady, (that would be the publisher who I still hadn't seen since arriving back in town some weeks ago). "She's going to be bullshit about it," Martin said.

"Hmm, I know what you mean," Saunders said as his right flipper pushed two more glasses of ale their way.

"Why'd he do it?"

"Hmm, know what you mean," Saunders muttered again, obviously not even paying what little attention his gnat-like skull would allow, preferring instead to swill the tall glass in one gulp.

The two left soon after, leaving me in no doubt there would be hell to pay tomorrow. That suited me fine. In fact, I'd finally gotten the break I was waiting for all afternoon. If my mother was in anything like the mood I'd left her in the last time we met, I'd never see tomorrow. Thank god for small mercies.

It was not a particularly long or even unpleasant drive to my mother's house. It was only a couple of miles from the town along the eastern shore of the Big Puddle. It was the big end of town where anyone who was someone, resided. The homes had first been quaint lakefront cottages, but they were now grand enough for those who made their living from squashing the hopes and dreams of others. The first grand home one approached belonged to the Morgans. They had made so much money from twisting the truth in courtrooms across New England that they were able to parlay this skill into another profession that required quick thinking, guile and very, very thick skin – politics. The latest member of the clan, Mrs. Eustace Tucker-Morgan, was New Richmond's Mayor and willing to tell anyone who was dumb enough to listen that she'd one day be Governor. Their palatial home had a touch of *'Gone with the Wind'* about it, complete with towering white columns and huge windows that would not have looked out of place on Buckingham Palace.

The next lakeside cottage looked more like a prison than a home, which was appropriate, since it belonged to the Chief of Police who was currently being investigated regarding numerous less-than-honorable activities, too many to mention here. It featured bricks, millions of them covering everything from every inch of the three-story building to its Berlin Wall-like perimeter fence and even the long and winding driveway. I would not have been surprised to learn that they sat and slept on brick furniture.

Next came the James' family estate. Though their fortune was founded on paper, reams and reams of newspaper, when it came to construction, they preferred something a bit longer lasting. It lacked a moat, but contained just about everything else one would expect from a castle. It wasn't one of those castles built to draw admirers, though. Quite the opposite. It seems the earlier members of the James Gang were at least as concerned about keeping neighbors out as they were about letting everyone in on the latest breaking news stories. So much so that they fashioned their beachhead homestead out of stone – or should I say boulders. Many of these large rocks apparently had been moved from nearby quarries, sometime during the late eighteenth or early nineteenth century. They supposedly enslaved generations of friendly Indians to build their castle for them. The exterior's unusual light granite brown shading featured bold streaks of red, which so another story went, were all that remained from the blood spilt by hundreds of Indian laborers drip, drip dripping down its façade like so many sorrow-filled teardrops.

Enough of the architectural appetizers. Time for the main event – the holiest of holies; the cat's whiskers and pajamas all purring as one. The legendary Winslow Estate, so named after the town's most famous (and infamous) natives who unhappy with their lot alongside their Pilgrim compatriots at Plimoth Plantation, upped and schlepped west in search of greener pastures. Of course, they didn't settle in New Richmond right away. A few years passed before they made it to this wild frontier town sometime in the early 1720s. I had started doing research on this part of the family tree at the town's library, though hadn't gotten too far. I didn't mind that, though. I actually spent a bit of time working at a large library in between reporting gigs in Indiana. It was at Indiana University's multi-story monster on its Bloomington campus. Instead of putting books back in their proper places, I spent far more time taking other books out and poring over their yellow-stained pages, soaking up accounts of days and nights gone by in the lives of such luminaries as Mark Twain, Stephen Crane and Washington Irving.

Here is what I did know about my mother's patriarchal past. The grand poobah, Edward Winslow, was a printer and author, so anyone looking to lay blame for this lame story can pin it on him. He also was a bit of a wheeler dealer and wound up criss-crossing the pond which bridged the Old and New Worlds, with various business schemes before dying of fever during a military expedition to capture the island of Hispaniola. His son Josiah, after whom my mother's father and Uncle J.R. were named, had been an early Governor of Plymouth Colony.

Ensuing generations decided it was far safer to remain in New England where it was much easier to control one's fate. Few people died of fever in the colonies, though I do seem to recall a fair number springing off their mortal coils due to run-ins with pissed off Indians, bears, venomous snakes, ultra-cold winters or some combination of the above.

It was while building this grand estate that I now was approaching, that my great, great, great, great, great grandfather decided there was a dollar or three to be had from real estate. Christ, he probably gave away a free turkey with every house lot, but whatever it was, he very quickly became recognized as the area's prime land overlord.

My history lesson was interrupted by a big dark sedan zooming by me at the front gate. I hit the horn, or what was left of its feeble siren. The noise was drowned out by the screeching tires cutting hard to the left out of the drive.

It was practically pitch black out and with the idiot's bright headlights shining in my eyes, it was nearly impossible to tell who was behind the wheel. I did, however, believe it to include the heads of two people – probably women judging by the big heads of hair.

I won't bore you with a lot of detail about the house. Suffice it to say the word big isn't big enough to cover it. How big is it then? Big enough to fit my not-too compact Toyota easily through the front door. Big enough to include a six-car garage; detached carriage house that could comfortably sleep eight; Olympic-size swimming pool outside and nearly one as big inside; full-size tennis court; 18-hole golf course, you get the picture. We're talking BIG. Rumor had it that each floor had its own zip code. Put another way, my mother could eat a meal in a different room each day and probably not see the same one for six months. For all of its grandeur, it now was graced by only one person – perhaps not the last in the Winslow line, but certainly about as close to the rear end as you could get.

"You're late," boomed the voice of dear mama.

"Yes, sorry about that but I nearly got run over by your rude guests," I replied hoping she'd spill the beans on the unknown vehicle's driver.

"Your dinner is getting cold," she said equally coldly.

"Ah, there's nothing like a good-ol, home-cooked meal," I said. "Especially when it's from Mario's," referring to the area's most popular restaurant.

"Save your material for the newspaper," my mother replied. "It's cold out here." Her shadowy form still cut quite a figure – even in the moonlight. She had long, wavy dark hair; deep blue eyes setting off her olive skin; long legs and most of all, at least according to all my high school pals – the deepest, sexiest voice on the planet – or at least in the Greater New Richmond area. She made many men, and women, quiver. She mostly just made me feel uneasy and queasy.

"So, how ya been, ma?"

"Cut the crap. When are you going to grow up?"

"Excuse me, I thought we were going to at least try to be civil."

"You think you're so smart, don't you?"

"Never really understood why they called it the 'Civil War'. Can't think of anything civil about war, can you, Mom?"

"Let's cut to the chase, shall we?"

"Yes, let's. Okay, I'll agree to stay here but only if I get the big bedroom and can swim naked in the pools."

"I just had a visit from Connie, I mean, Mrs. Wheeler-James--"

"Connie, is it? And what did ol' Connie have to say for herself?"

"Not a lot, but she did have a little to say about you and your next feature story on Olde Richmond Plantation."

"That's not even typeset yet. If they pull that story, I'm out of here! Aww, to heck with you, I'm outta here, anyway. Great to see you, Mom. Let's do this again real soon – like in another lifetime?"

And with that, I stormed out of the house in a re-run of the exit I'd made just about 15 years ago to the day. Heck, even we Winslow-Adams-Bedrosian-Johnsons had to have some family traditions.

Chapter Eight

"Yeah," I coughed into the phone which had been ringing for about 20 minutes non-stop.

"Hey, Walt, that you?"

"Yeah, who's this?"

"Lou," as in Lou Cassals, fellow '*Record*' reprobate who'd I'd met at the 'Final Edition' last night for a drink or three.

"What time is it?"

"Time for you to get out of town, sunshine. Can you hear that noise?"

While I had to admit I did hear a fair bit of yelling and screaming somewhere out on the main street, it didn't seem any more or less than a typical Friday or Saturday night's activity outside one of the town's many pubs.

My muddled brain then realized, of course, that this was a timing issue. Most yelling and screaming took place in the wee wee hours after some hotshot had downed two too many alcoholic ego boosters. This verbal assault was occurring at the ungodly hour of 10 a.m. on a weekday! I slowly got out of bed and headed toward my tiny balcony. My eyes were greeted with the sight of some 50, maybe 100 people standing beneath the newspaper's front door howling and screaming for all they were worth.

I went back inside and picked up the phone. "What have we done now?" I asked.

Lou laughed. "Aren't we modest. They're all here for you and what you said about ORP!"

"You're shitting me, right?"

"No shit, man, and if I were you – I'd be making a move for someplace safe – like Australia – pronto!"

"You figure it's that bad?"

"Put it to you this way: I just saw Marty and Saunders head down to the Publisher's office and no one but no one ever goes there unless it's a bad thing – especially at this time of day. Christ, the woman's a bat as far as anyone knows preferring to only come out after dark."

"Thanks for the tip off. I just remembered I have to be in southern Connecticut for my next story, anyway," I said.

"Good move."

"Hey, Lou, any sign of Hugh Jackson?"

"You're kidding, right?"

"Yeah, guess it's a bit early for him, too."

The phone went dead. Before heading south, I couldn't resist wandering among the protesters incognito and figuring out what all the fuss was about. Donning my Cincinnati Reds hat and dark sunnies, I headed out along the sidewalk on the opposite side of the street from the newspaper. Police had cordoned off the road in both directions. The protestors included among others, the Mayoress, assorted long-time ORP employees and a couple of guys who worked part-time at 'The Record' as copy-editors. The rest of their time was spent in the company of a couple of other guys named Jim Beam and Jack Daniels, both of whom seemed in good spirits on this fine fall day. One guy carried a sign that read: "Nothing reads like a broken *Record*", while others performed rather imaginative chants. One went:

"ORP IS GOOD; ORP IS GREAT. WE WANT TO SET THE RECORD STRAIGHT."

The bluer version went:

"ORP IS GOOD; ORP'S GOT CLASS. USE THIS PAPER TO WIPE YOUR ASS."

And oh yes, there was one other notable attendee – my mother who was leading the crusade against the newspaper in general and moi in particular. Okay, so the Partridge Family we most assuredly were not. Even I had to admire her guts for getting out there and attacking her own flesh and blood. But then again, this trait seemed to run in both sides of the family, so she gets no credit for creative thinking on that score.

It seemed like a good time to retreat post haste to my apartment and prepare for a quick trip south of the border. The last thing I remember is looking up at the paper's front window and seeing Lou Cassals gesturing me to turn around. The only next image I have is of a four-legged, furry blur of a freight train launching itself toward me at a speed approaching Mach 1. It was my neighbor's trusty sidekick who ran full tilt before launching itself into my backside like some heat-seeking missile. The resultant collision knocked me into one protestor and then another and then another and before long, I was at the bottom of a very-pissed off pile of ORPies.

Fortunately, I must've blacked out because I don't remember any part of the fight. I came to in my favorite watering hole with Mel, the owner, hovering over me with a couple of cold cans of beer pressed to my face.

"Hey, Walt, you okay?" she asked.

"Am I still alive?"

Mel smiled. "Fraid so."

"Am I still employed?"

"Now that's a tougher question. But I'll see what I can do. I don't like losing good customers," she said. "What was with that dog?"

"Ohh, he was just fooling around. Did anyone get hurt?"

"You mean, besides you? I don't think so. But the police did take your mother and the dog's owner away."

"You're kidding, right?"

"Nope. Quite a sight really. Never knew your mother had it in her. She bolted over to the pile and grabbed the dog in a headlock. The dog went limp until this old lady showed up and started banging on your mother with a handbag that must have been filled with bricks," Mel said.

"By the time the police separated them, the rest of the crowd had turned into spectators. Except for you of course, who was out cold," she continued.

"Then what?"

"Well, I dragged you in here and then the police took the two female combatants away, along with the dog."

"I better go see how she's doing," I said.

"Who?" Mel asked.

"My mother, god bless her," I replied.

"I thought my family was fucked up. You guys take the cake," Mel said.

A proud smile came over my face. Don't know why, really. Guess it was good to agree on something regarding my clan even if it was a rather dubious distinction.

My head had stopped throbbing by the time I got to the police station. Hard to say whether it was the effects of the cold beer cans on my forehead from the previous few minutes or the previous night's alcoholic level finally leaving the system, but at least I was feeling a bit better. That is until I entered the station and heard my mother and Louisa May screeching like two wounded pole cats. Even the police were unsure how to handle this one.

"Give me a minute with her," I said to the attending officer, a semi-regular drinking buddy at the 'Final Edition'. He winked his approval and also gave me a look as if to say, "good luck."

"Whoa, Mom, Mrs. May - time out!" I yelled.

The two ladies stopped in their tracks and turned on me. Both began shouting in unison.

"Mrs. May, are you alright?" I asked.

"Why, yes, dear, I'm fine. But I can't believe this she-devil is your mother. Why, she has none of the grace and dignity of your Uncle Josiah."

That did it. The mere mention of my uncle's name, let alone the way in which he was portrayed, was enough to start the fight all over again. This time, though, I grabbed my mother and pressed her against the wall. My police pal did the same with Louisa May on the opposite wall.

"Now, Mom, calm down or you'll wind up staying here for a few nights," I said.

"I'm fine, dear. But who the hell is this faded film star?"

"My neighbor at The Lincoln," I said.

"Figures. No wonder you prefer living there over my home," she said dripping with sarcasm.

"Hey, you should talk. One minute, you're protesting against me; the next minute you're trying to protect me?"

"Yes, well, you're still my flesh and blood and I would do anything to protect you," replied the winner of the Triple AAA anti-maternal mother award for the past three decades. I swear, if someone had agreed to carry me for the nine months prior to birth, my mother would've put her Joanna Hancock on any piece of paper.

"Thanks for your concern, but I think I like you better when we're fighting," I said.

With that, she broke into a laugh and lay her head on my shoulder. 'Love you, Walter,' she said.

"Me too, Mom. Let's get outta here," I said.

"Sorry about all the fuss," she said. "But I really was upset by what you wrote in that story. You have so much talent. Why do you always have to make everything sound so awful?"

"The truth always hurts," I replied.

"Has Connie spoken to you yet?"

"I've not yet had the pleasure, though I do look forward to it if for no other reason than to call the region's most powerful woman – 'Connie'," I said. "I'm actually leaving town for a few days and catching up with Dad in New London."

"Now?"

"Yeah, any messages?"

"For him? You have to be joking," she said returning us to where we left off some time last night.

"Great. Can we agree to disagree for now then?"

"Absolutely. But I want to see you when you get back. There's still much to discuss – about a lot of things," she said.

"No problem," I said preferring not to think about what her last statement meant. What 'lot of things' could we possibly have to talk about?

Before leaving town, I checked in on my neighbor to see how she and Rin Tin Tin's evil twin were doing. Both were doing fine. The dog, who I also now learned was named 'Flynn' after her favorite actor – (Aussie icon Errol Flynn who she also no doubt knew intimately), even came up to me for a gentle pat. I also called the newspaper to catch up on the latest developments with Lou, but he was out on assignment. Hugh Jackson also had not shown up for work yet. I did learn that Marty James was keen to talk to me, but I quickly hung up before he could grab the phone. My last call was to Mel at the bar to check on any insights she had into the day's events.

"Far as I can tell, you're still employed, though only just. Jury's still out on what to do with Jackson. I'll have a quiet word with my mother when next she stops by," she said.

"Your mother drinks? In the bar?" I asked not fully believing anyone so high and mighty would ever stoop so low with even lower lights like me.

"Oh shit, yeah. But she picks her moments. She's not really all that bad – or hard to figure. If it makes money, she's in. If it don't, she's out. Simple as that. For what it's worth, my advice to you is get out of town for a couple of days and let things settle."

"What about Marty?"

"He's the least of your worries," Mel replied. "Now get outta here."

"Thanks, I owe you."

"Damn right, you owe me. Thanks for reminding me. You owe me for those two cans of Bud I put on your face to revive you," she said.

"Stick them on my tab, you big softy Melinda Constance James."

"You ever repeat that name to anyone else and I'll deck you so hard you'll need a fricking keg wrapped around your head to reduce the swelling," she said just before the line went dead.

Chapter Nine

The phone did ring one more time, but I let the machine take it. "Walter, if you're there, please pick up," announced another familiar female voice. "I need to talk to you," said Jenny Lawton, my old flame. "I, well, just call me, soon?" she said before giving up.

I certainly had a way with the unfairer sex, though I rarely had my way with them. It was a part of my game that could use a lift, though now was probably not the best time to work on it. What could she possibly want with me?

I blocked it out of my mind and headed south for the Connecticut border. It was an easy cross, just a few minutes along a deserted, old two-lane divided highway. Besides, I always felt much closer for some damn reason to this small neighbor of the Massachusetts Bay Colony. Maybe it's the fact that it's the only state along the eastern seaboard in which one of the country's largest highways, Route 95, actually runs east-west rather than north-south. Must freak foreigners out when they look on the map from New York City and see that to get to one of the state's main attractions - Mystic Seaport – they must take Route 95 north when in fact, this small seaside town is east of The Big Apple.

Maybe it's the fact that Connecticut is home to the country's first newspaper, 'The Hartford Courant', which opened for business in 1764, making 'The Record' look like a journalistic toddler. Other firsts include the first insurance company, the first dictionary, the first revolver, the first hamburger, the first portable typewriter, even the first pay phone. It also claims a slew of other more unusual firsts like the first lollipop, Frisbee, ice-making machine, tape measure, cotton gin and atomic-powered submarine.

There are other bits of its make-up that always interest me, though. For starters, the state's territory is split nearly perfectly in half by the Connecticut River. While nowhere near as big as the mighty Mississippi, the Connecticut manages to do something few other waterways can claim: It very neatly divides the haves from the havenots. Any would-be gold diggers reading these pages would do well to stick to bars and pubs on the river's western shores if they're looking to hook a whopper. While not a perfect form guide, let's just say there's a lot more wealth on the western front than in many of the areas I knew best back east.

The state's homey inhabitants also had another trait that makes them downright lovable. While early settlers tended to hark back to the old countries for inspiration when it came to naming places and natural landmarks, they certainly didn't play favorites when it came to bastardizing the originator's nom de plume.

Take the very quiet and out of the way inland eastern hamlet of Versailles. It's unlikely that either Louis XIV or Marie Antoinette would've stopped by for a croissant and coffee. And not just because there are no fancy castles, graceful promenades or gold-encrusted fountains found there. No, the ol' King of France would've schlepped right by his New World namesake quite simply because it's not called vair-SIGH. It's known as vurr-SAILS. Then, too, some other bright British spark setting out by boat from New London named the area's largest river after their favorite old home waterway – the Thames. You guessed it, rather than call it the TEMMS, locals prefer The THAMES. Nothing pretentious about this crowd.

Connecticut also has boasted a rich Indian history, though little if any record of these inhabitants ever made local newspapers, let alone history books or even Hollywood movies. Perhaps they were not as colorful as their Plains and Western brethren who captured people's imaginations as much for their less kinder moments as for their good deeds. For some reason, though, I greatly enjoyed reading about the early settlers and their native counterparts. I even found some old gravestones deep in the backwoods of my grandfather's ranch, paying homage to fallen pioneers from the early 18th century who were cut down by allegedly angry Indians. I also enjoyed tramping around in the adjoining Indian reserve near the Big Puddle's northeastern rim where it was not unusual to come across large mounds. Dig down into these mounds and it was not uncommon to unearth fine examples of arrowheads surrounded by millions of shells. These mounds were basically the

Indians' garbage dumps where they obviously threw all the shells from the region's original clam bakes.

Today, little evidence remains of the rich history enjoyed by the area's original settlers. Instead, most of their sites have been turned either into huge gambling halls or housing developments while still other sites along the southern shoreline now boast towering temples dedicated to the State's top dogs: Multi-billion-dollar Defence contractors like General Dynamics who churn out monolithic steel-clad, nuclear-powered denizens of the deep to keep the Russians at bay.

All this thinking about the State's rich history led me to selecting a far more laid-back, rustic rumble through some of the eastern half's rich array of small, near-deserted towns, many of which had dried up when water wheels were replaced by electric power. There were few signs of recent developments such as 7-11s, McDonald's or Kentucky Fried. Instead, there was usually a row of small one-story, peeling weatherboard homes, an old gas station, complete with mechanic (permanently off duty) and a small grocery store filled with canned goods left over from the last World War. Still, there was something appealing about these villages. There was something worth admiring about places that, whether they had done so consciously or not, repelled any moves to bring them into the 20th century, preferring instead to recall an era when a horse's hooves set the pace. There probably was a story in finding out why so many (or was it so few?), people still called these places home. Places like Surrey Hills, which is situated about half-way between New Richmond and New London.

The one thing that did work in these areas was the local pay phone. I suspect because for many of the locals, it was the only form of communication with the outside world. Figured I'd give ol J.R. a ring and try to catch up with him while I was in the area.

"Hey, how are ya, buddy?"

"Just great, J.R. What you up to?"

"You shoulda been here yesterday. My old pal Bob was in town."

"Bob?"

"Bob Mitchum, you chump," he said.

"The actor?"

"Don't know any other Bob Mitchums, do you?"

And therein lay another of my dear uncle's fabulous traits. In addition to buying and selling baseball cards, he claimed to know many luminaries from the sports and entertainment fields, though I'd yet to actually meet one. In addition to Big Bob, there was Sammy Davis, Red Sox legend Ted Williams, even a young brash Aussie golfer named Greg Norman, among others who had obviously spent time in the company of the great J.R. Winslow IV.

"I'm afraid to ask how you know him, but just wondering if you're around for the next day or so?"

He was and then proceeded to drop a story idea on me that just might top all the other ones combined. More on that later.

For now, it was back in the Toyota for the last leg to New London and a visit with yet another member of the dysfunctional first family.

A smile always came over my face whenever I visited with my dad. You see, I always picture him as a young man – the man who stole my mother's heart – at least for the time it takes a heart to beat. She always said he reminded her of Omar Sharif who was *big time* at the time they were dating. Dr. Zhivago and all that jazz. And therein lies the reason for the smile.

Because I found it unlikely that Omar ever worked as a short-order chef at HoJo's in New London, Connecticut. Then again, I don't recall Omar ever having a budding beer belly, balding head or thick glasses preferred by his New World double. This picture was completed with the perfunctory HoJo's hat (you know those stylish ones that make everyone look like a demented Shriner), white shirt and slacks and matching apron, complete with stains from god knows what fake food.

"Dad, good to see ya," I said approaching him gingerly for fear the stains would rub off on my two-day-old L.L. Bean jumper.

"Good to see you, son," he says before placing his Popeye-like forearms around me in a bear hug.

"Is this someone I should be jealous of, hon?" came a female voice from behind us.

I turned and began to wonder what part of the Twilight Zone I'd just entered. There, before me, was a female version of my father – except for two noticeable differences: She had more hair on her head – and arms than my father – but far fewer front teeth.

"Hi Connie. You've heard me talk about my son, Walter. Walter, meet Connie."

"Hi Connie, nice to meet you," I said lying through the perfect set of enamels contained in my skull. "Friends call me Walt."

"Give me a hug, sugar," said Connie.

She squeezed me the way wrestlers do while waiting for the three count from the referee. "Ooh, you're a thin one," she said in a tone that was filled with disappointment.

"Yes, I just don't get to eat as much fried food and ice cream as I'd like," I replied.

Connie gave me a blank look. No, that's not right. It was more than blank. It was far less than blank. It was vacant. No, that's not right, either. It was a black hole look, totally void of any understanding of who or what stood before her. I envied the hell out of this woman.

"Connie is my head waitress," my father finally chimed in, trying to fill the black hole.

"And I also give him head," Connie added which showed just the right amount of class for the occasion.

"How nice for you both," I said wishing I was somewhere else; anywhere else.

"Connie, can you give us a minute?" dear old dad offered. Connie turned and went through the swing door into the dining area.

"Christ dad, is she a keeper or what?"

"Don't start, smart ass," he said. "Come down to do another story on your old man?"

"Ah, no. Just to catch up and let you know how Pop is going."

"Ahh, he's fine. Old bastard will outlive all of us," he said in obvious disdain for his own fatherly figure.

Getting back to his earlier comment: My father actually had graced the pages of 'The Record' some years ago. It was not while he was in charge of the night shift at the New London HoJo's. It was some other godforsaken Eastern Connecticut town the name of which thankfully had escaped me. What made my Dad newsworthy was not the fact that he worked at Howard Johnson's. No, it was far worse than that. The story centered on the fact that he worshipped the organization. He loved working for the food firm so much that he changed his Armenian wog name from Torkum Bedrosian to Howard W. Johnson and his only son's as well. And to make it even worse, he insisted that the authorities at town hall add the "'s" on the end of the name so it matched perfectly with the restaurant signage. And to make matters worse still, (though the reporter didn't use those words at the time), he painted the roof on his own house orange, just like the ones on the restaurant. I can still see the picture of dear old dad, dressed in his company whites, pitched precariously on the roof of our house in whatever shithole town it was, all the while pointing to a menu. Yes, that was a proud moment in the Bedrosian/Johnson's clan.

At some level, though, I admired the guy. I mean, he was going nowhere fast as a farmer and obviously didn't have a marriage so he picked himself up and wandered down the MassPike, stopping in at the first business he saw and asked for a job. It happened to be a HoJo's and they hired him on the spot as a dishwasher. He took this as an omen, which it was, in an odd sort of way. Dishwashers, that's the human variety I'm talking about, come and go at HoJo's practically on a daily basis. It's a thankless job that never ends – particularly during the morning, noontime and evening rushes. Like most back-room jobs, there's no one there to thank you for a job well done. There's only someone there to give you hell when something goes wrong. At least that's what Dad tells me. He happened to drop by this particular eating establishment just as his predecessor was walking out, drip, drip, dripping from one too many sprays of water on him rather than the customers' plates during that day's lunch hour.

Dad slowly worked his way up the HoJo pecking order, culminating in his current position as short order chef/assistant night manager. Anyone working the grill was considered something of a star. Not sure why exactly. Maybe it harkened back to caveman times. You know, he who makes fire, makes merry. I dunno but I do know the story of how he earned his assistant managerial stripes was nothing short of comic genius.

One of his many hats in this role was conducting routine inventories on food stocks. It was not uncommon to go through 100 or more hamburgers and hot dogs (each) on a busy night, so it was important to know how many were still in the walk-in refrigerators. His predecessor (and mentor) on the short-order grill was a man of prodigious passions. His name was John Colter and no one knew much about him except that he preferred being called 'Big Johnnie'. We didn't even know why he liked that nickname, since he was quite short – so short in fact that he often needed to stand on upside-down milk crates to reach the plate shelf next to the grill. He had equally short arms and stocky legs that bowed as if from carrying great weights around on his shoulders. If you could believe some of the women who worked at HoJo's, he apparently oozed sexuality and though he wasn't everyone's cup of tea, nearly everyone got a piece of Big Johnnie whether they wanted him or not. Few diners, for instance, would have been impressed with the way he 'spiced up' the tuna salad. Traditional mid-day sandwich favorites like tuna and egg salad, were often made up in advance and crammed into square metallic bowls that when not kept on the benchtop next to the grill, were stored in the walk-in frig. Big Johnnie, who was known to sample most menu items regularly, used to say that these pre-mixed recipes lacked "zest," complaining that they often tasted like sawdust. So, when the spirit moved him, he took great pleasure in working his sexual instrument up into a lather and then inserting it into the tuna salad container and injecting his own splash of DNA into the recipe. Gave the tuna salad a "bit of raw protein," was his favorite explanation. I still wince every time I pass the tuna aisle in the grocery store.

Big Johnnie also didn't take rejection real well. If and when any diner deemed it necessary to return a sirloin or hamburger for not being cooked well enough, he'd throw the offending piece of meat on the greasy, dirty kitchen floor and step on it several times. He then would pick up the newly-tenderized piece of meat and spit on it – three or four times - before placing a new sprig of parsley on it and hitting the bell which alerted the waitress that her order was ready for picking up. All the weeks I watched this ritual, I never once saw one of these orders come back again.

It was his penchant for HoJo's hot dogs, however, that would prove to be his undoing. HoJo's hot dogs came in large boxes, like the ones long stemmed roses come in. Must have been 50 or so in each box. Big Johnnie routinely helped himself to one or two of these boxes and took them home for his own family barbecues. Everyone knew he was doing it, but no one would snitch on him. So, Dad, in his own style, set a trap. He ordered in a couple of extra boxes and marked them 'Special Order'. Big Johnnie took the bait and as he so casually did, walked out the back door cradling one of these hot dog boxes on his right shoulder.

Now, Big Johnnie should have known something was different on this night, but his arrogance knew no bounds. He always stole the dogs on a traditionally slow night, usually a Monday. On this particular Monday night, there were cars all over the back parking lot. That was because my father had called in the local police who were waiting for their quarry. No sooner had Big Johnnie come out the back door with another slab of hot dogs on his shoulder when a large spotlight hit his face. He stopped cold and the smile that seemed to constantly grace his round face – turned sour. An officer turned on a bullhorn – "Stop where you are. Drop the dogs!" he said. Big Johnnie did as he was told and gave up without a whimper. I asked my Dad some time later whatever happened to Big Johnnie. He said he wound up delivering flowers, many of which came in long narrow boxes just like the dogs. What goes round, comes round.

My Dad was considered a hero by management (and a bum by staff) for catching the hot dog marauder and was quickly promoted to management.

He never got to meet the original Howard Johnson – thank god. I hate to think what the media would have made of that meeting.

"Can I make you a tuna salad sandwich or somethin?" Dad offered.

I winced once more at the thought of Big Johnnie's protein-filled recipe. "No, I'm fine. Just thought I'd stop by and say 'Hi', but I can see you're pretty busy, both with the business and in the female department."

He blushed. "You like working at the paper?"

"Yeah, it's okay. Think I'll stay a while," I said.

"Good, that's good. Seen your mom?"

"Yeah. Still the same. We spoke for two, maybe three minutes, then wound up springing her out of jail and haven't spoken since."

"You two. Two peas in a pod," he said.

I actually hadn't thought of that before, but he was probably on to something there. Perhaps that's why we did fight so much. But even more peculiar was how the heck those two ever ended up together in the first place. But that's another story.

"You better get outta here before Connie comes back. She wants to fix you up with her daughter."

"Hey, that could be fun. Maybe we could double date, eh?"

Before he could respond, I felt someone grabbing me from behind. I feared it was the return of Connie 'Haystacks' Calhoun. Fortunately, it was only Uncle J.R.

"Gotcha," he said.

"Hi J.R.," my father said. Though my mother and father hadn't worked out – the relationship between them was quite strong.

"G'day, Howie. What's cookin?" he said.

Dad ignored the question, preferring to find out what the two of us were planning.

"Well, I promised the boy here a very special treat the next time he was in town," J.R. teased.

"Yes," I said. "Tell me more."

"We're gonna clean up," he said.

"Clean what up?" my father asked.

"I'm gonna introduce the boy to the center of the frickin universe," J.R. said.

"Ah, yes, do tell me more about this wondrous place?" I said.

"Sure. It's Fred's Laundromat on Colman Street," J.R. said.

The mind boggled at just what dear old' J.R. had in store for me, but unfortunately, I was unable to find out any more about just why and how this innocuous looking and more-than-slightly run down Laundromat held the key to the universe. My own universe back in New Richmond, once again flared and required immediate attention. Tales of inter-galactic daring do, it seemed, would have to wait for another day.

Chapter Ten

I rather foolishly made one last call to the newspaper to see what was going on. As usual, I rang my own extension, figuring Lou Cassals would pick up. I got Martin James instead.

"Where the hell you been?" the editor asked.

"Just checking out the universe," I replied.

"Get your ass back here now – pronto!" Martin screamed down the line.

"Can I ask why—"

The line went dead before I could find out why my presence was required so urgently. I opted against returning directly to the newspaper, preferring to check in on my demented neighbors at The Lincoln. I was greeted by Louisa May's dog who was camped on my doorstep, all the while growling softly at me. After thanking her for being such a gracious doormat, I turned the knob and found a rather odd looking throw-rug laying before me. If I didn't know any better, it looked like Hugh Jackson.

"Walter, is that you dear?" came Louisa May's sturdy whisper from the doorway.

"Yeah," I replied not knowing what else to say.

"I didn't know what to do, Walter. This rather surly gentleman began knocking on your door early this morning and refused to stop."

"What time was that?"

"About 3 a.m.," she said.

"3 a.m.?"

"He kept shouting something about cats and Marsden," she continued.

"I see. Well, thank you for looking after him. It's okay. I sort of work for him."

"Oh, I see. Well, he should learn some manners. Let me know if you would like me to do anything else," Louisa May said.

"That's fine, ma'am. You've done more than he – or I – deserved."

"Come, Flynn. Time for your walk," she said.

I thanked her again and shut the door not knowing what to do next. I didn't have to wait long. The throw-rug for once wasn't throwing up in front of me.

"What the fuck…Where am I?" my esteemed some-time editor asked.

"Would you believe in the drawing room of your favorite feature writer?"

Hugh turned over slowly all the while rubbing his eyes. He gazed at me and didn't appear fazed in the slightest. "That you, Johnson?"

"Hey, don't mind me, I only live here."

Jackson ignored that retort. He'd heard them all before and then some. "Yeah, sorry about all this, but it occurred to me that you should know a few things."

"Oh, so at about 3 a.m. it occurs to you that I should know a few things? Am I allowed to ask about what precisely?"

"Work and life," he replied before asking if I had any whiskey.

"Let's try something with a bit less bite. How about coffee? You spill the beans on work and life in that order," I replied hoping he'd forget about the earlier alcoholic order.

"I got thrown outta the house," he said, ignoring my last comment.

"What house?"

"My house, you idiot. My wife threw me out," he said.

I was surprised by this information. I knew he'd lost one wife. Didn't sound overly promising for his second go, either, but then again, I never figured him as the marrying type.

"And this has what to do with me precisely?" I finally offered.

"I'd had a long conversation with Connie," he began.

"Connie? As in Constance Wheeler-James?"

"Yeah, that's the one," he said still rubbing his eyes.

"Wait a minute. I'm totally lost here. You start talking about your wife and then jump to Connie?"

"Yeah, the two are not unrelated. You see –"

Hugh's confession was interrupted by the very annoying sound of my phone ringing. I debated whether or not to answer it and then decided to pick up. "Walt, is that you?"

"No, it's not Walt. It's his evil double – who the frack is this?"

"Jenny. It's me, Jenny."

"I'm a bit busy right now, Jenny. Can I call you back?"

"It's important, Walt. I need to talk to you."

"So you said in your last message. Look, I'm sorry about what happened five life times ago, but if it helps, I'm sorry, alright?"

"No, it's not that. It's something else. Well, it's a couple of things," she said.

"Look, Jenny. Fine. I'm late for work right now and I've got a bit of a situation here so can we meet tomorrow?"

"Oh, I didn't know you had someone there," she said assuming that my visitor was female.

"It's not a girl, Jenny. Not that it's any of your business. It's a guy friend of mine and no, I'm not gay if that's what you're thinking."

"Walt, don't be like that. No, this is serious. Well, I do have something to say about me – and you – but the other is about your granddad. It's important, Walt."

"He's not sick, is he?"

"No, it's not that. But we need to talk."

"Okay, alright. Tomorrow. Can I please go now?"

"Thanks, Walt. See you then." Click.

By the time I turned back to face my esteemed *'Record'* colleague, he'd fallen fast asleep again on the floor in much the same position as before, only this time he was lying face up. I decided to leave him there and get over to the office. Whatever he had to tell me about work, life and Connie could wait. Jeez, all these great offers: Uncle J.R. holding the key to the universe while ol' Hugh boy has the key to my job and my life. Who could ask for anything more?

Martin James for one. "Where the hell you been?" called out the editor from the entrance of the 'Final Edition'.

"I told you. Discovering the mysteries pertaining to life, work and the universe," I yelled out from across the street in front of the newspaper.

Martin ignored my remark and motioned for me to join him in the bar.

"Oh good. I like these sorts of meetings," I said.

"What'll you have, Walt?"

"A beer would be great," I replied.

"Walt, it's about time we go over some of your work."

"I didn't know we had a formal review process?"

"No, it's not formal. It's just, well, it's just—"

Martin's comments were interrupted by his sister Mel informing him that he was wanted back in the newsroom – pronto. "Oh, shit. Okay, ahh, Walt, stay here and have a drink on me. I'll catch up with you later on."

"Yeah, sure," I replied. "No problem." Jeez, did I have the plague or something? I couldn't find out nothing about anything.

Mel came over and joined me at the table. "I could see where that one was headed so I got rid of him," she said.

"You're kidding, right? Christ, he'll be madder than heck when he comes back," I said.

"Nah, he'll forget all about it. Besides, it's the old lady that needs to talk to you."

"Yeah, so when do I get to meet her? It's easier to get an audience with the fucking Pope."

"Don't worry. She'll find you," Mel said knowingly.

"What the heck does that mean?"

Mel shrugged her shoulders. I opted against pressing the issue.

"Hey, I ran into Hugh Jackson earlier. He mentioned something about him and your mother. Got any insight into that little number?"

"What?" she bellowed. "You gotta be kidding. Do yourself a favor. Get outta here before Marty gets back. Go somewhere. Anywhere but get outta town for the day. It'll all be cool by tomorrow," she said.

"If he comes back, tell him—"

"Hey, leave it to me. I know how to handle him," she said.

And with that, I finished my brewski and left via the back alley. No point in taking any chances. Figured it was a good day for a ride in the country.

Chapter Eleven

The leaves had long since left their lofty perches on the trees that enveloped the old road to granddad's ranch. With the additional chill in the air and the pewtery, gray sky, it was clearly evident that the season's first wintry blast was not far behind. I didn't give a stuff about Jack Frost, though. I couldn't feel a thing thanks to my old travelling companion – Jim Beam - who graciously jumped up off the shelf from behind the bar as I exited out the back door. I made a mental note to add the cost of the bottle to my tab, which at the rate I was going, would soon exceed the outgoings from Liz Taylor's bridal dowries. What difference did it make if I would soon be unemployed – once again – only this time from one of the world's worst newspapers? I mean, where do you go from '*The Record*?' The alternative wasn't worth contemplating.

My addled brain shifted to thoughts relating to Jenny Lawton. Why was she so hell-bent on seeing me? What the frack was so important – not only about her and me who had never been a couple even when we were supposedly together, but about ol' granddad? Had he killed again? Learned another word? What indeed?

It was nearly mid-day when I got to the farm. There didn't seem to be anybody about. It then occurred to me that I'd forgotten to ask Jenny where we would meet, rather stupidly assuming she would be at the farm. And since I didn't have her number, nor knew where she lived, it was unlikely I'd be able to track her down. I'd no sooner reached the front door, though, when Jenny pulled up in a brand new Toyota Celica sports coup.

"Quite flashy for a farm girl," I offered nodding at the car.

"Yeah, it gets me from A to Z," Jenny replied, breaking into one of her patented smiles. When her face lit up, I could remember why I found her so desperately cute all those years ago. Even though her hair was now tinted blonde and fell down over her shoulders, her face still glowed like that of some impish pixie. With huge brown eyes, tiny, turned up nose and chubby lower lip, she still looked more like a young child, rather than a grown woman. It wasn't her smile or even ample bust that had attracted me to her all those years ago. No, it was her legs – the most beautifully-crafted pair that had ever been moulded. Not to thin or thick, they were head turners from the time she was 14 and showed no signs of letting up – even beneath the rumpled track suit pants that encased them at present.

"Thanks for coming, Walt," she said.

"Always glad to oblige," I replied. "What's he done?"

"Nothing, Walt. Nothing, really. Let's take a walk out back. Okay?"

"I drove like a maniac for nothing? I haven't even seen him yet. Do you know where he is?"

"Calm down. Judging by the smoke coming out of the chimney, I'd say in his workshop over the garage. He spends a lot of time up there. He says because he likes woodworking. I think it's because it's the only place where he can keep warm," Jenny said breaking into one of her patented little-girl grins.

I decided to change the subject, in part because I wasn't really all that interested in my granddad's problem, and also because the ol' pilot light was starting to flicker again for the old flame. "So where you working?"

"I'm an exercise instructor at a nearby gym," she said quickly.

"Hey, I'm not interrogating you," I said.

"What difference does it make?" she replied. "Besides, there's something I've been meaning to tell you for a long time," she said while grabbing my left arm and motioning to sit down beside her atop a rather dishevelled stone wall.

"This sounds serious," I replied.

"No, not really. Well, I hope not. I just wanted to tell you how much I cared for you all those years ago and how much I missed you and yes, hated you for leaving."

"Join the queue, Jenny."

"No, I'm not trying to put you down. It's all so confusing and hard for me to explain, but please let me try."

I gave her a reassuring nod and she continued. "I realized after a while that you really weren't coming back and I felt guilty, because I felt I had driven you away."

"You? But you had nothing to do with it."

"I know that but after our last night together—"

"Hey, I'm the one who feels guilty. I never should've tried to make…"

"Shhhhh, Walt. I know you would not have done anything that we would have regretted. Then again, I'm not so sure I would have regretted it if we had."

"Thanks, Jenny. But this is all rather past tense and not really important for the here and now, is it?"

"I'm not done with the history lesson yet. You see, as much as I thought I loved you, I couldn't truly love you then."

"Now I'm the one wearing the cap of confusion."

"This is harder than I ever imagined, Walt, but the fact is, I was afraid that if we made love and had a child – it too might be born…"

"OHHHHH, now I get it! You were worried that your unborn child might only have one ear and turn into another freak show like me? Is that it? You waited 15 years to tell me what I've known all my life? That I'm a fucking freak? Thanks, Jenny. Thanks for filling me in on a real old piece of news. Thanks a lot," I replied and got up to go.

"Walter, please! That's not what I meant. You didn't let me finish," she said dragging me back down onto the unforgiving rock fence.

"Oh, there's more?"

"Please, Walt. Don't be like that. I really cared about you and yes, at the time, I was so confused and hurt and worried about something as stupid as a possible birth defect that I let it get in the way of my true feelings. After you left, well, let's just say I had a few relationships – one of which ended in giving me a beautiful child. And little else. None of these men ever, ever treated me with the dignity and respect that you did. And each time I started going out with someone else, I kept comparing them to you. To you, Walter and what made that so weird was the fact that you and I never really had a relationship."

I kept waiting for her to take a breath, but she didn't. "What I'm trying to say now is that try as I might to move on after you left, I never did. I tried but never found anyone who actually treated me the way you did. I just hope to god it isn't too late to try again."

I was left dumbfounded, and speechless, by this revelation. "I'm waiting for the 'but'."

"There's no 'but', Walt. I guess if you want one then it would be, 'but' I'm not trying to pressure you," Jenny said.

"Thanks. I mean, well, I don't know what to say," I said.

"You could say you'll think about what I've said?"

"Ah, yeah. Yeah, sure," I said rather unconvincingly.

"Are you seeing anyone right now, Walt?"

"Who, me? You gotta be kidding. Between getting thrown in and out of jail, drinking every last can of Budweiser in the tri-state area and running all over the countryside chasing front-page stories, there isn't much spare time for girls. Ooops, I'm lying again. There is one lovely lady I'm seeing. Her name is Flynn and she's gorgeous though her breath smells rather ordinary. And her voice can get scratchy, but she's beautiful."

"Really. Does she work at the paper?" Jenny asked hesitantly.

"No, next door at The Lincoln, but I don't think she's much of a threat to you."

Jenny's eyes let me know she was still confused as to Flynn's true identity.

"Flynn is truly marvelous – every one of her four legs. She's my neighbor's pet dog, though don't ask me what kind she is. Even Flynn has figured something out about me."

"Which is?"

"The grass is no doubt greener in the next pasture," I said.

"This Ms. Flynn sounds like quite a gal to work all that out," Jenny said.

"Oh, yeah. But seriously, Jenny, you'd probably not be interested in me if I you got to know me better."

"Why is that?"

"For one thing – we never had the chance to give it a chance, if you know what I mean. We were both living at home and going out on occasional dates. It's a bit different living together – as I'm sure you've learned. Besides, there's nothing special or unique about me except for the fact that I was born without an ear. Or, born with only one if you want to put a less negative spin on it. And I hardly think that's worthy of any praise."

"Does that really bother you? You don't really think you're a freak, do you?"

"It's not important, Jenny. Let's just say I came to understand real early in life that I'm not perfect. Nowhere close. And that's okay."

"Who is perfect, Walt?"

"That's not the point, Jenny. I don't know many people who face their imperfection from DAY ONE the way I had to. Nor have to keep having people remind you of it. I mean, there are people who lose some limb or whatever through injury or accident, but it's far rarer to wind up without something as common and noticeable as an ear from birth. It took a lot of soul searching to deal with this shit. And no one, not any one, can help you get through the 'Elephant Man' stares; the nasty names; the cold shoulders as if you're carrying the plague. It took me a long time to figure out that that was the hand I was dealt and that if I didn't want to end up either completely insane or totally inane, I had to take control of the situation. And where it got me was the realization that I'm okay and those who think I'm not, can go and, pardon my French, get fucked."

"Fair enough."

"I don't know if it is or not, but it's all I got so it has to do," I replied.

"You realize of course all you've managed to do is make me love you even more," Jenny said.

I leaned over and gave her a hug. She smelled good. She smelled Shalimar good.

"Woooo-Hooooooooo, wooooo-hoooooooooooo," came the high-pitched coo of my grandfather who had quietly ambled up near us. "Goddamned bastard!" he replied to no one in particular, least of all me who he obviously neither saw nor heard. I think he was chasing after a stray calf or one of those legendary Turs or Mouflons from the old country.

Jenny got up and went over to take him by the arm. She handled him as if he was made of glass. The girl had class, even if she did think I was something special. "Come with me, Mr. Bedrosian. It's me, Jenny-girl and your grandson."

"Woooooo-hooooooo!" he said again finally realizing who was nearby. He usually saved this particular whooping noise for single women who happened onto the property. He obviously had expanded its usage now to include stray and/or imaginary animals which was not a good sign.

"You and Jenny-girl up to something no good?!" he asked hopefully.

"Maybe, granddad. Maybe," I said smiling at Jenny. She grinned back.

"All I get is a lot of talk from your grandson. Very little action, Mr. Bedrosian. Can you talk to him? Otherwise, maybe you and I go out on a date, no?" Jenny said.

"Woooooo-hooooo!," came the reply. God love him. He may have been 80-something years old, but he still had the testosterone of a teenager.

Jenny handed him over to me before checking the time on her wristwatch. "Oh, shit, I have to run, Walt. Can you take over?"

"Yeah, no problem. What's the rush?"

"I have to pick up Howie from my Mom's before going to work," she said.

"Howie?"

"Yes, my son."

"You named your kid Howie?"

"Yeah, didn't you know?"

"No, I didn't," I said.

"Don't flatter yourself, Walt. It's not after you," she said, referring to my nickname while in grade school. Friends called me 'Howie' which I later decided wasn't too dignified and absolutely refused to be called 'Howard', so changed it to 'Walt' not long before leaving New Richmond.

"So why did you pick it then?"

"I just liked the name, that's all," she replied.

"Okay, fine. Anyway, wasn't there something else you wanted to tell me? About him," I said nodding toward my grandfather who was now trying to decide if it was Jenny or me who was holding onto him.

"Oh, that. Yeah, well, this might not be such a great time," Jenny said walking away from the very odd Armenian couple.

"C'mon, Jenny. I haven't got all day. Just spill it," I said.

"Okay, there's an envelope sitting on the kitchen table. It's from the State Revenue Service. They've just sent another notice regarding a large tax bill that has not been paid. See you later, Walt," she said as if she were talking about the weather.

"What? What did you say?"

"Bye, Walt. See you soon. Gotta run. Call me, eh?" she replied ignoring my plea.

"Jenny-girl, good girl, eh?" grandfather cooed.

"Yeah, great. Just great," I said before being left dumbfounded and speechless for the second time in less than five minutes. "Hey, grandpa, why did you come out here?"

"I lost something," he said turning his heard toward me. "I lost something close to me."

"Not yet you haven't, grandpa. Not yet," I said not knowing what the heck either one of us was talking about.

Chapter Twelve

I helped grandpa back to the farmhouse and put the kettle on for a cup of tea. The letter from the Massachusetts State Revenue Service lay on top of a huge pile of mail – mostly junk leaflets on a small windowsill looking out on the yard we had just walked across.

"What bother you, Torkum?" my grandfather asked.

"Nothing, grandpa. Nothing. Drink your tea," I replied. I wasn't sure what was more disturbing – the size of the money he now owed the tax collector or the fact that I even cared in the slightest.

"Jenny-girl nice girl," grandpa said.

"Yes, very nice. Say grandpa, how long you been here on the farm?"

"Oh, many years, no back look," he replied.

"How would you feel about moving someplace else for a while?"

"What? You crazy, boy? Me, no move. Make something go right here," he replied.

That ended any idea of getting him to consider moving gracefully. He'd hardly been anywhere else since moving across the ocean some 60 years earlier. But how the hell had he racked up a tax bill of nearly $23,000? How could this no good piece of shit land be worth that much? But then, why was this my battle? Why did I even care what happened? Good riddance to one of the world's least appealing pieces of unreal estate. Even a four-lane divided highway would look better? Besides, what self-respecting retirement village would open its automatic doors to an aged Armenian assassin?

^^&&TTTT%%$$#ENNMM[{]&6^=)(8&^&%^5%M.

Uh-oh, just what I needed. Another visitation from St. Vartan. He who relies on Nature's gifts, is the wealthiest man alive. Apparently St. Vartan was making his own feelings heard regarding the Old Man's predicament. "Okay wise guy, so you cough up the $23,000 large to cover the bill," I said to St. Vartan.

"Who you talking to, Torkum?" my grandfather said.

"Ahh, no one, Pa. Just muttering to myself. Drink your tea while I get the stove going," I said hoping like heck he didn't know what I was talking about. I didn't want him worrying about the money. I just needed to figure out a plan to buy him some time and it was obvious St. Vartan didn't intend on springing for the bill. Sure, he could drop in at a moment's notice and give me these wonderful sayings filled with all sorts of great sentiment and feeling, but were they worth anything? I got the fire going in his old cast iron stove and slipped the bill in my jacket before he saw it. He probably wouldn't know what it meant anyway, but no point taking any chances.

I had well and truly sobered up during the drive back to my apartment. It was nearly dark as my aged Corona negotiated the small, windy back roads. My mind kept drifting to the huge pile clearly stamped 'Unfinished Business' continuing to stack up. Now added to the list of J.R. and the unlocking of the universe was Hugh Jackson's insight into life and work; pretty Jenny's offer of unbounding love pour moi; and now the very real possibility of the same pour moi having to sort out the nasty tax situation and living arrangements for a non-house trained octogenarian.

I finally made it back to The Lincoln, parked the trusty mode of transport and headed up to the apartment. I fully expected to find Hugh Jackson still passed out on the floor, but to my surprise, the only things lying on my carpet were five cans of beer. Scratch that – five empty cans of beer. The only ones I had left in the house. Glad I was able to quench his thirst before he departed. He did leave a note of sorts. In typical Hugh Jackson style, there was no beating around the bush: "Always lead with the cats."

That was probably the best advice anyone ever gave me, though I wasn't sure whether he was referring to the secret of good news writing, living life, both, or neither. It would have to wait till our next encounter, whenever or wherever that might be. He didn't seem to be working at the paper any more, though nothing had been announced.

Louisa May likewise had left me a note, offering to fix me a meal whenever I got back. Sweet lady. I was slowly coming to appreciate her concern and interest in my disquieting desperate life. I almost envied the alternative enjoyed by her and her trusty companion – that is, a life ruled far more by peace and quiet respiration.

There also was one message on the phone machine. It was from Jenny once again telling me how much she cared about me. Truth be told, it wasn't all her fault regarding our 'failed' earlier relationship. Though I hadn't raised it with her, I too had had a couple of relationships while in the Mideast and more or less ruined them by not letting either woman get too close. While I wanted to believe the problem stemmed from their inability to deal with a 'handicapped' partner, I didn't help matters much. I had to hand it to Jenny for coming clean and expressing her concern over the physical appearance of any child of mine. I too did not want to give any other human being the same burden and for that reason, shied away from carnal relations with any women in the baby-making mood.

My jangled ramblings were once again interrupted by the unblessed ringing of the phone.

"Hello, son," said my mother's unsoothing voice.

"Hi, Mom, how's your day been?"

"What's wrong?"

"Oh, nothing a few hundred cans of beer can't sort out," I retorted.

"It can't be that bad, Walter, surely," she said.

"Surely, it can be," I replied. "But why the call? Something I can help you with?"

"No, not really. Just wondering if we can catch up to discuss a few important matters."

"You too?"

"What do you mean?"

"Is someone trying to take your house away? Is your job in jeopardy? Has anyone told you that they love you lately?"

"Walter, have you been drinking?"

"Not nearly enough."

"What are you talking about?"

"Nothing, Mom. Nothing," I said just as a loud pounding noise descended on my front door. "Gotta go, Mom. There's someone at the door. And there are a few things I want to talk to you about, too."

"Do call me soon, son. I'm worried about you," she said.

"So am I," I replied and hung up.

If ever there was a day when one believed that there was no way that things could get worse – then welcome to my nightmare to end all nightmares. For there, standing, or should I say, leaning in my doorway was none other than dear old Dad.

"Thought I'd find you at the paper," he said with a strong slur in his voice.

"Nah, I try to get away – if only for a few minutes each day. Keeps the edge on my writing," I said.

"Huh?" Dad replied.

"Nothing. And where's the little lady love?"

"Aww, she didn't come."

"What a shame. I was so hoping we could do some more bonding," I said.

"Don't get smart, wise guy. I got something big to talk to you about," he said walking in the door slowly, cradling a couple of six packs of beer.

"By all means – please do come in," I replied not knowing what else to say. "But if you've come to ask whether I approve of your betrothed – the answer is a resounding 'yes, yes, yes, big fella."

"You can be so weird sometimes," Dad replied.

"Ahh, yes. As opposed to other members of the family who are just plain crazy," I said. I certainly was getting some homecoming. For longer than the last decade, I had experienced few situations that rivalled any of the ones literally crossing my threshold. I hadn't laid eyes on any family member for years. Probably only spoke to someone remotely related on a monthly basis and now, they were everywhere: In my apartment; in my face; even in my dreams! I wanted to go out and strangle Thomas Wolfe for writing about not being able to go home again. It wasn't that you couldn't. It was that you shouldn't!

"What's on your mind, Dad?"

"I don't know how to say this so I'll just come out with it: Howard Johnson's has asked me to run their newest restaurant in Connecticut."

"That's great, Dad. So why the long face?"

"I'm just not sure I'm ready for this honor."

"C'mon, you're kidding, right? You were born to run a HoJo's. You got more HO and a lot more JO than any guy I know," I said, half-admiring my poor rhyme.

"It's all kinda sudden, you know?"

"Have you told what's her name yet about this development?"

"Who, ya mean, Connie? No, I haven't. I haven't told anyone yet. Only you cuz I wanted your thoughts on it."

"Not sure I see the problem. It's more authority and I assume more money than before. What's not to like?"

"For starters, it's nowhere near New London."

Now, to someone used to the relative closeness of nearly everywhere in New England, 'nowhere near' can mean 10 or 100 miles. Both can be a long way away, depending on circumstances. "That may not be so bad. Is it over the other side of the state?"

"No, it's north of New London in Willimantic," he said, before continuing: "I don't hear a lot of good things about that area."

"C'mon, Dad. It's still Connecticut for Christ's sake. If it were Ohio or Indiana, I'd be advising you to bail, but any place in Eastern Connecticut can't be all that bad, eh?" I decided not to spoil this occasion by telling him he'd also have to make room for granddaddy, too.

"Maybe you're right. So you'd take the job?"

"Who, me? No way, but then again, you already know how badly suited me and restaurant aprons get along."

The poor man's Omar Sharif smiled broadly at that one. "Hey, c'mere – give your old man a hug," at which point the front door, which hadn't been closed completely, was burst open by Louisa May's four-legged advance scout – Flynn, the wonder dog.

"What the fuck is that?!" Dad yelled as Flynn bowled straight into the back of me knocking us both over onto the floor. There were now cans of beer sprawling over various parts of the room, while my father and I tried to get off one another as quickly as possible.

Not quickly enough before Mrs. May entered the room and let out a shriek that would've woken the dead – or even the deaf guy in the apartment on the other side of mine.

"Ohh, my dear god," she exclaimed all the while pulling on Flynn's collar.

"Sorry, Mrs. May but my father just told me some great news and we were sharing a couple of beers when Flynn knocked us over," I said.

"This is your father?" Mrs. May asked, breathing a bit easier at this development. Given that the last two times here she found different men sprawled on the carpet, I probably would've begun wondering the very same thing she was.

"Yes, it is. Dad, this is my neighbor, Mrs. Louisa May. Mrs. May, Dad."

"He's a very nice boy you have here Mr. Johnson," she said.

"Howie. Please, call me Howie," Dad said.

"Well, we won't keep you any longer. I apologize for my dog's rather rude behavior, but she seems to have taken a very definite liking to your son," she said as just the glimmer of a smile came over her face. "But then, he seems to have this effect on women of all ages," she added rather ominously, obviously implying she knew a lot more than she was letting on.

"Nice meeting you, Mrs. May," Dad replied as the lady and her tramp closed the door behind them.

"What the frack was that?" Dad asked.

"She's okay. She actually hit it off pretty good with J.R.," I said.

"You're kidding, right?" he asked.

"Well, yeah, I am," I said.

"Anyway, you think I should take the job?"

"Hey, you gonna be an assistant manager and work in New London all your life?"

"You're probably right. I just hope I'm up for it. It'll mean longer hours and a lot more responsibility," he said.

"You can handle it, Pop. Heck, we Johnsons are sturdy stock."

He smiled again. "Thanks for that. I better get going back home. I gotta break the news to Connie."

"Yeah, great. Thanks for dropping by, Dad," I said debating whether I should say anything about his own father's plight. I decided it could wait for a day or two. "Say, what's Connie's last name?"

"Mack. She's Connie Mack," he said proudly.

"You're kidding, right?"

"No, why? What's wrong with that?"

"Ask J.R. the next time you see him," I said.

"You can be so weird sometimes," Dad said pulling the front door shut.

I was beginning to think it went with this territory. For those of you who are unfamiliar with baseball, Connie (actually he was born Cornelius Alexander but was known only as 'Connie') Mack was one of the game's most revered player/managers from the World War I era. While Dad's make and model was undoubtedly priceless, I made a mental note to ask J.R. how much the original Connie Mack might be worth.

Chapter Thirteen

It is with great concern and pity, yes
pity, that I felt for your unsuspecting
readers when I read a recent copy of 'The
Record'. While I have little doubt there
are countless other Walter Johnsons in this
country, there is only one such named
person (hopefully!) that writes with as
much bile and bad feeling as the
aforementioned WJ. This most offending
piece had to do with the unveiling of a
beautiful statue at one end of your lovely
township. While no one I spoke to about the
statue could find any fault with it or
regarding the esteemed gentleman it
portrays, Mr. Johnson preferred to find his
own way, any way, to bring down this
historical figure and demean his memory via
comments from unsuspecting passersby. I
would just like to say this sort of
behavior is precisely the stock and trade
that he plied while working in my hometown
of Cincinnati, Ohio, attacking any and all
who tried to better any community activity.
Do yourselves a favor and rid your town and
paper of this one-man cess pool before he
infects your pleasant village and all that
it stands for.

Sincerely,

Linda Bourgeois
Cincinnati, Ohio

❧

"Catching up on your weekend reading material?" said a deep voice
from behind the bar. It was still quite early on a rather dreary late

autumn Sunday evening. The voice sounded familiar, yet totally alien. I looked up expecting my gaze to be greeted by big Mel, my favorite tavernkeeper. I was half right. It was none other than the woman who was currently paying my salary – the elusive Mrs. Constance Wheeler-James herself.

"Ah, well, no not really, ma'am," I said in my best caught-off-guard voice.

"It's alright, Walter. If you didn't get up some people's noses, I'd worry about you more," the esteemed Publisher said. "Buy you a drink?"

The woman sure knew how to keep me off balance. "Ahh, yeah, great."

Without asking, she reached for a bottle of scotch from the top shelf and poured out a double shot – neat. She emptied a similar amount into another glass for herself and downed it in a flash. I blinked hard to make sure I was really awake. This just wasn't happening, was it? For weeks now I'd wondered when this moment would arrive, never dreaming of course it would happen on a quiet weekend evening in an even quieter drinking establishment.

"Been meaning to catch up with you before now, Walter. Interested to know how you're enjoying your work back in the old home town," she said.

"Ahh, great. Just great," I replied unconvincingly all the while hoping beyond hope that Mel, Marty or practically any other living creature – including Mrs. May's wonder dog Flynn, would come flying through the door.

"You're a bad liar, Walter," she replied breaking into a grin. "But thanks for the effort." My eyes caught two competing bright reflections from mein host – one emanating from a gold ring about the size of a ping-pong ball on her right hand and the other from an equally large gold necklace dangling from her chest. Despite being in her mid-to-late 60s, the woman still cut quite a figure though she was obviously adept at keeping people guessing not only as to her whereabouts or thoughts, but even her dress size. Most times I had laid eyes on her, she would be wearing a one-piece garment, usually all in one solid dark color and almost always with some sort of long scarf around her neck. That obviously was her daytime business attire, preferring something a bit less formal for her stint behind the bar. Her starch white hair done up in her trademark bun was offset beautifully by a dark blue turtleneck and matching loose-fitting slacks. With her tortoise-shell, half moon reading glasses dangling merrily around her neck, she would not have looked out of place in front of a one-school classroom. She certainly didn't look like any barmaid I'd run across.

But this setting, so the story goes, is where it all began as she inherited the pub from her father who worked hard all his life so that his daughter might do better. Well, she did in a way. She wound up marrying the one guy who spent more time in the establishment than her father – Martin James Senior who died a few years ago, no doubt from the insides of his liver caving in from alcohol overload. She obviously was a quick learner, however, and picked up the news game in a hurry. She even wrote a column assessing various community projects – for better though mostly for worse – over the past few years. She was never going to threaten George Will, but she could turn a phrase and carry an argument.

I lifted my glass in her direction and then skulled it. I looked again around the room to see if there were any other patrons. The place was empty, leaving me the only idiot foolish enough to be drinking with the boss. Never a good move, particularly when they owned the bar.

"Thanks for the drink, ma'am, but I really—"

"Hey, c'mon, Walter. Don't go yet. I have a proposition for you. And hopefully one that you can't resist," said the lady spider to the fly.

"Ahh, that's great, but I really do—"

"It won't take long. And then I promise to let you go. Deal?"

"Ahh, sure."

"Great," she said reaching for the same bottle from the same top shelf and pouring two more double scotches. The door opened and I turned quickly hoping beyond hope this person would give me the help I needed to escape.

"Hey, Walt, how goes it?" said her daughter Mel.

"Oh, great, Mel. Just great," I replied.

"I see my mother has you in her clutches. Best leave you to it then. Looks like a business meeting, eh?" Mel said.

Her mother never said a word or moved one iota, but obviously somehow let her daughter know that this was indeed a private meeting. I made a mental note to ask her some time how she did that.

As the 'meeting' unfolded, Mrs. Constance Wheeler-James began talking faster and faster. At least that's how it seemed to me. Or may be that was just the six hours worth of beer prior to the two double shots talking. It sounded promising, at any rate. Sounded even like she liked my work, which was a switch from my experiences at other rag sheets.

In fact, for probably the only time in my life, things were actually looking up. I left this rat hole of a town more than 15 years ago, because nothing and no one gave a crapola about anything – especially me! I had a mother who was consumed in letting everyone know about her family tree, though the lower limb that I occupied had mysteriously fallen off some years back. My father likewise didn't seem to pay too much attention to me or anyone other than his well-known namesake who had a penchant for 28 flavors of frozen milk and barn-sized buildings with orange roofs. I even had trouble getting dates back then, but oh how the worm has changed!

What once seemed like a town that any mug with two good legs and half as many decent arms to wave down passing traffic to hitchhike on outta there, now seemed like a community that made Dorothy's Oz look about as colorless as an early episode of 'I Love Lucy'. I had a mother and father bonding with me in rather odd ways, but bonding nonetheless; I had a boss who bought me drinks and well, what else do you want from a boss?; a neighbor's dog whose version of affection was launching herself at me as if she was a canine bowling bowl and I her favorite 10-pin; a casual mentor who broke into my house and drank my booze while passing on pearls of wisdom; and a curvaceous, young woman who now says I'm the only guy in the universe capable of making her moon glow. It was hard to fathom just what the magical moment was that turned it around for yours truly. I didn't plan on spending a lot of time delving into this issue. The irony of ironies now was that everyone – even people like 'Linda Bourgeois' whom I'd never met in towns I once cruised like Cincinnati – were hanging on to the one-eared guy's every word!

And though one side of the genealogical ledger read like a Who's Who of Losersville Unlimited, the maternal side of the family had guys who had been world leaders and opened new frontiers. Surely, it was the likes of Edward Winslow and John Adams now channelling their deeds through my veins? And the more I read about their exploits, the more I became convinced that my recent return to the home front was not only fortuitous, but fate-filled.

I stopped my mind from wandering just long enough to hear the publisher say she wanted me to tackle much bigger issues and "not to get caught up in the less important, day-to-day flotsam and jetsam journalism preferred by many of my peers." I also think that at least once during our 'Off-the-Record' session regarding '*The Record*', (a word play even I had to doff my non-existent cap to), she put down many of my journalistic colleagues, claiming most of them wrote as if they 'hadn't had a vowel movement in weeks'. She also told me not to worry about her son too much and to simply let him know what I was working on, along with some idea of when copy would be ready. "And if there's any problems, LET ME KNOW!"

Yes, it was all coming my way – big time! I motioned to the bottle on the top shelf. The publisher deftly grabbed it once again and poured the same two double shots – without spilling a drop. We raised our glasses one last time and drank to our mutual budding hangovers.

I detached myself from the bar stool with the sort of skill and aplomb one could safely compare to that of a day-old baby. How I managed not to break my neck will remain another one of life's mysteries, though as I headed for the door, I had one burning question that had to be posed to my esteemed Publisher/Drinking Buddy: "Say, Mrs. Wheeler-James?"

"Yes?" she replied.

"Has anyone ever called you Connie Mack?"

Chapter Fourteen

It occurred to me as I approached the newspaper the next morning that there were more cars in the adjoining parking lot than most work days. Most reporters, I suspect due to their drinking habits, preferred starting work in the afternoon until late at night. I quite enjoyed getting up early, the remnants of a mis-spent youth on the farm no doubt, just so I could avoid dealing with most of my so-called colleagues.

The minute I opened the newsroom door, I remembered something that the publisher had told me the night before about a mandatory staff meeting to outline new newsroom responsibilities.

"Glad you could join us, Walt," Martin James said with just a hint of disdain in his voice. There were about 12 staff members sitting at their desks around the outside of the newsroom. Martin James stood in the middle with his trusty sidekick Jack Saunders standing guard next to the door. "I'll let the others bring you up to date on what's already been said, which brings us to your good self."

"Can't wait," I said.

"In addition to his regular work, Walt will take over responsibility for the CD coverage," Martin said.

The blank expression on my face, along with half the others, encouraged Martin to spell it out a bit more clearly: "That's Community Development stories," he said with such emphasis that it sounded like some terminal disease.

"When did I take on this role?" I asked.

"Apparently last night," Martin said, curtly referring to my drinking meeting with his mother.

"Oh, is that what I agreed to?" I said, raising a laugh or two from my esteemed colleagues.

"I'll fill you in on what we're looking for after the meeting," Martin said. "Is there anything else I need to cover?" he said turning to his sidekick. The sidekick's head wiggle suggested there was nothing else. "That's it. Back to work!"

I was no sooner wondering just what else I agreed to last night when Lou Cassals passed by. "Jeez, I thought I got stuck. I'm now city editor on Friday and Saturday nights."

"Wow, what a star," I said.

"Yeah, well, I had asked for a raise, but I didn't figure on that. Sadly, it'll mean no more Friday afternoon booze-ups," Lou said.

"Shit, you're already towing the company line. Fucking management scum," I said.

"Yeah, but what about you? How drunk were you last night?"

"What do you mean?"

"Agreeing to take over the 'Certain Death' beat? That's the kiss of death beat, you stupid shit," Lou informed me.

"Oh, is that all? And I thought it was something fatal. Why is that?"

"You're kidding, right? Who the fuck in their right mind wants to take responsibility for the one beat that the publisher and her deranged family use to push their own plans for the town's future?"

"Maybe I should go now."

"Yeah, like Hugh. He's gone, you know?"

"Really?"

"Really. Marty didn't say much. Or even who fired who only that as far as he was concerned, Hugh Jackson no longer had a 'role to play in '*The Record's*' day-to-day activities', whatever the hell that means."

"Hmmm. How sad," I managed at last.

"Did you ever catch up with him?" Lou asked.

"Not really. He did drop by, literally, the other night at my place. Never mentioned anything about leaving, though" I said.

"That's Jackson, for you," Lou said.

"Hey, Johnson, gotta minute?" Martin called.

"Yeah, sure boss," I said. "Better run. Got to find out what else I agreed to last night."

Martin motioned me into his office which doubled as a phone booth. His pal Saunders had already planted himself in the other chair that could fit in the room in front of Marty's huge, fake antique desk.

"Can I sit on your knee, Jack?" I said to Marty's first mate. Saunders grumbled something that sounded like a school-yard swear word before slowly getting up and leaving.

"Thanks, Jack. We'll only be a minute," Marty said.

"I do hope it was something I said," just as Saunders slammed the door behind him.

"It's a shame you didn't get here on time, Walt."

"Yeah, well, I got caught up in rush hour."

"Very funny. I just want to let you know that you may have pulled one over on my mother, but I'm running this place and don't you forget it."

"Sorry, did I miss something?"

"Yeah, wise guy. You missed something, alright. For starters, your fearless mentor is gone. For whatever reason, Jackson thought you had talent."

"And you?"

"Hey, this room stinks with talent," Marty said.

"Is that what that smell is?"

"Hope you're up to the CD beat. It's a big responsibility and so far, everyone else has failed – miserably."

"Gee, thanks for the pep talk – and your support," I replied.

"Still, you will have help," Marty said.

"Great, who?"

"My brother and Gail Gerard who has come on like gang busters over the past few weeks," Marty said.

"She has, too. She came on to me last week at the bar, but I was busy puking at the time and turned her down."

"Funny man, eh? I want you to sit down with those two ASAP and get a handle on what's been done to date and how you'll approach the task. And when I'm not here – Jack will be your guide."

"Jeez, you're sweet talking me now. I'll only agree to this death sentence if you give us our own space to work in away from all the other wordsmiths."

"No problem. You can have all the room you want – in The Morgue with Wall."

"Really? That much. You're too kind. Far too kind. I don't know how I'm ever going to repay you, boss," I said with my swollen tongue firmly planted in my cheek, before adding: "Who could ask for anything less?"

"Scramola, wise guy. And come back to me before long with a list of stories you and your team will be working on."

"Aye, aye, Captain. In fact, I'm already working on a big one," I lied somewhat convincingly or so I thought.

"Good. What is it?"

I hadn't counted on him asking that question. "Ahh, it's all about this city of similar size to New Richmond in southeastern Connecticut that has gone through a similar redevelopment scheme. I thought I'd have a look around down there and see what shakes," I said not having a clue what I was talking about.

"Sounds good. Keep in touch," Marty said just as the phone rang. "Oh, hi mother," he said into the phone while waving me out of the office.

"I'll be on my way," I said getting up and leaving as quickly as I could. Jack Saunders stood just outside the doorway.

"He's all yours again, Jacko," I said, heading quickly for the main entrance. Not quickly enough, though, as my new Girl Friday – Mason James – blocked my exit.

"Hey, it's great we'll be working more closely now," Mason said.

"Took the words right out of my mouth, Mase," I replied.

"So where do we start?"

"Huh?"

"You know, on the CD beat. What should we do first?"

"Oh, that. Well, it'll take a bit of brainstorming when I get back, but in the meantime, it'd be good to see who owns what downtown."

"Yes, that's a great idea," Mason replied.

"Is it? I mean, it is, isn't it?" I replied.

"I'll get right on it," he said. "And I'll get Gail to help."

"Good thinking, 86. I'll be back in a couple of days and see what you find out."

"No problem. See you then," he said.

Lou and a bunch of others called out next, but I kept moving for the exit as fast as I could. I needed air. Lots of it. Maybe it was to escape the stench created by all the talent supposedly concentrated in the newsroom. I had a good giggle over that idea. Stinking, rotten talent. I'm sure Hugh Jackson would've loved it, too.

Despite the run-in with young James, I'd bought myself a couple days grace by getting as far as I could possibly get from this hellhole, which suited me just fine. I'm sure Marty and his Mom thought they'd corralled me by sticking me with the impossible beat. If I was paranoid, I'd think they stuck young Mason on me to keep them up to date on my activities, but paranoia was the least of my failings. It was more likely that they wanted me to baby sit the poor bastard.

Still, if they thought that this beat would beat me, they had another thing coming. They forgot one important thing: It was only an impossible beat to someone who took these lunatics seriously and believed there was a 'possible' right way to cover the beat.

I knew otherwise. It didn't even matter that they also were lumbering me with some of the deadest of the dead wood in the whole of the news business. They thought I was like the others that came and went. I was,

119

in one respect: I liked a drink and cared little for rules. But what they hadn't realized is that I not only liked a drink and cared little for rules: I loved to drink and I cared not one iota for rules or for playing the game. Where was I trying to get to from here? The *New York Fucking Times*? The *Boston Bitchin Globe*? Not bloody likely. No, this was the last roll of the dice for my time as a reporter and I was going to give it the same sort of effort as my glorious ancestor – dear Mr. Winslow – Mayflower Monsieur extraordinaire. Okay, so getting dumped from a perfectly shithouse rag is hardly in the same category as my ancestor's antics in the then New World. But this was my own special voyage and though perhaps not as grandiose as his historic exploits – it already had revealed things to me that a few short months ago, would've seemed impossible.

I was the captain and now even had a crew to order and obey on this bold mission.

There was no better place to begin this maiden/final voyage, than with the only man who knew more about all matters maritime than myself – Uncle J.R. That is, following a couple of quick pit stops before setting sail.

Chapter Fifteen

I didn't have the exact address for Hugh Jackson, but I owed him a visit to pay my last respects. I knew he lived on the west side of New Richmond. If the eastern shore was the place inhabited by the privileged, then the western side, whether it was near the water or not – contained the less well off. Huge mansions fit for families of 1-4 on the east side gave way to shabby, three-story walk-ups, inhabited by 1-4 families. Nothing looked good as new over here. Whether it was a kid's front teeth, the sign on a restaurant or the grill on a car, there were sure to be holes – huge gaps that had been knocked out by waves of violence fuelled by too little work and too much alcohol.

I found the street where Hugh said he shared a small apartment with his second missus. It was not half-bad as far as streets in this part of town went. There were some that were worse off, but few in better condition. Fortunately, my trusty steed fit right in here. After a few death-rattling chugs, the engine conked out and I mounted a series of recently-laid concrete steps. It was a duplex and with no names on the mail boxes, I guessed which one he would live in.

"Go away," said an elderly female voice from the other side of a steel-grilled door.

I went away. Wrong again. The door of the second unit was open before I even got there.

"What do you want?" came the aggressive opening from a woman I figured was Hugh's wife. She was a good deal taller than him and about the same age, but that meant she could be anything between 45 and 65.

"Ah, hello, would you be Hugh's wife?"

"Who wants to know?"

"A friend," I said.

"Oh, great. That narrows it down. Hugh has lots of friends. What he doesn't have is lots of money," the woman said, coming down heavy on the words 'lots' and 'money' and in that order.

I suspected there was some tension in their relationship and that it emanated from a disagreement over finances. "Yeah, that could be but I was wondering if you knew where I could find him?"

"Got any beer on you?" she said.

"Huh?"

"If you did, he'd find you, the fucking pisspot," she said.

"Look, I'll just be going," I said.

"Yeah, that's it. You're all the fucking same."

"Yeah, thanks. Thanks a lot," I replied.

She slammed the door with such force that the heavy steel knocker on its front fell to the ground. It made a thud that rivalled the slamming of the door, but the occupant could not have cared less. She'd obviously done this before and also didn't much care for callers.

I called off my search for Hugh Jackson and decided if anything, I'd like to warn him about returning home before Ms. Mt. Vesuvius erupted, but I suspected he already knew that.

Upon getting back into the car, I realized I was also near the street where Jenny apparently was living. Though I didn't get over this part of town that often, the streets were few but close together. I hoped to catch her before heading to the gym.

Jenny's place was about two miles west of Hugh's address and just a few yards from the New York State line. It was less crowded than Hugh's area, but not much classier if that made any sense. In fact, the area if anything, had gotten worse in recent times due to a mile-long stretch on the New York side known as 'Silicon Alley' and it had nothing to do with the computer chip industry. Twenty years ago, it had been mostly seedy bars and adult book stores that had now morphed into a seemingly seamless series of strip joints, featuring such classy names as the 'Trepid Fox' and 'Pussy Galore'.

I knew about these places only through reputation and by Hugh's insistence that I do a story on why these joints were multiplying so quickly and threatening to spill over into Massachusetts. He had a theory or three, at least one of which had to do with the hunch that some big business development was about to hit New Richmond. These stories came up a lot and usually about six months out from an election, which was about how long before the next one was due. Still, I said I'd look into it and even though Hugh was no longer among us, I made a pledge to get onto it right after I got back from southeastern Connecticut.

I found the row of apartments where Jenny lived. They were fairly new because when I was growing up, this region had been part of the Myer farm property. It was never much of a farm, though. Always thought old man Myer would've been better off letting it go for developments. There were still pastures some distance behind the row of apartments, but they now looked more like an after-thought or part of some new-fangled suburban petting zoo rather than a working farm.

The apartments seemed in good order and even had nicely-kept shrubs and flowering plants in their postage-stamp-sized front yards, no doubt enhanced by the many years worth of cow manure plowed into the soil. I saw Jenny's car parked outside one and took a chance that it would be hers.

I knocked confidently at the door which to my surprise, was opened by a woman, but not the one I'd had in mind.

"Can I help you, sugar?" said this comely black woman with flaming red hair.

"I must have the wrong address," I said and started to turn away.

"Depends, sugar. You looking mighty right to me," she said.

I turned and smiled and kept on walking.

"You lookin for Jenny?" she said.

"I am. Do you know her?"

"I do that, honey. She's inside sleeping. You wouldn't be Walter, would ya?"

"I am. Are you psychic?"

"Not even Catholic, sugar, but if you wanna come in, I'll see—"

"Walt, is that you?" Jenny said rushing to the doorway.

"Yeah, I thought you might be up," I said.

"Oh, yeah, I just haven't been sleeping too well lately, that's all," Jenny said, brushing her roommate aside.

"Do you wanna go get a coffee?" Jenny said.

"Ah, yeah, but you're not even dressed," I said trying not to look at the sight of a beautiful, semi-naked woman who apparently found me attractive.

"The place is a mess, Walt. Do you mind waiting here and I'll be back in a jiff," she said. "I gotta pick up Howie from my Mom's anyway."

"Yeah, sure. No problem," I said. "Perhaps your roomie can keep me company?"

"Honey, I can do more than just keep you company," said her demure roommate with the biggest brown eyes and most luscious lips I'd ever beheld.

"He's mine so don't get any ideas!" Jenny called out from the hall.

We shook hands and giggled much the same way school kids do.

"So, you work with Jenny at the gym?"

"Gym? Is that what it's called?" Anita said.

"I don't follow," I said before the light finally clicked. God, what an idiot I'd been. There was no gym. She was working at one of the strip joints on Silicon Alley. Anita also realized that I had not been let in on this secret before now and pulled me close.

"It ain't what you think, sugar. Really it ain't. She's a good girl."

"Define good," I said.

"We all gotta make a living, honey," she replied.

"Thanks. I needed that. Can you let Jenny know I had to go. I'll call some other time," I said.

"No, don't go. C'mon, man, she digs you," Anita called.

I got in my car as quickly as I could and drove off not wanting to think about what had just happened. I'm sure there was a perfectly good explanation, but I didn't really give a damn. Not now, anyway. Hell, she could probably get me a lot of good juicy info for my expose on the Alley when I got back from Connecticut. So it went in this thing called life. I had some good times and some less than good ones. And then there were the extra special cases like today. Wonder when Jenny planned on letting me in on the secret? At least I didn't stumble across her while doing research for my article. And so it went. For every action there was a reaction. I don't know why it took a genius like Newton to figure that one out. Then again, it took an ignoramus like me to figure out the corollary to that beauty: For every action, there could be a reaction or there could be a FUCKING REACTION.

And then there was this: If something or someone appeared too good to be true – RUN.

Roll on Connecticut.

Chapter Sixteen

The farther I got away from New Richmond, the less I really cared about all that had been left behind. I wasn't worried about the job, Hugh's whereabouts or even good ol' Jenny. I began to wonder just what the heck bugged me about her being a stripper. Most guys would kill to have a woman who knew how to shake it. Besides, who the frack was I to question her morals? Not exactly ol' Mr. Sermon-on-the-Mount Moses myself.

I decided to focus more on two other matters, both of which had strong family ties – which seemed ironic given my kin's rather dyslexic series of anti-social sensibilities.

I was curious as hell to find out what this story was that J.R. had in mind. I sure hoped it really was something and not just another one of his excuses for a booze up. I didn't need any excuses for that.

And the other was just how the heck I was going to help my grandfather come to terms with losing the farm. There must be something I could do, even if it was just to delay the matter. Buy some time and hope the old man either keeled over while hoeing his greens or milking his cow or became so senile he didn't know what was happening. Neither was very pleasant, but they beat the alternative. There was one last family matter to sort out: Find out why the heck my mother was so against me having any 'relationship' with her side of the family except its one and only black sheep – J.R. How the heck could the past come back to haunt me, or her, for that matter?

J.R. was well and truly in party mode by the time I reached his seaside abode in the quaint one-time fishing village called Victoria. It was located on the rocky shoreline of far southeastern Connecticut, wedged between the equally-quaint and far more historic villages of Mystic and Stonington. It was nearly four in the afternoon and surprisingly warm given that the calendar on the wall said Christmas was less than six weeks away. He had on a Hawaiian shirt with matching sun visor like the ones worn by pro golfers. His dark slacks looked as though they hadn't been cleaned since the war – pick a war, any war. Music was blaring from his two-bit stereo – it was '*The Last Waltz*' by The Band.

"G'day, Wally boy, how's it goin?" came his familiar greeting.

"Oh, great. Just great. So what's the story?"

"Whoa, slow down, boy. You're gonna thank me when you hear this one, but you gotta understand a few things first. You know, scene setting, I think is what you guys call it," he said.

"Hey, all I know is that it has something to do with a run-down laundromat in New London. Don't tell me, Mickey Mantle once got a suit pressed there," I said.

"Funny boy. You're gonna thank me when I tell you," he said.

"I'm sure I will. Don't I always?" My mind began drifting back to the many times when as a young lad, my mother would drop me off at J.R.'s boat while she dropped anchor at her family's beachside mansion at Stonington. I must have been mad, but I always preferred J.R.'s floating, one-room hotel to a multi-storey palace that would have made Gatsby feel not so great. In fact, very little had changed over the years except the amount of moss and god knows what other inhumane bacteria taking over the bottom of his unseaworthy ship and the number of empty beer cans and wine bottles rattling around on the open deck.

J.R. ignored my last comment and went over to turn down the music. He then grabbed a couple of cold beers from his fridge and motioned for me to sit down on a couch that technically could seat three, but currently was inhabited by more books and magazines than any army could hope to browse. There also was a dilapidated pizza box and some dirty clothes and dishes.

"How much you know about the Navy?"

"Hmmmn, they're the ones who like to play with boats, right?"

"Yeah, them's the ones. But did you know that every day of every year, we have secret missions being conducted all around the globe to keep our eyes mostly on Mother Russia's activities?"

"Have you stopped taking your medication again?"

"Don't believe me? Ask yourself: Why are we building more underwater military hardware than ever before? There are more nuclear subs being built in nearby Groton, Virginia, Washington State and god knows where else. Why?"

"Okay, but what the heck has this got to do with Fred's Laundromat in New London?"

"All shall be revealed. But first, take a look at some of this material and then we'll take a ride." J.R. pulled open the middle drawer of a large, three-story filing cabinet. He scooped out a bunch of manilla folders brimming over with information. He threw them down on the semi-empty pizza box next to me on the sofa, but not before giving me a heads-up on what each file contained. The first one contained news clippings from newspapers up and down the eastern seaboard and beyond; the next featured photocopies of articles from books and magazines; while still another contained photos of various ships and subs; and the lucky last, (which was by far the biggest of the bulging files), contained what looked like notes – both in longhand and type, from the master himself. I was in for a long night.

"I'll go down to the store and get us some extra beers while you have a read."

And with that, he was gone leaving me with an impossible pile of papyrus to pore over. I was beginning to think this might be a good opportunity to escape, but to where? I was in no hurry to head back up north. Interestingly, the music playing in the background sure seemed appropriate: It was The Band's Richard Manuel giving it his all on 'The Shape I'm In'.

It's funny but I sort of already knew a lot of the stuff J.R. wanted me to glean from his clipping files. He'd talked about these matters on and off for the past 30 years, though I rarely paid full attention. I still was having a hard time accepting the fact that there were games of cat and mouse being played underwater by squads of highly-skilled submarine crews from the USA and the USSR. What did they have to learn about one another they didn't already know? Were they playing high-speed games of chicken under the sea? How did they keep score and what was the prize?

J.R. returned more quickly than I'd planned, but I had another idea on how to bone up on the matter at hand. I decided to stay a couple of days and dig in when the sun came up tomorrow or the day after. For now, we decided to pay a visit to his, and mine, favorite watering hole – 'Ye Olde Salty' – just off the main drag of bucolic downtown Victoria. I'd loved Victoria from the first time I laid eyes on it when I was in my early teens. I don't think it had anything to do with the quaint, wooden shops that lined its one and only main street. I don't think it even had anything to do with the way it looked in the dead of winter when practically everyplace else looked forlorn and hollow – Victoria gave off vibes that only happy and self-confident selves do.

Take New Richmond as the other end of the scale: It featured so many buildings either beyond or near demolition stage that it just screamed 'GET ME OUT OF THIS LIVING HELL!" Just what effect this situation has on its residents is hard to qualify, but I'm guessing that there's a few more suicides and nasty incidences occurring for no other reason in New Richmond than its inhabitants don't feel comfortable in their immediate surroundings. May be that's a bit harsh, but surely one's environment does indeed have some effect on the psyche?

Then again, may be we can blame it on the water. New Richmond wrapped itself around a fresh body of water, while Victoria's ribbon of picture-postcard homes nestled up against part of the salt-fed waters of Long Island Sound. This meant not only did the salt-soaked water give off an odor that you could see and touch, but often included fog so thick you could eat off it.

Perhaps it was all that nautical nature in my genes coming to the fore again. All I did know is that I didn't get the same feeling whenever I dropped by my Mom's monolithic 'home away from home' in neighboring Stonington. No, there was something more primal; more immediate about Victoria that pulled me in time after time.

It didn't hurt that it also had one of the best bars I'd ever been in. Returning again after being away for so long, it started to become clear as to just why I found 'Ye Olde Salty' so appealing. For starters, there were never any tourists around. They preferred to stick to the safe bet bars with all-too-predictable names (and fare) like the 'Lobster Tail' and 'Clam Bar'.

Then there was its no-frills wooden bar that was always good and sticky with beer and blood stains from the previous year's worth of boozing and brawling. The kitchen seemed perpetually closed so you made good with packs of stale pretzels and potato chips and healthy dollops of Irish whiskey and Australian beer. It was the only place I knew that stocked Aussie beers and not that watered down Foster's lager, either. I don't know where the owner got this stuff from, but it had names like 'Crown' and 'XXXX' (pronounced 4X) and actually had some bite, compared to the piss they passed off for beer in America. I also didn't know what his job ads said, but they must have insisted on hiring only women who had long since given up on men, life and practically anything else that seemed important to the bar's patrons. These women, who were never easy to gauge how old they were, (but suffice to say were somewhere between 35 and 71), rarely smiled and exhibited even less emotion. It wouldn't have mattered if World War III had started in nearby Victoria Harbor, these gals just weren't going to get excited about anyone or anything.

Most of all, though, it was its feisty and feral owner – John Jefferson ('just call me J.J.') another ex-Navyman who had lived in this area all his life. He never talked about his past. He didn't have to. It was written in his face that featured more wrinkles than an Agatha Christie murder mystery. He also had tattoos of anchors on each of his oar-sized forearms and a voice that must have been pre-recorded and stuck in those fog horns that blew on particularly foggy nights.

He had one other endearing trait, which either he picked up from J.R., or passed on to him – a love for baseball cards. "Are we starting a Mickey Mantle binge (that's at least a four-day booze fest) or something bigger?" he asked as we came through the door. "Hey J.R., I need another Koufax to complete my 1964 Topps collection." J.J. pointed to a wall behind the bar that was plastered with cards that were all obviously from a particular year's collection. Koufax was one of the best pitchers in the game in the early to mid 1960s and surely would finish off anyone's collection. Of course, not that I was an aficionado or anything, but I didn't have the heart to tell J.J. that he was most certainly deflating the value of any of these cards by not only sticking pins in them, but letting any and all local reprobates smoke, spit, puke and perform any number of other bodily functions on various parts of the bar's walls, ceiling and floors on a near nightly basis. It was a great place to hang out.

"Will that cover us till Friday?" J.R. asked in his best bargaining voice.

The look on J.J.'s face suggested that it would. And it did. I don't remember much more about that night. Only that J.J. knew all about the laundromat story and that our drinks were being paid for not by dollar bills with pictures of famous 19th century presidents like Jefferson and Jackson, but by the contemporary color photograph of a most unlikely baseball hero - one Alexander 'Sandy' Koufax – a Jewish left-hander who could throw a lightning bolt that would have made Thor green with envy.

I knew what those batters who faced Mr. Koufax must have felt like. Some batters said that Koufax used to throw 'radio balls'. They could hear them; they just couldn't see them. While I heard J.R. and J.J. telling me things, I just couldn't see what they were getting at. That is, until J.R. and I piled into his old Buick convertible and set sail for nearby New London – and a particular establishment allegedly set up to wash and dry people's belongings.

"Did you read any of that material I left for you?" J.R. screamed as we headed over the divided, five-lane bridge that connected New London with Mystic, Victoria and their immediate neighbor, Groton.

"No, not really, but I have a feeling you're gonna tell me," I said.

"Hey, you're the reporter, but don't you think it's weird that despite the billions of dollars we spend every year on not only building the world's biggest and best submarines, and another billion dollars on keeping their movements hush-hush, that it's relatively easy to figure out where they are?"

"Yes, I know you've been telling me this, but what the hell has this got to do with the laundromat?"

"You'll see, you'll see," is all J.R. would say and promptly turned up the volume on his tape deck, currently featuring the dulcet tones of Bruce Springsteen, belting out a song titled '*The Promised Land*'.

I gave up fighting J.R. Or thinking about what lay ahead. He wanted me to trust him and that I would. At least we had that if nothing else. What I didn't expect was for him to drop me in front of Fred's Laundromat and speed off leaving me very much alone in the middle of Colman Street – not exactly the most inviting place for interlopers to be, after dark on a full moon. I heard him yell something as his four-wheeled steed pulled away from the curb, but failed to catch it. I needn't have worried. Rather than bore you with a lot more detail, here's the opening of the article that appeared in *'The Record'* the following Saturday.

SUBMARINE SECRETS COME OUT IN THE WASH

With water views in sight from practically any vantage point in New London, Connecticut, it's not hard to see why the place is drowning in marine mania. There's the General Dynamics-Electric Boat shipyard – where the world's biggest and fastest nuclear subs are built; the Naval Submarine Base, the world's first and biggest home away from home for not so ancient mariners; and the U.S. Coast Guard's Academy where it trains the next generation's naval gazers.

Despite all of these maritime matters, it's the submarine fleet – the so-called 'silent service'- that draws the most attention.

With cold-war animosity between the United States and the Soviet Union at sub-zero temperatures and sinking fast, both sides have unleashed scores of unsavoury agents seeking any information that could expose the other's underwater underbelly. Given the uber secretive nature of the submariner culture, however, you would think it would be almost impossible to uncover anything of value.

Indeed, call the local Navy PR office for help and you get any number of pleasant-sounding helpful souls keen to give you whatever you want, so long as you don't want to learn anything about the submarine service.

When I asked if a particular nuclear attack submarine from the Los Angeles class of vessels had left New London, the reply was: "We can neither confirm nor deny that report."

"Okay, I know it left port because one of my buddies sails on it. I just want to know roughly when I can expect it to return. He owes me money," I next asked, hoping the additional personal detail might make them a bit more helpful.

"We can neither confirm nor deny that report," came the monotonous reply.

I don't think the response would've changed if I'd suggested that his wife and children had been abducted by aliens and spirited away on a flaming dessert spoon. You had to admire this group's unwillingness to waiver from the party line – no matter what. There's a certain logic to this attitude. Billions of dollars have been invested in these high-tech denizens of the deep. Equally large sums have been allocated to keep unfriendlys (see Mother Russia) in the dark.

So it may come as something of a surprise to Rear Admiral Hyman Rickover – the father of the Nuclear Navy – that the fate of his fleet, or at least those that hail from New London, comes down to a hungry, rusted clothes dryer falling off the wall at Fred's Laundromat on Colman Street.

"Gotta quarter?" asks the pudgy red head who is wearing what must be the last clean blouse and blue jeans left in her cupboard.

"Excuse me?"

"Can I borrow a quarter? I need it to dry my panties," says this woman with a grin that suggests she's solicited money before. Before long, my clothes-drying associate, known by everyone in the greater New London area simply as 'Tess', and I are enjoying a couple of not-so-quiet drinks when top secret information starts getting passed around like a hot joint.

"I know where she is," says Tess boldly.

For those not familiar with the ways of marine affairs, all ships, regardless of whether they ply the seas above or below the surface, are female. In this instance, we're talking about a 688-class attack submarine – the USS Cincinnati. "Where is the dear girl?"

"She just left Scotland bound for the Arabian Sea," Tess says as if she knows precisely where the hell that is.

"And how do you know such things?"

"Because my Danny Boy is aboard. He's a cook on the ship and calls me whenever they reach port," Tess offers before providing more intimate details about how so many Navy wives help wile away the time while their men are anchored offshore.

It's only after a few more questions that Tess becomes concerned that she may be giving away state secrets. "Why are you asking me so many questions about the sub? Are you a spy or something?"

"Nyet," I reply, but of course, if I was a spy, it was already well and truly too late. I daresay if the Navy wants to avoid any further sinking feeling regarding the secrecy of its underwater activities, it'll need to get a lot more serious about the information its diligent crew members pass on to unsuspecting family and friends.

Editor's Note to Rear Adm. Rickover: Divert funds from Ohio-class cost overrun slush fund to upgrade washers and dryers at Fred's in New London.

❧

The story went down a treat getting picked up all over the country and sending shockwaves throughout the Navy and U.S. Armed Services Committee meetings. That was nothing compared to how the evening ended up, which I shall do my best to relate to you now.

Tess and I hit some bar called the 'Whaler's Rest' under a bridge not far from the Coast Guard Academy. I could spend a lifetime describing the ambience of the place, but two words probably covered the highlights quite nicely: Shit hole. It did have one redeeming feature: cheap drinks which Tess seemed to inhale before they ever reached the glass. With each gulp, I got a new/different insight into her psyche which ranged between Coal Miner's Daughter to Bride of Frankenstein. Both she and Danny, her one and only, hailed from some godforsaken town in western Oklahoma. Neither of them had ever seen an ocean before ol' Danny boy set sail on a submarine. She said this proudly, though not sure it would ever make a great endorsement or poster for the submarine service. Then again, I made a mental note to ring up my mates at the local sub base and/or Washington in the morning to get their view on the matter.

I don't know how we got to her place – a shabby apartment situated on the middle floor of a three-story house within walking distance of the bar, but I'll guess we somehow stumbled there. And, though I found this woman scarcely attractive when the evening began, gentlemen, I must say she looked mighty fine by its end.

All I could see was Ann-Margret with about 60 extra pounds and a few less teeth, but hey, it was Ann—Fucking – Margret! We dispensed with the pleasantries rather quickly, preferring to get right down to business. I don't know who was hornier, nor did I much care. It didn't take long to figure out whether there was any sexual chemistry between us. If she had been an oxygen molecule and me a couple of hydrogen molecules, we would have made TNT. The next thing I remember is entering this she-devil with little else on besides my socks and shoes and my jeans wrapped around my ankles.

Not sure how ol' Danny boy would have appreciated the sexual callisthenics I was currently conducting with his missus, but I told myself he was more than likely screwing himself silly whenever his ship hit land in or around the Arabian Sea. Fortunately, Tess didn't turn on the lights. There was just enough left over from the outside street lamps to help guide the way, though it's unlikely that even Blind Willie would have had trouble negotiating this woman's ample curves.

If nothing else, the lovemaking finally shut her up. I thought she'd never stop talking while we were out drinking. Her words were now replaced by a series of the sexiest groans and moans my good ear had ever heard. The effect these utterances had on me was quite extraordinary, encouraging, nay, demanding me, to thrust harder and harder and harder.

"Ohhhh, ahhhh," she moaned.

'Yes, you bad. You big, baaaaad man', I thought.

"Ahhhh, ugghhhhh," she moaned again and again, each time with a bit more passion until, well, until I thought that we were about to explode together.

But then, just as her moans and groans continued speeding up in rhythm with my action, and just as I was about to enter that most sought after sexual state, her moans and groans became even more urgent, until, it became apparent – even to me – that she was not experiencing ecstasy – rather, a heightened state of well, unwellness. Such unwellness I had never encountered before while in full flight, but there we were – both exploding though a dual orgasm like this I doubt had ever been achieved before in the history of mankind. I certainly hope not anyway as I'd no sooner let fly when she fired salvo after salvo of the foulest smelling vomit rockets I'd ever seen.

Her performance took a bit of the shine off the evening. I managed to roll over on to the floor before realizing that my pants were down around my ankles. I had no idea what happened to my shirt. I stumbled toward the doorway, trying to remove her stomach remains from my chest. I finally found the front door and quickly opened it while pulling my pants back up. I heard muffled groans coming from the bedroom, but there was no way I was going back in. This may seem like a bad time for a confession, but yes, I do admit to being chivalrous. I do believe in holding doors for ladies and giving them my seat if the bus is crowded, etc, etc. Somehow though, I don't think the 'Guide to Chivalry' included any words or actions deemed appropriate in my current circumstances. And frankly, if by not going back inside led to any demerit points from the Chivalry Police, well, too fucking bad. Tess had delivered me with the ultimate comeuppance and that was enough for me.

It was pouring rain when I got outside. That was the good news because the rain washed away any remaining items of unpleasantness still hanging around. It also kept my mind off the events of the last few minutes which kept me from mimicking my latest conquest's foul endeavors.

The only problem now was figuring how the heck I was going to get back across the river to J.R.'s boat. He wouldn't mind me calling him if I could find a pay phone, but that didn't seem likely in this neighborhood. I somehow stumbled my way back to the bar where it all began some hours earlier, but of course, it was now shut tight. There was a pay phone nearby, but the steel cord had been severed. As luck would have it, a car pulled up, and a window rolled down slightly. A guy with a short haircut took one look at me and began rolling the window up again.

"Hey, wait," I said.

"Yeah?" he asked.

"I know this doesn't look very good, but would you be heading back across the river?"

"Ahh, may be, but can you tell me if the phone works?"

"Nah, I'm waiting for the Wichita Lineman. He should be here any minute," I said hoping he'd see the humor in my comment.

He didn't but decided to take a chance on this half-naked himbo before him and opened the back door. "Thanks a lot and let me start by saying I don't usually run around on rainy November nights half-dressed."

He laughed and leaned over, before asking where I was going.

"Would you believe, Victoria," I said.

"No problem. I live close by at the Sub Base," he replied.

And with that I started laughing for the first time in a long while. How ironic. Saved by the very guys I'd not only figuratively screwed well and truly in the paper, but literally screwed – at least one of their own 'one and onlys' – just a few short moments ago. Life doesn't get any better than that.

My new-found sailor friend Andy, who hailed from Lawrence, Kansas, yet another landlocked state, (must check on this with the Navy when I get back to New Richmond), loaned me a blanket, a Navy blanket to take a bit of the chill off while we left New London behind for Victoria.

By the time we got to J.R.'s watery pad, there were no lights on in any of the nearby houses. When I looked at the clock on Andy's dashboard, I could see why. It was 3.30 a.m. I thanked Andy very much for the lift and headed quickly for the back of the boat, which was lit up like a Christmas tree. Springsteen's '*Born to Run*' was blasting out of the speakers as I came aboard.

"Hey, man, good to see you. I was getting worried," J.R. says calmly as if I'd just been out for a stroll around the waterfront.

"What? That's it? That's all you can say after setting me up with that mad woman?"

"Hey, consider yourself lucky. At least her friend Holly wasn't with her," J.R. replied. I didn't even want to know what that meant. "Go have a hot shower and I'll get us a couple of brandies," he added.

Good ol' J.R. Could always count on him – for better or not so good. Not sure when he ever slept, but one thing was for sure: he did indeed deliver me one helluva story. It was what went with it that just didn't sit so well. 'Details, mere details', J.R. was wont to say in these situations.

Chapter Seventeen

THWACK. Ker-PLUNK. THWACK. Ker-PLUNK. THWACK. Ker-PLUNK. It was these two sounds – always in that order – that awoke me, though not from any sense of surprise or bewilderment. I'd experienced these same two sound effects dozens of times over the years while visiting Uncle J.R. The 'THWACK' was the sound made when his prized Number 1 club – supposedly autographed by Bobby Jones, though just as easily could have been Tom or George for all I knew (or cared) – collided with some unfortunate golf ball being jettisoned into the murky depths behind the boat. No prizes for guessing what made the 'ker-PLUNK' sound. It occurred to me that at some time in the not-too-distant future, a frigging dam comprised of millions of soggy golf balls would take shape creating a tidal wave to wash over Victoria's narrow, meek laneways.

Not sure if he ever actually played on a proper golf course. This could have been the only form of the game that he'd ever played, preferring the calm, still waters of Victoria Sound over the rough and tumble of any improper golf club. Hell, there were no queues out here and the greens fees were, well, waived. But the truly neat part about his private driving range was his innovative 'tee'. Because he was playing from the back of a barge, there was no grass or even astro turf. Instead, he'd glued two bath mats together back to back. This meant he could set up several balls at the same time on the suction cups facing up while their compatriots down below held onto the ship's contours for all they were worth.

"Mornin, J.R.," I said finally dragging myself up from down below.

"G'day," he said while in mid-swing, probably aiming for the 17th green at Augusta. "Feelin better?" he asked after watching his latest missile splash down some 150 yards away.

"Better than what, dead? Maybe, but I'll need to get back to you on that one," I replied.

"That's the spirit," he said followed by yet another THWACK, ker-PLUNK.

I opted against recalling any other events from the previous evening, preferring instead to turn my efforts to another issue that had been bugging me. I'd come back 'home', among other reasons, to find out more about the puzzling combination of DNA strands that not only came before me, but ultimately led to my own non-perfect creation. While my folks had proven less than helpful in this quest, I figured who better to approach this topic with than J.R.? Hell, he'd given me so much over the years, including in more recent times – one helluva story.

"J.R., can I ask you something?"

"Sure you can, only it better not have anything to do with the family," he said obviously reading my all-but-empty mind.

"How'd you know?"

"How'd I know? How didn't I know? Ever since you been home you been asking about this shit. Want my advice? Forget about it!"

"Why?"

"Because it ain't worth it. There's nothing to it," he said.

"How can you say that? How could you not want to know more about your ties to an American President – not to mention the fuckin Mayflower?!"

"I'll tell you why. For the first and last time: You wanna know why I never gave a damn? Okay, here it is. You ever been on a boat with 300 fucking rednecks, most of whom couldn't read or write, let alone tell you who the frack John Adams was or wasn't?" he asked.

"So?"

"So? You don't get it do you, Mr. Writer? Let me draw you a map. The last thing you want anyone to know about you is how 'special' your background is. It's bad enough being from New England – let alone the relative of some First Family and early President when you're stuck on a sardine can with a bunch of guys who are still fighting the Civil War. Forget what they tell you about people looking up or admiring those who can claim great ancestors. Most people despise the hell out of you for that and will do whatever it takes to pull you down," he said.

"C'mon. It couldn't have been that bad, J.R.," I said.

"It was worse. And if that wasn't bad enough – take a good long look at your mother, boy. And her father, and his father before him," he said.

"And?"

"I don't even want to go there. They're nothing but no good. And not one of them ever did anything for anyone but themselves. That ain't right. And it ain't living. You wanna go do your family history? Great, go find out about your Dad's side. At least they're down to earth."

"Down to earth? My grandfather murdered some guy," I said.

"Awww, grow up. Do you know that for sure? How do you know what he did or didn't do? Did you ever ask him? Did you ever spend more than two minutes talking to his pals from the old country? No. And you call yourself a reporter? And even if he did do it – do you know the circumstances surrounding the event? For all you know, he was backed up into the corner of some frickin stone hut protecting three others when someone came at him with a machete. Go do your research before you judge the man," he said before returning his attention to the small white balls lying on the bathmat below him. He'd dropped his driver and was now standing over the balls with a seven iron.

I'd never heard J.R. speak so passionately about any topic that didn't involve copious amounts of alcohol. He truly meant it. And he was probably right, but it didn't solve my problem. And it didn't make it go away.

I packed up my car and headed back to the boat one last time to thank J.R. for his hospitality and for the story – regardless of its unfortunate ending.

"Need any money?" J.R. asked while in mid swing.

"Nah, not unless you got a couple of Babe Ruths handy," I said.

"Now that's serious tender," J.R. replied. "Will a Gehrig and a Lazerri do?"

I wasn't sure whether he was serious. I thanked him again, got into my car and planned on making just one more detour before returning to New Richmond—namely to the old man's new digs in Willimantic, Connecticut. In some respects, I was happy for Dad and hoped his reward for all those hard years slogging it in the thankless jobs in the HoJo's chain, paid off. In other respects, I envied the hell out of him for this opportunity, because I was damn sure it was never going to happen to me. In fact, I hadn't been in a town in the past seven years that would take me back. There was probably a reward to anyone who did catch me inside the city limits of Cincinnati or Indianapolis.

J.R. was probably right regarding leaving his side of the family alone. I had to admit I was never really close to anyone on his side of the family except him. Maybe he was telling me in the kindest way possible – leave well enough alone. The only thing was, I could no longer just turn my back on any part of my past. Not any more. I know no one was going to understand this irrational quest to uncover everything I could about the various bits of bone, blood and spit that went into casting my one-off mold. Someone had to pay for letting me loose on this unearthly paradise. And I intended to find out who. It may have been fine for J.R. to let things go. He'd lived most of his life and come to terms with whatever demons lurked in his and his family's past. I was a long way from coming to terms with anything. All I knew it was time to face up to the cold, hard truths, no matter how ugly it got. And given what lay ahead – on both sides of the family tree – it was guaranteed to get real ugly. While it might have been difficult figuring out how to locate the 'cats' that Hugh Jackson always called for to go in the lead to any news story, my family tree was purring with feline fervor. Finding the lead wasn't the problem. Sifting through all the crap that had built up over the generations on both sides was proving particularly difficult and judging by the strong emotion still attached to these familial ties, as evidenced by the reaction of the normally placid J.R., it was going to make writing any story for 'The Record' or any other paper for that matter, pale in comparison. Sinking the Navy's supreme submariner was child's play compared to exposing the bare roots of the Bedrosian/Johnson/Winslow/Adams family tree.

Chapter Eighteen

"Fuck off."

"Normally, that expression is not used among family, but I'll take them in the spirit they were meant," I said to my father who was seated at a desk that was nearly as big as the tiny room in which it was placed. In fact, I don't know how they got the damn thing in unless they built the glass framed walls around the desk.

"FUCK YOU!"

"That's more like it, Pop," I replied, shutting the door to his new office in the recently-opened Willimantic, Connecticut HoJo's. "But seriously, what can you tell me about granddad's early days?"

"I got serious problems here and you wanna know about Pa's childhood?"

"What kinda problems?" I offered, trying to butter up the contact, (a technique I'd been led to believe worked on reliable snitches, though it had never worked much in my experience). It was early afternoon and admittedly, the restaurant was a bit light on customers. At least the one that was sitting at the counter was enjoying his cup of coffee and a large slice of what appeared to be apple pie.

"You name it. No good workers, late food deliveries, no customers," he shot back.

"Is that all? Say, where's Connie?"

"You had to mention that bitch's name to me?"

"No, don't tell me you've split?" I said, hoping beyond hope I'd never see that toothless wonder's Jack-O-Lantern-like grin again.

"She left me for the late night bread delivery man, do you believe that? When I asked her why, she said because 'I was too good for her'. Believe that?"

"I do, Dad. I truly do."

"Fuck you. Get outta here. I'm not in the mood for you and your stupid questions today," he said.

"Fair enough, Pop. I understand. Maybe some other time," I said, but knowing deep down there would never be another time. I said goodbye, shut the door to his office behind me and walked out, but not before asking if there was a pay phone nearby. With his head firmly lowered on top of his desk, he motioned toward a darkened hallway to his right. The pay phone hung just outside the staff's changing rooms. There were three or four young girls getting ready for their shift. The door was just open enough so that I could see one of them in little more than a bra and panties. She knew someone was there and didn't bother trying to cover up. I turned away before it could have been considered anything more than a short leer. Though the door to the guys' change room was closed, the people in the next county could have heard the sound made by metallic locker doors slamming shut. I finally got the number for the paper dialled, but was having trouble hearing anything due to the heavy metal jam next door.

"Hey, Lou, how goes it?"

"You gotta ask? "Hey, nice job on the Navy. We've already had four calls from Rickover's office and a dozen more from the Sub Base and the story hasn't even run yet," Lou said.

"Anything else?"

"Ah, yeah. You're Special Investigation Squad members are running riot. Mason is on to some huge extortion racket and Gail Gerard is working on a story that's so big she can't tell anyone about it!"

"Can hardly wait," I replied. "Anything else?"

"Oh, yeah. I almost forgot."

"Well, give it to me, baby," I said.

"The Mayoress called and left me her private number," Lou said.

"And this is supposed to impress me how?"

"Because she didn't leave it for me, dummy. It's for you and she wants you to call her ASAP," Lou said.

"Ah, yes, yet another member of the fairer sex whose caught the Walt Johnson bug big time, eh?"

"Walt, I don't know how to tell you this, but she's not known as the 'Black Widow' for nothing," he said.

"Black Widow, my ass. Her husband is still alive," I said.

"Is he? Is he really?" Lou replied before hanging up.

Actually, the timing of her call could not have been better planned. She wanted something from me and it wasn't my body. She probably just needed some good press to win another election or help get her into Congress for all I knew. But what she didn't know was how she could help me, and more importantly, my grandfather. While I doubted there was any way to get the State to back off from all the taxes it said was owed, perhaps she could buy us some time.

At that moment, the young lady who had been providing me with the floor show earlier emerged, fully garbed in the HoJo blue and orange. I don't think they supplied the chewing gum.

"Hey, ever been bitten by a black widow?" I asked.

"Fuck off," she said in between chews.

"Seems to be a catchy phrase around here," I said and decided to take her up on hers, and my Dad's offer to leave.

Chapter Nineteen

The weather had turned decidedly colder – at last. But then, winter was what being a New Englander was all about. It got cold, damn cold, during the winter months in southern Indiana and Ohio, but it still never seemed the same. New England winters were honest; genuine cold if that makes any sense. The others seemed like limp imitations. Sure, summer could be nice, but there was never enough of it to keep you well and truly satisfied. You want summer, head to almost any other part of the country. Okay, sure, so the autumn leaves are great in New England. Millions of trees' leaves turning into a rich kaleidoscope of reds, browns and yellows. But they are gone in a matter of days, soon to have all their color sucked out of them by Mother Nature's own white-out. Again and again. Some people think New England has four distinct seasons. That's crap. There's only two: Winter and the rest.

I was about to ask my latest drinking companion her views on this decidedly New Englanders-only topic when she blurted out: "I'm not even going to dignify that remark with a comment."

"Excuse me? What comment? I didn't say anything," I replied quickly trying to erase any and all previous thoughts.

"Oh come now, you needn't play shy thing with me," said the woman whom prior to 15 minutes ago, I'd never beheld before in my current or any previous lifetime. She was probably in her mid to late 40s, had dirty, shoulder-length brown hair, a face that was so round it would make many circles jealous and the dirtiest set of fingernails I'd ever seen.

While I had decided to sneak back into town, I opted against heading for my usual watering hole, preferring instead to stick to the only remaining bar in Richmond Heights. It was called the 'Last Call Cafe', which was a neat play on words given that the bar's only competition was the town's cemetery.

"She bothering you?" asked the bartender, a relative giant of a man whose hands neatly held five large empty beer glasses each.

"No, not really," I lied.

"Let me know if she does. Cuz Darlene knows she's not supposed to bother people," said the man in a voice loud enough to have been heard by the tenants in the nearby crypts.

"Hey, I don't need to be insulted," my latest femme fatale declared before quickly downing the remainder of her ale and departing.

"What was that all about?" I asked, given that that now left just me and the bartender in this fine drinking establishment.

"Aww, she's alright. Just a bit loopy sometimes from the meds they give her over at the nut house," he said.

"Nut house? You mean the Almshouse? Is that still going?"

"Not much. Last I heard they was trying to shut it down."

"Where would all those people go?"

"You're sitting in one of their favorite places," came the reply. "That and the graveyard next door."

Many towns were finding it difficult to take care of their poor, elderly, insane or physically handicapped residents. The big deal now was either finding them outplacements or throwing them out altogether which didn't seem like much of a solution.

"But then, this place has done alright thanks to the quiet neighbors next door," said the bartender flicking his head toward the cemetery's front gate. "People are sad to lose someone, they come in here to drown their sorrows. People are happy to get rid of someone, they come in here to celebrate. What's not to like?"

"Yeah, great," I said, placing two bucks on the counter and heading for the door. "Did Darlene really know what I was thinking?"

"Depends," said the bartender.

"On what?"

"On how much you had to drink."

"I don't understand."

"Exactly," came the reply. I decided to leave while I was still behind. The sun was going down fast and I wanted to make a quick visit to the cemetery. It was the comment that Lou had made about visiting the Black Widow that got me to thinking about another lady who undoubtedly loved me more than any other woman on the planet. It was my grandmother, Takouhi Manoukian Bedrosian, though everyone knew her by the nickname 'Taki'. It was said that her Christian name meant 'Queen, wearer of a crown', and there surely could not have been someone more befitting a crown than her. In fact, with her long, thick dark hair, (which even in old age remained more black than gray), and deep, dark skin and matching piercing brown eyes, she could have easily been mistaken for a member of some great Plains Native American tribe.

Though totally uneducated and unaware of most things involving day to day life in Massachusetts or the United States in general, Taki had a gift for sniffing out phoney people. She always said that the Mayoress, for instance, was a 'no good woman', though never elucidated on what she meant by that. For someone with little formal education, however, few people could more accurately gauge a person, any person's, inner soul, than my grandmother. I don't know how she did it. But she always knew before me if the girl I brought home would be worth pursuing or not. She was equally adept at picking political leaders, even though she would not have known if the person was running for local dog catcher or President of the whole shooting match. She had little time for Eugene McCarthy. Said he had 'no heart', which pretty much echoed the sentiments of many who followed his semi-meteoric rise in national politics. Indeed, who didn't come away thinking McCarthy was a nice guy who just didn't have the ticker to take over the country's top job.

Getting anything out of her now was going to be a bit more difficult than usual for the simple reason that she had died some 11 years ago. It had been some time since I'd last paid my respects and there were few other people still alive that I would rather spend my time with than her.

I always got a kick out of her gravestone. It was like no other. There must have been 300-400 headstones in this cemetery. Most were your standard blocks of granite, complete with deceased's name, dates, etc. My grandfather had a different image in mind. He had the biggest damn rock he could find in one of his back fields and hauled it to the cemetery and placed it upright at the head of her grave. It stood nearly five feet tall and looked more like something some sculptor had thrown away rather than a neatly polished tombstone. In the failing light, with its slight lean and twisted mid-section, it almost looked like someone trying to pull themselves out of the ground. Could there be a better headstone than that? Near its top were four simple words – 'FOR TAKI…MY ROCK. ' It would mean nothing to practically everyone, but that was not the point for my grandfather. It meant everything to him. Just as she had.

It was at that precise moment that I realised how little I did know about my grandfather. Rather than look at all the things he'd accomplished and even done for me growing up, I never could get the image of him killing some helpless soul for some unknown reason. This one stupid act clouded everything about him. I'd been thinking a lot about him recently, though. Maybe J.R. was right. Maybe there was a very logical and valid reason for his killing action. Coming to this grave site again, now, after many years of being away, gave me a clearer insight into the man. Life had been hard for him in the old country. As hard as the large stone tablet that stood before me. It didn't get much easier in Massachusetts and yet, in spite of all these obstacles, he found a beautiful woman, married, raised a son (and a grandson), bought a small farm, tended to his fields and after the sun went down, retired to his workshop where he carved beautiful pieces of furniture from his own forest.

My head was spinning with questions. How does a guy with this sort of sensitivity, kill another human being? Where does the urge/ability to commit the ultimate sin, come from? And why is it that in all the years that I knew him, I never saw him swat one of the legions of flies that buzzed about, let alone kill anything any larger?

And why now, when I'm still trying to work out why oh why I can't forgive him for a crime that occurred before I was even born, am I being asked to save him from a fate that would probably kill him if he knew what was going on? It was all getting way too strange, but I swear, as I stood there shivering from the wintry cold, a tear fell from the uneven end of my grandmother's rocky edifice to the cold, hard ground below.

Chapter Twenty

"Set it up," I said to my favorite tavernkeeper as I walked through the door of my equally favorite New Richmond watering hole. It was going to be a great day, I decided, and it had nothing to do with the fact that the latest edition of 'The Record' had my story on the Navy plastered all over the front cover.

"Great story, Walt," Mel said as she placed a cold mug of my favorite Aussie beer in front of me.

"Yeah, should be getting the Naval recruiters down here any time now," I replied. I swallowed half the mug's contents in one gulp. Though still only early morning, there was nothing like that first alcoholic beverage of the day. I began to think I may have a drinking problem. But as dear Uncle J.R. used to point out: "It's not a drinking problem. It's a drinking solution."

My next swig was interrupted by this tall, thin young man dressed in an ill-fitting suit and holding a copy of 'The Record' under his arm.

"Excuse me, are you Walter Johnson – the reporter?"

"Depends," I said to the young man.

"On what?"

"On whether you're buying the next round," I replied.

A look of horror came over the man's face – the kind of look more usually associated with such disasters as a house fire, car accident or family death.

"But it's only 9.30 in the morning," the man said.

"Yes, but it's after midnight in Sydney, Australia. So what's your point?"

The man nearly fell off the bar stool.

"Look, kid, if you're not buying the next round – I'll get it but believe me, you'll thank me for it after the interview."

"How'd yo know I was here for an interview?"

"Hey, I'm a reporter – remember? Besides, the regulars don't start piling in till at least 10 a.m."

"So what's he like? Martin James, that is," the kid asked.

"A fucking asshole," said the editor's sister Mel while washing a bunch of glasses from the night before.

"Don't mind her, kid. She's kin. But between you and me – she's dead right."

The young man tried to settle into the bar stool next to me, not sure of what to say next. In addition to the paper, he carried a small satchel which probably contained numerous clips from his recent days as a reporter for his college rag.

"Where'd you go to school?"

"Northwestern. Just graduated with Honors from the J-School," he said proudly, pulling out the clips from the leather satchel.

"Save them for Marty," I said.

"You write real well," the kid said. "That's the sort of stuff I used to do in Chicago."

"Really? You must be something. Why the fuck would you come here if you don't mind my asking?"

"I've got a job in Cleveland at the '*Plain-Dealer*' but it doesn't' start till summer. Just thought I'd get in some practice," he said with just a hint of disdain as if he was doing us a favor by coming here.

At this point, one of my new cell mates – ol' Wallace 'Wall' Edwards hobbled into the bar and hoisted himself onto the stool next to me. I hadn't actually seen him in the bar before, but then again, I didn't make it a regular habit of dropping by before work.

"Hey, Wall, how goes it?" I asked.

He grunted in what I assumed indicated an affirmative manner.

The kid, who was still debating whether to take a swig from the glass of beer placed in front of him, leaned over and snidely asked me if he worked at the paper.

When I indicated that he did and that he was one of the best reporters ever to grace the tri-state region – the kid started laughing – and not in a jovial, friendly sort of way. "You must be kidding," he says to me.

I turned to Wall and asked if he could get me some smokes from the machine down back. The instant he had reached the end of the bar and had his back well and truly to us, I turned to the young wannabe newsman and told him in as polite a fashion as I could muster at this ungodly hour – to kindly get the hell out or risk being beaten within an inch of his miserable little life.

"Excuse me?"

"What part of the phrase 'FUCK OFF' don't you get asshole? Get outta here before I beat the living shite out of you!"

The kid's eyes opened widely, ditto for his mouth, but nothing came out of either organ. He simply removed himself from the bar stool and stole away into the light of day without ever finding out what life would be like as a reporter in the mean street of New Richmond.

"What happened to your buddy?" Wall said throwing the pack up on the bar in front of me.

"Aww, he didn't feel so good. Bit of a pussy," I said.

"Lot of it going around," Wall replied.

"Hey, Walt, thanks for scaring off the clientele," Mel said from behind the bar.

"He wasn't a big drinker anyway."

"I could've broken him in," she said as a dirty smile came over her face.

What was happening to me? Since when did I ever give a shit about what anyone thought of anyone else – particularly regarding the riff-raff I worked with at '*The Record*'? I worried more about this rag-tag bunch of no-hopers than I did about my own family, though that wasn't saying a whole lot.

"Say, Wall, you ever do much reporting on New Richmond's development plans?"

"You mean the 'CD' beat?" he said, smiling broadly.

"Yeah, that's the one," I said.

"I did but that was quite a few years ago," he replied.

"Got any thoughts on where it's heading or better yet, where it should be heading?"

"You gotta keep one thing in mind about New Richmond," he began leaning over as if he was letting me in on a big, big secret. "It's all about the water."

"The water?"

"Yep. Forget what anyone tells you about the redevelopment of the city center or the re-jigging of Olde Richmond Plantation, blah, blah, blah. New Richmond begins and ends at the waterfront," he said.

My next question was interrupted by the late arrival of Martin James, obviously confused as to why a certain young hotshot reporter was not waiting for him.

"Mel, wasn't there a young guy waiting for me in here for a job?"

"Nope," she replied, trying to keep a straight face.

"I could've sworn this guy rang me from downstairs and I told him to wait for me over here," Martin said.

"Oh yeah, there was a young guy in here," I offered.

"And?" Martin said.

"He said something about having bigger fish to fry. Said we weren't up to his elite journalistic standards," I said.

"Fucking asshole. Who the fuck does he think he is?" Martin said.

"My sentiments exactly, chief," I replied.

"Nice piece on the Navy. I'm glad to get out of the office. Phone's ringing off the hook this morning," he said.

"For or against?"

"Both. They're 'for' the Navy and 'against' you," Martin said, showing a rare glimpse of humor.

"I like it. I like it a lot. Well, guess I better get up there and see who I can trash today," I said.

"Yeah, and while you're at it, can you find out what your two charges are up to? Gail has hardly been in the newsroom since you left and Mason is acting even crazier than usual," Martin said.

"Hey, am I writing stories or babysitting?"

Unfortunately, my query coincided with the mother of all belches emanating from 'Wall Street's' mouth.

"Have you got a permit for those?" I asked, patting him on the back.

He leaned back and grabbed my hand. "Remember what I told you, son. It's all about the water," Wall said in his best whispering tone.

"What's all about the water?" Martin asked.

"Ahh, the derivation of a good belch," I lied. "You need water. Lots of it. Mixed with alcohol in just the right combination to achieve maximum belch drive," I lied again.

"You two are nuttier than the fruitcakes already up in the newsroom. Go to work," Martin said.

"Yes sir, chief," I said, helping Wall off his stool.

"Cut the 'chief' crap, too," Martin said.

"Okay, but I have to stop the 'sir' then, too," I said.

"Get outta here!!!" Martin screamed throwing a half-filled mug toward the front door.

It took us a while to get across the street. Not because of any heavy traffic. Rarely was traffic a problem in downtown New Richmond. It had more to do with the patches of ice on the sidewalks and Main Street. Trying to keep my own balance was bad enough, but looking out for my octogenarian colleague was even tougher, even with the aid of a cane that he used the way skiers use their poles for balance.

I knew from the minute we hit the front door, though, that the newsroom was not in its usual early-morning hibernation mode. Like any good (or bad) morning newspaper, even those that came out twice a week, little happened before noon. In fact, it usually required no more than one guy, may be two, to handle all incoming calls, visitors, etc.

Except today. Phones were ringing on practically every empty desk. Martin's sidekick, Jack Saunders, was busy yelling at someone while my youngest charge, Mason, was deep in listening mode to whoever was at the other end of the phone.

Mason motioned me to pick up a phone – any phone while somehow also managing to welcome me back to the newsroom.

"You're a dead man," responded the caller to my 'Hello, Walt Johnson speaking."

"Now that's a great way to start the day," I replied.

"Fuck you, ass-wipe," the pleasant-sounding gentleman said.

"May I ask what I've done to put you in such a sad, sad state to start your day?" I asked.

"Scum like you shouldn't be breathing," he said.

"Gotta hand it to you, pal. You don't mess around. But seriously, is it something specific I've written or are we just commenting in general on the declining standards in the use of the English language?"

"We're watching you, dickhead. Fuck off," he said before hanging up.

I'd no sooner hung up the receiver when the phone rang again.

"Fuck you, asshole," I yelled figuring it was the same guy calling back.

"Excuse me? Is this '*The Record*'?

Ooops. "Ahh, yes, how can I help. Forgive my colleague for swearing. He's not himself till at least 3 p.m.," I said.

The caller ignored my attempt at covering up. "Could you please put me through to Mr. Johnson?"

"Ahhh, I don't see him right now. Could I perhaps get him to return your call when he arrives?"

"No, that's okay. I'll call later. When do you expect him?"

"Ahh, it's hard to say. What day is it? Wednesday, yes, well, let's see, say, not sure he works on Wednesdays."

"I'll call again," the man said purposefully.

"Sure, no problem. Can I ask who is calling?"

It must have been a party line because I could hear one line clicking off. "Yes," this other, much younger sounding voice said. "You can tell him that Rear Admiral Rickover would like a word."

"You're kidding, right?" I said.

"No sir, we don't kid. Can I please have your name?"

"Why, sure, yes, it's – say hold on – here comes Walter Johnson now," I said pointing toward Mason James who, even in his usual state of confusion, was looking more confused than ever.

"Great, I'll hold," the young voice said.

I tried changing my voice as best I could. "Hello, Walt Johnson here."

"Mr. Johnson. We've seen your story in today's paper and found it most distressing," the young man said.

"I would think so," I replied.

"Admiral Rickover would like to have a word," the young man continued.

I kept quiet awaiting the tones of the Navy's most feared commander coming on the line. I debated whether to open with the query as to why he was called a 'Rear' Admiral when it would seem the most logical place to lead from was the front.

"Mr. Johnson?" said this rather scratchy, high-pitched voice.

"Yes, who's this?" I said, fearing the worst and forgetting all about funny word play with his Rearness.

"This is Admiral Rickover."

"How do you do, Admiral," I said.

"We found your article most enlightening."

"Thank you, sir," I said.

"Yes, in all my years of dealing with the media, I can't recall ever coming across a story that has been so poorly constructed and carried out as yours," he said.

"I'll keep that in mind for future stories. But then, I don't expect you get the chance to write a lot of articles in your line of work, Admiral," I said.

"Don't get smart with me. It's very dangerous having someone like you running around loose," the good admiral said. "It's also a most seditious act and if we were at war, I'd recommend you be locked up immediately."

"Phew, thank god we're not at war then, eh? Say Admiral, I appreciate the call and all, but I really must be going so if there's nothing else, I—"

"How dare you, you insolent fool. I expect your newspaper to write a full apology in the next edition or I will contact your superiors and demand satisfaction," he said.

"You do that, Admiral. We'd love to have a letter with your John Hancock on it in our humble rag. If you like, I'll even start drafting something for you," I replied.

With that, the line went dead, leaving me with the younger one's voice again. "That was most insulting," he said.

"I agree. Doesn't he know it's rude to hang up on someone?" But there is something you can do to make it up," I said.

I think if the guy at the other end could, he would've hung me with the telephone cord at this point. "And what might that be?"

"If Rickover is a Rear Admiral, what do they call you because you seem to constantly be coming up his behind?" I said.

The second line went dead, though I sensed there was still someone else listening in.

"Who was that?" Martin James said walking into the newsroom.

"Just Rickover calling to complain about the story," I said.

"Admiral Rickover? You shitting me?" my well-spoken superior said.

"No, I'm not shitting you and yes, that was him and the good Admiral is demanding a full retraction or he will call you and demand satisfaction," I said.

"Good god, nice going, Johnson!" Martin said.

"Hey, that's why I'm making the big bucks, right?"

"Never mind that, can you just make sure that Mason and Gail stay out of trouble?"

"Stay out of it or stay in it?" I said.

"Oi, nice piece," said Ian Ross, our token Aussie who handled editing and head-line writing duties for me, among other esteemed writers at the paper.

"Yeah, thanks, Ian. Truly love your headlines, man," I said.

"No worries," he said. He had a million and one great expressions that were slowly but surely working their way into the day-to-day conversations of most 'Record' writers. 'No worries' was such a classic phrase. So much more evocative than our 'no problem'.

"You bin workin with Gail? Her stuff has started to shine," Ian said.

"Ahh, no, I can't say that I have, but then again, I've been out a fair bit. What's she up to?"

"She's bin workin on a series of 'streetscapes' in which she delves into the lives of many of our more infamous street people. Didn't think she had it in her," he said, handing me her latest work. A profile of some local idiot who claimed he'd been abducted by aliens, not once, but twice.

"Got a headline for that one yet?"

"Not yet, mate but when I do, you'll be the first to know," he said.

"Great. Know where she is now?"

"No idea, mate. But she's also looking hotter than ever," he said breaking into a broad grin.

"You dirty bastard," I replied, just as someone slapped me on the back.

"Good to see ya, boss," said Mason James. "I started working on that story you told me about before you left."

"And?" I said.

"Well, I'm not sure where it's headed," he said.

"That's a good sign," I said. "Or a bad one depending on what you've discovered. Refresh my memory over a coffee, would you, Mase?" I had no idea of what story I'd suggested to him before leaving for Connecticut.

"You know. About who owns Main Street," he said.

"Oh, that story," I said as if I knew what the hell he, or I, was talking about. "And what did you find?"

"That's the part I don't understand. It belongs to all sorts of people," he said.

"Yeah, like who?"

"Not so much whos, but whats," he said cryptically. "They're fancy sounding corporations like Acme This and ABC That, Inc."

"That's good. Keep digging," I said not knowing what else to say. I'd never done any story like this before. "I've got to go out for an interview, but will be back later," I said to no one in particular.

"Right, boss," Mason said returning to a legal-sized sheet of yellow paper with a bunch of names and numbers all over it.

That was yet another great thing about newspapers. How many jobs allowed you to leave the building under false pretenses? You could only lose so many grandmothers or run out of gas a few hundred times in any one life time.

I headed straight for my favorite watering hole. It was still early – not quite 11.30 a.m. which probably was worth a celebration of some sort, anyway. Besides, anyone who wasn't supposed to be there was in the same boat as me, so was unlikely to say anything to management. Then again, the Publisher was probably better off with me in the bar than at the paper. At the bar, I was delivering pure profit while in the newsroom it was anyone's guess just what 'pure' I was delivering.

"Jeez, you really love this place, don't ya?" yelled out Mel.

"No, I really love you, baby, but you keep turning me down," I replied as a beer glass filled with some sort of amber fluid alighted right in front of me.

"Flattery will get you everywhere," she said before returning to another lost soul at the other end of the bar.

Time passed quickly. Either that, or I must have passed out because by the time I got outside, the street lamps were starting to come on. I decided it was a great night for a stroll so I started walking home. Then again, what choice did I have? I hadn't gotten far when I sensed that I was being followed. My 'sixth' sense was on full alert because whatever car was behind me started flashing its high beams while a horn that would have woken the dead in Alabama blared repeatedly as well.

"Hey, you, get in the car," yelled this guy who was getting out of what must have been the only stretch limousine in the county. I figuratively patted myself on the back for having such keen senses. Christ, if they were any sharper, every psychic in America would be sweating on when I planned to muscle in on their turf.

"Sorry, I don't ride with strangers," I replied turning my back on the car that was bigger than my apartment. I was starting to get a wee bit freaked out by this development. Was he from some Rickover goon squad or perhaps my mate with the chilling death rattle phone call? Alas, my concerns were lowered a few notches when a slightly familiar female voice called out. "Oh, Wally, yoo hoo? It's me, Wally. You're dear Aunt Stacey," came the siren's call.

I didn't have any Aunt Stacey. It was none other than Mrs. Eustace (call me 'Stacey') Tucker-Morgan – New Richmond's Lady Mayoress. Women, they just couldn't help themselves when it came to me. "Oh, hi, Aunt Stacey – how are ya?"

"Don't get fresh, young man! Please do get in the car. We have sooooo much to talk about," said another deadly spider woman to the still same old fly boy.

"Normally, I'd say 'yes', but this is a school night and I really must go home and do my homework."

"I won't take 'No' for an answer. Just one drink and then I'll let you go. What do you say?" she said, opening the car's door while rattling a couple of champagne glasses.

"Oh, what the hell. My first class is gym, anyway," I said climbing into the back of the limo.

"Great," she said before adding: "Home, James!"

"Is that really his name or do you just like saying that?"

"No, that's his name. James Dunn. His father performed the same job for my husband's father so there's history," she explained.

"That's really neat. Say, my mother and you are both mothers. Does that mean we have some history, too?"

"Don't be rude, Walter. Just sit back and enjoy the ride. We have much to discuss," she said as her tone became all business. I tried convincing myself that that was fine by me because I had some business to conduct with her, too. It didn't take long to reach the front gate of her, well, her husband's family mansion. I'd been here hundreds, well, tens, scratch that, maybe a handful of times for pre-Christmas drinks with my Mom and her father. That must have been 20 years ago now. I doubted whether egg nog and Christmas biscuits would be on tonight's menu.

"Do come in and make yourself at home, Walter. I just want to get out of this uniform and into something more comfortable," she said racing for the stairway that could have handled four lanes of divided highway traffic.

It was funny. Here were all these huge houses sitting one after another and combined, probably housed fewer people than half a floor of The Lincoln. I looked around the room she'd left me in. I guessed it was her husband's office as the walls boasted more books than most state library buildings. The room, which was large enough to double as a basketball court, complete with bleachers, was strangely silent this night. The only other 'people' in the room were four huge portraits: One each of the current Mr. and Mrs. Morgan, probably dating back 20 years and a pair featuring their predecessors, dating back to the 1950s or so. Quite handsome people, and I meant that in a most unflattering way – especially for the women, who though unrelated, both had jaws that would've made any amateur boxer lick his lips.

All of a sudden, one of the walls of books moved. I was starting to get creeped out. Was I having hallucinations again? How the hell did the thing move? When it stopped rotating, there was a large bar complete with stools and top shelf Scottish labels like Glen Livet and Glen Fiddoch on show. I doubted Jim Beam or Jack Daniels ever got a sniff in this joint. There also was a large fridge tucked under one end of the bar. I opened it and grabbed the first bottle of green beer I could see. It was a Heineken and there were enough replacements to keep me happy for a couple of months easy.

"I see you helped yourself to the bar," came the Lady Mayor's voice re-entering the room again. I don't know what she'd been wearing in the car as her outfit was covered by a floor-length mink coat. I doubted she wore see-through tops and skimpy little skirts to the office though. Ditto for the shoes which were the highest heels I'd ever seen any woman try to walk on. It was very strange for me to see her as a woman. Up till now, I knew her only as my Mom's best friend; tennis buddy; etc. She even had a daughter who was about my age, but died tragically in a car accident about three weeks before high school graduation. She was a beautiful girl. Much too good for the likes of me and most of my pals. Not that she ever said that. She just was better in every conceivable way. My mother said that her friend Stacey changed after that. Both she and her husband, Jonathan, successful lawyers for the area's two most prominent law firms, tried drowning their sorrows with countless cocktails. Why wouldn't you? The death of an only child is never easy. At any rate, it was most odd for me to be in this house again and in such different circumstances. Mrs. Morgan was not an unattractive woman, though probably on the wrong side of 45 now. The stiffest thing about her appearance as noted earlier was her face, which still could grace the side of any Rushmore-sized mountain and retain its rocky appeal. She did, however, have a body to match any Hollywood siren. What once had been sharp, curvaceous edges, however, were now slowly losing their never-ending struggle with gravity. Even her legs, which could have given Betty Grable's a run for their money, seemed a bit stockier, shorter now than before. Regardless of how she looked, I kept trying to remember her as my Mom's best friend and not someone I ever spent much time thinking about in any other way.

"How's Mr. Morgan these days?" I said trying to get my mind off what she wasn't wearing.

"Not well, I'm afraid, Walt. He used to be so much fun but now he comes home by 6 and is tucked up in bed by 7.30 p.m."

So much fun, indeed. It was said that in his prime, ol' Jonathan Morgan could drive to New York City while preparing his briefs, argue and win two separate cases before the Second Court of Appeals in Manhattan and be in some luxurious drinking establishment by 3 in the afternoon, looking down Madison Avenue while looking up some young waitress's skirt. He was quite a guy. Every woman, and most men for that matter, wanted to get know this guy. He made James Garner look ordinary. Though blessed with great size and stature, and a thick head of hair to match, his athletic prowess was nothing to write home about. His bedroom antics, however, were legendary, claiming more notches on his belt than a posse of Casanovas. Even without the looks, this guy would have been a stud, due to his quick wit and way with words. Girls loved him, because he oozed so much class. When I did it, it was just another sleazy move. When he did it, he made them feel like they were giving it up for the King or something. I'd heard that he had gone downhill in recent times. It would seem that all the grog and hard living had caught up, leaving him with little more than hazy memories of times when he ruled all who walked before him. The mantle had now been passed to his all-too-passionate wife who as you may have guessed, also had something of a reputation.

"Be a dear and fix me a drink, Walter," she said, sitting down on a large leather sofa somewhere across the room.

"Sure, what sort of beer do you drink?" I said.

"Oh, never mind. Just pour me a glass of chardonnay and come sit over here. I'm lonely," she said.

"Jeez, you don't mess around. Won't the help come by or your husband at some point?"

"I doubt it. 'The help' as you call them have the night off and Jonathan has had the night off for some years now."

"I should warn you, though. A couple of beers and I can't get it up," I said.

"That's okay. We'll keep you to one then," she said smiling.

"I've already had four earlier this afternoon," I replied.

She laughed a throaty laugh. "You crack me up. Connie said you had a delicious sense of humor."

"Connie? Oh, you mean my boss?"

"Yes, that's right. Now Walter, it's been so long since we had a good chat," she said.

"We never had a chat," I replied to Mrs. Tucker-Morgan. "I barely know you."

"That's not true, Wally. You know that's not true. But I must say, you have grown into quite a handsome young man," she said eyeing me off like some hunk of beef in a butcher's window.

"You, too. I mean, you're a very attractive lady, but I don't think there's much point in going down that track," I said. "With all due respect, it's a bit like 'The Graduate', ain't it?"

"I knew you were going to say that. Well, let me tell you right now that there was less than 10 years difference between Dustin Hoffman and

Anne Bancroft in real life," she replied, arguing a case she'd obviously argued before.

"Fine. That's fine. Can we just get down to business?" I said.

"Yes, good idea. First, let me formerly welcome you back to your home town. We are so glad you decided to return."

I looked around for the rest of the 'we' but saw no one but the four silent faces in oil above. "Oh, it was nothing really. I really had nowhere else to go. I'd already been thrown out of most states east and west of the Mississippi."

"That's not what I hear. I hear you were a very popular reporter at your last job," she said.

"Oh, yes. I was until I wrote a story linking two members of the town council of some northern Cincinnati suburb to a child porno racket in Covington, Kentucky. That went over a real treat. It seems that sort of thing is not only okay in some parts of Cincinnati and most bits of Kentucky, but encouraged," I said.

"Well, fortunately we don't have those sorts of stories out here," said the Mayor with the mostest. "By the way, loved your piece on the Navy."

"Thanks. Rear Admiral Rickover and his crew apparently had some problems with it. The death threats haven't stopped all day," I replied.

She ignored this statement, preferring to steer the conversation back to something she knew a lot about: "Tell me, did you fuck that young lady you wrote about in the story?"

Normally, little amber ale ever spends much time in my mouth. It's simply a short stopping point between my lips and the bottom of my stomach, but it just so happened her audacious comment came just as I was swigging the last few ounces of my first cold one in about an hour. I spewed this lovely imported ale's last few gulps all over the leather sofa, just missing her by inches. "Excuse me? Did you just say what I thought you said?"

"Don't be coy with me, Walter. I could tell from the way you talked about her that you two got it on."

"What are you, my mother? Besides, a gentleman never tells," I replied.

"Neither does a lady, but I'm not one and nor are you a gentleman if I'm any judge of character!" she said.

"Jeez, Mrs. M, I'm blushing now," I said heading for the safety of the bar.

"Pour me another glass while you're up?"

"Sure thing. So what is it you wish to know?" I said trying like heck to get her off her obviously favorite one-track, sexually-oriented mind?"

"I believe that Connie has entrusted you with the very important task of getting to the bottom of what's going on in New Richmond," she said.

"Really? You two talk about me? Jeez, I'm getting a big head now."

"Don't be silly, Walter. It's a big job and we felt it needed someone special to put things straight."

"We? Do you run the paper with Mrs. Wheeler-James?"

She obviously had revealed more than she was supposed to. "Ahh, no, nothing like that. It's just that we have regular meetings, along with some other prominent citizens and from time to time, *The Record's* handling – or should I say mis-handling of this matter, arises."

Good catch. The woman wasn't a politician for nothing. In fact, at one time, she'd been seriously touted as a gubernatorial candidate. "So what can little ol' me bring to this adventure that no one else can?"

"It's simple, Walter. You are one of us. You have grown up here and seen what it once was and hopefully could be again."

"I don't follow. As far as I can remember, New Richmond, with all due respect, was always a shit hole. It just stinks a bit less these days," I said.

"That's unfair, Wally! We're working hard to breathe new life into the old girl."

"But to what end? What's here? A statue to some ancient gin rummy who stole everything he ever wrote from Thoreau and a broken down semi-breathing, living hysterical museum that should have been read the last rites years ago."

"Granted, it's taking longer than we'd hoped, but soon we will be making a series of announcements that will put us well and truly on the map again," she said.

"Do tell," I said.

"No, that's for me to know and you to find out. But in the meantime, we'd like you to find out who has been buying up downtown and to what purpose they have in mind."

"Surely, you know who 'they' are?"

"Not really. That's where you come in. But I'm happy to help in any way I can," she said, taking the glass from my hand while opening her legs wide enough to let me see that there was nothing between her and that thin skirt.

"I'll keep that in mind," I said trying not to stare at the good lady's very public private parts. "Say, you could do me a favor," I said.

"Yes, you mentioned that in the car, name it," she said.

"Well, do you remember my granddad's farm in Richmond Heights?"

"I don't think so," she said not altogether convincingly.

"Yeah, well, he has this 50 acre run-down farm on the other side of the Indian land and the State is threatening to take it off him unless he coughs up outstanding land taxes," I said.

"How much are we talking about, Walter?"

"I'm not exactly sure, but it could be $25,000-$30,000."

"I can write you a check now if you like," she says as if we're talking about pocket change.

"Ahh, no, that's okay. I'm just wondering if you can have a word to the boys in Boston and get them to lay off – at least for a while until I can figure out some sort of payment plan."

"No problem. What are friends for? Now, how about a night cap?"

"Aww, look, I better be getting back to my apartment. I haven't been there in a while and I just want to make sure the pot plants are still dead," I said.

Her throaty laugh reappeared. I had to admit it was rather sexy, but I'd promised myself that after the last little fiasco in New London that I wasn't going to fall for that trap again. At least not in the same week. "You kill me, Walter," she said.

"I hope not, Mrs. M," I replied. "I'll just call a cab."

"No you won't. I'll have James drive you home. It's the least I can do now that we're going to be working so closely on this little 'CD' project," she said.

"Thanks," I said heading for the door as quickly as my drunken legs could go. I didn't look back, preferring to wave as I headed for the front door.

"Don't be a stranger, Wally," she yelled out.

I left feeling like I needed a long, hot shower. The more I thought about our conversation, the less I thought it really was about sex. There was something else going on there. For starters, she never once mentioned my mother and I knew they were real close. Or at least they had been. Not to mention all that stuff about her and Connie talking about me. Even her use of the phrase 'CD' was odd. That was a term used only in the newsroom. No, everything was not what it seemed. She may have been nearly nude, but there was nothing nakedly obvious about what the hell had just happened.

Not long after I got into my apartment, the phone rang. "Hey, Aunt Stacey, thanks for—"

"Walter, is that you?" boomed my mother's voice.

"Oh, hi Mom. Jeez, you're up late."

"Never mind the time. Who's 'Aunt Stacey?'"

"An old girl friend," I said, stretching the truth only a teeny weeny bit. "What can I do you for?"

"We need to talk and I've been wondering where the heck you've been," she said.

"No problem. I'm happy to come around now if you like," I said.

"See you tomorrow for dinner," she replied before the line went dead.

I'd no sooner hung up than the phone rung again. "Hi Walter, did you make it home okay?"

"Ahh, yes, thanks Aunt Stacey."

"Sure you don't want that night cap?" said the Lady Mayor who obviously had had a couple more drinks since I'd last seen her.

"No thanks, but thanks for offering," I said, before the line went dead again.

I'd no sooner put the receiver back in its cradle and headed for the bathroom to clean myself up when it rang again. The place was busier than Grand Central. "C'mon, Stacey, it's late—"

Again, there was an eerie silence at the other end. It obviously was not my favorite 'Auntie'. "Mom, is that you?" I said.

"You're a dead man," came the monotoned voice I'd heard earlier in the day at the newsroom.

"Oh, c'mon man. Give me a break. What did I do to you?"

"It doesn't matter. You're a dead man," the robotic-toned man said again.

"Fine, thanks. Can we make it for the weekend, because I'd hate to miss out on my usual booze-up with the guys on Friday?"

The phone went dead again which was fine by me. Earlier in the day this man's gruesome threat had bugged me. Now it was just pissing me off.

Chapter Twenty One

"Open up. Police."

I couldn't believe it. Christ, was I going to be arrested for not having sex with the Mayor or may be for having sex with that crazy New London woman? Or was it something else? Whatever or whoever it was, it was still too damn early for my liking. The digital alarm clock read 9.45 a.m. Way too early to be entertaining house guests – even if they were cops. But wait a minute. It could just be the crazy nut who keeps leaving me creepy messages.

"Go away!" I shouted.

"Open up. We need to talk to you now!" came this voice that sounded as if it were used to getting its own way.

I grabbed my favorite Louisville slugger, a Rod Carew model which sported a real thin handle and a super thick barrel. Not much good for hitting cheap singles, but just perfect for going deep to left, right or right in the center of some madman's pineapple. I opened the door slightly, hiding my secret weapon behind my back. My eyes were greeted by two uniformed officers – one male; one female.

"Hello, Mr. Johnson is it?"

"It might be. What the hell have I done now?"

"Ahh, nothing, sir. We just need your help getting into your neighbor's apartment."

"Why?"

"Have you seen Mrs. May recently?"

"Who? Oh, you mean Louisa May? Ahh, no, but then I've been away the past few days – why?"

"Some friends of hers called to say they hadn't heard from her and when they knocked on the door earlier this morning, all they got was a very angry dog barking and growling.

"That'd be Flynn," I said. "She can be hard to handle."

"That's why we came here. Understand you get along with the mutt," said the male whose name tag read 'Ritter'.

"No one gets along with Flynn except Mrs. May," I said.

"Look, we're losing valuable time. Do you have a key to her door?"

"Yeah, here it is," I said throwing it out in the hall.

"We'd really appreciate it if you'd open her door for us," Officer Ritter said.

I still wasn't convinced they were who they said they were. Any baboon can rent a cop suit. I opened the door and showed them my weapon. I may not have been able to take them both out, but I was confident I could make a lasting impression on at least one of their brain pans.

"Whoa, now slugger. Please put the bat down. We're police officers," said the female whose name badge read 'Sauta'.

"Yeah, how do I know who you are? I got guys ringing me threatening to kill me at all hours of the day and night. How do I know you're not 'him?'" I said before realizing how stupid that last statement sounded.

"Just open the goddamned door," Officer Ritter finally said.

I opened the goddamned door. Two things struck me immediately: Flynn the Wonder Dog and a very strong, pungent odor that didn't bode well for my neighbor's well being.

While I wrestled with Flynn on the ground, the officers entered the apartment and found Mrs. May, sitting in her favorite chair. Judging by the smell, she'd been sitting in that same position for about three days.

"You can go now, Mr. Johnson. Please take the dog with you if you don't mind," Officer Sauta said.

"I, I, can't believe it. I can't believe she's gone," I said.

"Thanks again for your help, sir," she said, closing the door behind her.

I was finding it hard to get Mrs. May's last look out of my head. It was so, well, her. So calm and serene. Everything she did oozed serenity. She made the Dalai Lama look like a crackhead on speed. I wished now that I'd told her how much I had appreciated her acts of unkindness, but would just have to hope like hell she had known that.

Officer Sauta popped back in a while later. She wanted to know if Mrs. May had any family. It was a simple question but there was no easy answer. She'd never spoken about anyone to me, but surely she had not been on her own forever. I remembered seeing pictures of a guy and a couple of kids on the mantle, but they were old pictures. Everyone looked like they'd fallen out of a *'Leave it to Beaver'* episode. What was that all about?

I vowed to do the one thing I said I would never do again after my time in Cincinnati. That was where my illustrious journalism career began and in stereotypical fashion – my first job was to write obits. The thinking of the day apparently was that someone who couldn't talk back would be an easier story to write for a beginner than those who could. Talk back, that is.

But I proved this theory well and truly wrong. First cab off the rank was some middle-managing, middle-aged guy who'd had a heart attack at his desk and cashed in his chips without passing go. He died on the only job that many of his fellow Cincinnatians would have truly envied – and no, I'm not talking about during the throes of sexual passion. I'm talking about dying for the one company that took nearly every citizen's fancy in 'Cin City' – Procter & Gamble. The only thing was, I didn't know that. I wasn't a local. Not even close. And not only that – I didn't give a rat's ass about a company that cleaned up on washing powder. I cared so little that I misspelled Procter.

BIG mistake. Mucho Biggo Mistako in Cincinnati – the one and only home town of P&G. It didn't take long for everyone in the rather large newsroom and probably in the entire tri-state area for that matter – to find out just how little I knew about my subject. I'd say the article had left my hand for oh - a whopping three or four seconds when the proverbial hit the fan.

That's about how long it took the assistant editor – a gray-haired, burned-out dwarf of a man who hadn't written a word since World War II, to ring a huge cow bell that he kept under his desk. I was to find out that this was the one thing this man lived for. Not ringing the bell literally. Rather, ringing the bell of some snot-nosed, young brat like me, both literally and metaphorically. No one doubted the man's genius at picking up on the typing and/or grammatical mistakes of others. A trait that I truly loathed – particularly when I was the 'other'.

"Listen up, Ladies and Gentlemen. I have a NEW winner in the 'Barnsey (that was the only name he was known by – probably the name he was given at birth), Cavalcade of Fuck-Ups'.

I turned around to see to whom he was referring hoping like heck it wasn't yours truly. Alas, it twas I.

Barnsey motioned to me to join him in the middle of the newsroom. "Son, you are a winner!" he hollered.

"A winner for what?" I asked naively.

"For the biggest fucking mistake any writer for the misbegotten can make in this town," Barnsey said to a growing swell of chatter and giggles growing around the room. "Listen up, people. What's the one word no one gets wrong in Cincinatti?"

A chorus bellowed out: "P-R-O-C-T-E-R."

"Don't you ever forget it, asshole," Barnsey said to me just in case I hadn't heard the Mormon Tubercular Choir in the background. What did I learn from that mistake, you now ask? To not get stuck writing obits for one thing. And to not get stuck writing obits ever again for another.

That is, until now. I owed Louisa May Alcott May something. I owed her a lot. She was one of the few people, male or female, who gave me things unconditionally. That was pretty special. So I grabbed Flynn's lead, shut the door and headed off for 'The Record's Morgue. The Morgue. Even Mrs. May would've loved that one.

++__))(((****JJJJJGH^^%$TTY^666TGGFHH. Oh great, another visitation from the Sainted One. Then again, who would know more about the arts of death and dying than dear ol' St. Vartan?

__))((*&*&^&^^^YYYY77655RRFFF446JJJJJJJJJJJJ%%$$#####%. HONOR THY DEAD FOR THEY WILL BREATHE NEW LIFE INTO THE LIVING. PAY SPECIAL TRIBUTE TO THOSE WHO DEDICATE THEIR LIFE TO GIVING, BECAUSE THEY GET MUCH MORE IN RETURN…

I wasn't sure about any of these concepts from the 'V' man, but strangely enough, I sensed he was about to pay me a visit regarding her passing. I'd had a few of these feelings in recent times and was coming to the belief that he was trying to tell me something. Something about my own past perhaps? Or lack of future prospects? Whatever it was, everything was starting to spin faster and faster – even faster than dear Flynn was now dragging me along Main Street.

I didn't know what to do with Flynn so I dragged her through the front door and up the stairs to the newsroom. Lou Cassals greeted me.

"See you have your new girlfriend with you. She's quite a looker, Walt," he said.

"Fuck you. Help me get her into the Morgue before anyone else sees her."

"You gotta be kidding?" he asked.

When I gave him my best 'No, I'm not kidding' look, he shrugged his shoulders and helped me escort Flynn into the library, which was its usual empty self – except for the room's caretaker, Wall Edwards. The old man was so busy cutting articles out of recent editions that he failed to see Flynn pull up right beside him. Lou kept right on walking by the Morgue toward the men's restroom. I whispered 'thanks' to him and got a one-finger salute in return.

"How ya keepin' young fella?" Wall said, peering out over his glasses at me.

"Not bad, Wall. Not bad. Did you know a lady named Louisa May Al—"

"Mrs. May? Everyone knows Mrs. May. Why, what's up?" he said.

"Ahh, well, she died and I was just wondering if there might be some clips on her so I can put an obit together?"

"No? Did she really? What a shame. Great lady. Ahh, hell, son, there's been a couple of volumes on her. I'll get them for you," he said still not noticing the very large dog curled up next to his chair.

"Watch out for the—"

Before I could say 'dog', Flynn jumped up, pushing the old man over onto the hard floor whereupon she began licking him within an inch of his life.

"Flynn, get off! Get off him!" I yelled while pulling at her collar.

"It's okay, boy. She's not trying to hurt me. Is that Mrs. May's dog?"

"Yeah, do you mind if she stays for a while?"

"Not at all. Hell, I love the damn things. Make more sense then most people," he said just as Martin James walked in.

"Well, look who's here. The Prodigal Son himself," he said just as Flynn turned her attention to him. "Hey, what's this dog doing in here?" Martin said just as Flynn launched herself onto his abdomen.

"Ahh, she belongs to a neighbor who died earlier today and I'm just watching her until I can figure out where to keep her," I said. "I'm just getting some material to write an obit."

"An obit?" he said, ignoring the dog's affectionate moves. "I'm not paying you to write obits."

"You'll want him to do this one, Martin. It's for Mrs. May," Wall explained.

"Louisa May died?" Martin asked as if she was better known than the Pope.

"Yes," I replied. "What did she do that made her so famous around here, anyway?" I said.

"Get him the clips, Wall," Martin said. "Make it good," he added before turning to walk away. "And make sure the dog doesn't come in here again."

"Like I was saying. The dog makes more sense than most people," Wall said motioning toward Martin. "Frickin' asshole," he added.

"It's alright, Wall. He's got a right to be pissed off about the dog. But what makes Mrs. May so special?"

"Take a look for yourself," Wall said placing four business-sized envelopes that were bursting at the seams in front of me.

Here's the short version: Mrs. May grew up in New Richmond, the only child of two rather ordinary parents – Mr. And Mrs. Jack Alcott. Upon graduation from New Richmond High School in 1931, she took up teaching until meeting and marrying an equally ordinary chap named Vernon May a few years later. The Mays had two children, a boy and a girl who became the center of their lives. The stories portrayed a family that was perfect in its ordinary qualities. They lived in an ordinary part of town in an ordinary house. They probably even had an ordinary cat and dog. The Mays' extraordinarily ordinary life turned upside down in the early 1950s when the family, which had just recently purchased a new car, were involved in an horrific accident. It was one of those warm, sunny days in late spring and she had packed a picnic for them to enjoy at a nearby lake. (This information was dutifully provided in a well written news story by Wall Edwards). The accident occurred while they were driving home. 'A-c-c-i-d-e-n-t'. Now there's a strange word. It all depends on your point of view and the timing. The police used it because they had no other way to describe what happened at the time.

A man named Norman Potter lost control of his vehicle and slammed head-on into another vehicle that contained the May family. There was no bad weather; unforeseen obstacle such as a deer or some other animal straying onto the road. It was just an accident.

What came out in stories written later by Wall Edwards and others proved it was anything but an accident. Norman Potter driving a vehicle was not only an accident waiting to happen, but a guaranteed death notice for someone who happened to be in the wrong place at the wrong time. Enter the Mays'. Exit three family members in less time than it takes to blink. Vernon and their two children, son Samuel and daughter Ruth, were killed instantly. Louisa May survived with little more than a slight concussion and twisted ankle when she was thrown from the car.

Wall told me that the police later said that Potter had been picked up on drunk driving several times, but always got off with a light sentence. This time he survived, but suffered a fair bit of brain damage which saw him placed in the 'Almshouse' not long after the tragic smash. One week to the day after the accident and one day after burying her family, Louisa May visited the drunk's bedside and not only took care of him, but paid for his hospital bills!

Before cutting to this most extraordinary act of kindness, there was something else drawing me into the story. And it had nothing to do with my dearly departed neighbor. There was another force at work; there was another story circling in the background that needed time to expose itself.

I asked Lou if I could have another couple of days to get him the story.

He gave me a very puzzled look. It was the kind of look someone gives you when you tell them that you're thinking about voting in the next Federal election. No, scratch that. It was the kind of look someone gave you when you said you were voting for Ronald Reagan in the next Federal election.

"Let me get this straight: You not only want to write an obit, but you want extra time to do it?"

"Hey, he said he wanted me to 'make it good'," I replied.

"I really am starting to worry about you. Look, fine by me but if Marty asks what you're working on – I ain't gonna cover for you," Lou says.

"Thanks, big guy. You're a star. Besides, Marty wants the story, too," I said. Lou turned to walk away. "Hey, do you know who runs the Almshouse these days?"

Lou motioned toward Wall Edwards. "Ask him," he said.

I asked him. He told me. I grabbed Flynn and walked back to the Lincoln to pick up my car and take a drive. A drive back in time to a place that would have fit more snugly into the day-to-day existence of any one of my early forebears. No, that wasn't quite right, either. I was going to visit a place that would have gotten Queen Elizabeth excited – and I'm not talking about the reigning English monarch – I'm talking about the earlier model - the 17th century Tin Lizzie model to be exact.

You're probably wondering what early English monarchs, the Almshouse and Mrs. May's demise have in common. This was precisely the question I kept asking myself, but not just about this story. Everything I came in contact with seemed to have stories within stories. It never seemed like that before. Hell, when I covered the wet t-shirt contest out in the Mideast, there was no hidden agenda – so to speak. It was just a breast-fest, pure and simple. When I stuffed up the spelling of Procter in that obit in Cincinnati, it was just another fuck-up by the world's most prolific fuck-up. Not now. It was hard to tell where a story began or ended. They were running all over one another like the freeways wrapped around Los Angeles.

Speaking of roadways, it's probably more important that I start concentrating on the drive at hand. Particularly with my hairy co-pilot in the passenger seat, constantly trying to lean over and lick me. I rolled her window down a bit which got her mind on other matters like trying to bite the gusts of wind blowing into her face. That gave me time to think a bit more about the history lesson fast forwarding to the recent past present in front of me.

One of New Richmond's first buildings was a then small stone fort on the northeastern edge of 'The Big Puddle'. It had been built as the early settlers first major foothold in Massachusetts' wild western frontier. It survived several raids by the French and Indians throughout the latter part of the 17th and early 18th centuries before converting from a fortress to keep unwanted people out – to a place to keep equally unwanted people in. Enter the 'Almshouse', which derived from an ancient English social institution more commonly referred to as a poorhouse or workhouse.

It was during the reign of Queen Elizabeth I that the so-called 'English Poor Law' was passed to provide shelter for the old and the infirmed. This was 17th century speak for finding a place to keep the human flotsam and jetsam out of the way of more decent folks. This great sense of responsibility by the many to take care, (see remove) of the lame and the sick, sailed across the sea when the Pilgrims settled in the New World.

There was only one road into the Almshouse. The very same one that drifted by the Murderer's Row of killer estates mentioned earlier, including the Police Chief's, the Lady Mayoress' and yes, dear ol' MaMa's mansion. I blew a kiss to each and every one as we sailed by and decided if time permitted, to stop by to see the old lady on the way back. My mother would love Flynn, especially if she peed on her prized rose bushes.

I kept getting the radio static buzzing sensation in my head, but this time, there was no Vartan. Just noise. It was really strange, but it was almost as if it was willing me to visit the Almshouse. Maybe it was just Flynn farting for all I knew.

An elderly man was fiddling with the flag flying limply in a grassed in area inside the facility's large circular drive. It was too early to be taking it down. He was in fact moving it half-way down the pole. Bad news travelled quickly in these parts.

∓

I'd forgotten just how large an area the Almshouse consumed. In addition to the main building, which was probably the oldest surviving structure in western Massachusetts. And why not? Its long, narrow body was composed entirely of boulders taken from the surrounding woods. While the tile roof had changed over the centuries, not rain, hail, snow or flaming arrows were going to pierce its sturdy girth. It still even had its unique round oval windows which obviously had been concocted by some long lost landlocked sea lover. He may not have been stretching the marine motif too far given the building's close proximity to the Big Puddle's edge. It gave the building a natty nautical lilt, though how any ship forged from solid rock was going to float would have been an interesting journey indeed. There were other buildings nearby, none of which were anywhere near as grand or as imposing. These had probably been built to handle any number of agricultural products grown by the inmates, ranging from corn and wheat to peas and tomatoes. Not long after it had stopped being a fort, the facility was turned into a place for the area's less fortunate to take up residence and tend to the fields behind the main building. These poor farms were seen as a way for communities like New Richmond to save money by providing for the needy efficiently and collectively. They may have gotten room and board for nothing, but in return, they basically worked as 'free' slaves to grow their own food and whatever was left over, was on sold to the local community.

This set-up didn't last long, however, as in addition to the poor, these facilities attracted other unwanteds like the blind, elderly, orphaned and mentally unstable. Ironically, the thing that killed off many poor houses around America was the Great Depression as FDR's bold New Deal offered new job opportunities for the less fortunate than had ever been provided before. Then, too, separate facilities were popping up to cater for other sub-groups like orphans, the elderly and the mentally ill.

Which brings us to the property's most recent manifestation, namely as a no-frills public hospital. I say no-frills, because there were few pieces of cutting edge equipment ever installed there. There was no intensive care capability; no heart or blood specialists hanging out a shingle there. It was just the health facility of last resort again for those members of the society who were not known for rolling a lot of sevens and elevens.

Which brings us to Mrs. May, or more precisely, the son of a bitch who killed her family. It didn't take a genius to figure out where the ambulance was going to take him. He had 'Almshouse' tattooed on his butt from Day One. Few patients who went into the Almshouse with serious ailments ever came out again alive. It just wasn't the kind of place that boasted great survival rates. In Potter's case, he'd had a fair bit of brain damage before the accident which when combined with his latest tragedy, gave him the mental capacity of a pulped orange.

Mrs. May became something of a cult figure when she showed up not long after the accident and not only took personal charge of his case, but paid for his treatments and, when the last rites were performed, picked up all the funeral charges.

It's funny how some people react to personal tragedy. For many, including yours truly, I would have either taken out my rage directly on Mr. Potter with the aforementioned Rod Carew Louisville Slugger, or internalized the whole nightmare by slugging down a case or three of the worst scotch ever bottled.

Not Mrs. May. She not only exorcized her own demons, but took care of everyone else's, too. Over the next 10 years or so, she became a cross between Florence Nightingale and Eleanor Roosevelt, tending to the sick by day, challenging the community's political and health officials by night, to do more for the sick and needy. She was not just a talker, but a doer. One of Wall Edwards' stories described how she sold her house and put most of the proceeds toward bringing more nurses and modern equipment to the Almshouse.

As I walked in the front entrance, there was a huge glassed-in cabinet on one wall. It contained photos, hundreds of photos, most of which dated back to the days of black and white, with famous dignitaries, semi-well-known sports personalities and other public figures of some note, chatting with patients or admiring the Almshouse's fine-trimmed lawns. The photos contained one other near constant: the smiling visage of one Mrs. Louisa May Alcott May. I truly had been blessed to have known her, even though I knew so little about her.

Flynn became very agitated on her lead and practically tore the arm out of my socket.

"Flynn, my favorite girl," announced this squeaky little voice which emanated from a square-shaped man who in his prime, looked like he could have gone a few rounds with Sonny Liston. In fact, he had gone a few rounds with Sonny Liston which in part explained why he had such a squeaky, little voice.

"You know this dog?" I asked incredulously.

"Know this dog? Why, son, this dog knows this place better than most of us. How glorious to see her again," said the man whose pugilistic features, including his crooked nose and cauliflower ears, belied someone who would use the word 'glorious' in any conversation.

"Of course, I should have guessed," I said, before reaching out the arm that had not been overly extended by my four-legged companion and mascot of the Almshouse. "I'm Walt Johnson, Mr. Walker," I said.

"Milt Walker," he declared just in case I didn't know him. But know him I did because in a town the size of New Richmond, there are few people whose fame ever spreads far beyond the community's own boundaries. Milt Walker, on the other hand, had been something of an unreal contender for the heavyweight crown in the late 1950s and early 1960s. I say 'unreal' because his main claim to fame, apart from winning hundreds of toothless title belts, including the prestigious 'New England's Prize Heavyweight' for a record eight times, was as a sparring partner for Sonny Liston in the lead-up to his inglorious demise against the then little known lip from Louisville, Cassius Clay. Liston took out a career's worth of aggression on the hapless Mr. Walker whose rather pedestrian pugilistic career reached its zenith when the then Champeen of the World landed a vicious right cross into the challenger's voice box, which resulted in his now famous squeaky voice.

There were no TV cameras rolling that afternoon, but several newspaper photographers who captured Mr. Walker's unique retirement 'speech'. It seems hungry sportswriters, ever searching for new ways to describe Liston's punching power, asked Milt how he felt about going a few rounds with the champ. Unable to talk and with his right glove removed revealing a pulp of a fist spurting blood, he calmly finger-painted the word "finis" on his left glove and shoved it into the nearest cameraman's lense. The rest as they say, was history – especially for Mr. Walker's boxing career.

When Milt Walker returned home a few days later, there were no ticker-tape parades or 'welcome home' parties. To make matters worse, he apparently suffered a broken hand and punctured lung along with a squashed larynx in his final ring fling, but when he checked into the local hospital, he was summarily dismissed due to overcrowding. He wound up, you guessed it, at The Almshouse, where he very quickly became something of a celebrity who upon recovering from his wounds, dedicated the rest of his life to helping those who were far less fortunate than himself.

"You're probably thinking how some punch-drunk jamoke like me got to run such a prestigious estate?" asked the very well-spoken, punch-drunk jamoke from New Richmond.

"Ah, no. I wasn't actually thinking that," I lied.

"It's alright, Walt. I'm used to it. I don't actually run the place. I'm just helping out while the big boss is in Boston with the Lady Mayor fighting to keep the place open," he said, though my mind wandered to thinking if the big boss spent the better part of the trip trying to keep the good Lady Mayoress' hands, legs and any other moving part to herself.

"You want to learn more about Mrs. May?" Milt asked at last.

"Yes, I do. She was quite a lady," I said.

"Come with me," Milt said, bending the index finger on his right hand ever so slightly. He took me into his tiny office that looked as if it had been wall-papered with photos of Mrs. May. "I've had a lot of time to think about Mrs. May and what she meant to her people," Milt began obviously referring to the patients and staff at The Almshouse. "I know you will make this sound better, but for me, she was an ordinary woman blessed with an extraordinary gift to help those who could not help themselves."

My mouth fell open. It was the most beautiful sentiment anyone had ever expressed about another human being before.

"Did I say something wrong?" Milt asked.

"No sir. That is the most wonderful quote anyone's ever given me," I said. "It will become the opening of the article if that's okay with you?"

Milt put out his two big mitts and cupped my face in his. "Thank you, son," he said.

Unfortunately, dear readers, I must now make a confession. I've given you a lot of this background about The Almshouse, (none of which of course appeared in my story on Mrs. May's passing), as a trade-off, because I knew that I would be unable to share with you the actual obituary itself. I know this may sound strange, but the article was far too personal and yet, fell far too short of its mark (in my humble opinion anyway), for me to share with you. If you wish to read it, you'll need to look up that particular issue of 'The Record' for yourself. Just ask for the one with the Page One obit.

I will, however, share with you the headline of the article, which was the work of that crazy Aussie, Ian Ross, who edited most of my stuff. It read simply: "NEW RICHMOND LOSES LITTLE BIG WOMAN."

I loved that heading and I trust she would have, too. I even think St. Vartan liked it, because he never 'said' a word to me either during the drive back to the newspaper or after the article was published. It was for me, the most difficult piece I ever had to write. It also was the most revealing. I was becoming more and more convinced that I had come back here not totally of my own volition. I know that sounds like a lot of New Age Mumbo-Jumbo, but there was some other power toying with me. Talk about a mis-match, I mean, I was hardly brain surgeon material.

And then, as if on cue, came the unmistakable gibberish jabberwocky of the one and only St. Vartan.

####%%%^^776588&&9*^5432%^&**(:#$%$#%^&& THE ROAD LESS TRAVELLED REQUIRES DEEPER REFLECTION.

Oh, yeah, that's a keeper. Thanks for nothing, big guy. What the heck does that mean? Christ, even St. Vartan is going all gah-gah on me.

XX((**&&^^%5$$#3366^^^. Oh no, not again. What now? WE CANNOT APPRECIATE LIFE WITHOUT EMBRACING DEATH.

Okay, yes, I admit that in some bizarre way, Mrs. May's death had opened up new avenues of investigation for me. I'd even learned a bit more about myself, which is not an altogether bad thing. I did have to admit that for most of the time, I had little or no clue what St. Vartan was talking about. You know you're in trouble when the voices in your own head sound crazy. Well, crazier than normal. Everyone hears voices, don't they?

I dropped by my favorite watering hole for a quite ale or three after completing the obit. Life was pretty stock standard for the next day or so as I plotted ways to avoid running into any member of the James family except Mel. My strategy for managing the 'CD' beat was based on three simple rules: Avoid, avoid and oh yes, avoid. I knew that sooner or later my luck would run out. So be it. I'd worry about that moment when the time came. I was bound and determined to sort out a few other issues that meant a heckuva lot more to me than what the future held in store for this two-bit town. Put it another way: I'd have been much happier to be accused to live a life of loud desperation rather than the type chosen by most – namely, that of quiet regurgitation.

Besides, I now had another being that I was wholly responsible for. For the first time in my tragic life, another being was actually relying, scratch that, counting on me. Big call. Big responsibility. Big Deal. Huge.

I was so affected by this responsibility that I decided to work from home for the next couple of days to let Flynn become a bit more settled. I'd be very happy whenever she decided to stop peeing and shitting on my one and only carpet and favorite bedspread. Funny, but I never noticed either foul smell in Mrs. May's abode. Perhaps that was why the smell of lilac and jasmine was so powerful in there?

The fact that Mrs. May had now left the building, however, did not mean she had left us entirely. In fact, she was still very much on the mind of one Matthew Tyndall, otherwise known as New Richmond's 'Mortuary Matt'. Who wouldn't kill for a nickname like that? Anyway, ol' M&M gave me a call the day after the Page One obit ran. Judging by the opening salvo, I'd say he was not altogether happy with the article.

"Since when do obituaries appear with bylines?" came his initial offering.

"Hi, Matt, how it's going?" I replied meekly.

"How's it going? I'll tell you how it's going. Not only do you 'steal' my words and take credit, but guess what – the dear departed didn't have two cents to rub together, leaving me with the bill." Okay, so I now knew he was upset, it was still unclear which burned him more – not getting any credit for the obit, (which was ludicrous because his work was little more than a series of phrases like 'born and raised in New Richmond;' 'wife and mother of two children;' etc, or getting stuck with the bill.

"Hey, Matt, if you ever want to give up the funeral game, let me know. I reckon there's a lot more words burning to get out of you, big guy," I offered in hopes of appeasing the savage beast. It was a very strange sideline that most funeral homes offered, providing local newspapers with rudimentary, dare I say pitifully pedestrian pieces of prose to accompany the recently departed. In my experience, I'd yet to find one obit supplied via any funeral home anywhere that expressed even one iota of life in it. There was more life in one of their plain pine boxes than in any of their obits, though I figured it wise not to raise this thorny issue with Mr. Mortuary himself.

(And no, dear readers, don't even think this is going to get me to share the obit with you. Forget about it!).

"You really think so?" he replied, obviously buying into my all-too-transparent attempt at sucking up.

"Oh, yeah, 100 percent," I said.

"Yeah, well I've been working on my writing – particularly during the winter months when it's too cold to go outside," he said.

"It shows. It truly does."

"So what about my money?" he fired back.

"Yes, that is a surprise. I wasn't aware that she had not pre-planned her burial expenses," I said as if it was a topic that came up every day between neighbors.

"Hey, I don't mind helping out, but no way am I wearing the whole 2,300 smackers," he said.

"How much?"

"$2,300. Where's that gonna come from?"

"Ah, could you leave it with me? I promise to get back to you soon. I do," I said not knowing whether I really meant to or not, but figured it was worth a shot.

"Yeah, but let me know because in my experience, once they're in the ground – there's no one to be found," he said, not realizing his marvelous turn of phrase.

I got off the phone as quickly as possible because Flynn was raising havoc in some other part of the apartment. So much so, that I have little time to spend on other major matters that occurred over the past two days. Here's the short version:

I called on Uncle J.R. to help with the outstanding debt for my dearly departed neighbor. He told me to drop by the family estate and open the foot locker under his bed in the bungalow out back. There, I would find all sorts of baseball cards, which when gathered up and sold at a local card fair, would more than cover the cost of the funeral. He also said the container contained some other 'gems', though he failed to say what these might be.

The only downside about getting the cards was I had to spend time with dear Mama, a treat I preferred to save up for next Halloween if possible. Still, I owed her a visit and she owed me a bit more info on the family tree. More on this visit shortly.

The night of the day that the obit appeared, I ventured out only to pick up enough booze to appease the wildest wildebeest. Everything went fine, (at least as far as I can remember), until Flynn went off her nut barking loudly at the back of the door some time after midnight but before dawn. I know this approximate time by the simple fact that I never ever placed any Springsteen records on the turntable till yesterday was over. (Don't ask why).

I looked out the window to see if any clues as to my late-night visitor would appear there. Not much to go on. The street was perfectly empty except for one vehicle – a starch white limousine that stretched from New Richmond to the New York State border.

"Yoo hoo?! Oh, Walter, helloooo, it's me, your Aunt Stacey," said the Lady Mayoress in her most unfetching voice.

I ignored her hoping like heck she'd just go away and molest some other misfit.

"Ooohhh, that's quite a bark you have there, tiger. I hope you're not entertaining some other lady?!" she said.

"Go away!"

"No, no, Walter. Do let me in. It's cold out here and I do have some good news for you," she said half convincingly. She was after all, a politician.

I opened up and closed down all in the same motion. It was quite a feat.

Chapter Twenty Two

I woke up the next day sprawled out on the living room rug. I sensed I was not alone, but calmed down when I realized the only other living being in the room contained paws, a bushy tail and a very loud snore. I still had my shirt, shoes and socks on, but nothing else. I didn't remember dressing like this so wondered whether I'd just gotten warm in the nether regions at some point in the evening or whether Aunt Stacey had performed some unspeakable sexual act during her visit. I decided the best course of action was not to think about the latter option, figuring I already felt sick enough.

Just then, the phone rang.

"Hi, lover boy. How you feeling?" came the familiar sound of the Lady Mayoress.

Ugh oh. "Ah, hi there, Ms. Lord Mayoress. Say, we didn't actually 'do' anything last night did we?"

"You're kidding, right, tiger? I'm cancelling my afternoon appointments so we can spend a bit more, how shall I say, 'quality time' together," came her reply. "I'm actually calling to make sure you're okay. You weren't feeling the best when I left, which is a bit of a blow to my ego," she said.

"You're kidding, right?"

"I don't kid about my sexual prowess, lover boy," came the reply. "I also was calling to make sure you did understand what I was telling you about your grandfather's farm."

"Ahh, I must have missed that bit," I said.

"It'd be the only bit you missed," she began. "Basically, you've got an extra 12 months to come up with the money. That's the best deal I could cut and trust me, that's pushing these guys about as far as you can go."

"Oh, that's great. Really great. Truly, I appreciate the help," I said.

"Oh, you'll pay for it. Don't you worry, darling. You will pay for it. Gotta run. Call me later, yeah?"

"Oh yeah. No worries about that," I replied before hanging up. I didn't know whether to laugh or cry – or both. Flynn wasn't much help, either, continuing to snore atop my beat-up, three-seat sofa. Christ, if only she could tell me how to come up with a spare $23,000 or better yet, tell me exactly what happened here last night. Then again, perhaps it was better left unsaid. After living with New Richmond's own 'Mother Theresa', the poor dog must have started wondering what she'd stumbled into.

I still hadn't caught up with dear old Mom, so gave her a call and told her I'd be over tonight with a 'guest' for din-din. She seemed not the least bit interested in either the fact that I was coming by or that I had a 'guest'. I then got dressed quickly and headed to the newspaper. While I'd been lucky in avoiding the James Gang to date, it was time to start going on the offensive and finding out more about just what my colleagues on the CD beat had been doing. I left messages for Mason and Gail and hoped like hell I got to them before anyone else. I told them to meet me at the bar for a drink. Nothing like an early morning spirit to level out the day.

Just as I was about to leave, the phone rang. It was Lou Cassals warning me about the James' – both the mother and son. It seems they were expressing some concern over the lack of progress with the CD beat. Bingo. The old sixth sense was certainly operating on all burners. There also was a message from a chap named Trevor Brown who ran The Almshouse. He wanted to catch up to tell me more about the property's steady decline.

With a menu like that facing you first thing in the morning – there was clearly only three things to do: Drink, drink and drink. In that order. I finally got out the door and decided to leave Flynn inside asleep. Heck, even if she woke up and decided to trash the place, there wasn't much left to trash. It'd probably improve the joint's re-sale value.

I walked briskly along Main Street and once again felt like I was being followed. In fact, when I turned around I did notice a car similar to the one that had been parked behind The Mayoress' limo the night before. It wasn't hard to spot: a VW hatchback sporting a pale orange tint that looked like baby vomit. Who the fuck would tail someone in such an unforgettable motor machine?

I kept walking and stopped by the bar before entering the newspaper building. Mason James was chatting with his big sister behind the bar. Gail Gerard was nowhere to be seen.

"Hi chief. Good to see you," Mason offered. Mel smiled before asking if I'd had any famous visitors recently.

"Why yes, I dined on Olivia Newton-John though her thighs were a bit 'Greasy'," I said.

"Hah, hah," Mel replied. "I was thinking of someone a bit more local."

"I'm sure you are but I can't help you there. The only company I keep these days is with my new four-legged companion. So Mase, what have you got for me?"

"Not much really. I thought I was on to something regarding a number of recent sales in the downtown area, but came up empty."

"What do you mean 'empty?'"

"Well, the lady at the town planner's office said it was not unusual for different businesses to buy and sell. It happened all the time," Mason offered.

"Did you get any of the names?"

"No, I figured there was no point."

"Why, because someone told you it was business-as-usual? Mason, go back there and tell her you want the names of every buyer and seller over the past two years," I said.

"Okay, but I—"

"Don't think about it. Just do it," I said as authoritatively as I could. I had no idea what I was talking about, but figured it was better to keep him busy on something, even if it was a dead end. "Where's Gail?"

"She's been real busy getting inside one of those strip clubs on Silicon Alley," Mason offered. "She told me to tell you to drop by this evening. She said she'd found out some interesting stuff."

"I bet she has though I doubt it'll help us on the CD beat."

"Can I get either of you a drink?"

"On the house?" I asked, which managed little more than a smirk on Mel's face. "Worth a try. No, think I'll try to save up for later in the week. Mase, can you get up to the newsroom and tell your brother that we'll have some big stories, starting next week?"

"We will?" Mason asked.

"Absolutely. Between you, Gail and me, we've got a whole bunch of stuff to write about," I said.

"Where are you headed?"

"I've got to go out to The Almshouse and meet up with the head guy before dropping by the Alley later on," I said. "Tell your brother not to worry. We'll deliver," I said figuring if my goose was going to be cooked, might as well make it burnt to a crisp.

I'd had every intention of dropping by The Almshouse that afternoon. I really did, but ended up getting sidetracked somewhere between the 'J' in Jack and the 's' at the end of Daniels. It was a pleasant enough way to spend the afternoon, (as well as the better part of my weekly pay check), drinking and chatting with various local bar-flies. I put it down to 'deep research' on the CD beat. It might not get me any front pagers next week, but it sure beat hanging around the newsroom waiting for the phone to ring or worse yet – getting a call from the Publisher or the Lady Mayoress – the thought of the latter one leading to the opening of a second bottle of Jack Daniels.

At about 3.30 p.m., I excused myself and toddled off toward The Lincoln. I was pretty drunk, but not drunk enough to remember that I still had to prepare for a dinner with ol' Mama. I also had to take Flynn out for a walk. The poor dog was so keen on getting outside that she burst by me the minute the door opened. I admired the strength of her in-door plumbing. While she was outside, I took a shower and tried to look somewhat fresh for my 'dinner date'. Not that she would care. She knew me too well. I looked out the window to see if Flynn was nearby, only to see that same old VW parked nearby. Maybe it was just broken down. Practically everything else was in the neighbourhood – especially the residents.

I whistled to Flynn who shot up the stairway three steps at a time. The phone rang and I decided to leave it for my answering machine. It was Gail Gerard. She didn't apologize for missing the 'meeting' earlier with me and Mason. Instead, she said it was important that I drop by some joint called 'Wild Cherry' on the Alley around 10 p.m. That sounded like as good an excuse as any to leave my mother's. "Oh, yes, sorry to do this to you, but I have to go now. I'm expected at a strip club where I'm to slip dollar bills up the clackers of several naked ladies. You don't mind, do you, Mom?"

The phone rang as I got out of the shower. I hoped beyond hope it was someone telling me I'd just won a million dollars. "Hey, son, how ya doin?" came the familiar twang of my Dad.

"Great, Dad. How are you?"

"Yeah, getting there. Just wondering if you can come by some time soon? I got some things to talk over. I'll buy you dinner," he said.

"If you mean you'll serve me that swill you call food in your restaurant – forget it. But yes, I'm hoping to get over your way soon. Have you heard from J.R. lately?"

"Funny you should ask. That's one of the things I wanted to talk about," he said.

"Oh, why?"

"It can keep. See you soon," he said just before the line went dead.

I continued getting myself ready for my meeting with Mom. I also combed Flynn's unruly mane. She looked almost presentable, not that that would make any difference to my mother. I dialled J.R.'s number to find out what was happening, but got put through to his answering machine. I wasn't in the mood for leaving any message. He was probably out either hitting golf balls into the river or picking up another mint Mantle or Maris baseball card.

It was nearly 6.30 p.m. by the time I started the drive over to Chez Winslow. Flynn was her usual excitable self when given the opportunity to go for a ride. Little did she know! My mother never liked animals. She never let me have a pet when I lived under her roof. She never really explained why, only to say they were only good for shedding and shitting where they weren't wanted. I never quite saw that as a good enough reason to avoid animals. Shitting and shedding were quite admirable qualities among most of the people I had run across in New Richmond.

I stopped at a local package store and picked up three bottles of red wine and a six pack of beer. The beer was for me. So too were the three bottles, but she didn't have to know that. Fortunately, I wasn't in the mood for getting too drunk. I also sensed that I had been followed for part of the drive, but the offending vehicle had veered off down a side street some time before I reached the family poorhouse.

Per usual, the front gate was shut tight when I arrived. I got out of the car and hit the buzzer.

"Yes?" came the throaty call from my mother.

"Avon calling," I said. The gate began to open. Before I could get back behind the wheel, Flynn was flying up the driveway toward a fluffy cat that must have hailed from a neighbor's house. I drove in as fast as I could, but couldn't catch the mutt.

It was pitch dark except for the light being thrown by the nineteenth-century-style 'gas' lanterns that lined the driveway. My mother was standing in the front doorway.

"Where's your other guest?" she said avoiding the usual ho-hum 'Hi, how are you?' greeting.

"That was her whizzing past after the cat," I replied.

"You brought a dog?"

"Not just any dog, Mom. Mrs. May's dog – Flynn the Wonder Dog," I said.

"Good god," my mother said before turning and heading back into the house with the perfectly unnecessary tag line: "Just make sure she stays outside."

"Aye, aye, mon captain," I said as Flynn bounded onto the front porch not via the steps, but from a perfectly timed leap over the five-foot high shrubs. I grabbed her collar and stuck her back in the car. I'd remembered her favorite blanket, hoping beyond hope that she'd just curl up and go to sleep.

As if to ensure I kept the dog out, my mother had closed the front door which in another life had no doubt kept marauding Huns or Vikings at bay. It was made from wood, but must have been reinforced with steel girders, lead shot or ballast from some British ship. Probably the latter given the family's close ties to Mother England – a topic I hoped to broach with my mother once again this evening.

Childhood memories for many are filled with idyllic scenes captured by New England's own Norman Rockwell. Mine were similar with one minor change: Scratch Rockwell's moniker from the lower right hand of corner of the canvas and etch in a name like Hieronymus Bosch, Goya or some other perfectly disturbing artist. Daydream believers need not apply. Never-ending Nightmares perhaps were more appropriate though still far too meek; timid. No, my childhood memories far exceeded any nightmare – night stallion perhaps? Or better still, night fucking bucking bronco.

Not long after I was born, my father was cast out of the Winslow property – with me close behind. The Winslows, it soon became clear, were not big on imperfection, and though no one ever said it, a one-eared mutt was not likely to figure highly in the Winslow Christmas album. Apart from the odd two-week stay during summer holidays, I rarely set foot in the place or had any contact with the Winslow clan.

Though my times at this address were fleeting, I did recall how big and domineering everything seemed. Everything, from the front steps to the back door was oversized, as if built by and for giants. Returning here for the first time in decades, little had changed.

While the front door was quite grand, indeed, it would have fit snugly beneath the Empire State's towering spire, it was nothing compared to the entrance that greeted guests once inside. Your eyes were nearly blinded by the immense sea of bright, white marble that encased the floor. A couple of football teams in full shoulder pads and helmets could fit comfortably in the foyer, along with the bus that brought them. A grand staircase, not unlike the one descended by Scarlett O'Hara at Tara, set back just to the left while on the right, lay what my mother's parents referred to as the 'Front Parlor'. It was an equally large room with deep rich green-velvet-covered walls. Different-sized portraits of various Winslow family members stared at you from their lofty perches along either side of the room's floor to ceiling windows. Though no one ever told me otherwise, I'd always believed that the more prominent members were regaled in larger, Gainsborough-style oils while lesser-lights made due with more modest models. The three most prominent figures were my mother's father, a very austere-looking, no-nonsense chap named Josiah Ross Winslow III, his parents – Mr. and Mrs. (Edward Josiah Boylston Winslow) and my great grandfather's parents – (Mr and Mrs Josiah Cotton Winslow). I barely knew my grandfather who seemed to treat most people the same way he treated his family – as servants, slaves or worse. Even my mother didn't like him, but ended up inheriting the place, I guess by default. His wife had died many years before his demise in the late 1960s, no doubt literally from a broken heart. While everyone in the Winslow family spoke glowingly of the late great Mrs J.C. Winslow, no image of her appeared anywhere in the house.

They made much of their money through real estate – or more precisely – through screwing little people out of their homes and then re-packaging their properties for sale to developers and other n'er do wells. It could explain why the front door had to be so heavy. There would have been a lot of people trying to break it down to get their hands around his long, slim neck.

I was probably 10 or 11 when he died. The few times I laid eyes on him, he reminded me of Washington Irving's Ichabod Crane. Tall and lanky with arms and legs to match, giving him the look of a human preying mantis. He also had big bulging eyes and with few original teeth left, meant his lower jaw often protruded over the top one, ensuring that all viewers knew they were not about to meet a happy, care-free, type of guy. He'd lost most of his hair by the time he reached 50 and what was left stood up as though he'd just stuck his hand in a light socket. The painter, and I had to give him or her credit, gave him an almost kind, benevolent smile which would have required great imagination. Ditto for the thick mane of blond hair and soothing look emanating from his huge bulbous eyeballs.

The rest of the room was filled with genuine antiques, much of the furniture having probably previously been owned by a guy named Louis or some other French-fried ruler. It all looked like some sort of layer cake with lots of big, billowing pillows and gold frames perched on thin, curved legs. They may have been great for sitting around, chatting about the latest haute couture out of Paris or Milan while sipping their Earl Grey. It certainly was not the sort of furniture I liked while watching the Sox on TV with a brewski or seven. There also were fine pieces of porcelain and gold-gilded clocks and the like stationed about the room, but it looked like so much brittle bric a brac to my uncultured pearly gaze.

If it all sounds like one of those dust-collecting museums you visited during school trips, you wouldn't be far off. The only thing missing were the 'Do Not Touch' placards and the ropes to keep you from jumping up and down on the uncomfy sofas.

I won't bore you with details of the rest of the house. Just multiply the Front Parlor by a factor of 50 and you'll get close to cluttering up the rest of the castle.

Actually, I wouldn't put it past my mother to install ropes around the furniture. She was a marvel at keeping people at bay. You might call it a specialty of the house - mother. I tried getting my mind off frivolous family squabbles and onto more positive issues when my eyes caught the figure of someone else standing at the end of the hallway – just in front of the kitchen where my mother was preparing what undoubtedly would be my last supper. I hadn't seen any other cars around so didn't expect any other guests.

"Hello, Walter. How are you?" called out the as yet, though not unfamiliar, other house guest. If I'd wanted my mother to pick out one more unwanted person to share a meal with, it would be with this one, which you will appreciate shortly.

"Ohh, hi Mrs. Wheeler-James. How are you?" How ironic was that? I spent the better part of the week trying to avoid the boss at work and now am about to wind up breaking bread with her at my mother's house. "Do excuse me for a minute while I go see how dinner is coming," I said.

"I see you've met our other dinner guest," mother said as I entered the kitchen.

"You could have warned me," I said.

"I knew if I did that, you wouldn't have come. Besides, I figure it's good for you to get to know her. She's a smart lady and can do you a lot of favors," she said.

"Favors? What kind of favors?" I asked.

"You know, Walter. It wouldn't hurt you to just try and fit in – just once in your life," she said.

"Oh, thanks, Ma. Appreciate the pep talk. Can I go now?"

"No. Go see if Connie wants a drink," came the reply.

"No problem. Can I call her Connie, too?"

She shot me a glance that said it all.

"I do have to leave around 9.30, though," I said. "I'm actually working tonight."

"Nothing you do would surprise me, Walter. Nothing," my mother said.

"So, Mrs. Wheeler-James, long time no see. Hope you're well and ready for a taste sensation tonight!" I said in my most upbeat banter.

Mrs. Wheeler-James handed me her empty martini glass and glared rather oddly at me. "Yes, I do rather enjoy your mother's creations," she said. "I do hope this evening won't make you feel uncomfortable. We needn't talk about work," she said, before adding "much."

I took her glass, smiled and returned to the kitchen. Visions of semi-naked ladies and dollar bills started looking pretty damn tempting.

"So what are you working on?" my mother asked while pointing to the half-filled martini mixer on the counter.

"Huh? Oh, that. Nothing really. Nothing I can talk about, I mean. Hush, hush," I said.

"What? C'mon, Walter. Your boss is here. Surely, she has to know."

"Ahh, no, she doesn't and that's good, because, well just because," I said with as much certainty as a dead man standing on the gallows with a cloth bag and noose snugly tied around his neck. "I was kind of hoping it was just us, though, because I wanted to catch up on family matters."

"You mean like your Uncle?"

"Well, no, but now that you mention him. What's up with J.R.?"

"Later, dear. Let's go talk to our guest. Besides, the chowder will be ready shortly."

I refilled the two martini glasses while draining the first of the bottles of cheap red I'd brought for myself. I had just about finished pouring when the distinctively rich voice of Mrs. Wheeler-James boomed out: "What's a gal got to do to get a drink in these parts?" she said putting on the worst excuse for a southern accent I'd ever heard.

I smiled and handed her the topped-up tipple. "Thank you kindly, Walter," she said.

"My pleasure, Mrs. Wheeler-James," I replied.

"Forget about that for tonight."

"About what?"

"The Mrs. Wheeler-James," she said. "Just call me Connie."

I was stunned by this offer. But not enough to turn it down. "I can't do that, ma'am."

"Why not, for god's sake?"

"Well, for one thing, I was brought up to respect my elders – no matter what - and for another, if we go down that path, sooner or later,

I'll accidentally call you by your first name in the middle of the newsroom and that wouldn't be pretty now, would it? So all things being equal, let's just maintain the status quo, if that's alright with you, ma'am?"

I don't know who gave who the stranger look, but both my mother and Mrs. Wheeler-James downed their second martoonis in one gulp. "I can see now who you take after, Walter," our dinner guest said, turning with a smile and heading for the dining room.

I still wasn't so sure. I didn't think I looked much like either of my parents – with or without the second ear. I also didn't think I acted much like either one of them, but if not, then who the heck was I?

"Really liked your obit, Walter. Everyone's been talking about it," Mrs. Wheeler-James said in between sips of my mother's homemade clam chowder.

"I still don't get why Mrs. May's so damn famous," my mother chimed in, just to make sure I didn't get too big a head.

"Thanks, Mom. Always appreciate the support," I said.

"Oh, now, she was a remarkable woman. And as Walt here pointed out – she ended up performing quite extraordinary feats from such an ordinary upbringing," the publisher said, proving beyond a shadow of much doubt that she had at least read the first sentence of the obit.

My mother opted not to say anything, but even her silence spoke volumes.

"I hope you can put as much passion into articles focusing on larger community issues," said the boss.

"Yes, ma'am. As a matter of fact, I have to leave shortly to start work on one of those pieces tonight."

"Really? How exciting. Speaking of which, I have to say I've never seen my son Mason so eager to get up and get to work in the morning. He can't stop talking about you and how you've helped him," Mrs. Wheeler-James said.

"That's very kind of him, ma'am, but I haven't really done that much. While we're talking about staff matters, could you tell me what happened to Hugh Jackson?"

Call me Mr. Timing. All the good will I'd been storing up was now well and truly shot. "Why do you ask?"

"Because he taught me more in six months than I'd learned in the previous 10 years combined," I said.

"I'm surprised to hear that, Walter. I think you'll find that you were already a far superior writer to anyone else at the paper. Hugh may have helped you in some minor way, but I assure you in the end, his influence was becoming far too unsettling for many people in the newsroom."

My mother remained quiet, but stared at me in such a way as to imply she hoped I would not press the matter any further.

"Oh, my, look at the time. Is it that late already? I must be going," I said, getting up from the table as quickly as possible.

"Oh, Walter. You haven't had the main meal yet," my mother began. "It's not even 8 p.m. and you said you wouldn't have to leave till 9.30."

"Yes, well I got that wrong. I have to go now. Thank you both for a most enjoyable evening. I'm sure you two have better things to talk about anyway," I said.

"Nonsense, boy. Sit down and enjoy your mother's cooking. You look like you need a good home-cooked meal," Mrs. Wheeler-James said.

"Thanks, but I must be going. I'll call you tomorrow, Mom," I said heading for the front door. I marvelled at how easily I'd handled the Dynamic Duo's plot to unsettle me. My victory, however, was short lived as my mother's figure suddenly appeared in the doorway.

"Just who the hell do you think you are?"

"Excuse me?"

"Who do you think you are coming in here as my guest and then proceeding to insult my good friend and your employer, I might add!"

"Oh yes, I forgot about her. My apologies for any concern I may have caused her – and you. I'll call and apologize to Connie in the morning," I said trying to get by my mother.

"You're really something, aren't you? You think you're so smart, Walter. Well, don't flatter yourself."

I sensed my mother was a wee bit angry. I also sensed it was not a good time to press her on the family tree issues that I harbored.

"Don't bother calling me again. Just stay away," she said.

"Thanks, Ma. You're great. Really terrific. I'm so sorry that I ruined your life in this dusty, two-dimensional museum you call home. I appreciate all the support that you and the other Winslows have given me over the years. Truly. And I'm sorry for being your one and only son, though appropriately enough, of a bitch," I said.

I knew I'd pushed it too far with that last comment. I regretted it as soon as it had left my lips. The reply, however, trumped mine and then some.

"You've got that wrong, Walter. You're not a SON of a bitch. You're a BITCH of a son," she said, standing aside and letting me leave without further incident or comment.

Bring on the naked ladies.

Chapter Twenty Three

"Five bucks."

"What?"

"Five dollar cover charge," boomed a voice outside of New Richmond's finest strip club called 'Wild Cherry'. I hadn't seen him at first because I thought he might be a cardboard figure or blow-up toy. I admit he was hard to miss, standing over six feet tall and about the same size wide in what looked like a very ill-fitting penguin suit. With his very round face and darkish complexion, however, in another time, he could have doubled as a cigar store Indian – only twice as wooden. Perhaps appropriately, the only noteworthy thing about his face was perfectly-formed grooves at the left-hand side of his mouth, obviously sculpted by countless cigarettes having perched there. His demeanor, much like his economy of movement, was without frills. I hypothesized from this that his personality would be equally stilted and colorless – as colorless as an inert gas.

"Don't you mean uncover charge?" I replied, testing my latest theory.

There was no reply, only a hand that looked more like a bear claw, complete with long fingernails, facing me in the palm-up position. I dutifully smacked a $5 bill into his mitt and told him to 'keep the change'. This was turning into quite an evening. It began with the unenviable task of breaking bread with one's boss, only to be outdone by one's own mother unceremoniously tossing him out of the family home - yet again – complete with killer tag line. Top that, you say? I had a feeling that if any joint could provide the fifth course to one's most unappetizing meals – it would be a place like this. And just for good measure, throw a cherry or two on top.

Apart from the vastness of the darkened room and the pulsating sounds of ABBA's '*Waterloo*' waling away from some unseen jukebox, Wild Cherry stood out like no other strip club I'd ever ventured into. I may not have been a connoisseur on the finer points of the country's strip joints, but I'd visited a fair few during my many nocturnal excursions while working in Cincinnati, (where the girls weren't allowed to take either tops or bottoms off so any hot-blooded guy high-tailed it over the river to Covington, Kentucky where the girls took off tops and bottoms – and that was just their false teeth). What always struck me about these joints, and I suspected it would have been a similar scene in most strip clubs, was just how few guys were usually there. Sure, they could get crowded on a Friday night or some other special occasion, but not very often. Here we were in the middle of winter with the wind chill nipping well below zero degrees on an ordinary Tuesday night and the place was hopping.

"Get you a drink?" came the voice of a lovely young lady draped in a sheet and little else.

"You buying?" I said, which went down about as well as the opening line with Mr. Personality out front. When I turned back, I noticed a very attractive black girl dancing on a nearby table. She looked vaguely familiar which seemed strange because I hadn't met any black women since moving back to New Richmond. Ohh, no, of course, I had met one. Lo and behold, it was the one and the same young lady – the one who roomed with my almost ex-girlfriend Jenny. She gave me a big wink and motioned toward the bar. I politely declined the offer from my new-found, toga-garbed lady and headed for the bar where I immediately ordered a beer and a scotch.

"That'll be $15," said this guy who could have doubled for the cigar store Indian out front.

"You're kidding, right?"

His return look clearly showed that he was in fact very serious.

"Must be pretty damn good stuff," I said.

"The best," he said, while also placing a glass of watery-looking champagne in front of my ex-girlfriend's roomie who deposited herself on the stool next to me.

"Thanks, sugar," she said, referring to the fact that I'd now obviously bought her a highly over-priced drink as well. "It's not really champagne. It's apple cider," she whispered in my good ear.

"Just call me Daddy Warbucks," I said.

"I just call you Sugar Daddy," she replied in a voice that left me with little doubt that she could call me 'wheelbarrow' and I'd be tickled pink.

"What do you think of my outfit?" she said, getting up from the stool and twirling in front of my now grapefruit-sized eyes. Her costume, if you could call it that, consisted of two thick, shoe-string-sized strips of yellow material – one almost covering her modest-sized bosoms and the other unsuccessfully attempting to keep even a blind man unsure as to whether she shaved parts of her body other than her armpits.

"Ahh, yes, very nice," I said trying like heck not to look anywhere but into her large brown eyes.

"You didn't even look. How can you tell?" she said.

"I'm a real good guesser," I replied before trying to change the subject as quickly as possible. "Sorry but I didn't catch the name you threw at the other girl."

"When I'm working, it's Cherie, but my 'real' name is Anita – Anita Bryant."

"Really?"

"Why would I kid about a name like that?"

"Fair enough. Well, Anita is a great name. And where do you come from – certainly not New Richmond," I asked.

"Austin, Texas," she said.

"I should have known – why you're the Yellow Rose of Texas," I said, referring to her yellow outfit which now looked like little more than three band-aids. "You're a long way from home. What brought you up here?"

"A guy – a rotten guy," she said.

"How long you been working here?"

"Why all the questions? She shot back, before adding: "Oh, that's right. You're a reporter. Doing a story? We got three rules we have to follow: One: No boyfriends allowed in the club; Two: No drugs allowed in the club; and Three: No talking to nosy reporters."

"Really?"

"Really," she said.

"Well, I'm not nosy so you can talk to me. Besides, I'm here to meet a friend."

"Boy or girl?"

"Now who's being nosy? A girl, actually – and not our mutual friend."

"Oh, hey, you know, Jenny still digs you. She'll be here later on. Don't tell her I told you, but she's got it bad, honey. Do me a favor. Take her out!"

"We'll see, eh? Is the place always this busy?"

"No, not until recently. Word is there's some big jobs coming up," she said.

"Big jobs – what, like construction jobs?"

"I guess, honey. I don't know but these guys are coming in from all over and they like spending money on girls like me," Cherie said, before adding, "which reminds me, I have to start dancing again. Care to come watch?"

"Ahh, I think I'd best find my friend," I said hoping beyond hope she didn't catch me admiring her figure.

She gave me her best little-girl pout pose and then kissed me on the cheek before departing. I ordered another boilermaker for myself while thinking about her comment regarding the influx of new blood in the area. Maybe Gail Gerrard was onto something here. Trying to find anyone in this packed joint was not going to be easy. Especially when every woman was surrounded by a rugby scrum of horned-up, drunken guys.

"Buy me a drink, sailor?" came yet another female voice. You had to hand it to these women – they knew an easy mark when they saw one.

"No thanks. I prefer drinking alone with the other 300 suckers," I said without even bothering to turn to look at the latest lovely.

"The least you could do is look at me, Walter!" the woman boomed.

While the tone sounded vaguely familiar, I couldn't match the face with the voice. "It's me, Walt. Gail, you idiot," said my journalistic colleague whispering the last bit which seemed rather pointless given that the noise inside the joint would have exceeded a jumbo jet engine at full throttle.

The reason(s) I didn't recognize her included such things as I'd never seen her in a Marilyn Monroe-style blond wig before; I'd never seen her with an inch of make-up; and I'd never seen her nearly naked. At work, she preferred loose fitting tops and long skirts or slacks. With her short, page-boy haircut, she often was mistaken for an effeminate guy, rather than a woman – which she obviously was. All woman.

"So, what do you think?"

"It's a great club. You thinking of working here full time?" I offered.

"No, silly. The get-up. The costume," she said.

"Oh, that. Why, yes, yep, I'd say you're a stripper alright." As in the case of the recently-departed Cherie, I did not know where to look so I focused hard on her forehead.

"Gee, thanks. Hey, buy me a cocktail, otherwise they'll start getting suspicious," she said. "And call me Topaz," she added.

"Topaz? Good one. All the same, this drink is coming out of your pay check," I said, waving the barkeep over to splash another glass of bubbly cider for my latest faux conquest.

"There's definitely something going on, Walt. These guys are mostly in from out of state. They're talking about some big construction jobs coming up in New Richmond, though no one's given me any specifics yet," Gail said.

"You look good as a blonde," I replied, still keeping my gaze above her painted eyebrows.

"Are you listening to me?"

"Oh, I'm listening. I just can't believe you're running around in a costume that contains less fabric than a book of postage stamps," I said.

"How would you know? You haven't even looked yet?" she said, beckoning me to take a longer gaze at her physique.

"I'd rather not if it's all the same to you. Don't get me wrong. I don't think there's anything wrong with you or your outfit. In fact, I'd say-"

"You're so sweet, Walter. Hugh said you were but I didn't' believe him," Gail said.

"Hugh? Hugh Jackson? What's he got to do with anything?" I said.

"Oh, nothing. Nothing at all. Stick around for my routine, will ya? We can talk more later though we can't do it for too long, oth—"

"I know. They might think I'm your boyfriend and that's a no-go zone," I replied, before adding, "just like taking drugs or talking to nosy reporters."

"You do do your homework, don't you?" she said, downing the rest of the cider and slipping away along the bar toward a narrow T-shaped catwalk where three girls danced suggestively above the admiring throng of cashed up/caged animals.

I likewise downed my second boilermaker while simultaneously ordering a third, hoping beyond hope that that was the last time that my drinking would be interrupted by a member of the unfairer sex. What a night. And to top it off, I still felt like I was being followed. I turned around but saw no one in particular staring at me. Why would any guy be staring at me unless he was queerer than Liberace's hair dresser?

The mere thought of that hairy predicament led to boilermaker number 4 landing in front of me at about the same time as a very large scream emanating from the mouth of Gail 'Topaz' Gerrard.

It probably would've been easier to swim across a crocodile-filled canal than barge through the packed-out club so I did the only thing someone with an alcohol-induced brainwave does – jumped up on the bar and run along it before launching myself onto the stage in front of my scantily-clad work mate.

I grabbed Gail as much to steady myself as anything else before realizing there was some sort of commotion just below us on the floor. Gail motioned toward the commotion which consisted of two men locked in a wrestling hold that may very well have earned either or both of them a place in the WWF Hall of Shame.

The crowd had parted when the larger of the two combatants let go of the other one, no doubt as a result of the latter's taking a solid bite out of his left forearm. I now had a clean view of the biter who I knew as none other than my ex-boss/mentor – Hugh Jackson, who obviously had more than just a passing interest in the young lady standing next to me. It now became apparent why the club did not like having boyfriends frequenting the club – particularly when their betrothed was doing their best to get a bunch of strange, liquored-up men, so worked up that they'd spend untold amounts of cash on quick flashes of female flesh combined with a dash or three of over-priced alcohol.

Before I could jump off the stage to assist my compatriot, the aforementioned cigar store Indian bouncer and another equally brawny chap, picked the two combatants off the floor and carried them over their heads toward a back entrance. I was turning back to see if Gail was still alright when a hand the size of Michelangelo's David landed on my shoulder and yanked me toward the bar. It was the bartender obviously enraged at my using his bar as an express lane. I decided against fighting back, figuring it would probably only invite any number of other hot heads to join into the frazzled fray. The next thing I remember was being unceremoniously dumped out the front door and being told to keep out. Gail 'Topaz' Gerrard was not far behind, obviously also being given the heave-ho for breaking at least one of the joint's Three Commandments.

"You alright, Walt?" she said.

"Yeah, fine. Hope Hugh's alright," I said.

"Yeah, I think they called the cops so he'll probably wind up at the station. Can you take me there?"

"Yeah, sure, but geez, why didn't you say something about it?"

"About what?"

"About what? About building an H-bomb. Why didn't you tell me you and Hugh were an item?" I said.

"It's a long story. Can we just go?" she said.

"Yeah, sure," I replied, picking myself up from the pavement and trying to remember where I'd parked the car.

"Hi Walter. Had fun?" came yet another familiar female voice.

I turned to see my almost-ex Jenny Lawton, standing in front of the club's entrance.

"Hi Jenny. It's me, Topaz," Gail added.

"Yes, I can see that. Do you two know each other?" Jenny asked.

"I'll answer that one, Topaz. As a matter of fact we do. We're husband and wife, not that it's any of your business."

"That figures," Jenny said.

"Jenny, don't listen to him. I just got chucked out but thanks for your help. I couldn't have done it without you," Gail said.

"Couldn't have done what without her?" I offered.

"Jenny here is the best dance instructor a girl could ever wish for," Gail said.

"You mean, you don't 'work' here?" I said to Jenny.

"Not as a dancer. I'm their instructor not that that should matter to you," Jenny replied. "You obviously have found someone very special. Good luck to you both," she added before racing into the front entrance and slamming the door behind her.

"Do I need to know what that's all about?" Gail said.

"It's complicated. Let's just get to the station and see how Hugh's going," I said.

We headed around the side of the club when I noticed two more rather unusual sights. The first was the small orange Volkswagen I'd seen following me on and off for the past few days, parked right next to my own vehicle. The second vision, and while I may not be the best judge of interesting moments, believed this one would have taken out most people's top prize, was the sight of some guy's legs flailing wildly out of the driver's window of my car.

When I got closer, I realized what had happened. My would-be tormentor had obviously tried breaking into my car for some stupid reason and been attacked by the world's best car alarm – Flynn the Wonder Dog. Flynn had probably been sound asleep on the floor in the front of the car when the guy broke the glass. Wish I could have been there to see what happened next.

"Get this fucking mutt off of me," I think the guy kept saying to anyone who might be nearby, though it's doubtful he could see anything with his head buried deep beneath the dog's furry coat.

"Get locked out of your car?" I offered.

"No, but for Christ's sake, get me out of here!" he replied.

"Not till I get a big apology and some understanding of just why the heck you've been tailing me – otherwise, I tell Flynn to turn you into a permanent chew toy."

At this point, I told Flynn to 'stop' which she did, much to my surprise. When the stalker realized he was no longer being assaulted, he hurled his body backwards until he was outside of the vehicle. The face looked relatively familiar, but it was hard to know for sure what with a fair bit of blood oozing out of various bites.

"It's me, Tom Keenan, the trolley guy," he said.

"From New London, Connecticut? Geez, you got a bit of spare time on your hands, eh?"

"Hey, you made my life a fucking misery after that story ran. I figured I owed you."

"And just what the heck were you doing here?"

"Just trying to smash your window, that's all," he said.

"That's all. I guess we're even now, right? What about all the death threat phone calls?"

"Phone calls? I never called you," he said, which meant I had at least one more admirer still out there.

"Those cuts look pretty bad. Here's what we're going to do, Tom. I'm gonna drive you to the Almshouse for treatment. You're going to give your car keys to this lovely lady who will follow us back into town," I said knowing that he had little choice in the matter.

"Great, just great. Just keep that psycho mutt off me," he muttered.

I motioned Flynn to get into the back seat while I helped Tom get into the passenger side. He handed me the keys to his orange chariot, which I then tossed to Gail and told her go see how Hugh was holding up at the station. "I'll join you at the station after dropping this guy off, okay?"

Gail nodded affirmatively. I waited for her to start up the Volkswagen and drive off before turning over my own engine. Besides, I first had to remove bits of glass from the driver's seat. Flynn all the while remained on guard in the back seat, staring intently at her prey and emitting a steady, low growl.

"Can we please get out of here, I think I'm dying," Tom the trolley man said.

"No probs," I replied. "Do you mind if I ask you a couple of other questions about some of those statues you created while we head to the Almshouse?"

Judging by the look on my poor passenger's face, he was obviously wondering if he had been better off when a more or less mad dog decided to use his head as a rag doll. I decided to proceed with my line of questioning: "How the heck did you come up with the idea of re-creating the Sydney Harbor Bridge out of trolley frames?"

Chapter Twenty Four

It was after 4 a.m. by the time I got to the police station. Tom Keenan's orange chariot was parked out front, but that was the last good news I would hear for a while. That and the fact that Tom hadn't been too badly hurt in his ill-considered attempt at payback. The nurse at the Almshouse said the cuts on his face were mainly from the window rather than from Flynn who also had left very few marks on his arms and hands. The news was less rewarding at the police station. The desk sergeant told me that Hugh Jackson had been released into the custody of some stripper and promptly took off. I didn't know where Gail lived so decided to go home and get some sleep before heading into the office. It was bound to be another interesting day at '*The Record*'.

It also obviously had been anything but quiet at Chez Johnson's second story residence during my recent absence. For starters, there was a large foot locker lying in front of my door way. It looked vaguely familiar as the foot locker that J.R. kept in his bungalow at my mother's house. Some people say it with flowers. Never one to be constrained by convention, my Mama – once again – takes matters to another level. And without even opening the rather large container, I was pretty sure this was her way of saying – 'Don't even think about calling me again'.

There also was a note stuck to the outside of the foot locker. It was hard to read but the signature looked very much like that of Ian, my Aussie editor mate at the paper, who, it now seemed, was my new next-door neighbor. If all of this was not enough, when I did finally get inside the door and turned on the answer machine, there was yet another not-so-subtle death threat. The good news – if receiving death threats can be seen as fortuitous – was that Tom Keenan was telling me the truth earlier when he said he knew nothing about these phone calls. The bad news was that there was at least one other person out there who was quite upset at some aspect – or indeed aspects - of my life. Alas, so it goes and so I took myself to bed – if only for a short nap.

I couldn't have been asleep for more than 15 minutes when I felt this huge mass sitting on my chest. "Flynn, go away," I mumbled.

"Oi, mite, it's me," which struck me as super weird given that Flynn not only could speak, but do so with a great Aussie accent.

I opened my eyes to see none other than Ian Ross standing over me. "Mite, (for some reason the 'a' always sound more like an 'i' when Ian says mate), it's time to get up. I just got a call from the paper and all hell has broken loose."

"What else is new? Can't it wait till noon?"

"Mite, it's nearly there now. Let's get going. I told Lou I'd get you in there before Marty sends out the storm troopers," Ian said.

"Thanks, mate. Appreciate your support," I replied.

"No worries. Where you been, anyway?"

"Would you believe researching a story at Wild Cherry till about 2 a.m.? The rest of the night is a bit of a blur."

"Oii, Wild Cherry, eh. Did you see any Maps of Tassie?"

"Maps of what?"

"Tassie. Tasmania. It's an Australian island, mate."

"I know what it is, but what's it got to do with Wild Cherry?"

"It has to do with the shape of the female's nether regions if you get my drift. It's shaped like Tasmania. Did you see any Maps of Tassie?"

"You're one weird dude, Ian. To be frank, I didn't see any 'Maps of Tassie' or any other Australian geographic features while I was there. I take that back. I do think one of the girls had shaved her private parts altogether. What do you call that?"

"That's sailing right up the Derwent!"

"I won't even ask what that means. How'd you get into Mrs. May's apartment?"

"Long story, mite. Not very interesting. I'll fill you in on the way. Besides, you owe me a couple of drinks for getting that fucking casket up the stairs!"

"Yeah, thanks – I think," I said.

I arrived at the paper about the same time as one of my dinner guests from the previous evening. No guesses for figuring out which one it was.

"Good morning Co–, I mean, Mrs. Wheeler-James," I said holding the door for her. The publisher brushed by me without saying a word. I had this effect on many women. Men too for that matter. I was truly catholic when it came to leaving people without speech. The same reaction, however, could not be said of her esteemed son when I entered the newsroom.

"Get the fuck in my office!" boomed Marty loud enough so everyone in the tri-state area could hear it.

"I'll just grab a cup of caffeine, if you don't mind," I said.

"Now!!!!" he said again loud enough to disturb the dead.

When I got in his office, Jack Saunders and a now quite-covered-up Gail Gerard were in attendance.

"Jack. Gail. Nice to see you both," I said.

Marty followed behind me, slamming the door to his office which sat in the middle of the newsroom like some giant fishbowl. "Just what the fuck are you two doing?"

"Ahh, can you tell me which two you're referring to, boss? Do you mean me and Jack or Gail or Jack, or—"

"Cut it out, asshole. You know damn well who I'm talking about. What the Christ were you doing stripping on Silicon Alley?" Marty asked Gail.

"Let me answer that one, Gail. You see, I've been in the closet for too long," I said.

"One more word out of you, Johnson and you're gone," Marty said, with Saunders repeating the word 'gone' for good measure.

"I was working on a story and for what it's worth – I was about to break something big," Gail said.

"Big, huh? Like what? Most of the girls have fake tits?" Marty said, which drew a laugh from Saunders.

"No, not that. But I'm not going to sit here and be treated like cheap trash. You either respect me for my journalism or go jump in the lake," Gail said quite sternly.

Her words caught all of us by surprise, though Marty recovered quickly enough to tell her that her services were no longer required at 'The Record'. It was Gail's turn now to be surprised. None of us saw that coming.

"Hey, hang on a minute, Marty. Give her a chance to explain," I said.

"Explain? Explain what? I've got enough problems explaining to my mother why two members of my staff as well as a recently-fired editor were involved in a brawl at one of this region's seediest night spots," the editor said.

"Does this mean you won't validate my parking chit?" I blurted out trying to lighten the mood. Before I could say another word, Gail got up and headed for the door. She stopped to shake my hand and then marched out the door, which she left wide open so we could all see her heading for the exit. She stopped long enough to turn and face the now large number of staff members gathered in small groups around the newsroom trying to figure out what would happen next. She started to say something, but then thought better of it, simply turned on her heels and left without saying another word. I hoped I could catch her before she got too far out the door to find out how Hugh was doing.

"That's Strike Number Two, Johnson," Marty said with his personal chorus echoing "'Yeah, two" in the background.

"You guys are good. Glad someone is keeping score in this place. So if memory serves me, that means I have one more chance?" I said.

"That's it. Make it good," Marty said.

"Oh, I will make it better than good. I'll make it gooder," I said getting up from the chair and heading out the door to catch up with Gail. I didn't know if anything could make it 'gooder', but I knew I at least had a decent profile of the Almshouse almost ready – even without interviewing its current custodian, Trevor Brown. I caught up with Gail outside. She started to cry uncontrollably.

"Hey, kiddo, don't cry. These idiots aren't worth it," I said.

"It's not that, Walter. That was my first real job in journalism," she said in between sobs.

"I got news for you, Gail. *'The Record'* doesn't count on anyone's list of 'real journalism jobs'," I said, which got her laughing a bit. "How's Hugh?"

"Yeah, he's okay. The guys at the station knew him pretty well and were quite happy to let him go not long after he got there," she said. "I'm sorry I never said anything about us being together, but that was his call."

"Yeah, no problem. Can we get together for dinner some night?"

"Ahh, no, but thanks. We're actually heading out of town tomorrow," she said.

"Already?"

"Yeah, well, Hugh's got a job interview for a small paper in an Indiana town nestled along the Ohio River," she said.

"Was 'nestled' your word or his?"

"I'm working on making my copy more interesting. Who knows, maybe I'll even get to write one or two stories out there."

"Sounds good. Well, stay in touch. Give him my best and tell him to call me," I said.

"I will," Gail said, turning to leave before adding: "Hey, Walter, take care of yourself and say goodbye to Mason for me? There is something big going down and I'd hoped to get to the bottom of it. Guess it's up to you now," she said.

I nodded knowing full well I was not up to that task.

"Oh yeah, I almost forgot. Hugh told me to tell you to 'lead with the cats'. He said you'd know what that meant."

"I do, indeed, Gail. I do, indeed."

Chapter Twenty Five

I headed back to the newsroom to catch up with Mason and make sure he was all right. Actually, he was probably the only reason I was still on the premises, if I could believe what his Mom told me the night before. The gap between what people told you and the truth was quickly growing wider than the Grand Canyon, but deep down I think she was being pretty truthful. Why would she lie to me?

I also wondered why everyone kept thinking there was something 'big' going down in this forgotten town. I didn't get the feeling those guys at the strip club were celebrating getting hired for some big, lucrative job. They just struck me as ordinary slobs out for a not-so-quiet night's worth of boning up on their southern Australian geographical features in between drinks. What could be more natural than that?

I decided to spend less time worrying about what may or may not be going down in town and spending more time on writing good stories. And on catching up with J.R. to see how he was doing. After spending some time with Mason and finding out he was okay, I popped my head into Marty's office and told him I had a good piece coming on the future of the Almshouse. He nodded and told me to get it in by tomorrow night. First mission accomplished, (that is, apart from writing the damn thing – a mere formality in the hands of a writer as gifted as moi-self). I then headed back to the apartment to find out exactly what family treasures were stored in my uncle's old Navy foot locker. Before I could get to it though, there were two more messages on my machine. One was from the Almshouse to tell me that Tom Keenan was ready for release and could I swing by and pick him up. The other was from my father wondering what the heck I was up to and could I stop in to see him as soon as possible.

I swung by the Almshouse and picked up Trolley Tom as instructed, but not before getting some time with the establishment's main man for a few more choice quotes to go in my article. I also figured out a good way to keep Tom quiet while I went south for a day or so to catch up with my Dad and Uncle J.R.

"How do you like farms?" I asked Tom when we finally got under way.

"Farms? Dunno. Never been to one," he replied.

"Great. Then you're gonna love this one," I said as we turned down the lane near my grandfather's humble country estate.

"You're kidding, right? Aren't you going to New London?"

"Not on your watch, pal. Besides, the doctor told me to make sure you got some rest and this is just the place."

"Where am I gonna get food?"

"Easy. The surpermarket is close by and the food is really fresh. The only thing is, you have to pick it yourself."

"I don't mind self serve," Tom said not getting my drift.

"Well, ah, I don't think you quite understand. You see that cow standing by the doorway?"

"Yeah."

"If you want to make a milk shake, you're going to have to get a hand on her utter and twist and shout for a few minutes."

"What? That's disgusting."

"Well, it's either you stay here for a day or so or, I re-introduce you to your worst nightmare on four legs. As it is, Flynn is making a mess on the seat drooling," I said.

"Alright, but you better be back tomorrow night," Tom said.

"See you then. Just let me check in on my granddad and I'll be on my way." I no sooner pushed the sacred cow out of the doorway when Jenny's younger brother Ethan emerged from the front entrance.

"Ethan? How ya doing?"

"What do you care?"

"Now that's the Lawton spirit. Speaking of which, how's Jenny?"

"Why don't you ask her yourself? She's just in now helping your grandfather," he said taking the cow by her primitive halter and leading her toward the barn.

That was a shock. I didn't see her car anywhere and wasn't really sure how this was going to play out, but after last night I did owe her an apology – at least. I entered the doorway and headed for the small sitting room off the kitchen. Grandfather was in his favorite (and only) chair while Jenny massaged his temples.

"Hey, where's the line form for one of those?"

"Hello, Walter. So nice of you to drop by. Where's your girlfriend?"

"Oh, that. Yeah, well, she's not my girlfriend. In fact, she worked at the paper, but got fired and is heading to Indiana with her real boyfriend. Did that make any sense at all?"

"Indiana, huh? Gee, isn't that nice. Didn't you live there for a while? May be you can go back and try again?" Jenny said while rubbing my grandfather's temples harder and harder. Another five minutes and I figured his head would explode.

"Hey, look, I made a big mistake about you and I apologize, okay?"

My grandfather realized they were not alone in the room. "Ooooyyyy, is that you boy?"

"Yes, granddad. It's me." He made a couple more whooping-type sounds which pretty much implied it was good to see me.

"Gotta make something go, boy," he said.

"I'm trying, granddad. I really am," I said.

"You're trying alright," Jenny said, not giving me an inch.

Just then, Tom the Trolley Guy stumbled into the room. "Oh yes, I forgot to mention that I have to leave town for a day and need to leave this guy here to recover from injuries suffered last night if that's okay?"

Jenny gave me a look of total disgust. "You're a real piece of work. You just don't get it do you, Walter? Yeah, sure. Leave another one of your problems behind – no offence to you, Tom. We'll take care of everything."

"Hey, it's not like that. Tom can explain how we met and I think you're going to like that story – right Tom?"

"Yeah, like," he said.

"Besides, if you wouldn't mind stepping out to the kitchen, I have something else to tell you," I said pleading with Jenny to join me.

"Anything to get you out the door," she said.

"Jenny, look, I'm sorry. I really am. But were you aware that my grandfather will lose the farm unless he comes up with $23,000 real quick?"

"What? You're making that up – surely," she said.

"Wish I was, but don't worry. I have a plan. Just give me a bit of time. And when I get back – I'll explain everything to you over dinner, okay?"

She nodded her head up and down as if in agreement, but only just. "Who is this Tom guy, anyway?"

"Oh, him. He's okay. He's from Connecticut but he'd been stalking me for the last few weeks, because he didn't like the article I'd written about his shopping cart sculptures."

"What? You're leaving me and your grandfather with some lunatic?"

"Lunatic's a bit strong. Marginally deranged might be better. Flynn's got his number though so I'll leave her as insurance. It'll be okay, honest. When have I ever let you down?"

"How long you got?" she replied.

By the time I got to HoJo's in Willimantic, Dad was still finishing off a late-night rush of orders from what looked like either a prison break or the losing side of a local softball team. He had about 50 hamburgers and an equal number of hot dogs frying like mad on the grill while another 'chef' sliced and diced sandwiches next to him. I took the time to start writing the Almshouse piece in the relative peace and quiet of his office. I finished the story in under two hours, but decided to leave it overnight before submitting in case any other bright ideas came to me while visiting J.R. Many great ideas came to me while driving or while visiting J.R. Then, too, other things happened to me while driving and/or visiting my uncle, too.

KKLLKJJ::K(*&&JKLLLL:::G222@@@@&*&&__)*(&**HH;;;'"JH GT5$$$##. Guess who? ONE CANNOT BE FOUND UNLESS HE IS LOST.

I got the feeling that St. V was muscling in on my own thoughts, but once again, wondered what the frack he was trying to tell me. Wish to heck he would just come out and tell me straight instead of playing all these word games with me.

"Sorry about the rush," Dad said, entering his office.

"No worries," as an Aussie mate of mine often says. "I took the time to draft another prize-winning article."

"It's going okay then?" Dad asked me.

"Why? You looking for a new short-order chef?"

"You? No way. You were the worst cook ever," he said.

"You always were a rock when it came to supporting me, Dad," I replied, letting him know that I was kidding - mostly.

"I only got a minute and then I gotta get these new guys started on cleaning up," he began. "I'll come right to the point: The doctors say your uncle has a brain tumor and it's too big to operate on."

Even though I heard all the words, I had trouble making sense of what it meant. "But I just spoke to him the other day and everything was fine."

"That's J.R. He don't want anyone to know or to make a fuss. Especially you or your mother."

"I can understand his feelings about Mom. They're widely shared by all the men in her life. But me? Why didn't he say anything to me?"

"Dunno, son. All I know is that he was going in for more tests today, but I haven't heard anything yet. Be good if you could see him. He likes you," Dad said.

"Yeah, sure. No problem. I'm just so shocked. I can't believe it," I said.

"It's pretty awful, for sure," Dad said. "Hey, before you go. What were you asking me about the farm and your granddad a while back?"

"Aww, it can wait. Really."

"You sure?"

"Absolutely. I better get going so I can catch J.R. Thanks, Dad and take care of yourself," I said.

"You too, son. You too."

Chapter Twenty Six

"Calling hours are over. Come back tomorrow."

I looked down at the weasely-looking guy behind the glass window of what claimed to be an institution for the sickly of southeastern Connecticut. He had a thin moustache under his equally-thin lips. It looked like a ring left by a recent cup of cocoa. His red hair was cropped short and slicked back with enough grease to cook all the birds for the First Thanksgiving. I decided to go gobble-gobble and see if I could get his weasely slits for eyes to blink.

"Do you see this?" I said turning my head to the left so he could catch the full fright of my ear-less head.

The weasel nodded without uttering a word. I had him.

"I lost it in Nam. But that's nothing compared to what the other guy lost," I said while turning my usually placid facial expression into something that would outshine Jack Nicholson's 'Here's Johnny' maniacal expression so wonderfully expressed in '*The Shining*'.

"I'm sorry for your loss, sir. Who you want to see?"

"J.R. Winslow," I said.

He pulled out a large clipboard and looked over the names. "Yes, Room 314. Go on up but don't say nothing to nobody."

"Anything to anybody."

"Huh?"

"The expression is 'don't say anything to anybody'. And I won't," I said heading for the elevators. I could be so cruel, but hey, there has to be some upside to the downside of being one ear short of a box set. I found J.R.'s room without too much trouble. He was asleep in a bed by the window. A couple of nurses had drawn a white curtain around the bed of the other patient in the room. They were having difficulty trying to give the patient a sponge bath. I tip-toed over to the window near J.R.'s bed and kept low so they wouldn't see me when they had finished.

J.R. never stirred. The only way I knew he was still alive was from the machines hooked up to him, spitting out data regarding his various life functions.

The cold, clinical sounds of the hospital's hardware were offset by the large bouquets of flowers on the table next to his bed and along the window sill. I recognized one card signed by the guys at his favorite watering hole. There was nothing from any member of my family – including me.

"What're you doing here?" J.R. mumbled.

"Just passing through," I said. "Just felt like some hospital food."

J.R. smiled. "Got any hooch?"

"Sorry, no. I'll bring some next time," I replied, just as the nurses pulled back the curtain of the adjoining bed. "What are you doing here? Calling hours are over," they said in near perfect unison.

"I'm not calling anyone. I'm visiting my dear uncle here," I said.

The two women looked at each other. They looked very tired and were obviously not keen to take on any more difficult patients like their most recent victim. "Okay, but make it snappy. The ward will be closing for the night soon," said the larger, and older, of the two nurses.

"Thanks. I won't be long."

"You're some kinda pistol," J.R. said, breaking into a grin and hollow cough simultaneously.

"Me? What about you? Were you ever going to tell me about your illness?"

"What's to tell? I got a tumor that went from the size of a gumball to a grapefruit in a week. My head hurts like hell and my vision goes from bad to worse in the blink of an eye. You're now up to date."

"Hey, man. You're all I got. The things we did. How about that time in Newport?"

"What time?"

"Remember, we were at the bar in 'Blood Alley' and you hit on those two middle-aged babes."

"Ahh, no, I don't remember that."

"Sure you do, Unc. They were from some town in East Bumfuck, Kentucky and you told them they looked like two thirds of Charlie's Angels, when in fact they looked more like two members of Hell's Angels, complete with arm tattoos, missing teeth and hairy armpits."

"Hey, thanks for stopping by but I'm not up to it, kid. I appreciate what you're trying to do and all, but the game's over."

"What? How can you give up like that? J.R., you gotta fight."

"I'm leaving you the boat. And practically anything else of value. Did that money get to you for that woman's funeral expenses?"

"Yeah, thanks. You don't owe me—"

"HEY, look, I'm dying, okay? So spare me the bullshit. Let me go. I wanna go. Do me two favors?"

"Yeah, go ahead."

"Say a few words at the service? I've told the guys you would. Told them you're good with words."

"Still lying for me. Thanks."

"And get them to play something by The Band at the service."

"C'mon, man. Don't talk like that."

"Just do it – okay?" I nodded in the affirmative. "Take care of yourself. And take care of your Dad and your granddad. Tell your mother to go fuck herself. No one else will."

Good ol' J.R. Even in pain he had a way of hitting the nail on the head – full stop. "I'll come back tomorrow. Get some sleep."

J.R. had drifted off before I finished my sentence. It would be the last time I'd see him alive. It would not be the last time he surprised me, though.

I headed back to New Richmond some time after midnight. I got in just after 3.30 a.m. and looked around for Flynn before remembering I'd left her at the farm. I heard loud music coming from my new neighbor's apartment. I drifted off to the sounds of some obscure Aussie band screaming about '*Khe Sanh*' – at least that's what I thought they were screaming about.

I got up early, guzzled down two cups of coffee while making a few minor changes to the Almshouse piece and then headed toward the paper to drop it off – hopefully before I ran into anyone I didn't want to run into. As expected, there was only a handful of people there, including the octogenarian day-time editor whose main task was to keep from falling asleep and Mason James who was busy working on yet another story that would never see the light of day.

"I hope that's the Almshouse piece," came the voice of someone I definitely didn't want to run into – Martin James.

"Sure is, boss. And it's a beauty. All it needs now is a great header. Leave it to Ian for that, eh?"

"What're you working on today?"

"Oh, another in my hard-hitting series on where oh where is New Richmond heading?"

"Can you give me any more details?"

"No, but it'll make my submarine story look positively amateurish," I lied.

"It'd better. Give you till next week to get it in."

"Piece of cake," I lied again. "Gotta run. See you later." As I left the newsroom, I was beginning to think I should have packed up and joined Hugh and Gail in Indiana. What was I thinking, promising not only a story by tomorrow night, but a page one stunner to boot?!

When I wasn't thinking about my uncle, my grandfather's farm, my mother, Mrs. May and Jenny Lawton – pretty much in that order though I'd lie if ever confronted by the latter - I'd been thinking more recently a little about Gail Gerrard and a lot about Hugh Jackson.

Before you start thinking may be I'm a bit weird, even for a guy who hears voices from centuries-old ancient Near Eastern warriors, let me explain why Hugh kept creeping into my thoughts. He had indeed taught me a lot about journalism, though little of it was from anything he said to me. Let me start again: This may sound particularly weird coming from one who makes his living from playing with the alphabet, but little of it had anything to do with words. It wasn't the words he used to explain what makes or doesn't make a good news story. Rather, it was the way he did it. Does that make any sense?

Hundreds of millions of words had been strung together by supposed experts in the ways of modern-day journalism, explaining any number of factors required in making a good news story. These so-called experts often started from the premise that any good story usually has two sides and that any good journalist must make sure both are given equal time to ensure accuracy, fairness and any number of other motherhood mantras.

I'd practiced this two-sided style in my first few years, but slowly started to realize that this approach was not only flawed, but downright dumb and boring. This approach perhaps had become de rigeur because of the ever-growing influence of TV reporting where their idea of complete coverage is giving equal time to 'both' sides of a story. But that's because their reports are by their very nature, vapid and lacking any semblance of the way the world works. Any organization that says it can deliver 'all the news that matters' in less than 30 minutes each evening must surely have rocks in its collective head. What Hugh had gotten across to me was that it was the reporter's job to not be an innocent bystander presenting both sides of a story, but to BE THE story. I was being paid to take a stand and present however many sides to a story there might be. And more to the point: focus on those bits of the sides that made it edgy and well, newsworthy.

I'd cite my most recent article on the Almshouse as an example of what I'm trying to explain, but it quite frankly, was not up to scratch. Like my Mrs. May obit, I'd rather not share it with you for any number of reasons, but mostly because it offered little in the way of interesting journalism. It did get a great headline, thanks to Ian Ross, which gained it a spot on the front page when it appeared. It read: *A FAREWELL TO ALMS.*

It doesn't get any better than that.

Or does it? There was one other lesson regarding good journalism that Hugh to a greater degree, and Gail to a lesser one – had imparted to me. That is, the importance of 'being there'. You can sit in a classroom or in a bar or any number of other places you might find comforting, but it's rare when a rip-roaring Page Oner will take shape in these venues. If you want the really good ones, you have to be out and about. I don't know what kind of story Gail would have come up with from her time spent collecting dollar bills off strange men, but that experience offered any number of golden opportunities that I'm sure she and Hugh could have extracted.

That was her 'being there'. Mine required a far less exotic locale, at least at first blush. My 'being there' occurred during the drive over to my grandfather's to pick up Flynn.

Chapter Twenty Seven

I'd made the drive so many times to my grandfather's farm that I swear there were wear marks in the road. Instead of taking the usual route out of town, I decided, for some unknown reason, to try a much-less-used route. It meant driving by Aunt Stacey's, my boss's and my ex-mother's houses, but I could live with that. Not far after their homes and quite a ways before you get to the Almshouse, there is this small, windy, unpaved country road. Few people used it because it often got quite bumpy in parts, but it in fact saved nearly 10 miles on the trip to Richmond Heights if you could stand the dust, flying stones, rattling and rolling. It was considered part of the 'Indian Reserve' and for that reason no doubt, was never treated as part of the town's responsibility.

The bumpy ride didn't bother me. How could it for someone so skilled in the ways of handling vehicles with so many major safety issues like bald tires, burned out headlights, non-working windshield wipers, etc. Just before making the turn, however, I noticed something that I didn't think was there when I visited the Almshouse recently. At the place where one usually sees a street sign, but not in the case of an unsealed dirt road, was a hand-printed sign that said simply: 'THUNDER ROAD'.

I stopped the car just before the sign, blinked, shook my head several times and looked again. The sign still read 'THUNDER ROAD'. It might have meant nothing to most people. But for anyone who had followed the meteoric rise of a young punk out of the mean streets of New Jersey, Thunder Road was the address for one of Bruce Springsteen's biggest hits. While I was pretty sure I wouldn't be running into either the Boss or the E Street Band down this dusty road, I was equally pretty sure that this smelled like a story. A very big story.

I made the turn and headed down the dirt track. I'd known about this road in my youth. It was mostly used by young couples seeking a quiet place to trade saliva and any number of other bodily fluids. I was soon to find out that its primary purpose had changed slightly. I knew this because no more than 50 feet from the turn-off, sat an elderly Native American man in a canvas-backed chair favored by beach-goers. In front of him was a fold-up card table that had all sorts of colorful pamphlets and other pieces of paper on it. Behind him was a large sign that read: "Welcome to America, the Land of Peace, Love, Justice and NO MERCY."

Bingo. Stop the presses. Now, before you start shaking your head and wondering how this possibly could be – there's one other question you have to ask yourself. How did I know he was an 'elderly Native American man?' Simple: Because on his head sat the biggest fucking Indian headdress I'd ever seen. His name, at least his 'Native American' tag was Chief Bear Claw – the Grand Poobah of the once almighty Menashocutts, (the most powerful tribe in all of western Massachusetts, according to one of his pamphlets).

After chatting pretty much about nothing for a while, I did what any good reporter would do. I asked him if he'd like to go for a ride to which he quickly replied: "I have waited a long time for you to come, my son."

Christ, I should introduce him to St. Vartan. These two would have a lot in common. "I'm sure you have. Then again, perhaps if you stuck this stand out on Highway 44 you'd get a bit more action, eh?"

"Got all the action I need right here."

"I'd love to stay and chat but I got places to be. You coming or not?"

"There would be nothing I'd like better. Nothing, indeed."

I helped him into the car. He didn't seem the least worried about his table, the papers on it or even the one-man tent pitched not far from his 'office'. He took off his headdress and very carefully placed it on the back seat. I noticed there was a sticker on the inside of it that read: 'Made in Taiwan'. He pulled out a beat-up baseball cap that had the faded but distinctive branding of the New England Patriots on it. How ironic. A local Indian wearing the insignia of the very crowd that more or less wiped out his and many other tribes in the greater New England area. The ironies continued with other parts of his wardrobe. His shirt was of the Country & Western variety – complete with pearl buttons. I won't go any further preferring to save it for the article. (And this time I promise to share it with you).

He then proceeded to stare at the side of my head, the way any number of others had before him. His reaction, however, was quite different. He didn't seem upset or horrified by the mangled mess where usually a perfectly-formed cochlear grows. A calm, knowing sort of smile came over his face. "It has been a long time, my son. Too long," he said and placed his left hand on my shoulder.

I not only was going to get one whopper of a story. I was going to get a soppy old Indian, too. Quite a collection of human flotsam and jetsam I was collecting: the Chief, Tom the Trolley Guy, 'Aunt' Stacey...My mind drifted toward other thoughts: Uncle J.R. – was he still alive? Jenny Lawton – would she give me one more chance? The list was endless. I drove without saying another word. I somehow knew the Chief and I would figure it out. Go figure.

While the Chief seemed to know me, I couldn't recollect ever meeting him before. Not far from the farm, however, he told me that his 'other' name was Larry Kennedy and that he'd been the janitor at Richmond Heights Junior High School when I was there. (The Junior High had long since closed down due to lack of numbers and been amalgamated into the New Richmond school system).

"Of course. Mr. Kennedy. I remember you now. You were always very good to me," I said hoping beyond hope I wasn't stretching the truth too much. Who remembers the guy who changes the toilet paper rolls?

"You were a very special child, my son. I remember seeing you reading all the time in the library – where your mother worked."

"You got one heck of a memory, Chief. Come to think of it, there were a lot of neat old books dealing with the area's early history. Wonder whatever happened to them?"

"All will be revealed, I'm sure," the Chief said, totally confusing me as to what he was talking about. I wished St. Vartan would make one of his 'house calls'. I really had to get these two together.

We said little else until reaching the farmhouse. "All ashore who're coming ashore," I said turning to the Chief who did not look well. "You okay, sir?"

"What is this place?"

"It's my grandfather's farm – in Richmond Heights."

"Powerful place. Much energy flying around," he said before asking if he could just sit there a while.

"No problem. I'll just be a minute grabbing the dog," I said.

grandfather was just heading out of the front door as I approached.

"Hey, Pappy, how ya doing?"

"Wooooo-hoooo, my boy, how are you?"

"I'm fine. Did Jenny leave my dog somewhere close by?"

"Jenny? She left a while ago with the dog and that other guy," who I took to mean Tom Keenan.

"What? She took my dog? Oh, shit. Okay, thanks, granddad," I said finding a note from Jenny next to the phone. It said she'd taken Flynn home with her and would drop Tom off at the nearest train station.

With these matters sorted out, I rang Lou at the paper and my father to check in on J.R.'s health. The news couldn't have been worse at either end.

"We're hurting for good copy. Got anything good in the pipeline?" Lou asked.

"I do and you shall have it next week. Hold the front page. It's a beauty," I said.

"It'd better be. Marty and Co. are still looking to string you up. The only reason they're stalling is because no one else is even coming close with good local news shit."

"It's nice to be wanted," I replied.

"Wanted is right though I'm not sure if it's better off being dead or alive in your case," he replied.

"Thanks, coach. And give my regards to Ian. Tell him we'll need another great header shortly."

"Any other hints?"

"Yeah, tell him to think Indian," I said before hanging up. I'd no sooner put the receiver back in its cradle when it started ringing.

"Hello?"

"That you, son?"

"Tis I, Dad. How'd you find me?"

"Just a hunch. Just wanted to let you know J.R. died a while ago."

"Oh, shit, no! Tell me you're fooling around?"

"No, he's gone."

"Jeez, he went quick," I said.

"You know J.R., when he decides to do something – he just does it," my father said. Truer words he never spoke. He told me there was not going to be any funeral. Only a memorial service in a few days time. "I think he wanted you to say a few words."

"Yeah, he mentioned something about that to me when I saw him. I just need a couple of days to work on a story and then I'll head over to pick you up on the way to his place, ok?"

"No problem. Take care, eh?"

I was stunned and not in the mood for dealing with Jenny and Flynn. I placed a call to her place only to find she hadn't arrived yet. I got her roommate who asked if I'd recovered from the recent visit to her work establishment. I assured her I had and asked if she'd tell Jenny to hang on to Flynn for a few days.

"No problem, Sugar. She'd do anything for you. Matter of fact, so would I," said Ms. Bryant which almost made me wish I wasn't such a nice guy.

"Thanks. Tell her I'll call soon," I said and hung up.

The fact of the matter was that since visiting with J.R., I'd started thinking about how hung up everyone is about coming 'first' or 'last'.

Anyone can be the first to do something. First in line; first man on the moon; first guy in high school to get laid. Yes, it's very special coming first. It's much harder to be the last one, and yet, it can also be special. Remember *'The Last Picture Show'*? *'The Last Tycoon'*? *'Last Tango in Paris'*? How about The Band's *'The Last Waltz'*? Lastly, we may never have remembered a certain young Hebrew man's first meal, but are we ever going to forget his *'Last Supper'*?

It seemed like a very appropriate intro to my latest story. Who gets to spend time with the last leader of anything – be it a company or country? Who could deprive me a look into the mind of a man who, for better or worse, represented the last gasp of a group of people who had roamed around North America for thousands of years before the Europeans decided to cut in?

First things first, though. When I went back outside, the Chief was nowhere in sight. Neither was granddad for that matter. The next few minutes, hours, days, were quite a blur. It was as if I was in a dream that involved several chats with the Chief and a whole bunch of other people. I know not how I did it, but here's the story that ran the next week.

The Very Last of the Menashocutts

Hollywood has a lot to answer for.

For many of us, the only image we had of Native Americans occurred in movie theatres where countless numbers of athletically-built, long-haired men covered in face paint, conducted cock-a-hoop war cries while straddling saddle-less horses against the backdrop of Arizona's breathtaking Monument Valley or across the Great Plains of the Midwest that were teeming with boundless buffalo herds.

Enter Chief Bear Claw, the latest and undoubtedly last great leader of the once proud and powerful Menashocutts, a tribe who called the greater Western Massachusetts region their own. For more than 4,000 years, this tribe resisted all comers from neighboring clans like the Oneidas to their west, Algonquins to the east and Mohegans and Narragansetts to their south, as well as with encroaching colonials.

There may not have been any Sitting Bull or Crazy Horse, but there were tales of great warriors capable of performing superhuman feats, such as carving out The Big Puddle from the teardrops of another tribe's fallen chieftain.

It was a far cry from the living conditions of Chief Bear Claw – the very last of the Menashocutts.

The Chief resides not in some grand wigwam surrounded by hundreds of followers on some equally grand piece of God's earth. He sits alone on a rickety, canvas-back chair in front of a faded, fold-up card table covered with amateurish brochures and pamphlets in the last known piece of unreal estate colloquially referred to as 'Indian Reserve' in this area. It's actually a 500-acre holding that fronts onto The Big

Puddle, but contains little in the way of useful trees, grasslands or other flora. The only people who frequent the area tend to be young lovers in search of a quiet place to lock lips and other bodily parts safely away from the prying eyes of friends and family.

Behind the Chief is a one-man tent where he obviously lays his weary 83-year-old head in the evening, and a whopping big sign that was stuck on a wooden post behind his makeshift office in the woods. It reads: "Welcome to America – the Land of Peace, Love, Justice and NO MERCY."

The Chief greets the interloper respectfully and invites him into his humble off-street address. He stands up slowly no doubt from the great weight of the magnificent headdress currently adorning his balding head. Although he wears coke-bottle thick glasses, his vision remains 20-20, recalling the visitor from another time in another place. Indeed, 20 years ago, the Chief was better known by his colonial handle – Larry Kennedy – who held down a job as janitor at the long-since-departed Richmond Heights Junior High School.

Following this school's amalgamation into the New Richmond school system, The Chief spent the next few years providing a similar service at the Almshouse, but that position dried up, too. When asked where he lives, he points to a small tent pitched behind his 'office'. Though a one-time janitor in the white man's world, Chief Bear Claw has been the custodian of the Menashocutts, a once proud clan that now numbers somewhere between 8 and 21, depending on your definition of how much blood in one's veins must flow from a

Native American ancestor, for the past 40
years.

Despite his advancing years, this Chief
continues to fight battles on all fronts –
from a variety of comers. Indeed,
descendants from an off-shoot of the
neighboring Oneidas on the western side of
the not-so-great lake claim the Menashocutt
real estate from some bloody battle fought
centuries before. Meanwhile, continuing
attempts by various unscrupulous local
developers to carve off huge chunks of the
Indian Reserve for yet another series of
unearthly boxes inhabited by commuters who
are keen to be seen (for some reason) to be
living close to nature while working in
congested urban centers like Hartford,
Worcester or Boston.

Still other Indian tribes like some to
their south in Connecticut, can't
understand what the Chief is waiting for.
In fact, they're reportedly deep in
discussions with state and federal leaders
to convert similar unused rural parcels
into garish, Las Vegas-style casinos.

Chief Bear Claw has heard all these
stories, and more, for many, many years. He
slowly removes his headdress and places it
on a well-worn tree stump near the table.
The colorful war bonnet contains a 'Made in
Taiwan' label in its inner lining. In its
place he proudly wears a beat-up, faded
baseball cap with the New England Patriots
logo on it, an ironic choice given that it
was these very guys who spelled the end for
his and many other tribes in the northeast.
It is not the only irony contained in his
outfit, though. He also wears a loose
fitting leather jacket with fringe – a
Country & Western shirt, complete with
pearl buttons, faded blue jeans and Black
Keds sneakers. His stride has become

something of a shuffle, in part affected by his advancing years though no doubt impacted by a meeting with a bullet while working for the U.S. Army in France during the Second World War. When he talks, he often sounds like he's trying to whistle – a situation he attributes to loose-fitting dentures.

When he does open his mouth, he chooses his words carefully, as if he's being charged for each one by some higher vocabulary authority. When he speaks, it comes out like a parable or some other wise, age-less piece of wisdom. 'Deal with your past or it will deal with you', is a pretty typical example. You could say he wasn't much in the chit-chat department. Better still, he was full of chit, but not much chat.

It's perhaps fitting that so much of the conversation, or what little he shares with his visitor, recounts the tribe's great past deeds. He tells his guest of many glorious victories by their one and only semi-well-known leader, Chief Wachuquin, who not only maintained the Menashocutts' rightful place on top of the local Indian pecking order, but even worked to bring the warring factions from New York State and Connecticut together for one last stand against the unwanted advancements of wave after wave of pesky colonials in the 1760s. This move failed and the proud Chieftain was captured and held prisoner at nearby Fort New Richmond, now the site of the Almshouse.

This was not the end of the Chief's claims to fame, though. According to his 20th century incarnate, Chief Wachuquin won over many of his warders, some of whom helped him escape into the wilds of outer Western Massachusetts. It was reported that a small group of local settlers, mostly young women, joined the outlaw Chief on the run.

These 'weekend' warriors were just that though, apparently returning to the fold within weeks due to lack of proper food and hygiene.

"This was the beginning and the end of our once great tribe," Chief Bear Claw says. "Chief Wachuquin was eventually murdered by soldiers and his body never recovered for proper burial. We have led lives of utter loss and confoundment ever since."

Local historians, archaeologists and anthropologists alike, disagree, delighting in telling any and all who might listen just how lively these Indian land claims can be. They delight in taking small groups of university students into the bowels of the Indian Reserve and sucking out all sorts of evidence revealing lives of untold worth and forward thinking by these Native American pioneers.

"Tribes like the Menashocutts figured prominently in conducting the sort of eco-friendly developments we can only dream of today," says Professor Bryan Harvey, noted anthropologist and Native American Scholar at nearby Western Massachusetts State University.

It's difficult for many less learned folk to grasp just what the heck is so wonderful and 'eco-friendly' about a group of people who left behind little more than a handful of arrowheads and pile after endless pile of shells shucked from countless numbers of clams along The Big Puddle's shores.

While Hollywood prefers to invent the sort of tribes that we all would like to think inhabited the Great Plains, attempts to re-create the lifestyles of their northeastern brethren weren't much better. Indeed, what school child has not read 'Last of the Mohicans?' by James Fenimore Cooper. The Coopster's classic tale got more than just a few facts wrong beginning with the name of the tribe. He somehow confused the Connecticut-based Mohegans with the Hudson Valley dwelling clan called the Mahicans and created the very fictitious Mohicans. The Mahicans were so upset they pulled up stakes and moved to Wisconsin where they are now known as the Stockbridge Indians.

They've probably amounted to a lot more than many of the local tribes, though. I must have missed the book detailing the 'Great BiValve Hunt of 1846' or the Frederick Remington bronze showing an Indian rounding up a bunch of marauding molluscs. While their Great Plains colleagues were leading lives of screaming desperation, those of their northeastern brethren were more like ones of quiet respiration.

This is not to say Chief Bear Claw intends on giving up without one last almighty fight. It's a rather odd fight given that he's not asking for much. He doesn't want a whopping big Las Vegas-style casino. He doesn't even want a bingo parlor or risk a game-of-chance hall. He's just looking for a little bit of love and hope from his not-so-friendly neighbors in New Richmond.

Like the sign says: 'Welcome to America, Land of Peace, Love, Justice and NO MERCY."

These are the words that give him solace; keep him anchored and strong for the fights ahead. And when asked from which ancestral leader these great words were taken, Chief Bear Claw turns and says: "I stole them from a Bruce Springsteen bootleg album."

తిం

The phones were ringing hard and fast at the newsroom after the story on the Chief ran. Mostly positive but then again, there were a few more calls from mean-sounding guys who wanted to do unspeakable things to yours truly. Most of that was fine by me. I could count the number of times I'd had bodily contact with a woman over the past few months on one finger. So getting the crap kicked out of me might not have been every guy's idea of a good time, but in my book – any attention – regardless of gender – counts.

I left the office around 7 p.m. and headed home to pack some clothes and head south to pick up Dad on the way to pay our last respects to J.R. I still couldn't believe he was gone; couldn't believe we'd never spend another night knocking down beers while trying to figure out who would make the Sox' all-time, all-star team. These discussions inevitably disintegrated into all-out brawls, because of our inability to agree on whether the Bambino should be included and if so – did you include his hey-day years with the Yankees or not? Ever the purist, J.R. argued it was only his time with the Red Sox that counted. I preferred the more cosmopolitan view that it was his time as a better-than-average pitcher in Boston that laid the foundation for his later exploits while in the dreaded Yankee pinstripes.

There were a couple of surprises waiting for me when I got home. One was Flynn the Wonder Dog, greeting me at the door with a classic flying hug and the smell of a woman coming from the kitchen. In fact, it wasn't just any woman – it was Jenny Lawton preparing a very lovely meal for me - complete with candles, though I don't think they were part of the meal.

"Hey, how'd you get in?"

"I have a special relationship with the super," she said.

"What, you shine his walker?"

"Something like that," she said in a way that made me wish I needed a cane.

"How do you like your steak, mister?"

"Ahh, Jenny, I hate to tell you this but my doctor told me I have to stop eating red meat."

"Really, how awful," she says as if I had to give up something really important like breathing.

"Nah, I just paint them green and Bob's your uncle," I said without realizing my faux pas.

"You bastard!" Jenny screamed running toward me.

"Ohh, thanks for the hug. Really. Between you and Flynn, who needs sex?"

"And who said anything about sex, fella?"

"Not me. Certainly not me. No, unfortunately I do have to leave soon."

"What is it this time?" she said.

"I'm sorry, baby. My uncle, J.R. died and I need to get down there for the funeral service."

"Oh, I'm so sorry, Walter. I didn't know," she said coming over and giving me another big hug. "It does seem a little odd though."

"Why? What do you mean?"

"Well, there was one letter under the door when I came in earlier. And it's from J.R.," she said, just as the door opened again. This time, though, it was my neighbour Ian.

"G'day, mate. Thought I heard voices in here."

"Ahh, yeah, Ian, this is Jenny – Jenny, Ian."

"Hey, if I'd known you were busy, mate – just say the word and I'll leave," said Ian, a guy who never, ever left any group of more than one alone.

"Okay, the 'word,'" I said though Ian seemed not to hear.

"Hey, got any beers?"

"Would you leave if I said 'yes?'"

"You're a riot, mate. Truly. I gotta have a beer. Anyone else?" Ian said grabbing a bottle of my beer out of my refrigerator.

"Nice of you to share, mate," I said.

"No worries," he replies.

Where is that accent from, Ian? England?"

"No way, - Australya," he replies.

"Okay, sorry to break up this geography lesson involving Commonwealth nations, but I really must be going. Say, Ian, why don't you stay and eat my dinner and drink all my beer?"

"Mate, when you put it like that – it sounds awful," Ian says warming to the idea.

"No problem, really. Just don't take my girl," I said, winking at Jenny who winked back at me.

"When's the service?" Jenny asked.

"Tomorrow morning. I should be back by the weekend," I replied. "Can you take care of Flynn till then?"

"I don't know. It's a big ask," Jenny said. "But then again, at least she's house broken. More than I can say for her owner."

I grabbed my overnight bag and quickly threw the first two semi-clean shirts and underwear I could find in it before heading for the door. Jenny gave me one last hug and handed me J.R.'s last letter. "Don't forget this," she said.

I stuffed the letter in my jacket pocket, leaned over and gave Flynn a pat on her head and shut the door behind me.

I'd had so many ups and downs with Jenny now, I was beginning to think we'd never get any time alone. These thoughts were soon shoved aside by J.R. and whatever words of wisdom he had waiting for me in the letter. I got in the car and placed the bag on the back seat and the letter on the passenger seat beside me.

It was a quiet drive to Willimantic to pick up Dad. He likewise wasn't in a very chatty mood, but couldn't help but notice the letter. "Is that from J.R.?"

"The one and only."

"Aren't you going to open it?"

"Why don't we wait till after the service?" I said. For once, my father agreed with me. May be things were looking up after all. It was well after midnight by the time we reached J.R.'s moored house. In many ways, his special seaside retreat seemed like a lot of things in J.R.'s life – a flamboyant concoction containing a bit of truth and a whole bunch of fantasy.

I remember him telling me how he got the idea for the floating home while travelling through China. J.R. said the so-called 'Marble Boat' was first built in the mid-eighteenth century at a lakeside pavilion near Peking. Its Chinese lines were dropped a century later when it was destroyed by Anglo-French forces and then ironically rebuilt in Western style. Perhaps even more ironically, according to J.R., was that the second owner of the great vessel, some old dowager empress, 'borrowed' money earmarked for the country's naval fleet to erect this floating monument, complete with Mississippi-style paddlewheels. J.R. said it was the ultimate statement of man and nature coming together. And so, the concept of his own unseaworthy abode was born.

I suspect there is a stone boat of some description moored in a harbour near Peking. But whether it was quite as fanciful as the one he described, is anyone's guess. Then again, I had a hard time believing some of the other things he used to tell me like his claims to being friends with Hollywood stars, international sportsmen and other biggies. That was all part of the J.R. charm, though. They were almost child-like fantasies. A bit of fun that didn't harm anyone. It certainly was a welcome relief from the cold, hardened personalities preferred by his sister and father. Speaking of which, I wondered if my mother would make an appearance. The betting line among the two men who knew her best – namely dear ol' Dad and myself, both opted for the long odds on that event.

It was spooky being on the boat without J.R. I kept hoping I'd hear him hitting golf balls off the roof. Or, strolling along the deck humming along to some forgettable tune by The Band, Bobby Darin or Barry White.

There was nothing but the overwhelming sounds of silence. We each drank a couple more beers from the six pack we'd brought for the ride. There wasn't a lot to talk about. Mostly vivid memories about time spent with J.R.

"You know, J.R. really loved you. I sometimes felt a bit –"

"You don't have to say anything, Dad. I loved him, too. As I do you," I said and headed for J.R.'s bedroom. I didn't bother getting undressed. I just kicked off my boots and fell on the mattress. A light was flickering on his answer machine so I hit the button to see who had left the last message on J.R.'s phone. It was his mate from the bar – J.J. – actually calling to tell me to come on down to 'Ye Olde Salty' when I got in. He had a surprise for me, he said. My life was just full of surprises – few of which I really wanted.

I called back and thanked him for the offer, but wasn't sure this was quite the right time. It just didn't seem right without J.R. I then realized that the letter was still in my jacket pocket. I couldn't help myself any longer. I took the envelope out, tore it open and out fell a pair of baseball cards. No surprise there. No, the surprise was in realizing which two cards they were. J.R. had somehow squirreled away what looked to be the rookie cards of Mickey Mantle and Willie Mays from the 1951 Bowman series. You didn't have to know a lot about baseball cards or baseball for that matter to know these cards might as well have been gilt-edged. Even with my rudimentary understanding of card values, they'd probably bring close to $10,000 on the open market.

A piece of paper fell out from in between the smiles of the game's two biggest names from the 1950s and 1960s. "Sorry I couldn't get to the bank. Hope these cover your neighbor's funeral costs," it said. Christ almighty. Who would or could do such a thing? No one but J.R. Hell, these two cards would not only cover Mrs. May's expenses, but probably give me enough to buy The Lincoln if I wanted it. It also went a long way toward paying off my grandfather's debt.

"Hey, Dad, you awake?" I yelled out.

"Barely," came his reply.

"Get dressed. We're going out," I said disembarking from J.R.'s bloated barge. There was little traffic on Victoria's one main street. It was well after midnight. Victoria looked a lot like many small New England seaside towns. Busy as hell during the day with people, mostly tourists, darting in and out of one after another quaint clothing and craft shops with names like 'Ye Olde Craft Centre' or 'Fashion Flaire'. At night, the place closed up tighter than a tick's bum with only a handful of restaurants and bars lighting up the night. Except for tonight. While there were very few cars, there were people – mostly men – everywhere. It looked like either the Red Sox had finally won the pennant or Gay Liberation had arrived. In fact, they were all coming or going to 'Ye Olde Salty' where J.R. was holding court – even in his absence.

I found a parking space on a nearby side street and then swam upstream against the throng of beer-soaked Victorian men. We could only get to within a few yards of the pub's door when someone yelled out my name:

"Yo, Walter – over here!"

It was J.J. – the pub's gregarious owner pointing toward the other side of the street. "Hey, thanks for the call earlier, J.J. My Dad and I greatly appreciate–"

"Hey, Walt, lighten up. There's plenty of time to drown our sorrows tomorrow. Not tonight. Tonight is our celebration of the one and only J.R.!!!"

Who could argue with that sentiment? Even the local cops turned a blind eye to the bar's patrons spilling out onto the street with bottles of beer and mixed drinks. It was a great night and certainly kept everyone's mind off the reason we were all drinking ourselves into oblivion. I don't remember much about the rest of the evening. I don't even remember driving back to J.R.'s place. I do remember waking up with one heckuva hangover and feeling like I'd swallowed a couple of hand towels sprinkled with rusty nails. I got up, showered and shaved, probably in that order, and prepared to leave for the church.

I'd hoped to spend some time thinking about J.R.'s eulogy. It was too late for that. By the time we got to the church, it looked like a replay of the previous evening. There were people everywhere only this time there were men, women and children all over the streets. It was strange seeing all these strangers gathering to pay their respects to MY uncle. I'd never thought about him knowing other people, because so many of our visits were really quite quiet affairs, but he'd obviously made a great impression on more than just a few locals.

The service was being held at the town's Methodist Church which stood at the far end of Main Street at the top of the area's one and only hill. It was quite a steep hill though and I'm sure J.R. would've loved watching everyone, especially those with sore heads from the night before, struggling up the 70 or so small steps that lead to its front door. I don't know why this church was blessed with his final presence. I was sure J.R. didn't attend this or any other church regularly, or irregularly for that matter. He probably just liked their clam bakes better than the others. I introduced myself to the Minister, a chap named Thomas Dylan who ushered my father and me aside as the townsfolk piled in. He wanted to know how we were holding up and if we were pleased with the look of J.R.'s casket. Frankly, it was hard to see due to the myriad floral bouquets draped over it.

I did know he'd made a few last requests. He was particularly adamant about making sure the lid stayed closed. His reasoning was that he was hardly an oil painting while alive so couldn't imagine how unattractive he'd look when "death-warmed over." He also said that he hated attending funerals of good friends who did give you one last peek-a-boo. He never saw anyone "lying in a box who even remotely looked like the person when alive, so better to keep it shut tight."

Fair enough. We did add a few touches though, but doubt he would have disapproved. They included his favorite mashie niblick and his faded 1940s Boston Red Sox cap that apparently had been worn by The Splendid Splinter himself – Ted Williams. Someone, probably J.J., also festooned the box with baseball cards from varying eras.

"I'm very sorry for your loss," said the solemn Reverend. "I didn't know your Uncle well, but was certainly aware of his boundless community spirit."

Indeed, one after another local resident got up and paid their respects to J.R., revealing sides to the man I never could have imagined. He'd been the primary sponsor of untold little league teams, boy scout/girl scout troops, lobster festivals, clam bakes, church socials, etc. There didn't seem to be any part of the town's rich social fabric that he hadn't been intricately woven into.

J.J. got up and invited everyone to come back to his pub after the service to continue the celebration of J.R.'s life. A call that was heartily received by all. He also helped explain the reason behind a rather unusual 'guest' at the funeral. Just behind the hearse outside the church was the town's one and only emergency ambulance van, with its bright red and blue lights flashing. "J.R. left instructions for the ambulance to be ready just in case he felt better during the service."

It was then left to me to sum up. Talk about a tough gig. Fortunately, I knew that not only was he there to help me, but so too were all his friends. There were no empty spaces in the church. Every pew and aisle as well as the seats normally set aside for the chorus were filled. Most faces were unknown to me, though I did recognize a fair few from the previous evening.

I decided to keep it simple and short. I don't remember exactly what I said but I did compare J.R. to his great love – collecting baseball cards. He was sometimes a little off center, even a bit frayed around the edges, but he was rarely in anything but mint condition.

I then turned toward J.R. and his final resting place, bowed my head and walked toward the front doors. I had people laying more hands on me than at a bevy of Baptist revival meetings. Everyone wanted to shake my hand as if I had something to do with delivering this treasured identity into their midst.

Once outside, I sucked in a few deep breaths and greeted the faithful, along with the Reverend, my father and J.J. It was hard to remember them all, but one face did look familiar.

"Has anyone ever told you that you look like the actor Robert Mitchum?" I asked this rather distinguished-looking, gray-haired guy. He had on a dark blue suit, white shirt and matching dark blue tie. The ensemble was capped off by one of those dark felt hats that were worn by 1950s detectives like Sam Spade and Philip Marlowe.

"Occasionally," the man said, each syllable rolling off more smoothly than the one before it, before adding: "I just wanted to pay my respects. J.R. was a good friend." There was something oddly familiar about the way he delivered these lines. Short and punchy with a melodic rhythm. It was the same kind of dialogue delivered by any number of private dicks from those same 1950s' detective movies.

"Thanks. Thanks a lot," I replied and turned to the next mourner.

"Hey, Walt, did he say if he was coming back for a drink?" J.J. asked.

"Who?"

"Why, Bob of course," he said.

"Bob who?"

"Bob Frickin Hollywood Mitchum, you dickhead," he replied.

J.R. continued to surprise me – even in death. And there was more to come. Lots more.

Chapter Twenty Eight

My father and I had a quick beer at J.J'.s following the funeral and then headed back to the boat house. Dad was quieter than normal if that was possible. He did manage to tell me that he wanted to hang around Victoria for a day or two and clean up J.R.'s house boat. That sounded like a good idea. He also said he'd hang around until his ashes were ready for pick up. I gave him a hug, packed my trusty four-cylinder stallion and headed once more back into the unknown.

I took my time deciding to take a few different roads between Victoria and New Richmond. Actually, I got lost somewhere outside of Norwich and before I knew it, the roads became smaller and smaller until they were little more than tarred cow tracks. I finally stopped just outside of a small town called Aberdeen. I half expected to run into some guy on a trusty stead armed with a long pole asking if I'd like to join him in a 'wee joust'. Alas, there was no such offering on offer. Its one main street was so deserted that even the cobwebs had given up. There was a run-down brick building which had probably been a house of worship. The front doors were now hanging loose off their hinges and more panes than not in its arched windows now provided natural air conditioning. A nearby gas station sported a faded 'Sunoco' sign while its only pump had more rust than a 200-year-old nail. About the only place in town that still looked remotely lived in was a two-story wooden shack with a shingle out front that read 'Ted's Place'. Although the place had an inviting screen door, it was harder to open than a green chestnut. Once it did let go, though, it led me into a space more typically found within some 'living' museum like Old Sturbridge Village or Plimoth Plantation. If the owner could sell the smell of dust and mildew – 'Ted's Place' would be a millionaire many times over. It was hard to tell what 'Ted's Place' had been in any previous life, but it was now in the business of selling people pieces of once-edible Americana. In fact, the labels on many of the items were so faded, there was no need to check the use-by dates. Christ, they may have dated from Roman times.

"Help ya?" came a voice from behind the front counter.

"Got any coffee?"

"The best. Brew it myself," came the reply.

When I got to the counter, I finally caught a glimpse of who I assumed was the store's curator. He looked old enough to be Casey Stengal's grandpa, complete with overalls that were more white than blue due to their age and a Boston Red Sox cap that probably 'Remembered the Maine'. I noticed the rickety, wooden chair on which he sat was covered in yellowed newspapers. Right next to this seat was another just like it, only a very old gray cat that looked to be pushing the envelope on Life Number Nine. It had taken the man five minutes to get up from his chair and turn around to grab one of the plastic cups next to the coffee maker.

"Passing through?" came the next bit of repartee from my eighty-something host.

"Yeah. You Ted?" I asked figuring I just had to know.

"Ted? Hell no," came the reply. "He died years ago."

I decided not to press any further. The coffee, which was probably brewed during the 1930s, set me back the Depression-like sum of 35 cents. Not sure what it would taste like, but the trip back in time was priceless.

At least till I got back to my car and took the first sip. It would not have been acceptable as diesel oil, let alone coffee. I choked on the first gulp and threw the rest out the window. I turned on the radio to see if there was any score in the Red Sox game. It was Opening Day. It was the only game J.R. would attend every year. He said "there was nothing like it." It was the first and last time every season when the Red Sox were on equal pegging with every other team aiming to win the World Series. A time of renewal; rebirth; hope.

Instead of the game, though, my ear was greeted by Joan Baez's rendition of The Band's most poignant and sorrow-filled ballad – '*The Night They Drove Old Dixie Down*'.

I threw the empty cup on the floor and started to cry. Not weep. Cry, as in sob. I buried my head in my hands and leaned on the steering wheel and sobbed for what seemed an eternity. At long last, there was a faint knocking on the window.

"You alright?" asked Ted's spritely replacement.

"Oh, yeah. Thanks," I said, quickly wiping my eyes before another gush of tears flowed. The old man's baseball cap reminded me of J.R'.s.

"You wanna refill?" Ted's descendant asked pointing to the empty cup on the floor next to me.

I hit the ignition and left him behind in a trail of smoke. Not sure what sobered me up more quickly – the one misplaced gulp of Ted's chicory-flavored rocket fuel or the thought of a second helping. Anyway, I was on the road again and merrily sailing toward the Massachusetts state line when:

YOU MUST NOT DESPAIR AT THE LOSS OF ONE SO CLOSE. DEATH IS NOT AN ENDING. IT IS, IN FACT, THE ONLY WAY ONE CAN ENTER AN ENTIRELY DIFFERENT DOOR WITH QUITE UNIMAGINABLE POSSIBILITIES.

Oh great, now for St. Vartan's take on the meaning of life and death. It's oh so easy for some guy whose been in the ground for 1,500 years to give me the latest hot tip from the great beyond on why losing someone dear is really not so dear after all. I mean, hey, get a life! Even I had to laugh at that one. I'm sure J.R. would've loved it, too. For all I knew, he probably willed it to me.

It was after dark by the time my wonky chariot pulled up outside the Lincoln. I could see lights on in my apartment. Could I be so lucky as to finally get some quality time with my almost on-again-though-not-quite-since-we-never-really-were girlfriend? I raced past the front desk and up the main stairwell two steps at a time. I hesitated briefly outside my own door before seeing if it was unlocked. The door seemed to open on its own, but there was no one there. Well, almost no one. There was just someone at a particularly very low height.

"Hello," said this voice emanating from a small boy standing in my apartment.

"Ah, yeah. Hello yourself," I replied rather feebly.

"Mommy, there's a stranger at the door!" the kid yelled which immediately awoke Flynn the Wonder Dog from a sound catnap.

"Relax, kid. I only live here," I said trying in vain to grab him as he ran for the kitchen.

Jenny emerged quickly from the next room complete with a tight-fitting Budweiser apron over her equally-tight fitting sleeveless white top and blue jeans. "Oh, it's only Walter, Howie. He's okay. He lives here," Jenny said, breaking into a smile.

"I tried to tell him that but he didn't believe me," I replied. "So, this is the man in your life, eh? He's an awfully big, strapping fella," I said kneeling over to reassure the kid I was not some sort of monster.

"Howie, say 'hello' to Walter and tell him how nice he is to let you stay in his house for a few days," she said with pleading eyes.

"A few days, eh? Well, yeah, why not. But what's wrong with your place?"

"Nothing, it's just that Anita has been on a bit of a tear lately. Hard to know who she'll bring home next," she replied.

"Oh, I see. A bit like this place really. No problem. I'm gonna be at the paper a lot anyway, so you guys can have your space."

"He's not like Uncle Ian, Mommy," the kid says, referring to the wild Colonial boy from Down Under who obviously had already made a great impression on the kid.

"No, he's not, Howie," his mother replied.

"And just what does that mean?" I asked.

"You don't talk funny, I think," she said.

"I hope that's all it is," I said, leaning over and kissing her on the forehead.

"How'd it go?"

"Okay, I guess. J.R. would've loved it. I'll tell you all about it later. What's cooking?"

"Nothing fancy. Just some beans and franks. That's Howie's favorite."

"A true food connoisseur," I said heading for the refrigerator to grab a beer before dinner.

"Not sure there's any left. Ian and I had a bit of a long chat last night," Jenny said.

"Oh, really," I said opening the door knowing full well there had been nearly 20 bottles of Michelob in the frig before I left for Victoria. "You had a 20-beer chat?"

"Something like that. He's a very funny guy," she said. "Howie, tell him what Ian said about breakfast."

Howie's face looked a bit puzzled and then he said: "Oh yeah, he told me he'd had a dingo's breakfast."

"A dingo's breakfast. What's that?" I asked.

"A scratch and a pee," the boy said breaking into a laugh without fully realizing what he'd said.

"That's very funny. Good ol' Uncle Ian. A regular laugh riot," I said.

"You're not jealous, are you Wally?" Jenny said.

"Who me? Nah, I mean, what woman in her right mind could resist this?" I said pointing to myself.

"I can't imagine," she replied, saying she'd put a bottle of red on the table that was ready for opening. While I fiddled with the corkscrew, Jenny got down the dishes and started serving up the meal. "Oh, you did get some strange calls earlier."

"Oh, like what sort of strange?" I asked.

"A couple of calls where there was no one talking, but definitely on the line," she said.

"Oh yes, they're my deaf mute fans just ringing to say 'hi'," I replied.

"And then there was a call from someone who sounded like the Mayor."

Ugh oh. "The Mayor? What makes you think it was the Mayor?"

261

"It just sounded a lot like her only she seemed a bit drunk."

"What time did she call?"

"Around 6.30 p.m.," she said.

"Yep, she was drunk alright," I replied. "What did she want?"

"She didn't say. Only that you were to call her as soon as you got in – no matter what hour it might be. She'd wait up for you," Jenny said.

"Oh, she's such a kidder, ol' Aunt Stacey. Isn't that funny? You have Uncle Ian and I have Aunt Stacey."

"A regular laugh riot, Alice," Jenny replied, imitating Audrey Meadows from one of my favorite shows – *'The Honeymooners'*.

I proceeded to do what any red-blooded tough guy does when his lady love is positioned under the same roof – I ripped the phone cord out of the wall to eliminate the chance of any further awkward circumstances arising.

And then, just when things were starting to look quite bright for this semi-nuclear, cozy Norman Rockwell-type family pose - when I couldn't help notice that the kid was barely touching his tasty meal, preferring instead to stare at me. And yes, it was that sort of stare.

"What happened to your ear?" the kid said finally.

"Howie. That's not nice," Jenny piped in.

"Hey, no problem. Or as Uncle Ian says – 'No worries'. It's very simple, Howie. I was born that way."

The kid didn't much like that answer, though. "Did it get lost somewhere?"

"Howie. Now stop," Jenny said.

"It's no big deal, Jenny. Really. No, it just never took shape. Any other questions?"

"No, that's enough, Howie," Jenny said cutting in though he obviously had one or three more queries just dying to get out. He wasn't alone. Most people did.

Jenny gave me that 'thank you' sort of look people – mostly women – can give when required. I did my best to give her a 'Hey, no problem' look in return, but it probably looked more like my 'Hey, I'm constipated' look.

After dinner, Jenny and I sat around and talked and got me to thinking how nice it might be to have her and Howie around on a more regular basis.

I was also thinking how nice it would be to have someone – preferably a member of the female sex – and even more preferably someone who had a body to die for like Jenny Lawton – to engage in well, sex.

"I guess we better be going to bed. You're probably very tired, too," Jenny said.

"When you say 'we', just who are you referring to?"

"Me and Howie," she replied.

"Of course. I knew that."

"We quite like the bed in your spare room," she said.

"No, no. Take mine – please. I'll sleep out here on the sofa as I want to spend some time going through this foot locker that my mother sent over and then get up early to get over to the paper to find out what's been happening."

"You sure?"

"Positively positive," I replied.

"Okay then. We'll get ready for bed. Good night then," Jenny said coming over and giving me a slow, soft kiss on the lips followed by an equally slow hug.

"Ahh, you sure you have to go to bed?"

"I do," she replied. "Oh, don't forget to call the Mayor."

"I already have. Forgotten, that is. She can wait till morning."

I waited till they were done getting ready for bed and then pulled out the foot locker that my mother had so graciously sent over to me. It contained some stuff from my childhood like Red Sox pennants, old term papers, even a small plaster mold of my hand done in the First Grade. There wasn't much stuff that I really cared to remember about my childhood so if this was it, so be it.

There also were some things that must have belonged to J.R – books mostly. There were a couple on the Navy's 'Silent Service' a few more on how to grade baseball cards and even a biography of Ted Williams. Pages of particular interest were marked by – what else – baseball cards, mostly of the Splendid Splinter himself.

Closer to home were some books on my mother's blood lines. There were some fairly simple biographies on John Adams, my favorite one titled *'John Adams: Atlas of Independence'*. For whatever reason, I never got very excited about this family connection. Perhaps because he seemed like such a boring prig of a guy wedged between the young country's twin titans – Washington and Jefferson. Indeed, the latter Virginian colossus even outgunning the Quincy lawyer while he was Prez, dethroning him after only one term in office – a matter that my relation never forgave him for till much later in life. Ironically, it was claimed that at his deathbed, Adams' last words were: 'Jefferson still lives', but it was untrue. Jefferson had died a few hours earlier, though in a bitterly ironic of ironic twists – the two men died on the one day of the year that they could practically claim as their own – the 4th of July. Talk about happy endings.

The foot locker also contained some lesser-known works on the Mayflower and Plimoth Plantation. There also was a copy of Marsden's famous history of New Richmond, which I'd read many times during high school for history class. If ever there was a style book on how not to write, this had to be it. Sentences droned on and on without any sign of punctuation. Then, too, he was extremely adept at recording the most obvious observations like: "Many members of the local Indian tribes were often referred to as 'Red Men', no doubt because of the reddish-brown shades of their skin." I'm surprised that little gem didn't have a frickin footnote after it.

I was finally growing tired from the events of the last few days when I sensed someone was staring at me. I turned to find little Howie standing not more than a few feet behind the table, with Flynn alongside him acting as his leaning post.

"Does it hurt?" the kid asked, obviously still keen to find out more about the missing ear.

"Only on the inside," I replied.

With that, he turned and went back to bed. I, in turn, was now wide awake and continued poring over the books in search of something, anything, that could help me navigate my way through the hundreds of millions of bits of genetic information that through some quirk of ungodly fate, gelled just long enough to create one of the sorriest creatures that had ever roamed the earth.

Chapter Twenty Nine

I vowed to make sure the next day would dawn brighter than its predecessor. In fact, it was positively radioactive through no fault of my own, I might add.

I had drifted off to sleep some time in the early part of the next day's early morning. To make sure I got a good night's rest, I did what any good, self-respecting one-eared geek does: I curled up on the world's most uncomfortable sofa with my back to the room and the biggest pillow I could find plugged up against my good ear. It's one of those few perks that never appears on the brochures that come with damaged human goods when leaving the hospital after birth. It used to bug the shit out of my ex-girlfriends at how soundly I could sleep. In fact, it was the lack of sound rather than the soundness that counted. Once I jammed my good ear into a pillow, the bigger and softer the better, the less able I was to hear anything short of a 21-gun salute being fired next to the bed.

There were times, however, when this 'perk' backfired. Indeed, one can only imagine the range of emotions I felt the next morning when I awoke to find Howie and Jenny screaming at the top of their lungs while Flynn the Wonder Dog remained atop what I assumed to be an unknown intruder.

It certainly was an intruder, and perhaps a most unexpected one, but under no circumstances could it be said that the intruder was unknown – unfortunately. My cunning canine friend had baled up none other than Mrs. Elizabeth Quincy Adams Winslow Bedrosian. (She'd failed to buy into my Dad's move to change his surname, denying her the opportunity for one of the longest names by any woman married to only one man in New England history).

"Hello, Mom. Nice of you to drop in," I said in my most sincere, insincere voice.

"Get this maniac mutt off me!" she screamed.

"Now, now. She won't play nice if you're mean to her," I said. Jenny had taken Howie to the opposite side of the room and was shielding him as if there was an explosion about to occur. Actually, it already had.

"Will you do something about this dog?!" my mother shouted again.

"She only wants you to apologize for being so mean to me. Say 'Uncle', no scratch that, don't say 'Uncle', say how much you loved your dear departed brother and I'll call the hound off," I said.

Even I was taken aback by this verbal assault. I got up from the sofa and gently pulled at Flynn's tail. She quickly jumped up on the sofa, but remained wary of her latest pray. I couldn't blame her.

"Thank you," my mother said, gingerly propping herself first onto her knees before regaining her full composure. "Please introduce me to your friends, or are they part of the family?" she said, turning toward Jenny and Howie.

"You got me, Ma. This is Jenny. You remember her. We used to date in high school. And this is her son, Howie."

"I thought you looked a bit familiar. And is Howie—"

"Don't push your luck, Mom. Why are you here?"

"I've been ringing your phone all night. Don't you know what's going on?"

"Afraid not. I pulled the phone out of the wall when I started getting more than three obscene phone calls in an hour."

"You truly don't know what's happened?"

"Apart from returning from a funeral at which you really should have attended and finding an unwelcome intruder in my living room, no, what's happened?"

"Look, I'm truly sorry about missing my brother's funeral. But I think you should prepare yourself for some rather rude treatment when you get to work today."

I went out to the balcony and looked up the main street toward the newspaper. It was still quite early. So early that rarely are there any cars parked on either side of the street. Not today. Not only were both sides of the street crammed with parked cars, but also other strange-looking, larger vehicles, with numbers printed on their sides. They were TV news vans, many of which I now recognized. There was Worcester's Channel 9; Boston's Channels 4 & 5 and Hartford's Channel 3.

"What have we done now?" I asked naively.

"It's not what the newspaper has done or not done. It's all about you – again," my mother said. "And if I were you, I'd get down there now to straighten out this mess."

"What mess?"

"What mess? You still don't know?"

"I still don't know what?" I said.

"It's your story on the Chief. No one can find him and now they're saying that you've made it all up."

"What? You're kidding, right? Surely, you're kidding."

"Connie rang me last night and asked me if I'd heard from you or knew anything about the Chief."

"Why would she ring you? You don't know anything about your own family, let alone what's going on in the life of an elderly Native American Indian's."

"That's not fair, Walter."

"Not fair? That's not fair?! I'll give you unfair, you no good—"

"Walter," Jenny cut in. "Please. Can we calm down here?" she said moving over toward my mother. "Please excuse your son. He's been under a bit of pressure lately."

"No thanks to her," I added.

"Why don't we all sit down and I'll go make some coffee. Walter, why don't you turn on the TV and see what's happening?"

"Good idea, Jen."

It didn't take long to tap into what some young gun from Hartford's Channel 3 was calling the 'biggest hoax in living memory', whatever that meant. "We're stationed right outside the '*New Richmond Record*' where we believe the Publisher – Mrs. Constance Wheeler-James – is about to make a statement regarding her newspaper's recent publishing of an article allegedly featuring a profile of the last Chief of the now near extinct Menashocutts tribe."

The mealy-mouthed, long-haired TV reporter continued: "We've spent the last few days talking to many officials in the New Richmond area and no one seems to know anything about this so-called Chief or even whether he ever existed. Even the reporter, Walter Johnson, has disappeared."

Jenny returned with three cups of coffee and a glass of milk for Howie. "What is it, Walter?"

"As best I can figure, not only have I fabricated the story about the Chief, but apparently I may not actually exist."

"I think you'd better call Connie," my mother said.

"Yes, that's a good idea. We should let her know that I exist anyway," I said.

I no sooner plugged in the phone than it rang.

"Walter? That you?" came the familiar voice of Lou Cassals.

"Ah, no, it's Billy Hoffa. Of course it's me."

"Have you seen the TV news?"

"Bout time we got some coverage in this town, eh?" I said.

"Pal, get your ass down here pronto. We need to find this Chief tout de suite and get these idiots off our back."

"Yeah, yeah, just let me get changed and I'll be right there."

"Great. Hey, one more thing," Lou said.

"Yeah?"

"He really does exist, right?"

"Who – the Chief? I think so," I said and hung up. I shut off the TV and headed into the bedroom to change my clothes. I debated on whether to go for the Calvin Klein double-breasted blue blazer and Brooks Brothers gray trousers or the Giorgio Armani two-piece black suit. I opted for the latest offerings off the half-price polyester rack from Marshall's.

When I re-emerged, Jenny and Howie were in the kitchen while my mother lay on the floor rifling through the foot locker she'd had delivered to my door.

"Can I help you with something? Looking for a Babe Ruth Crackerjack perhaps? Misplaced a 1951 Bowman's Mickey Mantle? Just what the fuck do you think you're doing?"

"Excuse me, Walter."

"Excuse me? How dare you! Get outta here before I get angry," I said in a tone that probably was heard in Harrisburg.

"I'm going, Walter. I'm not going to stand for this sort of rude behavior," my mother said.

I held back from saying anything else. Still, I was intrigued as to just what she was looking for. She hadn't seemed at all interested in her brother while he was alive. What was it in death that made her so damn curious? As the door shut behind her, I noticed that the last item she'd been looking at was the copy of Marsden's arid desert dry history of New Richmond. It seemed like an odd choice given that she, and nearly every other New Richmonder over the past century or so, would have their own copy. Not to be outdone, my mother probably had memorized by heart the bits concerning her beloved Winslows.

"Where's your Mom?" Jenny said racing into the living room.

"Just left on her broom. Something about having to get back to work before Dorothy and Toto showed up," I said.

"Now Walter, that's no way to talk about your mother. Especially in front of the boy," who happened to re-enter the living room at just that moment.

"What about 'the boy?'" Howie asked not really knowing who or what "the boy" actually was.

"Never you mind, Howie. Never you mind," Jenny replied, ushering him back into the kitchen. "What are you going to do about the Chief?"

"Don't know yet, but guess I better head on down to the paper and see what's happening. Can you stay here a while?"

"Yeah, but why?"

"Just because. I may need to leave town in a hurry and I'll bet you always wanted to know what it felt like to be hounded by a lynch mob," I said.

Jenny shot me a look that suggested she'd had better offers. I didn't doubt that. I could think of a half dozen or so better offers I'd wanted to offer her myself. Some time soon, I hoped. First things first.

The minute I hit the sidewalk outside The Lincoln, I could see walking straight up Main Street to *'The Record'* was not such a bright idea. There were so many TV news vans lined up, it was hard to believe anything else would make the evening bulletin.

I headed for the alley way next to the apartment house and marched along what in earlier days would have been the thoroughfare preferred by night cartsmen. It was perhaps befitting that the guy who found himself in the center of the biggest doo-doo in the town's inglorious history, should find sanctuary in narrow laneways once laden with the excrement unleashed by the local citizenry.

At long last, I recognized the back door to the one building where I knew I'd be welcome without fear or favor – the 'Final Edition'. Due to the early hour, there were few patrons, only Mel busily clearing away empty glasses from what obviously had been a very prosperous night before.

"Hey, what's a guy got to do to get served in this joint?" I said creeping up behind my favorite tavernkeeper.

"Ohhh, shit, you scared me, Walter. Where have you been?"

"Nowhere really, but can you possibly explain why this story has drawn all this attention?"

"Yeah, but jeez, you just missed the old lady and Marty. They're ready to kill you."

"It's nice to be wanted – dead or alive," I replied.

"I don't think 'alive' is an option right now," she said cracking into a smile. "But I do have to thank you."

"Why's that?"

"The only thing better than running a bar across the street from a newspaper, is running a bar across the street from a newspaper that is under siege by every other newspaper, radio and TV station from Boston to the Bronx."

Before I could say anything, Mel had set up a boilermaker in front of me. "On the house!" she said.

I thanked her and downed the whiskey and beer without taking a breath. "Okay, give. Why all the coverage?"

"Simple really. Didn't you hear about the 'Swiss Family Robertson' saga?"

"No, I missed that one. What was it?"

"About 18 months ago, this guy who had been the paper's Travel/Outdoor writer, published this fantastic tale about a family that had lived in New Richmond, but now led a nomadic existence living during the warmer months in State and National Parks around New England, before migrating south and doing the same in places like the Everglades over winter."

"Okay, so what's the problem?"

"Nothing really. Except when Child Welfare Services wanted to find this family of four, including two children aged between 10 and 12, it soon became apparent that they didn't exist. And because their surname was Robertson, they became known as the 'Swiss Family Rob—"

"Okay, I get it, but why would they just assume I'd done the same thing?"

"Well, apparently some reporter from Worcester had tried contacting the Chief and kept coming up empty. Then some schmuck from the Oneidas or one of them said no such person as the Chief existed and that set off alarm bells."

"And just who was this brilliant reporter who came up with this brilliant idea?"

"If I'm not mistaken, it's her on the TV now. And in fact, she's set up right outside here."

I went over to the TV and turned up the volume. "I'm reporting live from New Richmond, now known by many as the Big Mistake on the Not So Great Lake."

Catchy. Very catchy.

"I'm standing here in front of the building where many locals say, reporters like Walter Johnson, spend more time than in the actual newsroom. Yes, it's a bar, but not just any bar. It's the 'Final Edition' and is run by the daughter of the *New Richmond Record's* publisher, Mrs. Constance Wheeler-James."

"Not a bad plug, eh?" Mel says, obviously ignoring the blatant verbal assault on the reputation of yours truly currently in progress. I asked who the heck this woman was and Mel said her name was MaryElena Rabinelle who worked for Channel 9 News in Worcester.

"Despite contacting several local authorities, including the Police, Mayor's Office and even other indigenous Indian tribes, no one seems to know very much about the man who Walter Johnson featured in this recent front page story headlined – 'The Very Last of the Menoshocutts'.

"These sorts of situations are nothing new to '*The Record*'. It was not much more than one year ago when another reporter from the paper fabricated an entire story about a family supposedly down on its luck and living from day to day in National Parks up and down the East Coast. The so-called 'Swiss Family Robertson' saga shocked many readers which eventually led local Welfare authorities to try and contact this poor family. We now know of course that no such family existed and the reporter at the heart of this inventive fabrication, is ironically himself now living a rather nomadic existence in New York City, living off the kindness of strangers."

Doesn't this woman ever take a breath?

"What makes this alleged story even more bizarre, if that's possible though, is the fact that the reporter, as well as the supposed subject, has disappeared. I've been led to believe, however, that if he's in town, he's more than likely to be just on the other side of these solid oak doors so let's step inside and see what happens."

I had become so mesmerized by this woman's report that it hadn't occurred to me that she was about to enter the same space I was in. Fortunately, Mel saw it coming and shoved me out the back door before the nosy news hen hit the entrance.

"Thanks, Mel. Owe you one now!" I said, running back down the laneway for another five or six buildings and then jogging up the next alley toward Main Street. I could see that there were no news trucks or reporters around so I dashed across the main drag to the alley on the opposite side of the street, just a few doors down from '*The Record*'.

I didn't expect a particularly warm welcome when I hit the newsroom. But then, I guess it depends on what you consider 'warm'.

"Where the fuck have you been?" came the cry from the first person to see me – none other than Marty's right-hand man, Jack Saunders.

"Hi Jack-ass. Good to see you, too," I replied in as cool a voice as I could.

"You're in deep shit this time. Wait till Marty sees you," Jack said.

"Oooohhh, I'm shaking all over," I said. Unfortunately, it was not Marty that saw me next, but rather his very scary old lady, the Publisher herself who looked like she hadn't slept in days.

"Into my office now, Walter!" she said.

"Yes, ma'am," I replied without any further banter.

I no sooner got inside her rather large office, took a seat in front of her very imposing dark partner's desk while she picked up the phone, dialled and said "He's here" to someone at the other end of the line and then hung up.

"Do you have any idea of what we've been going through? You know how the media just love devouring one of their own when they smell fresh blood – especially coming so close on the heels of another disaster like –"

"Yes, I know, the Swiss Family Robertsons," I said.

Her door flew open and in came Marty with Jack Saunders close behind.

"Get out, Jack and shut the door behind you," the Publisher screamed at her son's second banana. "We need you to find the Chief and bring him in here so we can reassure our loyal readers, local community members and other interested parties that we are not some unruly rabble incapable of managing ourselves in a proper and dignified way," she said as calmly as someone in her current state of dismay could say.

I found her choice of words rather intriguing, but figured now was not the time to find out who she meant when she said 'other interested parties'. "Well, I'm happy to help but to be honest, I don't really know where the Chief might be."

"I told you that the bastard made it all up," Marty said.

"Thanks for your support, Marty. And just for that, I'm not inviting you to my next birthday party. No, I'm not saying that at all. It's just that we're not roommates. He was just a source for a story. Do you know where to find all the people you've interviewed over the years?"

"Most of them live in a house," Marty said.

"All in the same one? Well, The Chief doesn't own a house," I said. And from what the media swarm who've staked out his 'plain, run-down mobile home', he hasn't been there in a while. Leave it with me. I've got a couple of ideas. If I can't find him by the end of the day, then he doesn't really exist," I said in as funny a manner as I could muster.

Neither James laughed. "If you don't find him by the end of the day, it won't be just the Chief who doesn't exist," I heard Mrs. Wheeler-James say just as the door to her office closed behind me.

Chapter Thirty

It seemed like a longer walk than usual down the narrow hallway to the newsroom. It sounded particularly busy given that it was still long before the clock tower in the village square struck noon. Everyone stopped what they were doing, however, when I appeared.

"Okay, everyone, back to work. And no, I won't forget you now that I'm a big time star of TV," I said. I walked straight through the newsroom to The Morgue where my aging colleague, Wall Edwards, greeted me warmly.

"You is one for the books, you is," Wall said.

"I'll take that as a compliment."

"Ought to. Nothing worse than a media pack that smells blood. Only thing is, this time they're wrong. If anyone had asked me, I'd have told them the Chief exists," Wall said.

"You and I know the Chief exists, but the problem is in figuring out just where the hell he is. I called The Almshouse but no luck there. Ditto when I called the Police."

YOU MUST NOT LOSE SIGHT OF WHAT MATTERS, I heard a voice say.

"Did you say something, Wall?"

"Huh? Me? Not that I remember," he said.

"I was afraid of that." It was obviously my pal St. Vartan who somehow didn't even need any static to hit the right inter-galactic freeway frequency.

+++**&&^^%%$$%%#####"

LOOK NOT AT WHAT SURROUNDS YOU, BUT AT WHAT YOU SURROUND, St. Vartan continued.

What the frack did that mean? "Hey, Wall. If you were the Chief, where would you go?"

"Some place quiet. Some place safe," he said.

"You mean like a church – only for Indians?"

"Yeah, that's it. Good luck figuring out where that might be, though," he replied.

I swear at that moment I saw a great bolt of light flash through the Morgue. Perhaps it was a short in the century-old wiring in the ceiling. Whatever it was, it came with one last idea on where the Chief might be. I dialled my own number and hoped like heck that Jenny might still be there.

"Hello," came Jenny's sweet voice.

"Thank god you're still there," I said.

"Walt, what's going on? You're still all over the TV with everyone reporting that you made up the story about the Chief," she said.

"I know. Could you do me one more favor?"

"I've got to get Howie over to my Mom's. I'm due at work in a couple of hours," she said.

"This won't take long. Can you drive out to my granddad's and see if The Chief is squatting there? If he is, no, even if he isn't, can you ring me at the paper?"

"Okay, Walt, but you really owe me now."

"I'll make it up to you," I said.

"Promises, promises," she said and hung up.

Marty and his ever-present shadow Jack Saunders entered the Morgue. "Found him yet?"

"Hey, relax. He'll show up."

"He better. What do you want me to tell the press? They're practically pounding down the door to find out what's happening."

"That's great. All this free publicity. You should be paying me for this free exposure," I said.

"We're paying you to write stories. Real stories. And this better be for real," Marty said. Saunders nodded in agreement.

"Say, do you want me to do any of the interviews? I don't want to bother with the local stations, though. Is Jane Pauley here yet?"

"Why would she be here?"

"She and I are both ex-Hoosiers," I said. "I worked in Bloomington not long after she left. And now look at us. She's a star with *'The Today Show'* and I'm working at *'The Record'*. Two peas in a fricking pod," I said.

That got rid of Marty and his mate. Next came Mason who told me there was someone who wanted to speak to me.

"Is it a woman?"

"It is," he said. "Great, put her through to my extension in here," I said.

A few seconds later the phone on my desk rang. "Jenny?"

There was silence on the other end. "Ahh, no. My name is Sandy Bowman. I'm a Producer with the *'Phil Donahue Show'*."

"Well, well. Ain't this one for the books," I said. "What can I do you for?"

"We'd like to invite you out to Chicago to take part in one of our shows. We'll fly you out here and put you up in a great hotel."

"Would you now? And what's the theme? Undiscovered Pulitzer Prize winning journalists?"

"Ah, no, not exactly."

"What a surprise. What exactly then?"

"It's more about some of the issues involved in putting news stories together," she said.

"Oh, c'mon Sandy. You can do better than that. It's not really about putting news stories together. It's more about what tears them apart, right?"

"Hey, look, don't get mad at me."

"Oh, right. You're just the producer, right? What the hell does that mean? You aren't really the producer, are you? Your job is to call up schmucks like moi and get us to spill our guts in front of your half-dead audience and a few million others in the comfort of their own homes."

"Well, yes, I suppose."

"So you're not a producer then, are you? You're a Come Upper."

"A what?"

"A Come Upper. You 'come up' with the subjects to be roasted on your good show every day."

"Perhaps this is a bad time," Sandy said.

"Actually, it's a great time. Wish you were here. Look, I'd love to fly out to Chicago and meet Phil and the team. I'm a little busy here right now, though. Besides, I spent nearly 10 years of my life in that Gulag you call the Mideast and ain't keen on going back. Would you settle for a dog that can bark and fart at the same time?"

The phone went dead. I hope to heck Phil D. knows what he was passing up. I no sooner placed the receiver back in the cradle than it rang again.

"That you, Phil?" I said.

"It's me, Jenny," came the reply. "Whose Phil?"

"No one really. Phil Donahue," I said.

"You're going on Phil Donahue?"

"Nah, I turned them down. Offered them Flynn the Wonder Dog, though. Any luck?"

"Well, yes and no."

"Okay, what does that mean."

"Yes, the Chief is here alright."

"Great!"

"Not so fast. He's in some sort of trance down in the woods behind your granddad's house."

"What sort of trance?"

"I don't know what sort of trance, but all I know is when I tapped him on the shoulder, it was as if he didn't even feel it, let alone hear what I said."

"You'll think of something. I'm counting on you. I'd come down there, but I don't dare leave the newsroom. I'd be swamped by the TV wolf pack camped outside."

"What can I do?"

"Lie. Cheat. Whatever, but convince him that he needs to come back to town tonight."

"And then what?"

"Just drop him off at my place. I'll make sure Ian holds him and plies him with liquor till I get there."

"Walt, what is this all about?"

"You think I know? When I figure it out, you'll be the second person to know."

Lou Cassals sailed into the Morgue. "Any news, chief?"

"Funny. Very funny. As a matter of fact, I have located the good Chief."

"You're kidding, right?"

"Nope. I'm having him shipped back to town as we speak so we can hold a news conference tomorrow and well and truly shove it up all these bastards' asses," I said.

"That'd be great. Word on the street is that Charles Kuralt is possibly going back on the road to report on this one," Lou said, before adding that I should let the Publisher know the good news.

"Nah, make her sweat a bit more. Besides, we're now sitting on the biggest story this town has had in years and we're not even writing it. It's writing us!"

"Yeah, well. Let's make sure it doesn't backfire," Lou said.

"I'll do better than that. I'll do much better than that," I replied. "But I'm gonna need your help. And Ian's, too."

"Hey, one good deed deserves another. Which reminds me – can you spare me a couple of hours to bang out some good copy? We're a bit light on stories which is quite ironic given that the better part of the nation's media are camped on our doorstep," Lou said.

"No problem. It'll keep my mind off everything else," I replied.

I'd just finished off three small pieces for the Tri-State Round-Up page when the phone on my desk rang again. It was Jenny to say that the Chief was now safely tucked away inside Chez Johnson.

"I'll love you forever," I said.

"Not sure I want to be held to that. A hug would be nice, though," Jenny replied.

"You got it. I'll get Ian over there right away to take care of the Chief. He is okay, right?"

"Who? The Chief? Oh yes, just a bit quieter than normal," she said.

"How quiet?"

"As in 'not-one-word-for-the-whole-trip-back-to-town quiet'," Jenny replied.

"Ouch. That's quiet. I'll get Ian to lubricate him with a couple of Foster's finest lagers. That'll stop whatever's ailing him," I said.

"Great. I just need to be going."

"No worries. Thanks again. And Jenny – be watching the news tomorrow."

"I hope you know what you're doing, Walt."

"Me too. Me too."

I'd spoken to Ian and Lou about my plan earlier so after getting the call from Jenny, the next phase of what we were now calling 'Operation Overthrow' went into gear. It was hardly a complex plan. Lou wasn't even involved. All he had to do was look on sympathetically while Ian complained of having a terrible tummy upset forcing him to go home immediately. Once there, he would watch over The Chief and hopefully get him relaxed and ready for his first and hopefully not his last, major public appearance. Oh yes, Ian also had one other duty. To casually stroll up to Channel 9's intrepid reporter MaryElena Rabinelle after he left the building and let her in on an 'exclusive' story to unfold tomorrow morning.

What she didn't know is that we also had made the same invitation to every other news team to assure maximum coverage – and carnage. By convincing them all they had an 'exclusive', gave us two other advantages: First, that they would not discuss the supposed story with any competitors; and two, that they'd back off from trying to break down the doors of 'The Record', figuring it was now finally safe to put down their cameras and pick up their glasses of beer, wine or whatever other spirit moved them at the 'Final Edition'. He took off around 4.30 p.m. insuring that they would all get to do their live cross updates for the evening news. What a hoot. Because none of them had 'captured' me live, it was rather odd looking at photos they'd gleaned from earlier scrapes in the Mideast and even mug shots from the Richmond Heights High School year book. Flattering. Very flattering, particularly the ones with the mutton chop sideburns and pink floral shirts.

True to her muckraking roots, MaryElena even had a live cross with my previous employer in Cincinnati. This no-good gutter snipe named Adams, (no relation to my kin, I'm fairly certain), referred to me as a "first-class, second-rate reporter." She smiled sweetly into her microphone following this most unspeakable direct quote and said: "From New Richmond, MaryElena Rabinelle for Channel 9 *Action News.*"

I hung around till 8 p.m. finishing off a couple more stories for Lou before letting Connie and Marty know that everything was under control and ready for revelation in the morning. Neither of them, quite surprisingly, put up much of a fight. They too were keen to get rid of all the prying eyes of their near and not-so-near journalistic colleagues so that they could get back to doing whatever it was they thought they were doing at 'The Record'.

I also placed a call to the Mayor's office. "Hi, Auntie, how's my favorite political figure doing?"

There was a long silence at the other end of the phone. "Walter, what the hell are you trying to do to us?"

"Do to you? Why bring you publicity. You and Connie keep telling me that this town needs more exposure. What else can you ask for?"

"Is that supposed to be funny? What do you think you're doing?"

"Me? What do I think I've been doing? Not a lot but everyone still seems hell bent on stitching me up. I've been hung out to dry more quickly than a roll of wet toilet paper on a clothesline and you're looking for sympathy from me?"

"What do you want, Walter?"

"I love it when you use my proper name. It sounds so dirty," I said.

"What is it?"

"Nothing really. I've got a special surprise for you. Just be outside your palace around 10 in the morning and I'll take you to meet The Chief."

"You're kidding, right?"

"I'm not kidding. Tell your chauffeur to stay in bed, because I'm doing the driving and you're in for one heckuva story."

"What about the press?"

"Don't you worry. I'll make sure it only gets out to your favorite reporter," I said.

"MaryElena Rabinelle?" she said.

"Absolutely," I replied.

"I hope so, Walter. I really do for your sake," the Mayoress with the Mostest said.

"I hope so for all our sakes," I replied and hung up and headed out the door.

As expected, there were no reporters camped out on the doorstep. They'd all bought into the all-too-tempting promise of the 'exclusive' story to spend their time waiting for a glimpse of you know who. Judging by the yelling and screaming coming out of the 'Final Edition', it would seem most had decided to celebrate at my favorite watering hole. I fought back the temptation to drop in for a round or three, preferring to head straight home and find out what shape The Chief was in.

I needn't have worried. Neither he nor Ian Ross were in any shape at all. Both were passed out in the middle of the living room floor, surrounded by what appeared to be enough Foster's Lagers to sink the Titanic. I shook Ian without any response. Ditto for The Chief. Even Flynn seemed out of it, but hopefully not from drinking beer.

TAKE CARE OF THOSE WHO TAKE CARE OF YOU. STAND TALL AND THEY WILL STAND BY YOU. TREAT THEM WITH DISRESPECT AND THEY SHALL DESERT YOU.

At least St. Vartan was awake. He still wasn't making much sense which kept to the script – whatever that was. I picked up the empty cans and hoped there might be one with a little bit of liquid amber still inside. No such luck. Ian finally began to stir. The Chief remained lifeless.

"G'day, mate. How's it goin?" Ian asked.

"How's it going? I asked you to come here and baby sit the guy – not pickle him, you asshole," I said as calmly as I could.

"No worries, mate. Foster's never leaves a hangover. He'll be fresh as a daisy in the morning."

"He better be or you'll be pushing up daisies," I replied. "Did he ask or say anything before passing out?"

"Not really, mate. I've seen statues with more to say than this bloke, but once he had a couple of Foster's in him, he lightened up."

"What'd he say then?"

"Still nothing but a look of supreme serenity came over his gob and then he passed out," he added.

"Great. Just great. I sure hope to hell you know what you're talking about. Can you come back and drive him out to his 'office' on the Old Indian Road tomorrow morning?"

"No worries, mate. What time?"

"Better make it around 8.30 just in case I need help getting him up and about," I said.

"No worries."

"And the media are all lined up?"

"You bet. I told them to follow the beat up yellow Toyota," he said.

"Great. Thanks, I think. See you in the morning," I said gently pushing Ian out the door. "Hey, you wouldn't have a spare Foster's or three in your fridge, would ya?"

"Sorry, mate. The Chief drank the last one," he replied.

"No worries," I replied in my worst Aussie accent.

For the first time since I'd heard that now familiar Aussie expression – 'No worries' – I realized just how far from the truth it really was. No, worries were the one thing I had in seemingly endless supply.

Chapter Thirty One

"Do you want coffee or tea with your French Toast?"

As I neither heard the static before or after this phrase was spoken nor sensed that it held any deep-seated philosophical or metaphysical meaning, I ruled out St. Vartan as the speaker. Then again, perhaps I was having yet another installment in this recurring dream where I'm the only diner in a topless pancake parlor in Paris' Latin Quarter. No such luck as I opened my eyes to behold a fully clothed (thankfully), octogenarian Indian Chief standing before me with a plastic spatchelor in his hand.

"You're talking, Chief!" I blurted out, jumping up from the sofa which I'd squeezed close to the front door just in case he tried to make a run for it in the middle of the night.

"Why wouldn't I be?" he replied.

"No reason. None at all," I shot back before adding that I'd put a pot of coffee on and check to see if Ian was up yet, all the while guiding him along the narrow passageway to the kitchen. "Where'd you learn to make French Toast, anyway?"

"In the Army. About the only thing we had in any quantity each day was stale bread and the only way we could cover it up was to turn it into 'pain perdu'.

"Pain perdu?"

"Oui, French Toast, mon ami," he replied.

It was hard enough thinking of the Chief as an American GI, let alone as one who made his living by flipping flapjacks for fellow countrymen. Our chit chat was interrupted by Ian making his way into the kitchen and very ready to play his part in the latest adventures of Howard Walter Johnson's II.

"Sit down and eat. The French Toast is getting cold," scolded the Chief Chef or was it Chef Chief?

I'd managed one bite when the phone starting to ring in the front room. At least the caller was an ally. "Hi Dad, everything alright?"

"Yeah, I think so."

"Great. Can I call you back later, because I have one bitch of a day coming up."

"Yeah, no problem. I just wanted to tell you about the keys."

"Keys? What keys?"

"The keys to the safe deposit boxes that J.R. left in your name."

"Oh, those keys. I assume they're a bunch of baseball cards."

"Yeah, and something else."

"Dad, I haven't got time for 20 questions. What else?"

"It's a copy of that book by Marsden."

"Yeah, so what? Everyone, including me, already has a copy of that book if it's the one about the informal history of New Richmond?"

"Well, yes and no."

"Again with the questions. Just spill, Dad."

"It's got scribbling all over it," he said.

"You mean like by some kid from school?"

"No, more like notes. The kind of notes that I used to see you make on your term papers."

"Can you mail the book to me?"

"Yeah, if you like. I think you should see it."

"Okay, thanks. Everything else alright?"

"Yeah, fine. I just got back after three days straight of celebrating J.R.'s life. They know how to let it all hang out in Victoria."

"That's great, Dad. Hey, if you get a chance – watch the evening news. You may see someone you know," I said before hanging up. I didn't know what to think about the scribbles he talked about. Knowing my luck, they were probably just by some smart-arse kid scratching nineteenth-century obscenities in the margins.

"Who was that?" Ian asked.

"Just my Dad. Nothing serious for a change."

"Okay, so what's the plan for today?" Ian asked as the Chief served up three helpings of slightly cooled French Toast.

Before I could reply, the Chief cut in: "Did you grow up on your grandfather's farm?"

"Mostly, yeah. Why?"

"Powerful place. Can I go back there today?" the Chief asked.

"You certainly can," I said. "There's just one small favor I need to ask of you."

"Ask away, my son. I am forever grateful for you sharing that most magical place with me," the Chief replied.

"Okay. Well, you know how you've been complaining that no other media were interested in your story? Or in the tribe's story, I should say?"

The Chief nodded affirmatively.

"I think I've solved the problem," I said.

"Has he ever," Ian chimed in.

"How then?" asked the Chief

"If you wouldn't mind, I'll have Ian drive you out to where I first met you on the Old Indian Road. I'll then bring along a few reporters who are very eager to meet you."

"Are they ever," Ian chimed in again before the Chief quickly queried why the press would care now after he'd been trying to get their attention for years.

"I'll let them explain that, Chief. Once that's done – I'll drive you back to the farm."

"That would be most joyful. There is still so much for me – and you – to learn about that place's magic powers."

Ian and I exchanged blank stares. It was good to see that I was no longer alone in trying to keep up with the litany of bizarre events threatening to overtake any chance I ever envisioned of restoring some sort of 'order' to my chaotic daily grind. I cleared the table and checked the time. It was nearly 9.30 a.m. I took a quick look down Main Street from my front balcony. Despite the relatively early hour, there was not a vacant spot to be had along the town's main drag. There also seemed to be more people milling about than usual for this time of the morning. Or any other time for that matter in New Richmond. I thanked the Chief for breakfast and bade them goodbye while I had a quick shower and changed into some clean clothes. I never knew what to wear to special events like this. The only thing I did know is that it would still be quite chilly out there, even though the calendar had clicked over to April's initial day. April Fool's. How fricking appropriate.

I was in for another surprise though as I tried to make my way up Main Street. A police road block had been put up in the few minutes since I'd looked out my balcony window.

"Where you headed?" asked a young police officer.

"To '*The Record*', and I think you better let me through, because I'm the guy they're all here to see."

The policeman wasn't overly impressed with this answer, asking to see my driver's license which he grabbed out of my hand before retreating to his patrol car. He called someone – no doubt anyone who had been living in New Richmond for more than the past 10 minutes – and returned soon after and let me through. Apart from his dour visage, every other policeman that I passed grinned from ear to ear. I expect it was a similar look to the one preferred by executioners welcoming Louis #16 to the gallows, only they had the decency to cover their faces in black cloth. Merde!

It was absolutely bizarre how this usually quiet and unassuming thoroughfare now looked like Rio during Mardi Gras. There were cars and TV vans packed into every conceivable open space with hundreds of people of all shapes, ages and sizes darting to and fro as if it were a pedestrians-only, open-air mall. In spite of all the traffic, it was obvious that Ian had done a good job the night before alerting everyone to what sort of car I'd be driving. My humble yellow chariot had never received such looks from so many different people before. And if that wasn't enough – I swore a slow but steady cacophony of applause began resonating through the street as Flynn and I made our way, albeit slowly, along Main.

When I finally reached the front of the newspaper, I saw the Publisher and the Publisher-in-Waiting – waiting for me with one other person who I recognized from the TV – none other than MaryElena Rabinelle.

It was quite cold so I kept the motor running while I got out to introduce myself to Worcester's wild TV woman.

"Ms. Rabinelle, I presume. It's a pleasure to meet you," I said.

"At long last," she replied. "Is this the 'exclusive' you promised me?" she added pointing to all the other news teams ready to pounce.

"I'm afraid I had nothing to do with the media scrum. I did indeed mean only for you to come and meet 'The Chief'.

"We'd best be going then," she said. "I need to get back to Worcester by lunch time for another story."

"Walter?" said the boss.

"Yes, ma'am?"

"Do see that you take good care of Ms. Rabinelle."

"Absolutely," I replied to which her dutiful but dumb son Martin, nodded in agreement. I opened the door for my special guest and pushed Flynn into the back seat.

"And who might this be?" asked the reporter.

"My best friend and guardian – Flynn," I replied while getting into the driver's side and buckling up. All the other news crews likewise made for their vehicles.

"Great," she said rather unenthusiastically. "Make sure my sound and camera crew are behind us, eh?"

"I don't think they'll miss us," I replied knowing fully well there would be a conga line of vehicles piling up behind us.

It must have been a strange sight for anyone not involved in this media madness. It was difficult seeing more than a car length or two in front due to the sheer volume of people spilling out from the narrow sidewalks and from inbetween all the vans and other vehicles lining both sides of the street. Once I started moving, however, the townspeople parted as if they were playing the part of the Red Sea in the *Greatest Story Ever Told*, though I think that's stretching the Biblical analogy a wee tad. It was more likely they were all hoping beyond hope that I'd fall on my ass, thereby returning to the primordial slime pit with the rest of them.

"You've got quite a following," MaryElena said.

"Nah, it's just everyone likes a good lynch mob," I replied.

"So, does he really exist?" my not-so-grand inquisitor queried. I hadn't had much time to size her up, but first impressions went something like this. She was probably no more than three inches over five feet tall; had short curly dark hair surrounding a small, oval face punctuated by a long thin, ski jump of a nose. The one trait that stood out on this woman, however, was the eyes. They bulged out as if they were about 10 sizes too big for her struggling sockets, giving everything she gazed at a very, very serious stare. 'Intense' was one word you could use to describe her look. 'Mad as a cut snake' were a few more.

"You don't mess around, do you? Of course he exists," I replied. "We have a bit of a ride ahead of us. Can I offer you a beverage?" I added, grabbing a beer from behind the driver's seat.

"It's not even 10 in the morning," she replied.

"I know. It's really Bloody Mary hour, but it's hard to keep tomato juice fresh in the car. I can offer you a light beer. Just pour half the can out the window and voila."

Her stare became even more intense if that was possible following this last remark. It was an 'are you for real?' kind of stare.

"So what do friends call you – rabid?" I asked.

"Excuse me?" she said.

"You know – Rabid Rabinelle. Surely, some bright spark from the playground came up with that one?"

"No, you're the first, but that doesn't surprise me," she said.

"Yeah, well. If you haven't guessed already – I hold a black belt in tongue-fu."

"You hold a black belt in something," she replied.

"What do you mean by that? You think I'm some sort of idiot or worse based on what – a five-minute phone conversation with a drunken, derelict pisshead of an editor from Cincinnati?"

"Well, not really," she replied. "I guess from what I'd heard from various town officials and newspaper colleagues, I just expected you to be more, well, ordinary."

"Ordinary? Do I thank you for that one? Guess it beats 'first-class, second-rate reporter," I began. "The big question though is what do I get when you guys meet The Chief?"

"What do you mean, what do you 'get?'"

"For three days now you've all been implying that I've made this all up and that we're a bunch of third-rate podunks out heah."

"And?"

"And, well, for starters, when's the last time Worcester ever got mentioned with any phrase other than 'armpit of the earth?'"

"Hey, yeah, I know but a girl has to start somewhere. Besides, I'm already having interviews in Boston and Providence. I won't be in Worcester much longer."

"That's the spirit," I returned. "Me, I decided to take a different sort of career path."

"Oh?"

"I figured I'd work for the bigger papers first. Once I'd seen all they could offer, then and only then could I come back to this town – the town of my childhood dreams and nightmares."

She didn't know quite what to make of that reply. "I think I'll have that light beer," she said as a broad grin lit up her face. "You are something," she added.

"Just an extraordinarily ordinary guy. That's me," I said.

"Can you tell if my crew is still behind us?" she said turning to try and look out the now completely fogged-up back window to see if her camera crew was following.

"Don't worry. They're there – along with every other film crew within 500 miles of here," I replied.

We were nearing the turn onto the Murderer's Row of millionaires' estates when I saw Ian driving toward us from the opposite direction. He gave me a big toot and I did likewise.

"Another fan?" she asked.

"Just one of the perks of being an oversized fish in a guppy pool," I replied. "There's one more person we need to pick up before reaching our final destination."

"Anyone I might know?" she asked.

"I doubt it but she is a very important person in these parts," I said. I didn't have to say any more as the Lady Mayor was now visible to anyone – even to astronauts from the moon – judging by the bright red overcoat she had on. Hopefully, there were other garments underneath, but then again, that could make for an interesting journey if she was starkers.

"Mayor Morgan is joining us?" MaryElena asked.

"You know her?"

"Well, sort of. Tell me, is she on the level with this new project she's planning?"

"Ahh, which project is that?"

"Oh shit, she is! She hasn't even told you! Please don't say anything to her. She'll kill me."

"My lips are sealed. Besides, with only one ear, I only hear half of what anyone says."

"What?" my passenger asked.

"That's my line," I said turning my head so she could behold the one-eared monster behind the steering wheel.

"Oh, I'm so—"

"No need to be sorry, Ms. Rabinelle. Not your fault," I said. "But anything else you'd care to share with me regarding just what the good lady mayoress has shared with you, would be appreciated."

"I'm sorry, I can't help you there," she replied.

"Come, come, no need to hide behind 'confidential sources'. There are very few secrets in this town and sooner or later, it's all going to spill out." I was bluffing but hoped like hell she didn't know that. It did make me all the more keen to find out just what the heck was going on. And why oh why, the Publisher and the Mayor were so keen to make sure that the human cesspool known as New Richmond, smelled as sweet as a shit hole could.

The Mayor was waving her hand madly at us as we slowed to pull in off the road and onto her grand driveway. I jumped out of the car and opened the rear door behind MaryElena. It was hard to know whether the look of surprise on her face had more to do with almost being clipped by a run-down Toyota, or the realization of who else was in the car with me or the procession of other vehicles piling up behind us – or all three.

"My good lady, your golden chariot awaits," I said.

"Good morning, Walter. Hello again, Ms. Rabinelle and whatever this creature is sitting next to me," said Mrs. Morgan, using her small black handbag as a shield to keep Flynn off of her.

"Morning, Aunt Stacey," I replied jumping back into the driver's seat. "Don't mind Flynn. She only bites if you're wearing cheap perfume." I could see that even MaryElena liked that one.

"Hello, Mrs. Morgan. I didn't know you and Walter were related?" MaryElena asked.

"We're not, dear girl. I believe Mr. Johnson is just up to one of his schoolboy pranks."

"I love it when you talk dirty, Aunt Stacey," I began. "Besides, remember what you told me the other night when we—"

"So, Walter, just where are we going?" asked the Mayor trying like heck to change the subject.

"You'll see soon enough. I don't want to spoil the surprise," I replied.

"But I had just assumed—"

"Don't ever assume, ma'am," I said cutting in." Because when you assume something, you make an ass out of you."

"And me," MaryElena cut in, obviously getting the joke – again.

"Walter, dear. Just what is going on and why are all these cars following us?" the Mayor asked.

"All part of the plan. It's my way of giving just a little back to the town that has done so fucking much for me. Help yourself to a brewski," I added.

We were turning onto Thunder Road. In addition to delivering the Chief to his outdoor office, I had also asked Ian to collect one more person who would guarantee that this event would become an even bigger spectacle than anyone could hope for.

As I pulled up in front of the makeshift tepee, however, neither party was in view. There was still a bit of snow piled up along the roadside which made it difficult for either lady to get out. I ended up helping MaryElena get out from the driver's side while Flynn tugged gamely at the Lady Mayor's designer coat to coax her out.

"Walter! Walter! Get this mutt off of me!"

"Now that's no way to talk about my trusted companion. Say 'please' and I'll see what I can do," I said as MaryElena's camera crew, followed closely by several others, descended on the tepee.

What happened next was well, sheer magic – or madness depending on your point of view. Just as the news crews got up to the tepee's front flap, a very disoriented-looking Chief shuffled out from the back of a neighboring oak tree. He obviously had forgotten to put in his hearing aid and was busy trying to get his wrinkled manhood back into the hanger when the camera lights hit him. It was at this precise moment that my other surprise guest – none other than Sonny Liston's ex-sparring partner – Milt Walker – jumped out from the tepee and began throwing punches at any and all before him. I hadn't counted on his ferocity, though later he blamed his brain fade on all the cameras and lights flashing him back to his last-ever public appearance in the ring. Flynn the Wonder Dog also joined in, giving the scene more action and pathos than a cavalcade of John Ford westerns.

Mrs. Morgan somehow managed to get hold of the Chief and very deftly upped his zipper and fixed his headdress all in one motion. It was quite a feat given the number of bodies and pieces of equipment flying through the air.

Needless to say, we led every news bulletin along the eastern seaboard that night. Few news bulletins even mentioned the reason for the story in the first place, which was typical, since no self-disrespecting TV news reporter liked owning up to a mistake. They all pretty much covered the event as a piece of bizarre street theatre, complete with renegade Indian, punch-drunk prize fighter and a wild dog. At least no one was going to forget New Richmond in a hurry.

MaryElena did get her exclusive, though. The only way I could make sure she got the Chief alone for a couple of minutes was to tell the Mayor they were all interested to hear what the next Governor of Massachusetts had to say about herself. To get their attention she used Milt Walker as a battering ram to one of the TV vans whereupon Milt hoisted her up onto the roof in one big sweeping motion. She kicked off one high heel and grabbed the other one in her hand and banged it on the side of the van to grab their attention. It didn't hurt that once she took her three-quarter length evening coat off, she had on a very tight dress that began and ended somewhere about her navel. It was festooned with brown and black spots like the ones you'd see on a cheetah or some other big cat. So while she delighted the gathered media with god-knows-what, MaryElena quickly quizzed the Chief on his recent whereabouts and once satisfied, turned toward the camera and closed with:

'Was there ever any doubt that this aged warrior – the so-called 'Last of the Menashocutts' didn't exist? From Chief Bear Claw's last stand hide-out on the shores of the not so great lake in New Richmond, Massachusetts – I'm MaryElena Rabinelle for Channel 9 *Action News*'."

Chapter Thirty Two

How could I have been so bold as to think I knew anything? Now that I'm older though no wiser, I realise my words ring hollow, worthless. I regret ever having taken up the quill and shall spend the rest of my days seeking inspiration from some greater Divine being.

These were the most insightful words that Thomas Jason Marsden ever wrote – and unfortunately, no one, or at least very few, ever got the chance to behold. These were taken from the first set of 'scribbles' as my father so eloquently called them, on the inside cover of his non-seminal work on the history of New Richmond. Marsden's self-critique continued:

It is with much regret that I did not find the likes of St. Thomas Aquinas – Christianity's greatest orator – sooner. How deftly he takes on any and all comers from Plato to Buddha! He wrote more than 40 books and several beautiful hymns during his long life and yet, as the final curtain drew nearer, he no longer had the will to write. It wasn't as if he couldn't. He just wouldn't. It seems he'd had a vision of Heaven and decided that compared to the great glory of God, 'my work seems like straw after what I have seen'.

Though I vow not to publish again, I shall spend the rest of my infernal days in attempting to right some of the many wrongs that were passed off as the 'truth' in this pathetic tome of mine. I do this not for me but for thee…

How the frack does anyone top this? And even worse, the world never, ever got to read these pearls from the insipid pen of Thomas Jason Marsden. I don't even know if we ever find out who the 'thee' was. No matter. These scribbles were his '*Moby Dick*' and then some, but he died believing he had nothing left to offer. How pathetically sad. How did that make me feel? Who was I to write the sort of drivel I dished up on a daily basis for the rag of all rags – '*The Record*'? To make matters worse, I was being lauded and applauded. I even got a job offer from another paper in Massachusetts – '*The Worcester Telegram*', which would no doubt make my ol' flame from Channel 9, Rabid Rabinelle happy! No, it was all enough to make a man think about other ways to go – job-wise, that is.

Thankfully, the James Gang were leaving me alone after the Chief's Coming Out party. To be honest, I don't think they even thought the Chief existed there was so much negative press flying around. Hell, I even started to have doubts. I stuck to the newsroom as much as possible, mostly because I was positively embarrassed to go out and have people, mostly strangers, coming up and shaking my hand, slapping me on the back and treating me like some A-List Celeb. And there was T.J. Marsden coming to the end of a lacklustre writing career and finally seeing the light and not having either the will or the desire to share it with anyone.

I didn't have long to sit around feeling sorry for myself, though. That same afternoon, the Publisher called me into her office to ask me to write the lead story for the upcoming 'Foundation Day' celebrations. That wasn't going to be too difficult. This year marked the 300th anniversary of the establishment of New Richmond or as it was first called – New Richmond Plantation, way back in 1679. The date was April 15, which had become known for many things over the years – the day Income Taxes are due; the day President Lincoln died; and the night a huge chunk of ice gouged a hole in the hull of the Titanic spoiling its maiden voyage across the Atlantic. While nowhere as grand a day on the celebratory calendar as the 4th of July or Thanksgiving, the locals did relish in celebrating some of the town's finer moments, though trying to come up with any at present was next to impossible. Newcomers like my Lincoln Apartment neighbor Ian Ross, got more out of it than many locals. He said there were some really great bars and restaurants opening up along the waterfront, as well as attempts by local authorities to save many older buildings from destruction. He said it reminded him of a larger version of Deerfield, a tiny town to our northeast, in which houses, many of which dated back to the 18th century, stood out like beacons of an earlier, prouder age in American history. Deerfield was basically early New England's answer to a wild west frontier town, consisting of one street with buildings carved out along both sides and little else. It was there that early settlers huddled together from the cold and sometimes from even frostier feelings harbored by Native American Indians working in collaboration with bands of feisty Frenchmen. Ian said that New Richmond gave him a similar feeling though I never quite got that same sentiment. Everything and everyone in New Richmond just seemed to be either old or out of it.

When I wasn't in the newsroom I hurried home to read the next installment in Mr. Marsden's margins. Because they were scribbled, sometimes rather quickly and other times along such rough surfaces, 'reading' his copy wasn't exactly the right word. It sometimes felt more like deciphering the Rosetta Stone or Dead Sea Scrolls. I know the secrets of New Richmond couldn't hold a candle to either one of those great works, but truth be told – as in the Eternal variety – knows no boundaries. The whole truth and nothing but is solid gold in any miner's mind.

That is, except for tonight. I knew if I didn't take Jenny out for dinner, our official first date, I wouldn't get another chance for some time, as I was heading off again in the morning to close up Uncle J.R.'s stone boat, check in on my Dad and granddad and drop by Boston to find out more about the Winslow clan. I didn't think she'd accept my excuse that I'd rather be home, curled up reading a book than courting her, though my heart ached for the former. Maybe she'll have to leave early to take care of Howie or maybe she'll get food poisoning? Hey, I can dream, right?

I took Ian's advice and booked a table at the only restaurant in town that was the least likely to serve up any helpings of food poisoning. I booked us a table at the newly-renovated New Olde Richmonde Inne. It had been in the same spot since the 18th century and served several purposes, though rarely as an eatery. It had been an early stockade, hold-up for the local constabulary, even an early hospital before becoming a flophouse for most of the current century. That is, until someone saw beneath the 100 years' worth of grime and tears and saw the pearl that lay underneath, waiting to be exposed to the sunlight. That someone turned out to be Thornton 'Smoky' Burgess, the Chief Executive of the worst excuse of a living museum in all museumdom – Olde Richmond Plantation. Coincidentally, Burgess was also dining this night at the Inne and practically ran over to shake my hand even before I got to the table. 'Ran' was perhaps a bit of a stretch. Prancing over like some great, two-legged hippo was probably more apt. At first, I couldn't tell whether he was coming over to hit me, following on from the venom with which he greeted my recent article on ORP. But no, he was now just like everyone else in my world – seeking an audience with THE GREAT ONE.

Jenny was impressed with the star treatment, but it was all starting to bug the crap out of me. Still, I went along with the flow. May be my mate Lou was right. He told me recently that I was so used to being in shit that I didn't know how to handle acts of kindness – especially acts of kindness from complete strangers.

"It's so good to see you, Walter," gushed mein host before continuing. "May I call you Walter?"

"Walt's fine, so long as I can call you 'Smoky'," I replied. For those not familiar with baseball, Forrest 'Smoky' Burgess was a rather rotund player who started his career as a catcher with the Cubs in the early 1950s before becoming a bit of a National League journeyman prior to ending up back in the Windy City with the White Sox. What he lacked in speed, the Smoksta made up with a great eye and even quicker bat speed – qualities I was sure that Thornton B. lacked. I also had to smile at somebody up there, because I know ol' J.R. must have been laughing his fool head off from whatever height or depth he was watching over/under me from. Due to Smoky's, the baseball model's that is, rather couch-potato-like stature, he, along with the Bambino himself, were probably J.R's two favourite players. "It's not the shape of the man's figure that makes a good baseball player. It's the way he figures how to hit the shape right off the horsehide!" J.R. used to say when watching Smoky come cold off the bench late in a game and take his customary one at bat and more times than not – smack a ball hurtling at him at 100+ miles an hour and send it back with interest, either right up the middle or wrap it around the right field foul pole.

My temporary mind drift was re-directed quite suddenly with an almighty slap on the shoulder from the other 'Smoky' that rattled the fillings inside my head and those of anyone else within 10 miles of the table.

"I won't keep you and your date long, Walt. I just wanted to say how happy we are for you and how proud you make us all feel."

I was tempted to ask why I made them feel so fucking proud, but opted against it and just shrugged my shoulders, mostly in a vain attempt to get the circulation moving again.

"I understand you're going to be working on the main piece for the 'Foundation Day' celebration and to that end, we would dearly love to have you come by ORP and let me show you what's new and exciting," Smoky said.

"I'll have my people call your people," I replied.

"Again with the jokes," Burgess says turning toward Jenny. "He's a regular comedian. I also wondered if you could introduce me to The Chief, because I'd dearly love to have his input on how we can get the local tribes more involved."

"Happy to help," I replied hoping beyond hope that that was the end of it.

"Oh, and just one more thing."

"Yep."

"Well, we've been working hard to save as many of the old buildings like 'The Inne' as we can, but well, we aren't getting a lot of support from across the road," he said, referring to the Mayor's Mansion.

"Oh?"

"We know how well you and Mrs. Morgan get on. I was just wondering if you could put in a good word for us?"

Ka-CHING. The pay back cash register was ringing up big time now. So much for the free meal. In fact, worse was yet to come, but at least for now, Jenny and I were more or less alone, if you don't count the freaky-looking six-year-old twins seated at the booth behind us. They were both cross-eyed which made them doubly scary looking, even for a freak like me. Their parents obviously had no problem with them standing up on the padded seats and making faces at total strangers in the next booth.

"So, Jenny can't say I don't know how to treat a lady."

"Walter, you are so sweet to take time out to see me. I know you're busy and obviously quite famous!"

"Who – me? Nah, they're all just a bit loopy. It must be the weather. I mean, we've all had enough of winter, right?" Though we'd been together on this 'first' date for nearly 20 minutes, I hadn't had time to appreciate the vision that now sat before me. Jenny seemed more at home in blue jeans and a sweatshirt and little make-up. Tonight, though, she was showing everything off and why not? She was wearing a low-cut number, not quite the sort preferred by the gals from *Dynasty* or *Dallas*, but not far off. And when combined with her long, dark brown hair flowing in a Farah Fawcett-inspired, fly-away style hairdo, it wasn't too unkind to say that she was far and away the best looking lady in the house. Any house within 1,000 square miles I would have thought. And here I was thinking about passing this evening up and spending it all by my lonesome with a dusty old book.

"Was he right when he said you're writing the main story on 'Foundation Day?' It's going to be real big this year, isn't it?" Jenny asked.

"So I've been told. But really, it's not all that big a deal. What's 300 years when you compare it to Europe or Asia? We're just babes in the woods. In fact, we're still babes in the woods," I said. Gawd, was I nervous. Where was St. Vartan when I needed him for a line – any line would do about now. "Jen, I just want to say how gorgeous you look tonight and how speci-"

My all-too-awkward attempt to tell my dining companion how damn lucky I was to be in her company was rudely interrupted by my over-zealous host for the evening – again. He was simply informing us that we would not need any menus because he would serve us the specialities of the house.

I wasn't sure how to respond to this invitation, but thanked him kindly while grabbing the next waiter I could and ordering the most expensive wine in the house.

I should have guessed something about the type of menu that the restaurant would feature given that the waiters and waitresses looked like refugees from ORP. Christ, I hoped the food was fresher than 200 years old.

The first course was a thick pea soup, 'good for sticking to the ribs', said the witty waiter. He was right though the ribs weren't the only place the mushy stuff stuck to. I was stuck with the taste for days after the event. From there, we feasted on a greasy duck l'orange pour deux, along with mashed potatoes, mushy peas, corn and coleslaw. The meal was washed down with copious glasses of the house's finest white and red wines, served separately as far as I could remember. I don't remember dessert – only that it included some sort of melange of supposedly fresh fruit, rock hard ice cream and hot chocolate. I'm guessing that this menu would not have looked out of place in any soup kitchen along the East Coast. It was that tasty.

The only good thing about the evening was that there were no problems getting worried about lulls in the conversation, since we were rarely left alone. If it wasn't Smoky popping by for one thing or another, along with enough waiters and waitresses to handle a Presidential reception. Jenny didn't seem to mind the attention. I was glad one of us didn't.

After about two hours, the owner invited us for a cook's tour of the restaurant and their future expansion plans, once the lakeside development kicked in. I had no idea of what he was talking about, but gave him one of those looks that people do when they're trying to convince you they know what the hell you're talking about. Again, it was clear that even though no money exchanged hands, I was definitely getting the short end of the stick when it came to value for the evening.

This tour did open my eyes to a different part of New Richmond I'd never appreciated before. I know it was early days and that while the menu at The Inne was not going to threaten many junior high school

Home Ec classes, it did have a certain je ne sais quoi about it. And when I figure out just what 'sais quoi' means, I'll let you know.

Jenny and I spent the rest of the evening strolling along a newly-laid boardwalk that eventually will run from the western end of the town's lakeside frontage, just one building away from The Olde New Richmonde Inne, to the town's other end. It was a distance that totalled about half a mile, but for now finished abruptly just beyond The Inne's front steps. My stomach was making more noise than the waves lapping up on the shore with all the cheap wine and pea soup swishing around inside. Trying not to think about the waves of illness welling up inside of me, I tried to focus on Jenny and see how she was faring.

"Thank you for a lovely evening, Walter," she said.

"My pleasure."

"Would you mind if I called it an evening, though?"

"Are you okay, Jenny? Is it something I said?"

"No silly. No, not at all. I just need to pick up Howie from my Mom's and get to work a bit early tomorrow. Do you mind?"

"I do. I really do. I had big, big plans for you tonight, little lady," I said grabbing her around the waist and pulling her close.

"Did you now?" she replied, pulling away ever so slightly, I hoped not out of fear or concern.

"No, I understand. I just wanted to say how much I have missed you, though."

"I don't believe that, Walter. You're so famous. What do I have to offer?"

"Plenty, Jen. Plenty," I replied pulling her close again. This time she didn't pull away.

"Walter, you do know how I feel about you?"

"Good, I hope? Because I think I—"

"Shush," she said putting her finger to my lips. "There is something I did want to talk to you about though before I go."

Ugh oh.

"It's nothing serious – I mean, I don't think it is."

"Hey, I didn't like the pea soup either, but if you have some crackers when you get home, it should soak it up," I offered.

She laughed and said that wasn't it. "It's about your granddad and the Chief."

"Oh, you mean Crutch Cassidy and the Sunburnt Geezer."

"I think you need to go out there tomorrow."

"Why?"

"Well, The Chief has a lot of good qualities," Jenny began. "He's cleaning up the place a lot better than I ever had and he's good company for your granddad, but I think he's found one of those bills we've spoken about and got your granddad all worried about being thrown out of his own house."

"Oh, shit," I replied. "Yeah, thanks. I'll stop by there tomorrow before heading to Connecticut." Just one more forest fire to put out.

"Oh, yeah, just more thing," she said pulling my face down to hers and planting her moist lips on mine.

"Yes," I purred. "Anything."

"I think I know what's going on – or what someone's planning to do to the town," she said.

"Oh really? Blow it up, I hope," I said biting her lovely lower lip softly and as deftly as a totally drunken asshole could.

"No, it's worse than that, but it's only rumors so maybe I shouldn't say anything."

"You're kidding me, right? Of course you should tell me. I'm the fricking press for Christ sakes!"

"I better run, Walt. Maybe I"ll tell you tomorrow. It's probably not important – or not true, anyway," she said pulling away from me and heading to her car.

I wasn't sure what hurt more. Her pulling away or not telling me about the latest rumor. Try as I might though, she wouldn't spill. She got into her car, blew me a kiss and headed off into the night. It was only about 10.30 p.m., but somehow I felt as though my night was just beginning. I thought about heading back to the paper and waiting for Ian and Lou to finish so we could go out and put away a case or four of beers at the bar.

My evening took a sudden turn for the worse, however, when some idiot bore down on me with his high beams shining right into my eyes. "I've been looking all over for you," came a voice that sounded vaguely familiar from somewhere inside the dark vehicle before me.

"Aunt Stacey – what are you doing out here at this hour? Shouldn't you be planning how to re-decorate the Governor's Mansion or at least re-decorating the Governor?"

"Funny boy. Get in the car, Walter. It's time you and I had a chat. There's sooooo many things that we need to talk about," she said, slurring every other syllable.

Oh shit. Oh shit, indeed.

Chapter Thirty Three

"I'm glad to see you at least like women – even if you don't like more mature, experienced ones," she said with just a hint – make that a sledgehammer's worth of disdain - in her drunken voice.

"Yeah, well, call me old fashioned, but I prefer women who are unattached. You'd be my first choice if you weren't happily married," I said.

"Fuck you, Walter. I'll give you happily married," said the Mayor in a voice only Cruella de Vil of *101 Dalmatians* fame could rival – perhaps. She then told the driver, a young black man, to drive back to City Hall.

"What happened to your regular driver? Picked up for drunk driving?"

"Yes, as a matter of fact. Want a job? I pay my staff really well and am very generous with other fringe benefits," she said now adopting her far more natural Darwinian position as predator to prey.

"I don't think I could keep up with your demanding schedule," I said.

"I'm sure you couldn't, but we could give it a try, anyway," purred the lion to the three-legged lamb.

When I didn't bite, her mood shifted another gear. To a side of her that I knew must exist, but had never presented itself before. "No mucking around tonight, Walter. I need to discuss a few very important matters with you, which I'm sure you'll find interesting and enlightening," she said with nary a hint of drunkenness. That got me very worried about what might – or might not - be coming my way. I grabbed a bottle of whiskey from the small bar shelf to my left and took a generous swig. She never said a word. Not one. She didn't have to. She just smiled the smile of a satisfied Black Widow who had just applied the finishing touches on a perfect web. Before I knew it, our long, black chariot had pulled up in front of the darkened City Hall building.

"Glad to see you're doing your bit for the environment. Not a fucking light on in sight," I said.

"Don't worry, Walter. I won't let you bump into anything you don't want to," said the Mayoress.

"Can I get that in writing?" I asked, grabbing the whiskey bottle and jumping out of the car while my hostess leaned forward and told the driver to come back in an hour.

"Where do you park a boat like that?" I said as the limo pulled away from the curb.

"Anywhere I want, Walter. Now just stay here until I get the front door open," said the Mayoress carefully taking off her hopelessly high heels and walking barefoot up the front steps of the three-story stone building.

"Okay, Mom," I replied.

"Don't start, Walter. Don't start," she replied without looking back as she opened a small metal box next to the left-hand side of the building's two massive wooden front doors. I took a big swig from the whiskey bottle at the same moment that a light that would not have looked amiss at Fenway Park lit up the front of the building.

"C'mon inside, Walter. We haven't got all night," she said.

"I bet that's not the first time you've used that line – tonight," I replied racing up the steps as fast as I could just in case anyone who might know Jenny saw me with this middle-aged nympho.

The last time I'd been inside this building, Ike was President. It had been part of some Sixth Grade Civics teacher's great idea to bring 'Government to Life'. Great in theory but not so grand in practice as the only idiots dumb enough to take up elected positions were locally-inbred men whose only benefits were those doled out by Social (in)Security.

"Pour us a couple of whiskeys, would you Walter? I just want to freshen up and then get down to business."

That sounded ominous. "No problem, chief," I replied.

Her office was bigger than my apartment, complete with huge leather sofa in one corner, (which I carefully avoided so as not to give her the impression that I'd be an easy lay), and a desk that contained enough wood to build Noah's Ark. There also was a large table in the other corner near her private toilet that was covered in canvas. I went over and removed the canvas only to find a replica of the town, complete with a kidney-shaped piece of rubber painted blue supposedly representing the Not-so-Great Lake, I surmised. On top of this intriguing patch of blue was some sort of vessel with the name 'Inkota Princess' emblazoned on it. Was this the part of her Grand Master (or was that Mistress) Plan for New Richmond? I heard the toilet flush and her hand hit the doorknob. I was too slow to get the sheet back over the display.

"I should've known you'd help yourself. That's what I like about you, Walter. You see something you like and you go for it," said the Mayoress rubbing up close to me while grabbing the whiskey out of my hand and not spilling a drop. Quite a feat.

"What can I say? Just a natural-born thriller. That's me," I replied, downing my own drink in one gulp. "What the hell is this, anyway?"

"I'll get to that later. I first wanted to talk to you about the work you've been doing for this town."

"Work? What work?"

"Mr. Modest. Why, the stories about the Chief and getting us all that exposure," she said.

"You think I planned that media feeding frenzy with the Chief to get New Richmond a place on the map? The only person getting significant exposure out of that mess besides Milt Walker was your good self. When are you going to announce your run for the Governorship?"

"Who, me? I don't think so, Walter. I have much bigger plans in mind and I want you to share in the vision."

Ugh-oh. This was starting to get scary now. I decided to change tack. "Say, earlier tonight I caught up with ol' Smoky Burgess who said he was hoping I could talk you into getting his group more support for saving the older buildings around town."

"Stupid old fool! Where's the vision in that plan? I ask you – do you want us to just hold on to the past and give people more of the same old look or do you want something new and exciting that gets people wet just thinking about it?" said the Lady Mayor who knew a thing or three about wetness.

"Is this a multiple choice quiz?" I asked.

"Seriously, Walter. We have to stop looking back and start planning for the future. And our future is not in this town's inglorious past."

"But didn't you support the unveiling of that statue of Thomas J. Marsden a few months back?"

"Yeah, yeah, but that's different. He was at least something of a celebrity if only in the hearts and minds of New Richmond. But I don't think we should simply prop up the old architecture. I believe we should tear it all down and start again."

"What? Are you serious?"

"Totally."

"And who else is behind this brave new vision?"

All of a sudden – the Mayor's mood shifted. I sensed she'd spilled more than she was supposed to. And her next question proved it. "How's your grandfather holding up?"

"It's funny you ask, because not so well. I still don't understand how he got into such a mess, but I'm heading over their tomorrow to see what I can do."

"For Christ's sake, Walter. It's no big deal. We all fall behind from time to time. I'll give you the $23,000 to make it go away."

"To make all what go away?" I asked. And how did she know the exact amount required to pay off the tax man?

"Let's have another drink," she quickly said, changing the subject yet again. My head was spinning trying to keep up with the ever-changing direction of the conversation. One of us was crazy and it wasn't me. At least I hoped not. I didn't remember much more about that evening. I had a couple more whiskeys and remember falling toward her shit-house replica of New Richmond.

∾

The next thing I knew there was a knock at the door. I raised myself slowly from the couch – my couch! I had gotten back to the apartment somehow. "Coming," I said to whoever was there, hoping it wouldn't be the local constabulary again trying to break into my neighbor's digs.

"Walter? Are you alright?" Jenny said, leaning over and giving me a peck on the cheek.

"I am now," I replied.

"Walter, I just had to stop by before going to work. I just wanted to thank you again for last night and to tell you how great it was."

"It was good, wasn't it?" I said, returning the hug. A guy could get used to this sort of treatment – that is, until I heard the sound of another familiar voice coming from the bedroom.

"Walter, is that my driver? Be a dear and tell him I'll be right out," said Mrs. Morgan. The evening's ending was starting to come back to me and it wasn't looking good.

"Walter, how could you?" Jenny said pulling away from me as if I was covered in killer bees. "You bastard. I, I thought you were different. Truly different. How could you? How could you?" she repeated before running toward the stairwell as fast as her shapely legs could take her.

"Jenny, wait! It's not what you think!" Too late. She was gone.

"Oh, Walter. Was that the lovely girl I saw you with last night?" asked the Mayor entering the room with her matching black panties and bra on and little else. "I do hope she didn't get the wrong idea, though judging by the way she left, it would seem she did," said the cat which had just swallowed every fucking mouse in the tri-state area.

Me and women were becoming something of a multi-fractured fairy tale – at least as far as the sexual stakes were concerned. The one woman I truly wanted to make love to now looked like entering the realms of Never-Never Land while the only other woman, (discounting that horrendous night in New London with Ann Margret's toothless, evil and obese twin), I'd apparently bedded, more closely resembled the Wicked Bitch of the West. Perhaps even more disconcerting, however, was the fact that I couldn't remember a single instant of either of those sessions while I was still trying like mad to rub out any memory of the hugely forgettable foray in New London. I certainly had a way – as in 'way off' – with the ladies.

As disconcerting as my lack of luck seemed to be in the lovemaking stakes, it more or less seemed to reflect every other aspect of my miserable existence. Talk about lack of control over one's destiny. I had nada control over anything. I had no say; no voice in my own life. Forget about the feminine side of the equation in which I was being screwed, or more to the point unscrewed, my day-to-day existence was being destroyed by a 1,000-year-old failed Near Eastern warrior and by a century-old wannabe Native American worrier warrior. My thoughts and visions were so clouded by all this hocus-pocus that I couldn't even focus on a rare and beautiful vision (cue Jenny Lawton), even when she was served up to me on a silver platter.

And so, like any great fallen hero, I did the next best thing. I gathered up provisions and my faithful, four-legged sidekick, saddled up my trusty, rusty steed and set sail into gawd only knows how many more unnatural disasters – each one more intimately connected to my very own make-up than I dared to imagine. It was all spinning way out of control as if even the very bits of spit, blood and sinew that had congealed to form me were now nearing meltdown. Either that or I was the first known case of dyslexic NDA, er, DNA.

Chapter Thirty Four

I did try, albeit unsuccessfully, to reach Jenny later that morning, but gave up after getting her answer phone recording. Even that sounded angry so I had a quick word with my neighbor Ian who said it was time for me, Lou and him to have a 'real piss up'. That sounded awkward, but he assured me I wouldn't regret it, before setting out for Chez Bedrosian in Richmond Heights. For one of the few times in my life, I didn't enjoy getting drunk. Company and conversation were great. Drinks were cold and delivered with production line precision. The problem was I couldn't stop thinking about a lot of things, ranging from Marsden's intimate marginal notes, which had ignited my interest in local lore, to J.R's untimely death, that fuelled my longer-since flagging interest in the Winslow clan's part in my confusing genetic code.

Though it would be some time tomorrow before I ended up in Boston to learn more about this particular pilgrim's progress, I did take time out to brush up on the Mayflower at the local library. I can't take all the credit for this effort, though. Dear ol' St. Vartan paid one of his early morning visits, (didn't this guy ever sleep?), and proceeded to lay the following riddle on me: SEEK AND YE SHALL FIND. FIND AND YE SHALL NO LONGER NEED TO SEEK.

Like most of his ditties, this latest one left me no wiser. I made a mental note to ask the Chief if he knew any ancient Armenian dialects. He seemed to have a handle on practically everything else, including my granddad's farm.

I also kept thinking about the name of that tiny ship that the Mayor had on her miniature-sized model of New Richmond – 'Inkota Princess'. I knew that I'd seen that word 'Inkota' before and rang Mason James to see if he could track it down. I told him it involved some madcap conspiracy to take over the tri-state area which was all he needed to hear to investigate further. I also thought I could run it by the Chief if I didn't strangle him first for upsetting my grandfather. Just one more loose end in my life that was now more loose than doubling over due to a double dose of diarrhoea – doubled.

About the only thing I did know as I set sail that morning, was that for once in my life, I was not the most unprepared person in all of recorded history. No, that honor would have to go to – Drum Roll, Palease – Taa-DAAAAA!!!!! – the 102 poor sods who risked life and limb aboard a leaky raft in 1620 to start a new life in the not-so-New World. These guys (and gals), must have thought they were being transported to some ready-made 17th century English suburb. They brought no livestock, knew beans about farming, even less about forestry, carpentry, hunting and other basic survival skills. It was as if they had set sail for a three-hour tour rather than for a largely unknown vast continent on the other side of the then-not-so-known world. Why else would the ship's manifest have mentioned such ill-suited professions as tailors, shopkeepers and hatters (not to mention my own relative who made his living from smudging type on papyrus)? They even poked fun at their fearless military man – Miles Standish – who his colleagues referred to as 'Captain Shrimpe'. No, bon amie wasn't big on the menu among these early unsettled settlers. So, with few provisions and little idea of how to bring down wild game, just how did this bunch of ill-prepared misfits figure on making it in the New World?

My memories of times gone by were quickly fast forwarded to the ever present as I pulled up to the front of my granddad's farmhouse door. Everything looked pretty much SOP. Chickens who'd long since flown the coop were scratching all over the front porch; cows were coming and going – and going again – and again – wherever and whenever they pleased; and perhaps best of all – was the sight of grandpapa's favourite beast of burden – a massive ram with an even bigger set of horns and ego to match – calmly banging his head into the front door. Orwell's 'Animal Farm' had nothing on this place. I deftly ducked and weaved around the cow patties while keeping eye contact on the damn ram's derriere. I'd learned long ago there were many lessons to be learned on the farm, the most critical being to never lose sight of the damn ram. Better he sharpen his perpetually-scabbed forehead on wood, rather than on my own foreskin. I simply went around to the back door where my grandfather was busily arguing with something or someone.

"Yoo, hoo, granddad, it's me, Walt."

"Go away!" he replied, perhaps to me; perhaps not.

"No, really. It's me," I said.

"No talk now. I lose farm," he said.

"No, you no lose farm," I said mimicking his own dyslexic English brogue. "I promise. Where's the Chief?"

Before he could reply, I could hear Flynn barking in the distance. "Be right back, granddad," I said running out the back fearing that Flynn had run into the unruly ram- or worse.

"What is it, Flynn?"

And there, coming out of the dense undergrowth behind the house, was none other than the Last of the Menashocutts – Ol' Chief Bear Claw himself.

"Hello, Chief. Long time no see," I said.

"Powerful place, this. Powerful place," he said.

"Yes, so you've already told me. But it won't be if you keep scaring my grandfather with bad news – capice?"

"You don't' get it, do you?" the Chief said.

"Get what?"

"Are you not hearing the voices? Or should I say The Voice?"

I knew not how to reply to his query. How did he know about St. Vartan? He couldn't, could he?

"Have you not yet seen the light? Have you not yet figured it out? We are all here – right here – for a reason, my son."

"Okay, let's get one thing straight, Chief. I'm not your son. We're not related in any way or shape," I said.

A wry smile came over the Chief's face. "You are so sure of this, my son? You are so sure?"

"I'll tell you what I'm sure of," I said turning to make sure my grandfather was out of ear shot. "You mention to him one more time about the back taxes and I'll knock you clear back to Thursday even if it's only Tuesday – got it?"

"I understand, but do you?"

"Hey, Chief. Let's cut the crap. You're not even a real chief. Before last week, the last time I saw you, you were just plain Larry Kennedy – Richmond Heights Junior High School Janitor. Now, you're the last tribal leader of a well and truly pitiful band of miscreants who haven't got enough members to make up a basketball team."

"Strength does not rely on numbers for one is the most powerful number of them all," said the sage-old Sachem.

"Cute. Really cute, but I've had enough of the witty ditties and vaguely sage sayings. I don't mind you staying here until you find something better, but just leave my granddad out of this – okay?"

"I cannot, my son. It is beyond my control; his control; your control. Do you not yet see? Have you not been listening?"

"To what? And to whom?"

"You must figure this out for yourself, my son. And I pray it comes soon. You must find The Way. The Way of the Inkota," he said while turning to walk away.

"Whoa, Chief – come back here! Did you just say 'Inkota?' Tell me you just said Inko—"

Any discovery of just what 'Inkota' meant quickly became secondary as all of my senses, particularly those handling pain, went into overdrive having just received the full force of the damn ram's wham bam, no thank you ma'am. I landed about 10 feet from where I'd been standing with my face pressed hard into the dirt. I remembered little else before passing out – even an attempt by St. Vartan to reach me – went blank. I was off the air. Over and out.

I was having an inner out of body experience, if that makes sense. Or perhaps no sense as the case may be. Strangely enough, though, just before coming to, and I daresay this feeling must have come and gone in less time than it takes to blink – I understood everything. It was all clear. Everything – including the meaning of the word 'Inkota'. The only thing was that when I came to – I remembered nothing of this moment of perfect understanding. Well, almost nothing. I couldn't be sure, but I believe I saw the remnants of a page torn from an old book go whizzing past. But it was not the page from just any old book, it was—

"Hey, stop that!" I heard myself say, coming to and thereby kissing goodbye any chance I had of resurrecting just what pearls of insight that the ram's raid had instilled in me. When I awoke, it looked like some sort of bizarre, Off-Off-Off Broadway version of the *Wizard of Oz* in which the role of Dorothy was being filled by none other than me. I was awoken by the constant licking not by Toto, but you guessed it, by my trusty companion Flynn who was unably assisted in this pathetic pastiche by an octogenarian Indian Chief, (no doubt fancied himself in the role of the Scarecrow), and a half-deaf and blind rusting Armenian who we'll pencil in for the part of the Tinman. (Note to producers: Must work on these characters as well as the unimaginative use of a stray cow as the Cowardly Lion).

"My boy, you alright?" Granddad asked while steadying himself against his cowardly cow.

"Yeah, no problem. Just keep that damned ram away from me," I said trying to get to my feet. "What was it we were talking about before the ram butt in?" I said, turning to the Chief.

"You were not making a lot of sense, my boy. Better you get some rest," he replied.

"No, no. It was important. Very important. And not just to me or to the farm. It was bigger than all of that. I know it was."

"It will come back to you. But for now, you must get some rest. All will be revealed when the time is right," the Chief said.

Why did I get the feeling that practically everyone – from Jenny and the Mayoress on down to this saggy old Sachem – knew more about everything than I did? With one possible exception – the farm's owner.

"Why you no save the farm, boy?" he asked.

"I'm working on it, granddad. I'm working on it," I said without having a clue as to how or what the heck I was working on. In fact, it was I who was getting worked on and over in every possible way. Somehow though, I kept coming back to one very strange but overwhelming sentiment. That everything, from the fate of the farm to unlocking the mysteries of my own toxic DNA to the very future of New Richmond, was woven tighter together than a Sikh's turban.

And then, just to top it off, the Chief dropped yet another one of his half-Indian/half-Springsteen-inspired offerings: "May the Great Spirit Walk with you – the Great Spirit in the Night!"

My head was spinning, but it was hard to know what was making me dizzier – the after-effects of the ram's wham or the ever-growing number of loose ends piling up in my cranium. There was no time to lose, rather, every time to win. But it wasn't here – not yet, anyway. I wasn't exactly sure of anything except that I had to keep moving. How much worse could things get? At least if I kept moving, it would make it harder for the bad times to keep up – wouldn't it?

I walked slowly toward the car, asking the Chief to take care of Flynn for me while I was gone. I said I'd be back shortly, but had to make a couple of quick stops. He nodded – or at least I think he did. I also told him to come up with some good stuff for me to use in the articles I'd have to write later in the week for the 'Foundation Day' celebrations.

"No problem," he replied.

No problem. He was half right. There was no *problem* – there were problems, as in plural, and multiplying by the minute.

Chapter Thirty Five

"You look like shit."

"Thanks, Dad. Good to see you, too," I replied while moving numerous piles of papers from the only free chair in his office-come-broom closet. While Dad's appraisal was brutal, it was at least honest, which was more than I could say for much of what many so-called friends had been pushing my way lately.

"You look like you got hit by a Mac truck," he continued.

"Close, but enough about me. You mentioned something else that J.R. left behind?"

"Yeah, it's over there," he said pointing to a rather plain, garden-variety-type rusty tin box.

"That's it?"

"What were you expecting – a Continental?"

"I don't know, but it certainly wasn't this. What's in it?"

"Dunno. Couldn't find the key."

"That's strange – even for J.R. He always kept everything in its place and vice versa. Maybe it's still in his seaside palace?"

"If you're asking me to go for a ride – let's go! I've had enough of this shit, I can tell you," he said.

"Dad, don't tell me you've lost your HoJo mojo?" Before he could open his mouth, I already knew the answer. Any HoJo joint that he'd worked at – regardless of whether he was the junior janitor or the senior manager, was kept spotless – inside and out. Flower beds were kept well weeded and litter free. Rare were the bits of paper or drink containers found lying around in the parking lots or toilets. Even employees were told to make a good impression on the 'paying public' by keeping their uniforms 'pressed, presentable and clean'.

The first thing I saw after the faded candy wrappers wedged in the front doorway was the egg and ketchup splatter on his non-matching, off-white shirt and pants.

"I'm going, Richie. It's all yours for a day or so," my old man said to a guy who looked more like someone used to reaching for the soap in a prison's communal shower than for a successful small business operator.

"Is that guy trustworthy?" I inquired as Dad picked up the tin box and ushered me out of the broom closet.

"Who gives a shit?" Dad replied. Omar Shariff with attitude. Roll on, Victoria!

Before leaving, I did get to make a call to Lou Cassals to make sure everything was more or less under control at '*The Record*'. "No problem here, man. Just be back by Thursday with a couple of front pagers for 'Foundation Day' and everything's sugary sweet," he said before adding: "I think Ian wants a quick word."

"Yo, Walter?" my Aussie neighbor asked.

"Yeah, what's up?"

"Nothing probably but just thought I'd mention it."

"What?"

"Well, this older woman dropped by your apartment last night."

Ugh-oh. "What did she look like?" I asked hoping beyond hope he didn't describe the Mayoress.

"It wasn't the mayor if that's what you're thinking – or hoping?!" he began. "It's someone I'd never seen before."

"What did she want?"

"She claimed to be your mother."

"What?"

"She said you'd agreed to let her in to pick up some package you'd obviously forgotten to send to her."

"Is that so? You didn't let her in, did you?"

"I didn't have any choice. I thought she'd physically harm me if I didn't."

"What did she take?"

"Nothing that I could see. She left within a few minutes and never said another word – not even 'thanks'."

"That's Ma, alright," I replied. "Thanks for telling me."

"Yeah, sure. See you soon, eh?"

"Very soon. Thanks again," I said before hanging up.

"What is it?" asked Dad.

"Nothing. Nothing and everything if that makes any sense," I said.

"It don't make any sense at all," he replied.

For once I had to agree. So I did the next best thing. After checking my faded golden chariot to make sure I did bring along the book that my mother had probably been scratching around my apartment for, I stopped at the closest packie, picked us up a couple of six packs of Dad's favourite spritzer – Rolling Rock – and headed for the coast.

I hadn't had a lot of time to put things in perspective since J.R.'s passing. J.R. had been my 'go-to' guy ever since I could remember. With his passing, it had helped make things a bit clearer regarding my place in the dysfunctional Bedrosian/Winslow clan. Dad was my family – for better or – well, not for worse – just for better. And Mom, well, she just wasn't in the picture any more. Probably never had been, but certainly wasn't any more.

And though he'd never say it, the same probably applied to my father. J.R. had been the one constant in both our lives and now without his presence – it seemed only natural that we would somehow become closer. I didn't have to wait long to find out how this new relationship would work. In no time at all, we were one, two, three Rocks each down the road and rolling into Six-Pack Numero Duco.

There we were – a more unlikely road trip duo I could not imagine – sucking down cold ones, listening to the wind whistle through our thinning hair lines and rapping about women – something we had both had little success with; work – another thing we both had equally little success with; and well, nothing else really. Except taking turns trying to out-burp and belch one another. It wasn't exactly a Hallmark Card-type moment. It was much better than that.

Chapter Thirty Six

By the time we reached J.R.'s floating palace, it was after sun down so there was nothing more to do besides pop open a couple more six packs, crank up the music and start looking for the key to the tin box.

"I don't know why we're bothering," Dad said.

"Bothering to do what exactly?" I asked.

"To find the key. It's only a fricking old box filled with more of his stupid baseball cards," he replied.

"You don't get it, do you?"

"Get what?"

"He wasn't hanging onto baseball cards. He was hanging onto memories – precious memories."

"I don't get it."

"Okay, did you open those safety deposit boxes in the bank vault?"

"Yeah, so?"

"What was in them?"

"Hundreds of baseball cards. You know that," he said.

"No, I don't know that. What I do know is that they weren't baseball cards."

"Why is everything with you a fricking riddle? They were just old baseball cards. I saw them."

"They were precious pieces of communal social and sporting history, Dad. And you know what? They may not be worth their weight in gold, but I'll take a wild guess and say that all up – they're worth $50,000 or more."

"You're crazier than he was!"

"Perhaps. But if I'm right – the contents of your tin box may be worth even more."

I stopped to listen to the music for a minute, trying to figure out where he might have hidden the key. The Band's Rick Danko was giving it his all on one of the most endearing love songs ever written called '*It Makes No Difference*', which made me vow that I would somehow try to make it up to Jenny Lawton. If only she'd give me one more chance. "*It makes no difference where I turn. I can't get over you and the flame still burns. It makes no diff--*"

"Hey, I think I found it," my father yells out, killing the moment. When I turned to face him, he was standing in the middle of the boat's upper deck with a very faded key pinched between his stubby fingers.

"Where was it?"

"Where else? Sitting in the keyhole of the cabin door which I know doesn't lock," he said.

"Great hiding place," I said. "Okay, let's give it a try."

My father grabbed the box and inserted the key into the opening. It fit like a glove. He gave it a couple of quick turns before the tumbler clicked and popped open the lid. "I don't think I can look inside after what you told me earlier," he said.

"Give it to me, chicken," I said. "Now I know how Howard Carter must have felt."

"Howard who?" Dad asked.

"Never mind." I had sensed all along that there was something quite heavy in the box. We'd even shaken it a bit to try and get some idea of its contents. Thank god we hadn't shaken it too hard. It contained a faded baseball neatly packaged in a rather ordinary-looking plastic container. The top of the container perfectly held the ball in a see-through round sphere which sat atop a rather plain, gold-colored plastic base. On the bottom of the base was a note, stuck to it with scotch tape. I pulled it off and opened the faded piece of paper.

"Hi guys! I had wanted to tell you about this special baseball for some time now, but never found the right moment. It was my pride and joy and hope you'll like it too! I bought it off an old guy at a card show in Worcester in the early 1960s. He swore it was

the only one of its kind. I paid a lot of money for it - $35, if my memory serves me. It's worth a lot more now. DO with it what you will. May it bring you both as much joy as it brought me. Play ball!"

I put the note down and noticed something else in the bottom of the box. It was a picture frame that fit snugly into the rusty container's innards. I gently wedged the frame out and peeled off the manila envelope that had obviously been with its mate from the beginning. Inside lay something more precious than the Mona Lisa – at least to a Red Sox fan. It was a black and white photo of the team's two greatest sluggers – Ted Williams, and er, George Herman Ruth. It soon became apparent what the photo had in common with the ball. The first signature I saw was that of the younger star, the Splendid Splinter himself. Ted's signature was bold and strong like its owner. When I turned the ball over, there was a far less confident signature as if penned by either a small child or an old man. It took me a while to figure out but the image from the photograph gave it away – Babe Ruth. Talk about Yin and Yang. Few players cared more about hitting than Teddy Ballgame while the Babe could have cared less! And both for the Red Sox, even though a team out of New York might try to lay some claims to the latter's legendary career. I don't know which item meant more to me – the baseball or the photograph. It was one thing to have their autographs on the one object they both treated with utter disdain, but to have a 'live' photo recording the two in all their glories. There was Theodore 'Ted' Williams, perched on the dug-out's steps with a smile and self-assuredness many mistook for cockiness. The most splendid of splinters in his prime staring out at the world and letting each and every hurler on the mound know that they were only one pitch away from an early shower. The Babe, on the other hand, sported a forced grin that looked more like a grimace than a smile, framed atop a body obviously racked with pain from 10 lifetimes' worth of carousing, booze, nicotine and enough hot dogs to sink the Pacific Fleet.

"You're gonna tell me that isn't just a baseball, right?" Dad asked.

"You got it. This is your ticket out of HoJo's if you want it to be, Dad," I said.

"I can't believe that. He used to tell me about these cards and what they were worth. I never believed him," Dad said.

"Hey, and I never believed him about his mateship with Bob Mitchum!"

We clinked our bottles and proceeded to do what any good drunken fools do when toasting a fallen comrade – pledged allegiance to memories gone by, memories yet to come and most importantly – to another round or four of drinks at the local watering hole. J.R. would've loved it. Before leaving, we very carefully put the photo and the baseball back into their tin coffin, locked them up and placed the box back in J.R.'s full-sized safe which was disguised as a dishwasher. Who else would come up with such a clever design? The only thief who could work it out would be anyone who knew J.R. well enough to know he didn't have any plates or cutlery on board so if there ever was an appliance with no application – it was the dishwasher!

We got up relatively early the next day, considering we got back to the boat about the same time most people were heading to work. I decided to ask Dad if he wanted to accompany me to Boston, figuring he'd rather stay and keep making merry with the locals.

"Love to go to Boston," he replied.

"You're kidding, right?"

"Hell, no. Why not? It might be fun."

"Fun? You've got to be kidding? I'm going to be visiting State Government offices trying to figure out what's going on with grandpa's farm. Then I'm heading over to meet a bunch of stuffed shirts who can tell me everything I never wanted to know about the Winslows."

"Great! Let's ride!"

And with that, we were off. And as it turned out – we were way off.

Chapter Thirty Seven

I'd had a lot of time to think about the best way to attack both the taxing tax situation regarding granddad's farm and the good folks down at the Mayflower Mission about the early wanderings of the Winslow clan. I'd appealed to everyone I knew, (including St. Vartan for guidance) and came up empty. I'd tried to apply every conceivable approach I'd picked up as a reporter when facing a difficult story and came up snake eyes. It seemed in both cases that the chances of me achieving any kind of a breakthrough were so remote that it hardly seemed worth the effort. That is, until I asked my new fearless travelling companion how he might approach these vexing situations.

"How would J.R. have approached them?"

"Depends," Dad said.

"On what?"

"On what the other party looked like?"

"What do you mean?"

"If we get a woman – hit on her."

"And if it's a guy?"

"Just hit him."

With that, we loaded up the car, popped the tops on a couple of coldies and headed up the highway. It was nearly noon by the time we reached Boston. I knew where our first port of call would be – the Department of Internal Revenue – which was contained within a honey-combed-shaped office building known innocently enough as 'Government Center'. I wasn't sure where the Mayflower Mission called home, nor did I much care – for the moment. One hopeless cause at a time. I found a vacant block not far from Quincy Market with a huge sign out front: "SAFE THAN SORRY CAR PARK."

That sounded ominous, but then again it was the big smoke. "What's with the sign?" I asked the filthy-looking old-timer standing guard outside the lot.

"How the fuck should I know? You wanna park – it costs $10 bucks up front," the perky employee remarked.

"Why so much?"

"So much? Get outta heah – don't waste my time," the anti-gentleman replied.

"Okay, when you put it like that – of course I'll leave my car, its ignition key as well as the keys to my home and holiday home in the Hamptons," I replied.

"Help yourself to a cold one, too," I said figuring that would win him over.

"Great. You made my day, Ace," the not-so-smart ass says taking my tenner and stuffing it in his pants pocket. "Close at 6."

"6 p.m.?" I asked.

"No – 6 in the mawnin – of cawse 6 p.m.," he says further endearing himself to yours truly.

I grabbed my trusty satchel out of the backseat and stuffed the last two non-empty beer cans into it before handing over the keys to Mr. Personality.

"You want I should hit him?" Dad asked.

"Nah, save it for later, Cassius. Save it for later."

My usually non-verbal companion became quite the chatterbox on the way over to the Taxman's office. I was happy that he was coming out of his shell, but just not right now.

"Seeing anyone?"

"Not really," I replied.

"How about Jenny?"

"How about her?" I replied, hoping he'd get the hint.

"C'mon, she's nice."

"Hey, Dad. Yes, she's nice but can we concentrate on the job at hand?!"

He gave me the look he always gives me when he doesn't know how to process the information that he's been given.

"With all due respect, Dad, grandpa is in some big poo and if we don't get this thing sorted out – they'll chuck him and all the animals off the farm so just give me some time to think, okay?"

"Got it," he said patting me on the back.

Fortunately, or unfortunately for us, the appropriate line inside the tax office was nearly outside the revolving doors. Once again, it gave me time to think. The only thing was, I didn't know what to think about. The clock on the wall said it was getting near 1.30 p.m. by the time we got to talk to someone. It was a typical government office or large bank set-up. A number of tellers, most of whom never looked up trying like heck to handle as few patrons as they could in an eight-hour shift. They must give out an award to whoever didn't serve the most people each week. We finally got called and to be honest – it didn't look good. A very loud and quite angry-sounding voice called out – "NEXT!" referring to us.

When we approached the teller's window (or should I say cage?), we were greeted by the angry stare of a very, very large black woman whose name badge read 'Marrsha Brady – Customer Service'. Her bust was so big that the name badge pointed upwards making it easier to read for those customers who were dropping in from the ceiling. I debated on whether to say something really smart about her name, but thought better of it. I'm sure she'd heard it all before, though any large black woman walking around with the same name as a member of the hopelessly white-breaded Brady Bunch had to expect a little rain with her sunshine.

"Hello, Marrsha," I said trying on my best Uncle J.R. impersonation, while also trying like heck not to say anything about the unusual spelling. "Has anyone told you that you look like Aretha Franklin?" (I lied. She looked like three Aretha Franklins).

There was no greeting or acknowledgement in return for my weak attempt at a flirt. There was nothing except a very hard stare that was getting harder by the second. It was throwing me off whatever 'game' I may have thought I had. And that wasn't saying much. Before I could get the next words out – my companion, who'd I'd told more than once to let me do all the talking – started talking.

"We gotta beef with the taxman," he says in his best wise-guy voice.

"Beef is probably a bit strong," I said trying to appease the fiery tax god before us. "Perhaps a stringy little piece of chicken is more like it."

I waited for a reaction from my new best friend Marrsha. I was quite proud of my line. It deserved some sort of response, even the slimmest sliver of a smile would have sufficed.

There was nothing. Not a thing. Well, that wasn't exactly true. She did say something: "Name."

"Sorry?" I replied.

"Name. You gotta name?"

"Yeah, sure. I gotta couple, but it's not me with the problem – or him for that matter. Well, not directly –"

"Who then has the 'beef?'" Marrsha declared mercifully cutting into my babble-speak.

"It's my grandfather – well, his father actually," I said nodding toward my father.

"And does he have a coupla names?" Marrsha said, getting into the swing of the thing.

"Yes. Yes he does," I replied. "It's Torkum Bedrosian of Richmond Heights, Massachusetts."

"Spell that," she says.

"M-A-S-"

"His name. Spell his name," she says once again ignoring my humorous offering.

I spelled it and she punched the letters, one at a time on her keyboard. It sounded like a boxer hitting a punching bag repeatedly – rat-a-tat-tat; rat-a-tat-tat, etc. When she was done, she pulled her sausage-like fingers away from the keyboard after giving it one last almighty whack. After what seemed like an eternity, she said: "Looks like you owe $23,000 in back taxes."

"Yes, we're aware of that and we'd like to make restitution on…"

"Wait a minute, wait a minute," she said. "There's another message coming up on my screen. I've never seen this before," she says with the teeniest hint of surprise in her booming voice. She didn't strike me as the kind of person who liked surprises.

"I'll need to go talk to my super. Wait here," she said apparently to my father and me. Where were we going to go? Despite her enormous size, she dismounted the swivel chair as easily as a seasoned jockey got off his four-legged charger. I glanced again at the large clock hanging over the central doorway. It was nearly 2.15 p.m. and we were getting the opposite of nowhere fast - everywhere slow.

She finally returned with another dour-faced individual who looked very much like Wally Cox – only more mousey if that was possible. His nametag read 'Craig' which seemed fitting enough. Who the hell gives their kid that sort of lame-ass name? I figured it was time to take control.

"Hello, Craig. What's the verdict?"

"I'm rather baffled by this one," Craig began.

"Oh?"

"Well, are you sure there hasn't been any correspondence from any other Departments – in particular those of a Federal nature?"

"Look, can we cut to the chase, please? I have no idea what's going on and would really appreciate it if you could help us. We're here on behalf of my grandfather – and his father – because, well, how can I say this – he is not exactly aware of everything around him."

Both Craig and Marrsha looked even more puzzled.

"What I mean, is that, he's a first generation immigrant from a land far, far away from here. He doesn't speak much English and has even less understanding of this culture. He doesn't know the name of the current president or any other one for that matter. He doesn't drive a car, watch television or read books. He's never been to the hospital or to a Red Sox game. In fact, he wouldn't know what happens at a hospital or even who the hell the Red Sox are. He lives in his own world and relies on the kindness of strangers and other family members to pay the bills and look after him."

"That's all well and good but the fact remains he's apparently purchased a neighboring tract of land that is, well, how can I put this," Craig said. "It's just not for sale."

I looked at my Dad who was looking even more confused than me if that was possible.

"Are you sure you have not had any visits from any Federal authorities?"

"Not to our knowledge," I replied to which my father concurred.

"Well, unfortunately, there's not much more we can tell you. I will say, however, that we will still need the outstanding State Tax bill paid, but it will have to be co-ordinated with this other matter which I assume will present itself shortly," Craig said.

"Can you tell us anything else?" I said.

"I'm sorry, sir. I cannot," Craig said before turning to Marrsha and adding: "Would you please arrange a payment schedule with these gentlemen for the outstanding taxes?"

Ms. Brady nodded and perched herself back up on her stool, which I swear heaved a sigh of despair.

I assured my interrogator that we would pay the outstanding tax bill shortly, but were quite distressed at this turn of non-events. Marrsha seemed sympathetic. Almost human which was a bit scary. I thanked her for her time and turned to leave. The clock was now ticking past 2.35 p.m. and we had to make our way to yet another almost certain lost cause – the Mayflower Mission.

I felt a gentle tug at my sleeve. Ms. Brady Bunch had leaned forward toward the outside of her cage and motioned me with her right hand to come back to the window. Her eyes told me to look down. I looked down only to see her left hand pushing a small piece of paper toward me. I grabbed it quickly and turned it over. It had a series of numbers scrawled on it.

"Call me, sugar," she said, giving me a big wink and a smile.

Big lady. Small consolation.

Chapter Thirty Eight

"I'm gonna let you in on a BIG secret," said the guy sitting to my left at the bar.

Normally, anyone who starts a sentence like that is guaranteed to get your attention. Normally, it's someone who has inside information on something of interest like say, a little-known injury to the star player for the Celtics just hours before the big game. Or regarding an unfortunate mishap befelling a short-odds favorite in the next race at Hialeah. Unfortunately, I was a long way past normal. The guy sitting next to me happened to be my father, and he was convinced he owed me something for very kindly (and quickly) handing him the phone number of Marrsha Brady soon after leaving the Government Center.

"Dad, I don't think now's the time to talk about-"

"Why not? It's too late to go to that Mayflower Mansion or whatever damn hell that place is. Besides, we done enough for one day. I might even give that lovely little Marrsha a call later on." Amazing how much courage a couple of Coors could give a man.

It was now nearly 4:15 which meant we had 45 minutes to get to the Mission. Impossible? I found out it was not too far from the Government Center complex on Cambridge Street, so we decided to take a few minutes to freshen up over some liquid amber before dropping by.

"Alright, but I'm gonna tell you about the best fucking sex I ever had on the drive home," Dad said.

"Can hardly wait," I replied, hoping like hell he'd either forget, fall asleep or decide to stay behind and attempt to climb Mount Marrsha.

Everyone needed a challenge in life. Dad certainly had his in trying to woo Ms. Brady. I was beginning to think that this challenge paled in comparison to the ones facing moi. There was granddad's state tax bill as well as the Federal crime – whatever the heck that was, my family's genealogical disorders, Jenny, the Chief, St. Vartan, working at the newspaper and my mother. It suddenly occurred to me that despite their seemingly lack of overlap – they all seemed to be inextricably woven into the fabric of the one place in the world I sought to leave behind and never behold again – Grandad's farm.

After leaving Government Center, we walked a couple of blocks along Beacon Street where there was any number of nice-looking drinking establishments to choose from. We selected, or should I say, Dad selected the worst one of the bunch. That's because my father had a theory, not quite in the same league as one of Einstein's ideas or even Darwin's for that matter. He called it his 'Dear Beer' theory which simply hypothesized that the price of piss was directly related to the establishment's external appearance. The better the place looked on the outer, the more you'd pay for the beer in the inner. There was, however, at least one corollary to my Dad's theory which he obviously hadn't factored into his calculations. Anyone who was unable to pay, say, four bucks for a bottle of beer, was also less likely to spend any dosh on say, daily cleanliness products like SOAP. The proof in the pudding sat four stools to my left, the only other sod in this downtrodden watering hole. The only way I knew he was alive was from the fact that the level in the glass of beer before him kept decreasing at regular intervals. He didn't speak, but every so often felt the urge to let us know of his existence through some primeval burp, fart or both. He also brought with him the foulest B.O. I'd ever beheld. It was foul enough to clear the sinus passages of cold sufferers from Seattle to Sydney.

You couldn't fault the service in the place. You could, but why bother? I threw ten bucks on the counter and swear the bartender turned away. Judging by his slow reaction, tips were not high on his list of priorities.

Still, I didn't get angry or argue with Dad over his choice in drinking establishments. I didn't even take umbrage over this minor loophole in his prized theory on alehouses. That's because the joint we ended up drinking in, (I think it was called 'Muddy's Tavern' but could have been Maddy's or Middy's, due to the fact that the second letter had been comprehensively smudged out some time back, was more than likely to be the most unlikely place to run into anyone from the Mayflower

Mission. Judging by the dust on the bar stools and the long-since-expired dates on the bags of Cape Cod potato chips, I reckoned it had been some time since anyone except for B.O. boy to our left, had had a beer or two at Muddy's.

The Mission was situated in nearby Beacon Hill, which for those of you unfamiliar with the Massachusetts Bay Colony's capital city, was exactly the place you'd expect the country's earliest and most elite citizenry to be housed. Though only about one square mile in size, this pricey neighborhood was stock full of million-dollar-plus palatial mansions, accompanied by finely-cobbled brick sidewalks and nineteenth-century-styled gas lamps to remind people of how everyone got around when horsepower was generated by hooves, not petrol-fired engines. Some said it was fitting that Beacon Hill stood so high atop most other bits of Boston, so those who could afford to shack up there, could keep their high-priced snouts well and truly up in the air.

There was nothing particularly clever about the area's moniker. Many cities had a 'Beacon Hill' which usually coincided with one of the region's higher elevations so seafaring types could get their bearings from a well-lit, beacon of light. We were looking for a small street smack dab in the middle of the neighborhood called Oak Grove. And there, at just about 10 minutes before the clock struck 5 p.m., we reached our quarry. Surrounded by extremely well-kept Federal-style brick rowhouses, stood a solitary timber-framed structure. It was painted a bright shade of white with black shutters and black door. It was an extremely plain and unassuming-looking building that 200 years ago, would have still been a very plain and unassuming-looking building.

It wasn't what I'd pictured in my mind's eye – whatever the hell that meant. I never saw the Mayflower Mission as a black and white entity. It screamed color, and not just a brush of blue or shot of red. Rather, the whole fucking rainbow. But then, I'd put off this trip for many months, because deep, deep down I had serious doubts about this connection to America's Royalty, but even more worrying was whether I could handle it if it were true.

"What's wrong?" Dad asked.

"Nothing. And everything," I replied.

"C'mon, you fricking nut. We haven't got much time," Dad said, showing more interest in this endeavor than I ever thought possible.

"No, wait. Give me a minute to collect my thoughts," I said.

"For Christ's sake. It's a fucking library," he replied with just enough volume in his voice for everyone within the greater metropolitan area to know he wasn't much of a reader.

I walked up to the door and found it locked. I rattled the doorknob a couple of times without any success. The sign in the window clearly said the shop was opened between 9:30 a.m. and 5 p.m. Monday to Friday. There was a good 10 minutes to go before closing. There were no lights on and no sign of any human activity. Ironically enough, I was relieved. I don't know why exactly.

"That's it? You're gonna quit like some kinda poofta?" dear old Dad offered.

"Hey, it's no big deal. Let's go back to Muddy's and get a beer."

"Fuck that. We're going in," Dad said and with that, began ramming his shoulder into the front door like some human battering ram.

Before long, a window on the second story opened and a woman's voice yelled out: "What are you doing? I won't tolerate this sort of loutish behaviour. I'm calling the police at once!" she said.

"It's alright, ma'am," I said. "We're not engaging in loutish behavior. We're actually just here to find out about our roots," I said rather unconvincingly.

My comments were met with a look of amazement. "I'm coming down. Please move away from the door," the lady replied.

"See? I got us some action," Dad said.

"Thanks, Dad. Great work. Now go chew your bone in the corner," I said.

Before long, our second-story interrogator opened the door to the inner sanctum. "What exactly are you after?"

I wasn't quite sure it's exactly what I'd expected when I gave any time to thinking about what the Mayflower Madam may have looked like. One thing I can say for sure is that I didn't expect her to be holding a huge wrench and outfitted in mechanic's overalls. "Ahh, excuse me, but before we get to me, can I enquire as to who designed your wardrobe – Mr. Lubemobile perhaps?"

I at least caught our not-so-grand inquisitor off guard. "Oh, this, well, we were having trouble with the sink in our kitchen and since it had been so quiet, I decided to have a go and fix the problem myself," said our hostess (hopefully anyway).

"And did you fix the leak?" I asked.

"Not quite yet. But how can I help you?"

"I'm related to the Winslows," I offered with as much certainty as I could muster, figuring that would pique her interest.

"THE WINSLOWS?" the lady asked inquisitively.

"The one and only Winslows," I replied, before adding, "though not via the genes of my good partner here. Rather, they belong to my maternal side's offspring." I hated myself for trying to sound like I knew what the hell I was talking about.

"My dear young man. Surely, you must realize we receive many, many queries each year from people like yourself who believe they're related to one of the fortunate few who made it across the pond on the Mayflower."

I hated this woman with every part in my being if that was possible. But before I could reply, dear old Dad stepped in: "Hey, lady, my boy here wants to find out about his roots and if you don't give us a few minutes of your precious time – we'll make you regret you ever…"

"Hey, easy pops. She's the one with the wrench!" I said hoping to prevent some kind of offence that would no doubt have landed my father and me in jail with a roommate named 'Lucifer'.

This last comment finally raised a smile – albeit a slight one – on our blue-collared-attired, blue blood's face. "I take your point. Please forgive me while I slip out of these overalls. It's ever so impolite of me."

"No problem. My name's Walt. And this is my father, Walt Senior, if you like."

"Oh, yes, dear me," said the woman not knowing whether she should first put down the wrench or remove the overalls. She did neither and instead offered up her own name: "I'm Veronica Lincoln-Quaid, the Assistant Curator of the Mayflower Mission."

She then looked at me, then at Dad and then at her watch. It was still a good five minutes till closing. "Do come in gentlemen, but I'm afraid I can't offer any refreshments at this late hour. Hope you don't mind?" she said, opening the door a bit more and letting us into the hallway. "Make yourselves at home, I won't be a minute," she said while wandering off toward the back of the building. From what I could see, it really did look like a library, with its two front rooms featuring a series of ceiling-high shelves, stacked with books of all shapes and sizes.

I took Dad aside and told him to try and go work on the kitchen sink while I spoke to Ms. Lincoln-Quaid.

"She's not your type, sonny boy. Too much class," Dad offered.

"Yeah, I never deal with any woman who doesn't use stainless steel tools," I replied getting a laugh out of the old man.

"What's so funny?" asked our hostess who returned rather unexpectedly. It was hard to say how old she was, but it was probably somewhere between 45-50. She had jet black hair with light streaks of gray pushing through, tied up in a bun like the ones preferred by nineteenth-century schoolteachers. She wore tight-fitting black slacks and loose white blouse, continuing the exterior's penchant for black and white. She also wore large tortoise-shell-rimmed glasses that covered up her face which appeared to have little or no make-up and certainly no lipstick smudged over her pencil-thin lips.

"Nothing, nothing at all," I said. "Sorry we're so late. We ran into a bit of bother at Government Center," I said, now sounding more like some upper-class British twit than the true New World Ner-Do-Well that I really was.

"No problem. I don't usually close up early. It's just that it's been a particularly quiet day and I'd hoped to fix up our leaky sink. Unfortunately, I'm not quite as handy as I thought I was," said Ms. Lincoln-Quaid.

"My Dad here is a regular Mr. Fix-It. If you show him the problem, I'm sure he can tap into it real quick," I offered.

"Oh, that's not necessary," she replied.

"But it is," I retorted. "It most certainly is, isn't it, Dad?"

With that, they disappeared up a set of stairs behind the front desk. I tried to look busy and come up with what I'd say next.

"That's really sweet of your father. I think he will be able to fix it quite quickly. And now, how can I help you?"

"Let me try and start from the beginning. I'm Walter. Walter Howard Johnson II and the other chap trying to fix up your plumbing is my father, Walter Howard Johnson the First," figuring she'd be impressed not only by the numbering, but by the double-barrelled sounding names. It had to sound better than Torkum Bedrosian 1 & 2.

"You mentioned the Winslows. Can you explain your alleged familial ties with them?"

I let the 'alleged' bit slip through without comment. "It's really quite simple. My mother's line is connected to both the Adams' family of Quincy and to the Winslows. I just want to learn more about these connections," I said.

"The Adams', you say? How interesting. Where did you say you come from?"

"From New Richmond, in the far southwestern part of the state," I replied.

"Hmmm," she said. "Interesting. I can't vouch for the Adams family, but I'm almost positive that you could not possibly be related to the Winslows," Ms. Lincoln-Quaid replied.

"How can you already know that?" I asked.

"My dear young man. Do you have any idea how many requests like this we receive?"

"Requests like what?" I asked.

"From people believing they're related to one of the Mayflower's first arrivals. Do you not realize that there were only 102 souls on that maiden voyage? That's it. Just 102 people."

"So?"

"It's more likely that you are indeed related to two Presidents than you are to the Winslows!" began the Mayflower Madam. "If all the people who had claimed to have come on the Mayflower to these fair shores in 1620 actually had arrived on that tiny boat, it would have sunk without a trace before leaving the dock in England."

"You may be right in some cases, but surely as the decades elapsed and more and more descendants from the original 102 begat child after child – surely it would be possible for you to receive hundreds if not thousands of legitimate requests for help from legitimate relatives?"

"I take your point, but in some particular families like the Winslows – it just isn't possible. There were not that many family members who survived to adulthood and I've studied them quite closely over the years and know for certain there were no descendants who conducted their affairs in New Richmond," she said.

"So what are you saying?"

"I'm saying that just because someone told you about your past does not make it so. You may have something you were told by some mis-informed relative or even believed something written in one of the many poorly researched or, yes, worse, fraudulent documents that exist out there," she said.

"Okay, let's say I believe you. How do you know, as in absolutely, positively know, that I'm not related without even consulting one of the many fine books housed in this building?"

"Because you see dear boy, Edward Winslow and his bride, Susannah White had just four children, only one of which – Josiah – had children of his own. Why don't you take a look at this Winslow family tree which I personally have researched over the years while I check up on your father?"

I felt like I was back in junior high school. But then, she was making this sound all too plausible. While I was quick to apply any number of critical reporting techniques on stories involving New Richmond's slimy Mayoress or some other public official, I certainly hadn't spent any time checking out the facts regarding my alleged forebears. She could be right. No, she probably was right which then explained why everything in this place seemed to be color coded in BLACK and WHITE. Everything was crystal clear here. EVERYTHING. Except for me.

I didn't really want to look at the piece of paper in front of me. I wasn't in the mood for more bad news just yet. I put the paper down and took a stroll through the Mission. It was laid out like many old libraries. That is, rows of book shelves stacked beside one another behind the front desk. There also were several mini-booths along the three outer walls. Some were covered with books obviously belonging to some long-lost foundling. Others looked as though they hadn't been used since the War – Revolutionary, Civil or any other war for that matter. Above most of these desks were prints of the mighty Mayflower along with early images of Myles Standish and Co., doing their bit in the new colony. Again, I wasn't sure what I'd expected the Mission to look like. In some ways I'd half expected someone dressed in Pilgrim garb to greet me at the door and invite me in for a turkey dinner.

I could hear Ms. Lincoln-Quaid's voice. She was at the top of the stairs sounding as though she was ready to come back down again, so I quickly unfolded the large sheet of paper she'd handed me. It unfolded in much the same way that many road maps do. I'd hoped that there would have been many Winslows running around in the seventeenth century, which would have meant even more running around in the eighteenth century at the time that I'd been led to believed that one of them had pushed as far west as one could in the State of Massachusetts. As she'd mentioned, however, the original Winslow (Edward) and his wife – Susannah White – had just four children, only one of which appeared to have any children. This one child, Josiah and his wife, Penelope something-or-other, had one child – Isaac - who in turn had but two, etc, etc. Not only were the numbers way less than expected, but even worse – the names of the actual descendants didn't marry up with the one carried by my mother's father's line. Well, almost. It seemed the only thing my mother's father and the 'real' Winslows' had in common was the Christian name 'Josiah', but that was probably more due to sheer luck or pure deceit, depending on your view of the world. Me, I liked to keep my options open. I was neither a half-empty or half-filled kind of guy. I was glad to have a glass to worry about whether it had anything in it or not.

I looked and looked at the names hoping somehow that if I stared at them long enough, my alleged forebear's name would appear as if by magic. When I knew this was not about to happen, I calmly folded the Winslow map up and placed it back on the front counter. I wasn't angry. I wasn't even upset. Somehow, somewhere down deep I'd known this would be the outcome. I'd perhaps tried to hang onto the thought that at least my mother's side of the family was notable – given the rather notoriously dubious background of my father's father's lot. True to form, though, my day in Boston had not only unearthed a new tragedy on the horizon for the Bedrosian clan, but laid to rest any hope I'd had for staking a claim as a relative to one of America's First Families. I could have stayed an extra day and gone for the trifecta over in Quincy with the Adams', but figured I'd opened enough genetic sores for one 24-hour period. Who the heck wanted to claim allegiances to a President or two anyway? Given what we now knew about JFK and Tricky Dicky, the last thing I needed was some connection to the Adams Family. Besides, I had to get back to write some stories about New Richmond's 300 year celebrations. How pathetically ironic.

Dad soon came bounding down the stairs with Ms. Lincoln-Quaid in close pursuit. "He is a genius," gushed the Mayflower Mistress.

"That's my Dad, an irregular Renaissance guy," I replied putting my arm around him.

"Was the family tree of any value?" she asked.

"Totally. Perfectly. And you are 100 per cent correct. There has indeed been some rather unfortunate assumption on the part of my mother's family that they were related to THE Winslows. It would seem more likely it was just a far more common Winslow," I said.

"I'm so sorry. I wish it could have been a better result."

"On the contrary. You've solved a longstanding mystery which now gives me the impetus to determine just who the heck I am and where I came from even more!"

"If ever I can be of assistance – do call," said Ms. Lincoln-Quaid handing me her card while at the same time winking at my father.

"Thanks again," I said and headed for the door. When we got outside, my father put his arm around me in a consoling sort of way.

"It's okay, Dad. I had a hunch this was going to happen and I'm just glad it's finally been straightened out."

"I don't get it. We've been told all along that your mother's family belonged to the Mayflower. So if they didn't – who the heck were they?"

"A fair question and I think I know where to find the answer. And it's been under my fricking nose all along," I said as we made our way back to the parking lot to pick up our trusty steed and head back to the familial front line.

Chapter Thirty Nine

By the time we'd hit the MassPike, Dad was fast asleep, which was a blessing. I was not alone, though. As if to reinforce the day's events, a very apt tune by The Boss filled the airwaves. It's called '*Promised Land*' and in it he tells the listeners about a guy working for his father as a grease monkey. Although the gilt edges of his childhood dreams have been bruised and battered by life's litany of daily woes, he's implored to keep on keeping on in the hope that one day he will get his own slice of the American Dream.

You got that right, Boss man. And then, as if right on cue, the radio station tuned out and in tuned my favorite 1500-year-old Armenian wannabe warrior. I'll skip the usual opening, but rest assured, there was a sufficient amount of static preceding his 'visit'. His words were few but well chosen.

THE FARTHER YOU GO – THE CLOSER YOU GET!

Up until recently, these sorts of weird riddle clues would have left me clueless. No longer. While at first blush it would seem I was now farther away from sorting out any part of my genetic make-up than ever before, in fact, it was all starting to gel – if not quite nicely, then quite well, well.

We were making good time on the Pike when I sensed that Dad was stirring. "Pull over! Pull over!" he began yelling wildly.

"What's wrong?"

"Just pull over – now!" he said again.

We were about half-way between Boston and the next biggest city in the Bay State – Worcester, when we pulled over into the parking lot of a very dimly-lit Howard Johnson's.

"This is the spot!" he said.

"Spot? What spot?"

"The spot where your mother and I first met," he said.

"Oh shit, you made me pull over for that?"

"Yes, and now you're gonna hear my story. Let's get an ice cream – my shout," he said.

"Super. Can't wait, but don't start the story till we're back in the car. I don't want anyone else hearing this sordid tale," I said.

We got our cones and no sooner shut the car doors than he opened up like never before. "I was slinging hash in this joint in 1953. It wasn't even a HoJo's then – just some stinking diner, Zip's I think it was called."

"Yes, Dad. Good detail. I just love detail."

"It was late and there weren't many people in the diner when your mother walked in. She was drunk. Real drunk."

"How'd you know?"

"Cuz she started spewing all over the place," he said.

"Okay – got it. Move on."

"I helped clean up the mess and got her a lemonade to settle her stomach. I stuck her in one of the booths while I finished cleaning up the kitchen. She'd just finished her last college exams and was driving home for the summer. After about 15 minutes, she says she's gonna drive home. I follow her out to the parking lot and there sits this huge brown and white Pontiac convertible. A real beauty."

"Okay, so then what?"

"I offered to drive her home as my shift was over and I was in no rush to get back to the farm. I got her to New Richmond and eventually found the right address out there along the lake. I'd never been that close to a house that big before. You know what it's like – a frigging castle!"

"Yeah, castle."

"I left her sleeping in the car and went up to the front door. It must have been about 2:30 a.m. A very old and thin man answered the door. I figured it was her father. But it was the fucking butler who helped me get your mother out of her car and into her bed upstairs."

"Great story, Dad."

"I'm getting there. Hold on. Anyway, this butler, what was his name – James, Jackson –"

"I believe it was Jason, Dad," I said.

"That's it, Jason. Anyway, Jason thanks me again for my help and hands me a key."

"To her heart?"

"Huh? No, you idiot. It was a key to the room over the six-door garage. So, I went to sleep and didn't hear another sound till late the next morning when I heard a loud knock at the door."

"Ugh-oh."

"No, ugh-oh. It was just Jason again and he'd made me bacon and eggs with toast and coffee and left it outside the door."

"How sweet."

"It was nice and when I picked up the tray, there was a plain white envelope stuck underneath. When I opened it, a 50-dollar bill fell out along with a one word note: 'Thanks'. It was bullshit. I hadn't done it for a frigging reward!"

"No, you were after something much more valuable."

"Shut it, asshole. I got dressed and started walking down the driveway and toward the town. Before long, I could hear the Pontiac coming up behind me. There was your mother – fully revived from the night before with her long hair swaying in the breeze and the coolest pair of sunglasses I'd ever seen. I didn't care. I didn't like being treated like some dickhead, so I gave her the finger and told her to go away."

"You sly dog, you."

"Do get in, my knight in shining armor," she said.

"You don't even know my name," I said.

"I do – it's Sir Gallant!" she replied.

"No, it's Torkum," I said.

"What a beautiful name. Do get in, Torkum. If you don't, I'll get out and join you in your trek," she said, jumping out of the car while it was still in gear.

"Typical, Mom. A real free spirit," I said.

"I had to chase the fucking car down, jump into it from the back and grab the steering wheel to keep it on the road. I just barely got control before we both ended up in the lake."

"You and Mom?" I asked.

"No, me and the car!"

"You hero," I said.

"You think so? Not her. She was laughing her ass off, saying it's the funniest thing she'd ever seen. She jumped in the passenger's side and told me to 'Drive far, far away young man!'"

"Okay, cut to the chase. I can't take much more of this, Dad. She sounds almost human," I said.

"We drove all the way down to Victoria to J.R.'s houseboat. I'd never seen anything like that – or him – before in my life. We stayed down there a few days and had a helluva time, drinking and laughing mostly."

"And?"

"And, well, we drove all over Connecticut and Rhode Island drinking at bars by night and sunning ourselves on beaches by day. Then, on the last day, we wound up at some national park in Connecticut. I'll never forget the name of it – Devil's Hopyard."

"Now that's a winner of a name," I said.

"You bet. And that's where we first did it."

"Spare me the gory details, Dad, pa – lease."

"The only thing I'll tell you about that event was that it was where you were probably conceived."

"That'd be right. With a name like that – how could I go wrong? No wonder I'm such a fucking mess."

Dad continued. "We drove back to J.R.'s place, but he was out. He'd left a note telling your mother to call home. She did and her butler asked if she was okay and whether we should contact the authorities."

"Authorities?"

"Police. They wanted to call the police and stitch me up for kidnapping and rape," Dad said.

"Pretty harsh," I replied.

"She slammed the phone back into the wall and told me we were heading south."

"Why south?"

"Because she'd heard it was possible to get married quickly in Maryland, which is what we did. I don't even remember the name of the place, but it was just some podunk town hall."

"What'd you wear?"

"What we had on, I guess. No wedding dress or penguin suit for me, I can tell you that!"

The not-so-bright lights of Willimantic, Connecticut beckoned when all of a sudden the heavens opened up. It wasn't just raining. It was like giant buckets of water were being dumped over the car – over and over. The only problem being that my windshield wipers didn't like inclement weather. It was coming down so hard that without the wipers, I was in a quandary as to whether and try and get to the side of the road or keep going. I decided to keep going figuring if we did get to the road side, it could just as easily be down a steep embankment or worse. Without saying a word, Dad had leaned over the back seat of the car and found my old racquet ball racquet. It hadn't been strung in years, but I doubted he was looking to make any corner shots. The rain was still belting down when he leaned out of the front passenger side window with an umbrella in his right hand and the racquet stuck onto the closest wiper working it back and forth.

"Faster, faster for Christ's sake!" I yelled, hoping to keep his spirits up. I could hear him mumbling something but was drowned out by the storm. I doubt he'd even heard me. I hit the horn to see if that would stir him. He nearly fell out of the car from the sheer fright of the horn blaring at him. I could see our quarry now. The WILLIMANTIC, CONN exit sign beckoned when the only other car on the highway pulled up alongside me. It was a Connecticut State Police car and in most circumstances, these guys could be real sticklers for rules of the road.

I kept looking straight ahead, hoping they'd reward me for diligence and attention to detail. They seemed far more interested in the unusual hood ornament that was working the wipers wildly while holding onto an umbrella which was no longer operational, as the wind had sheared through its canvas canopy. I wasn't sure why Dad was still holding onto the handle. Perhaps it gave him balance. The officer on the passenger side pulled out a huge flashlight and shined it into my eyes. I tried to shield myself from this light which was making it even more difficult to keep the car on the road. Eventually, he shined the light on Dad. The light went out. I waited for him to tell us to pull over. Instead, the patrol car pulled away and left us on our own once again in the pitch darkness and the pelting rain. The exit ramp finally appeared and I gladly veered off. By the time we got to the end of the ramp, the pace of the rain had slackened off to a dull roar. I told Dad to come back inside.

"This has been truly enlightening, Dad," I said as we pulled up outside the restaurant.

"Yeah, great. Just great. I think you'll need a new racquet," he said smiling as he shut the door.

"Hey, you owe me an umbrella, too!" I said. "Before you go – did you ever get to meet Mom's Dad?"

"A couple of times, why?"

"What was he like?"

"First-class prick," he replied.

"I figured as much. Let me know if you want any help with Marrsha Brady – or do you have your eye on Ms. Lincoln-Quaid?"

"It's Ronnie to her friends, and who says I can't have them both? Make for quite a tasty sandwich, eh?"

Now there was a sight I tried to etch from my mind's eyes before it became branded into the memory bank. A more bizarre 'sandwich' I could not imagine than dear old dad, Marrsha B. and Veronica L-Q.

"Do me one favor, Dad?"

"Name it."

"Get back to J.R.'s when you can, round up all the baseball cards except for the ones in the special box with the old photo and baseball, and find out how much they're worth," I said.

"Where do I do that?"

"J.R.'s probably got flyers from recent baseball card shows or whatever they call them, lying around. I'm sure there's one every weekend somewhere in New England."

"Leave it with me," said Dad, smiling the grin of grinners. I was happy for him. I don't even know why he was so fucking happy. He was drenched from head to toe. He looked like a shaved walrus, minus the tusks.

As I drove off into the night, it seemed that my choices, biologically-speaking, had just gone from near 0 to ABSOLUTE FUCKING ZERO in one afternoon. Prior to today, I'd tried like hell to eliminate any ties which may have bound me to my Armenian roots. Thank god that my old man had had the good sense to do away with the drop-dead worst ethnic name possible in exchange for one of the country's premier, albeit ancient, baseball hurlers and/or the name of one of America's most beloved chain of dingy diners. That at least removed one major obstacle to going through one's day to day business without ending up on the wrong end of some back-handed comment or worse – a cold, dank stare. If you haven't guessed by now, life wasn't much fun growing up in good ol' Richmond Heights. If it wasn't bad enough growing up in that rural cesspool in general, and in the Bedrosian Hacienda from Hell in particular, I was never too far away from a near-daily reminder from my all-too-accommodating classmates that I A). Looked like a freak; or B). Belonged to some smelly, non-American clan of goat huggers; or C) Both A & B.

So who could blame me for hanging out on the slim hope that on my dear mother's side of the genetic pool, that I might, just might, have been able to claim a lane on the most prized shipping list of all time? Alas, poor Yorick, this was not 'to be' in this Shakespearean-sized tragedy – just a whole lotta 'not to be's' whirling around in my now perfectly presented past, present and pathetic future.

And now, in yet another cruel ironic twist – I was having to return to the scene of my most forgettable childhood memories and try to prevent my father's father from suffering the ignominy of being thrust out of what could only for him have been considered a paradisiacal place.

Before focusing on that drama, however, I had to face up to re-entering the rarefied atmosphere of 'The Record' and try to churn out enough copy to cover a double page spread (if not more!) celebrating the 300th year since the birth of this stillborn town. It was never quite that straightforward a mission, though. I was still having trouble digesting thoughts of my father's salacious 'sandwich' situation, not to mention what the heck my mother was doing breaking into my apartment (for a second time) and wondering just what the heck the word 'Inkota' meant.

It was too late to ring the farm. Ditto for thinking about what faced me at the paper in the morning. So I did the next best thing. I parked the car outside the apartment house and walked right past my door to Ian's to see if he was up for a beer or three at the bar.

"Matey, good to see ya! You're wet - good trip?"

"Yes, I'm wet and good's a relative term – particularly when you're using it in relation to any of my relatives," I said.

"That bad, eh? Let's grab a beer, mate," Ian said. "There's much to tell. Much," he said rather emphatically before adding with equal emphasis, "but I think you better have a look at your apartment first."

I knew, in much the same way when Ms. Lincoln-Quaid had handed me the Winslow family tree that I wasn't going to like what I'd see. I just knew. If I told you that the place had been turned upside down, it would not begin to describe just how messed up it really was. I didn't know where to look first – or last for that matter. Somebody or bodies had turned every piece of furniture upside down looking for god knows what.

There were bits of stuffing obviously ripped out of the bedroom mattress that were floating in the kitchen sink, inside the smashed TV picture tube, even stuck inside the refrigerator which now lay on its side in the living room.

"You got some powerful enemies, maestro," Ian observed.

"My mother did this?" I asked.

"No, that was a couple of days ago. This was some time last night which I missed because I was working late," Ian said.

"I can't imagine who the hell I've pissed off this much. Or what the fuck they're looking for. No time to worry about it now. Let's grab that beer," I said as Ian helped me pile the remains of what had been a perfectly first-class, second-hand lamp into the middle of the floor, before adding: "Does the word 'Inkota' mean anything to you?"

Chapter Forty

Ian and I got to the bar before Lou. In fact, we were well into Round Three by the time he joined us, looking like something out of a bad zombie flick.

"Thanks for waiting up," Lou said.

"You look like shit," I offered as an ice breaker.

"Now I know what you must feel like every time you look in a mirror. What's a guy got to do to get drunk in this place?" Lou said.

"Now you're talking!" yelled out Mel, our favorite tavernkeeper, who very gently placed three more long, tall glasses of liquid amber in front of us.

"So tell me, what's it like out there in the unreal world? Give me something – anything," Lou says.

"Hey, forget about what's out there, mate. You should see his flat. It looks like something Godzilla rolled around in," Ian says.

"Why?" Lou asks.

"Got me. I've got a couple of ideas, but it doesn't really matter. I was hoping to re-decorate the joint anyway."

"Oh, really? Since when did you have any money? It certainly ain't from working at '*The Record*'," Lou says.

"It certainly ain't, but enough about me. What's happening here?"

"Well, glad you asked. Since you've been gallivanting all over New England, I've been charged with the non-too-easy task of breaking in three new reporters who wouldn't know a news story if it fell into their laps. Add to this, the fact that we now are the proud custodians of the world's worst computer system and you have the perfect recipe for becoming an alcoholic, drug addict or Mets fan," Lou said as he placed three fingers in the air toward no one in particular, indicating the need for another round of drinks.

"Computers? How the hell did the James' get the dosh to afford them?" I asked.

"Who knows? Who cares? Just get ready for even more bedlam than normal – if that's humanly possible in this shithole," Lou said.

"Can see you're high on life," I said. "So what's wrong with them?"

"What's wrong with them, Ian? Do you wanna start or should I? I'll go. Well, call me old-fashioned, but I still prefer holding the story in my hand so I can mark it, cut it and paste it beyond recognition before handing it back to the idiot who 'wrote' it to take another stab at it," Lou said.

"What he said," Ian chimed in.

"Now, all you have in front of you is a tiny, gray screen that holds about 50 words. You spend half your life moving the copy up and down and all around trying to remember what was written before to figure out if you need to move it up, down or sideways. I tell you, I'm about ready to throw one of these screens out the fucking window," Lou says, downing his latest beer in one gulp.

"Yeah, but it must be nice to not have scissors and cans of paste all over the place," I offered.

"I love the smell of paste pots in the morning," Ian offered in the world's worst Robert Duval impression. "Seriously though, what I miss is the noise."

"What do you mean?"

"Without typewriters, there's no more noise in the newsroom except for the occasional fart or burp. The fricking computers make no sound at all," Ian explained.

"Sounds great. Can't wait to get in there," I said.

"Enough of our challenges. So how was your time away?" Lou asks.

"Great. Just great. I found out my grandfather's farm is about to be taken off him for some Government infringement I cannot even begin to figure out and I never was – and never shall be – genetically connected with the likes of John Standish and Myles Smith or whoever they were. Other than that, the trip was tremendous."

"You can't have everything," Lou said. "Did you give any thought to how you're gonna fill two pages tomorrow with cutting edge material on 'Foundation Day'?"

"I did and I have, though not sure what our fearless leaders will make of it. Course, we could always just turn it over to the Great Chief and let him talk about the old days cleaning the toilets at Richmond Heights Junior High School. Give us some real insight into the makings of a modern-day, rags to rags Chieftain," I said.

"You gotta be nuts. Hey, the old lady is mad as hell about you taking off. You better deliver."

"How do you know what she thinks?"

"Because she still comes around some nights to give the final approval on Page One."

"Really? What time is that?"

"I dunno. About 11.30 most times, why?"

"I would've thought she'd leave that with Boy Wonder," I said.

"Yeah, most Friday nights she does, but not on Tuesdays. She's almost always there."

"That's interesting," I said.

"What are you thinking?" Ian cut in.

"Nothing really, but what if something big happens after they've signed off?" I asked.

"What? You mean how does one literally stop the presses?"

"Yeah."

"I yell 'Stop Press!' and they stop rolling as if by magic. What do you think?"

"But does anyone else have the authority to do that?"

"Only Martin but he never does. It's never happened since I've been there, and it's unlikely that it ever will as I'm the only moron from editorial still around that late at night. It'd have to be a damn big story for that to happen. DAMN BIG," Lou said.

"So you wouldn't have to get any authority from the Wicked Witch?"

"Nah, I'd just have to pull rank over the press boys and get them to stop the run," Lou said. "Why, got something in mind?"

"No reason. It's just good to know," I said.

"Hey, hang around the newsroom long enough and you may figure it out for yourself," Lou said. "I gotta get some sleep. Can't wait to see what you come up with for 'Foundation Day'."

"Me, too," I said. "Can't wait."

Ian and I paid our respects to Mel who handed me a business card from a recent patron.

"What's this?"

"Business card from some New York guy. Figured you'd be interested," she said.

The card read: Lance Hale II, Senior Executive, Corporate Affairs & Marketing – Savage & Savage, Public Relations/Corporate Communications. The address was based on Park Avenue. What the heck would a big time Park Avenue PR hack be doing in this backwater?

"Did he say what he was doing here?"

"No, just drank like a fish and left a big tip," she replied.

I thanked mein hostess and weaved my way back to the apartment with Ian. Ian offered his couch to me but for some reason I opted to head back into the chaos that now filled my apartment. It suited me.

What didn't suit me was who I found waiting there when I entered. I knew something was wrong the minute I walked in because the light was on. I never leave lights on. I went to reach for the baseball bat I kept by the door. It wasn't there. When I looked up to see who was there, I realized a baseball bat would not have made any impression. A nuclear warhead would not have made any dent. It wasn't the bums who'd tossed the joint. It wasn't some crazed drug addict, hit-man or super-sized street thug. It was much, much worse than that.

"Hello son. We need to talk."

Chapter Forty One

"I knew it! A guy can't re-decorate without word spreading like wildfire. Well I'm not telling you who I've used! Forget it!"

"Fuck off, Walter. I need to talk to you," my humorless mother said.

"At this hour? Do you know what time it is? Better still – why do you keep breaking into this place when you have a museum's worth of shit to toss around at your own place? Or, better still yet, do you know what your name really is?"

"You're drunk," she said stating the bleeding obvious.

"I may be drunk, but I at least know who I am and what I stand for!"

"You're crazy," my mother replied.

"Not as crazy as you. Who were the thugs you paid to toss the joint? What the hell are you looking for?"

"Walter, I am not looking for anything. I'm just concerned, that's all."

"Concerned? This is how you show concern? Christ, I gotta put you in for a medal. I think they're still taking nominations for 'Mother Fucker of the Year'."

"I'm not listening to any more of your crap. Call me tomorrow when you sober up. We need to talk," said Mrs. Elizabeth Quincy Adams Winslow-Bedrosian-Johnson – or whatever her real name was.

"Please be careful where you step, you devil you. Or should I say 'Devil's Hopyard?'"

She had just reached the front door when I mentioned the site of her initial passion play with dear old dad. "Good night, Walter," was all she said and slammed the door. It was hard to know whether she was any angrier than usual from her reaction. I didn't really give a shit. I was still curious what the heck she was after, though.

I decided against cleaning the place up, hoping it would somehow magically return to its original state by morning. Either that, or perhaps the goons who had wrecked the joint could return and pulverize everything into bite-sized pieces.

I finally found the answering machine and decided to check it for any other potentially-important clues – to what I wasn't really sure. Sure enough, there were several calls – and all from women. The first one was from Jenny, sounding more like some lawyer acting on behalf of my grandfather than anything else. At least she still cared for one member of the family. Click. The second call was from the Lady Mayoress, obviously drinking alone and wanting to know where I was and who I was 'fucking' now. Click, click. And last but not least was the esteemed publisher of '*The Record*', simply calling to congratulate me on my recent work and hoping I'd be able to help out with 'a classic Walt Johnson piece of magic or two' for the special 'Foundation Day' edition. Click, click, click.

And if the click chicks weren't enough, I'd no sooner switched the answer machine off when a whole bunch of static filled my head. You guessed it – dear ol' St. Vartan, horning in to drop his two-cents worth. YOUR FUTURE LIES IN THE PAST is all he had to offer.

"Your future lies in the past," I yelled trying to imitate his scratchy whisper. "Just who the frack are you? Leave me alone! Go away and come again some other day – no, make that some other life time. In fact, make that someone else's lifetime," I said hoping to deliver the ultimate knock-out blow.

I swear I heard his static laughing at me.

At some point, things just had to start looking up. I tried finding some clean clothes to wear the next day to work, but wound up finding only a few warm cans of unopened beer. What better way to spend the rest of the early morning than drinking warm beer in the middle of my living room piled high with bits and pieces of my past? Was this what St. Vartan meant about my future lying in the past? Or was the key word 'lying' as in not telling the truth? I just kept downing the beers and when that ran out, I found a half-opened bottle of rotten scotch that the thugs had obviously missed. I don't remember much more about the evening.

When I woke up, my head was fighting it out with my back for who felt worse. I declared the competition a tie and promptly downed the last remaining can of room temperature beer. It was like drinking your own piss. May be that's how the fad started in Britain all those centuries ago? Who knows – may be some bright spark put in charge of engineering Stonehenge, for instance, ran out of beer and convinced the guys around the campfire one night that they could satisfy their thirst by drinking their own wee-wee. Christ, I was losing it fast. I had a quick shower and threw on the first shirt and pants I could find before heading to the newspaper.

It was still early – about 10 a.m. when I arrived and I was expecting the worst. There was an overwhelming sense of calm about the place, though, which was odd given that it generally thrived on complete chaos – like the kind found in my apartment. I'd never heard the newsroom so quiet before. Deathly so. Lou was right about the computers – even though they took up more space on the desks than their right Royal predecessors – they made no noise. Usually, there would have been few reporters in the newsroom that early to make any noise anyway, but today was different no doubt due to the special edition celebrating the town's 300th birthday. There also seemed to be, dare I say it, a hint of professionalism descending over the newsroom. Surely that couldn't be?

"Nice of you to show," Marty James called out.

"My pleasure," I replied.

"Don't know what makes you so special," Marty muttered.

"You talking to me?"

"Who else – dickhead? If it were up to me – you'd be gone. As in fired," he continued, assuming I knew what the hell he was talking about.

"Hey, thanks for the pep talk. Glad you're on my team," I replied, coming to the realization he must have been referring to his mother as my unlikely Lady and Protector.

"What you got for 'Foundation Day'? Martin next asked.

"Something special," I said.

"Can hardly wait. Tell Saunders what you got because he's in charge of 'Foundation Day' copy," he said.

"Oh, good. Glad to see the cream has risen to the top of the dung heap," I said, though Marty missed it having moved on to someone else.

I headed to the Morgue to start working on my contribution to this fine celebratory edition. Even my Morgue stablemate, Wall Edwards, was busy putting thoughts down, though still on his ancient typewriter. I still was unsure exactly what I was going to write, but figured I'd pull out some of the material I'd found in Marsden's lost copy of the *History of New Richmond*. From what I could see, there wasn't going to be much room left for me anyway, as it looked like at least seven other reporters were slaving away at copy when I arrived.

"You lucky bastid," Lou yelled out.

"You gotta be kidding," I said.

"No, it seems the boss lady got worried when you didn't show up yesterday, but instead of taking it out on you – ended up taking it out on everyone else, including her beloved son and heir-head – Marty. She outlined stories for everyone in the newsroom. Very organized – for once in her life," Lou said turning to make sure there were no James' in earshot. "And when she's not organizing copy, she's deep in discussions in her office with your old mate, the dear lady Mayoress."

"Really?" I said not really taking in what he was saying. "So I don't have to write anything?"

"Don't think so. If I were you, I'd bail out now and worry about coming up with something truly exceptional for next week's edition," Lou said.

"That's great, cuz I got to get out to the old man's farm anyway. Can you cover for me?"

"Yeah, but it's gonna cost you," Lou said.

"Name it," I replied.

"How about a real job with human beings?"

"Hey, I'm no miracle worker," I said, heading for the door. I felt a deep sense of relief on the one hand, because I really had nothing to offer word-wise, that is. On the other hand, though, I'd hoped to spend some time uncovering an angle or three that would have blown their socks off.

I kept thinking about St. Vartan's words. And I kept thinking about Marsden's autographed copy of his *History of New Richmond*. And about granddad's farm. Something kept telling me the three were bound together tighter than a mosquito's bum.

Chapter Forty Two

In my haste to get away from the newsroom before anyone else stuck me with some stinker of a story idea, I realized I hadn't caught up with Mason James in a while to see if he'd had any luck finding out about the meaning of 'Inkota'.

As per usual, I checked the 'mail room' at the bar across the street. Mel was busy as ever cleaning up the joint from the previous night's activities. But even the 'Final Edition' didn't look as disheveled as it usually did. To top it off, there wasn't a bar fly in sight and it was way past opening time.

"Wanna another job cleaning up a real mess – come by my place," I said.

"No thanks. This is bad enough," she said. "Hey, did you catch Mason while you were over there?"

"No, why?"

"He said he had some info for you. And figuring you'd come here before the newsroom he left me this note for you," she said handing me a small piece of paper.

'Inkota is an old Indian word (no great surprise there, I thought before returning to the note). Didn't find any meaning, but did find out it's been used by whatever company's buying up downtown properties – Inkota, Inc. Hope that helps," he said.

"Yeah, thanks," I said. "Hey, anyone else been looking for me?"

"What? Besides the drop-dead gorgeous models from the catwalks of Paris and New York? Nah, not really," Mel said.

"Their loss," I replied.

"Yeah, shame," Mel replied. "Come to think of it though, there were two guys – one white and one black – came in looking for 'some reporter from *The Record*' named Walt', a coupla nights ago."

"You're kidding, right?"

"Not at all, but I figured they weren't looking for your autograph so I made up some poop about you not working there anymore," she said.

"What'd they do then?"

"Had a couple more shots and left," she said. "One really odd thing about that, though."

"Yes?"

"Well, two things. First, the shots were from top shelf whiskey – Johnny Walker's Blue Label."

"What's so odd about that?"

"No one ever drinks from the top shelf in this bar except my mother!"

"And the second?"

"They drove off in a limo like the one used by the Mayor," Mel offered.

"Thanks. Thanks a lot," I said.

"You know those guys?"

"Sort of," I replied.

"What do they want?"

"I wish I knew. I really wish I knew."

The coincidences were becoming far too, well, coincidental. First, the Publisher is treating me better than her own blood. Next, my mother tries breaking into my apartment – twice – looking for something. When that fails, a couple of guys who probably work for the Mayor turn the place upside down and then turn up a few nights later at the bar looking for me.

So what was the connection between the Mayor, Mom and dare I say it – my Boss? I got back to my car only to find the passenger side window had been smashed, but nothing seemed out of place. Of course, the inside of my car always looked like it had already been in an accident so it was hard to know just what, if anything, had been removed.

I took a quick look around, but didn't see anyone waiting to pounce on me from the bushes. I simply wiped off the remaining bits of glass from the driver's seat and decided to head over to the farm before anything else could go wrong.

I took it especially slowly out of New Richmond hoping to find out if anyone was tailing me. Sure enough, there did seem to be one car, though it wasn't a limo. Then again, surely they wouldn't be that stupid, would they? Just for the heck of it, I stopped at the next gas station and placed a call. It was just after 11 a.m. so surely the person whose number I'd dialled would be hard at work? The car I felt had been tailing me, pulled in at the other end of the gas station. The driver got out and pretended to be checking the air pressure in his front tires. He had on a Yankees baseball cap and dark glasses, which given the overcast nature of the day at hand seemed a bit over the top, unless he was worried I might recognize him.

The person at the other end of the call picked up. "Aunt Stacey – is that you?"

"Why, Walter dear. How nice of you to call. Are you alright?"

"Why, shouldn't I be?"

There was silence at the other end of the line. "Whatever are you talking about, dear? Have you been drinking?"

"Not nearly enough, you?"

"Not without you. When are we getting together again?"

"Soon, real soon. Say a quick question: How'd you get to work today?"

"I'm not following you, dear."

"Well, did you drive yourself?"

"No, I came by limo like I always do, dear, why?"

"No reason. Say, that driver of yours – what was his name – Jimmy Dunn?"

"Yes, James. What about him?"

"Does he have a blue Charger?"

"Sorry, Walter. The Governor is on the line. Must run, bye," said the Mayor before hanging up.

I'll take that as a 'yes', I said to myself before trying to find another quarter to call the newspaper for back-up. It was at this point, dear readers, when something strange, or should I say even stranger than usual, happened. More recently, I'd not had so many visits from St. Vartan. At least not the formal one-way conversations he was so noted for. When I realized I didn't have any more quarters, and I now had no one to call for help, my first reaction was one of fear – as in seriously-stain-your-underpants kind of fear. I mean, these were two big guys and they were capable of doing whatever they wanted to me – especially out here on a near-deserted country road. Visions of drooling banjos and men whose IQs were exceeded by the number of teeth left in their mangy heads popped up. These sorts of visions didn't happen often, but when they did, they tended to hang around for a while like the smell of a prodigious fart. Not this time, though. No, in no time at all, the feelings of uneasiness were soon replaced by a steely sense of calm and total self belief.

Something, or someone more to the point, was taking control of my life which was fine by me, but usually they are someone tangible, like a lover, a best friend, hell, even a shrink. I was putting my life in the hands of the spirit of an ancient warrior whose last outing had ended badly (see killed) for himself and many, many of his devoted followers. I consoled myself, (or was that St. Vartan taking over again?), with the thought that someone, anyone, was better than no one at all. There even was a weird scheme hatching in my brain and it didn't seem to be coming from me. Did I just say what I thought I said? Christ, I'm starting to sound even whackier than The Chief, if that was possible.

I got back in my faithful four-wheeled steed and headed out again for Richmond Heights. Sure enough, the Charger likewise re-engaged in the pursuit. Glad to see his tire pressures were okay. It was at this point that the scheme became clear. Mid-mornings in Richmond Heights, particularly, through its rotten center, usually meant that it's one and only policeman and his patrol car were positioned behind the hedge in front of Town Hall, to nab drivers daring to go over the snail-like 25 m.p.h. speed limit that had been in place since Moses was a boy. Something, or someone I should say again, assured me that he would be ready and waiting for me today!

About two miles out of Richmond Heights, I started to slow down so the Charger had no choice but to creep closer to my trusty steed. I could now see Richmond Heights Town Hall's red bricks glistening in the morning sunlight. I could also see a vehicle parked neatly behind its huge hedge. Once I got past the hedge, I gunned the accelerator for all it was worth. It wasn't worth much, but we reached 50 in a matter of seconds. The Charger was forced to speed up as well and in an instant, I could hear the all-too-familiar siren of the local constable's patrol car.

The first part of the trap had worked to perfection. My hat, or should I say, my warrior's helmet, is off to you St. Vartan! There was still the problem of negotiating the ever-dangerous Darwinian Highway before I reached the farmhouse. This was that particularly nasty stretch of highway I told you about some time back in which cars, as well as many large trucks, travelled at speeds normally reserved for vehicles used in space travel. There were no stop signs or traffic lights on this bit of the ribboned highway, leaving it up to those crazy enough to try and cross the suicide strip to determine when it was best to give it a try. It was a lot like those times when you've come across a family of ducks merrily crossing a road with little or no concern about passing motor traffic. I envied the hell out of those quacks now, because I knew precisely how difficult it was to cross this little bit of roadside hell and just how easily I could become a piece of road kill beneath some 16-wheeler out of Wheeling, West Virginia, given the state of my decrepit four-door, non-lunar module.

As luck would have it, I could see there were no cars or trucks coming in either direction as I slowed down for the stop sign so I gunned it across. When I looked back in the rear-view mirror, I could see that the Charger had stopped and had to wait for a truck to go by before crossing over. If the Charger stopped there, the pursuit would be over; he'd get his speeding ticket and none of us would be any the wiser as to what was going on.

The Charger's charges were not about to lose me now so they charged over the two-lane divided highway with the copper in close pursuit. If only the cop knew they weren't running from him as much as they were trying to keep up with me! At the very least, I knew they'd now well and truly pissed him off and would be dealt with a lot more harshly if things worked out the way, I, and St. Vartan hoped!

I somehow managed to keep slightly ahead of the Charger and turned onto my granddad's dirt road. I hoped like hell there would be some sort of party to greet these bozos when I finally pulled up, but even St. Vartan wasn't giving anything away on that score.

I pulled the car up just outside the front door, but saw no one in sight. I got out of the car as quickly as possible and bolted for the sheep's pen. The Charger didn't pull up behind me, preferring instead to follow after me off the dirt drive and through the front yard. He was going at such a speed though that he lost control, skidded on a cow patty or two, and ended up piling straight into a century-old oak tree. The driver, the one I'm sure was James Dunn, remained slumped over the steering wheel, obviously knocked out – or worse – from the collision. His colleague in crime, a very large black man who I think was the other limo driver used by the Mayor, got out and began running toward me with the police officer in close pursuit.

Now the reason I'd run for the sheep's pen, I would think is fairly obvious. Because there, stationed calmly at the far side of the pen was my all-time-favorite skin head, gently banging his rock-hard forehead against the stone wall. When the ram saw me enter the pen, though, he quickly turned his attention away from the blood-stained stones along the wall, and began barrelling at me as fast as he could. At just the right moment, and in hindsight, I cannot explain how I knew to dive when I did, but dive I did in such a way that the ram missed me and managed to scramble the family jewels of my would-be attacker good and proper.

"Just what the heck is going on?" puffed the policeman, whose light cream uniform looked as though it would have been a perfect fit about 10 years ago. He looked like the Pillsbury Doughboy packing heat.

"Got me, officer. All I know is that these two guys have destroyed my apartment, broken into my car and now were tailing me at breakneck speeds from New Richmond to here," I said.

"Thanks for your help. I couldn't figure out what the heck they were doing back there at the stop sign. Help me get this one up. I'll cuff him and get him in the car and call an ambulance for the other one."

"No problem."

"You mind coming down to the station later and making a statement?"

"Happy to oblige, officer," I said.

In spite of all the commotion, there still was no other human being about. Finally, my grandfather emerged from his garage where he obviously had been mucking around in the workshop. And then, as if from nowhere, The Chief appeared - as if from nowhere.

"It is good to see you, my son," said The Chief.

"Is that all you have to say?"

"No, my son," he began pulling me away from the policeman and his suspect. "I have hidden the treasure that these two men sought."

"What? What treasure? How do you know about what's been going on?"

"My son. Do you not yet understand that I hear the Voice, too?"

Chapter Forty Three

"Chief, you're starting to scare me now," I said.

"There is nothing to fear but fear itself," The Chief replied.

"Great. It isn't bad enough you have to steal sayings from Springsteen tapes. Now it's dead Presidents. What's next?"

"It is good you have come. The others will be here shortly," The Chief said.

"What others?"

"The men in the dark suits. They said they would be back today," he continued.

"You're losing me, Kimo Sabe," I said.

"They are coming back to show us their proof," he said.

"Can't wait. In the meantime, where have you hidden this 'treasure?'"

"In the cellar – under the wooden palings," The Chief said.

"Palings? In the cellar? What the hell is a fence doing down there?"

"All will be revealed shortly," The Chief said as Flynn came running from god knew where and jumped onto my back knocking me down and smothering me with kisses.

"If only all women could take a leaf out of your book," I said trying to fend her off. "C'mon girl, let's take a quick trip to the cellar before these other bad men arrive."

Thoughts were racing through my head. My mother; the Publisher; even the Mayor and her mis-guided henchmen – were all involved in some plot – but what? And what was it that I had that they so desperately wanted? And who were these mysterious men in dark suits? And what were they coming to do?

I turned on the light to the cellar and walked slowly down the uneven steps. It wasn't much of a cellar. More like an uneven, open pit surrounded by rock walls and creaky floorboards overhead. I soon found the old wooden palings The Chief had referred to. They were indeed very old and unusual in shape. They certainly weren't the kind of fence palings found on any home built since the War – any war. They were far thicker and cruder like the ones found around forts in the old Westerns. When I asked granddad about them, he said he'd been digging them up for years and using them for firewood. Digging them up? In the cellar? Sure enough, I'd no sooner recalled that comment when I tripped over the top of one still buried snugly into the cellar's dirt floor. I picked myself up and lifted the top two planks from the most recent wood pile. There, almost glistening beneath the rubble, was the treasure – though not of Sierra Madre but rather, of Chez Bedrosian. It was Mr. Marsden's most unusual copy of the *History of New Richmond* – complete with edited notations. So this was what they were after? But why? Because they revealed the truth about my mother's non-Mayflower ties? Why would the Mayoress or the Publisher give a shit about some familial forgery? Why indeed?

Unfortunately, I was unable to get stuck back into the book before I was being called upstairs by The Chief. Our well-groomed guests had arrived. While I was pissed I'd be unable to read any more of the book – I was at least looking forward to finding out what the heck they were after.

"Gentlemen, how can I help you?"

"Are you the owner of this property?" asks this guy dressed in a dark gray suit, white shirt and gray tie. (I'll call him 'Mr. Gray').

"Could be. Who wants to know?"

"We're from The Department of the Interior – Native American Indian Land Claims Unit," says Mr. Gray in a flat tone to rival the blahness of his attire.

"You're who from where?"

"Listen. We've already been out here once. We're here to serve whoever is the rightful owner of this property for a major infringement of Native American title."

"Sorry. You're still not making any sense."

"Okay. I'll make it easier for you: Someone has been purchasing parcels of adjoining land to this property that were never, and never will be, for sale except by decree from the Federal Government."

"Hang on, pal. You're telling me that my dear, sweet, old grandfather who doesn't know that Audrey and Katharine Hepburn are not related, scratch that, who doesn't even know who Audrey and Katharine Hepburn are, has been buying up Indian land illegally?"

"That's it."

"Can you prove it?"

And with that – Mr. Gray's partner – who was equally non-resplendent in a solid black suit, white shirt and matching black tie, (I'll call him 'Mr. Black'), handed me several pieces of Xeroxed paper. They were copies of land deeds showing land purchases attributed to Mr. Sarkis Bedrosian but signed by some other person.

"This is all well and good but that's not my grandfather's signature."

"How do you know that?" queried Mr. Black.

"Simple. Because he never learned how to write," I replied.

Mr. Black and Mr. Gray turned simultaneously to look at one another and then without missing a beat, Mr. Gray piped up with: "The cheques, which amount to more than $150,000 over several years, belong to some local company called 'Inkota, Inc."

"You're kidding," I said.

Their matching blank expressions indicated that they were not kidding.

"He's been framed. Surely you can see that?" I said.

"It's not for us to decide. This matter will be referred to the State's Attorney's Office for trial. Consider yourself served," Mr. Gray said, handing me another official-looking-type document.

"Consider yourself served," I said trying to imitate his overly nasaly intonation while simultaneously re-creating the entire chorus form 'Oliver!', repeating the mind-numbing phrase 'CON-sider yourself', over and over. There were to be no ovations on this day, though.

Just a great sense that it was all getting weirder by the moment. My grandfather not only owed the State more than $23,000 in back taxes, but now was being accused of illegally buying up acres and acres of Indian Land. And in yet another irony of ironies, this so-called illegal property baron was providing shelter to the region's oldest surviving local Native American.

I thrust the subpoena at The Chief and stormed into the house. Granddad was busy peppering a perfectly good ear of corn with enough salt to start his own mine.

"Go easy on the salt, granddad," I said though it was apparent he not only hadn't seen me come in, but hadn't heard me, either. I nudged him gently on the shoulder, which caused him to turn around as quickly as a 90-year-old could.

"Hoo-hooo, my boy!" he says.

"Yeah, your boy," I said figuring it was best if he didn't know he now had the Feds as well as the State hot on his aged Armenian ass.

"What those men want?" he asked, pouring even more salt over the corn.

"Directions. They were lost," I replied, picking up the phone and dialing the newspaper, hoping beyond hope there might be some less tragic news happening there.

"Hey, good to hear from you, sport," Lou said.

"What's up there?" I asked.

"Well, let's see – it's been just another typical 'Foundation Day'. A shit-house parade; a bunch of stupid kids singing off key and The Lady Mayor then boring the crap out of everyone with some 'grand visions' for the future of this once thriving 'inland shore town'," Lou said.

"Inland shore town?"

"Yeah, do you believe that one?"

"Not really. Was that it?"

"Not quite," Lou began. "Turn on the TV – any TV and tune into Channel 9. I think you'll see someone from your recent past," Lou said before hanging up.

I turned on the set and saw a promo featuring my good friend and colleague Ms. MaryElena 'Rabid' Rabinelle – announcing in her weekly 'State Scoop' segment that New Richmond was to become the center of New England's largest inland marina complex.

It was all now starting to come together like a monumental jigsaw puzzle. The only thing was, the pieces were not all from the same puzzle. I did, however, have a few leads, not the least of which was something ol' Wall Edwards had told me many moons ago – 'The water. It's all about the water', he'd said.

I patted granddad on the back and headed for the door. I ran into The Chief on the way out and told him to guard the treasure with whatever was left of his life. I called Flynn but she did not appear. Strange given her love of riding. I told The Chief I'd be back soon. He winked at me knowingly – though just what he knew that I knew, I didn't know.

When I got back to the apartment, there were two more messages on my machine. One was from Marty James telling me to meet him tomorrow morning at 'the office'. The other was from Smoky Burgess at Ye Olde New Richmond Inne. He sounded absolutely apoplectic, which was a bit over the top – even for him. He said it was important for me to stop by – no matter what the hour. I had a few drinks to settle my nerves and made sure it was long after the serving hour before heading over to The Inne.

By the time I got there, the kitchen was closed, though the stench from whatever stew they had heated over and over again for the umpteenth night in a row still hung heavy in the air.

"Thanks for coming, Walt. Are you hungry?" mein host inquired.

I hadn't the heart to tell him that I'd rather eat someone else's vomit than risk another meal at his gastro bistro.

"What's up?" I asked hoping to get my mind off the thought of food.

"Were you there for the big announcement?"

"What, the one about New Richmond being the largest inland shithole? No, I missed it," I replied.

"Yeah, well, I think this document blows that little story out of the water," Smoky said while very discreetly pushing a manila envelope across the table.

"What's this?"

You'll see. Sure you don't want a drink or something?"

"Oh yeah, a double scotch – no ice - would work wonders," I said, ripping the cover off the folder. It contained a six-page document titled NEW RICHMOND: NEW ENGLAND'S GREATEST INLAND SHORE TOWN – Communications Strategy.

The author of this prized piece of PR was none other than Lance Hale II, Senior Executive with Savage & Savage – Public Relations and Communications' Specialists – New York New York.

Holy shit. This was dynamite which in the hands of the right journalist, (or little ol' me as it turns out), could prove fateful or even fatal to someone or some-more-than-one. It certainly wasn't well written. In fact, it did everything but communicate its message clearly. It was filled with gobbly gook like "The main aim of this communications strategy is to bring coherence to this great town's drive to restore itself as one of the state's – if not New England's – inland water pearls'.

It then went on to list a bunch of worthless bullet points under the heading of 'Principles:'

S&S will be open and honest in all communications

We will seek input from all parties and relay these messages back to the core stakeholders in PLAIN ENGLISH

We will ensure that all information is shared, accessible and inclusive to all interested parties

Blah, blah, blah, blah

"Gotten to the good bits yet?" Smoky said delivering the tallest double scotch ever.

"Hard to say. Why don't you save me a lot of time and spill," I said.

"In a nutshell – this lays out a bunch of plans – both positive and negative – to get the people of New Richmond to turn over all waterfront to some Marine Development Committee that will 'revitalize and reshape our tired shorelines'.

"Just how exactly?"

"Ahh, now that's the interesting bit. Because it would seem the good Mayor and whoever else comprises this so-called Marine Development Committee have been implementing this 'multi-leveled strategy' hook, line and stinker," Smoky said.

"I don't follow."

"You know that statue of Marsden put up a while back?"

"Yeah."

"That was Step One in the grand design. Next comes the move to pay homage to the local Indian tribes so as to gain pity and offer an apology for all the hardships that the Europeans have foisted on the Indians."

"And?"

"Well, today was the announcement of the next stage – namely, a grand Marina complex to rival that of 'Monaco or San Francisco', the good Lady Mayor actually said earlier – words taken directly from this document.

"Fuckin sick," I offered trying to get the bartender's attention for a refill.

"You ain't heard nothing yet," Smoky continued. "The next step will absolutely kill you."

"Kill me – please."

"Would you believe a floating casino?"

"Don't tell me – is it called the 'Inkota Princess?'"

"How did you know?" Smoky asked.

"Just lucky, I guess. Mind if I borrow this document?"

"By all means. Just don't let anyone know—"

"Hey, I never snitch on a snitch," I replied. "Thanks for the drinks."

"You gotta do something, Walt – before it's too late."

I didn't have the heart to tell him that we were well past late. I also didn't have the heart to tell him the really scary bits were well hidden down the back of the document. After getting through all this crap about the water and how best to 'exploit it to the good citizenry's advantage', was some truly spooky stuff that smacked of something like a cross between Tammany Hall and Tammy Faye Bakker.

Smoky hadn't drilled down in the document where plans were discussed about bringing the operators of the Almshouse into disrepute as well as passing on big news stories like today's Marina announcement to TV outlets rather than to the local newspaper, thereby 'bypassing any local resentment and ensuring wider, positive coverage throughout greater New England'. But then, in the last paragraph before its none-too-subtle conclusion, was the belief that New Richmond should let the planned casinos on Indian lands in southern Connecticut gain public scrutiny before blowing them out of the water – literally – with the proposed floating poker palace on what its authors cleverly dubbed 'The Bay State's Lake Champagne' (which was sure to go down a treat to those Green Mountaineers to the north who lay claim to the largest lake in the U.S. outside of the five Great Ones – Lake Champlain).

You had to admire Lance Hale II. He had a vivid imagination and an even more vivid way with words. What he didn't have was any sense of truth, justice or decency. But hey, who said good PR had anything to do with truth, justice or decency?

By this time, I'd long since left Smoky Burgess and his Inne far behind. I'd started walking home, but something or someone guided me toward City Hall. It was late – well past 9 p.m. and there were few signs of the revelry that had enveloped the town's tiny streets earlier in the day.

The only thing shining at this hour, oddly enough, was a light from the top floor of City Hall – which if I didn't know better belonged to dear old Aunt Stacey's grand office. I tried the back door and much to my surprise, found it unlocked. I couldn't find the light switch, but it didn't really matter. All I had to do was walk up four flights of stairs – which even in the dark and half drunk was not very difficult. What awaited me when I got to her office, however, sobered me up in a hurry.

I burst into the room figuring I'd give her a bit of a scare. I did that but hadn't counted on scaring the heck out of someone else who tumbled onto the hardwood floor as I roared into the center of the cavernous room.

"Walter – what the hell are you doing here?" The good lady Mayoress screamed reaching for some article of clothing to put around her semi-bare breasts. Her partner, a young man I'd never laid eyes on before, quickly scrambled behind the couch.

"Oh, my. What have we here? While I was unlucky enough to miss the celebrations earlier in the day, it looks like I've got a ringside seat for the evening's fireworks, eh?! Seriously, though, Aunt Stacey, I thought I was your one and only? How could you, you, you wanton tart?!" I said in my most hurtful voice.

"Walter, go now before I call the police!"

"Be my guest, dear. What would you tell them? That I stumbled in on your peccadillo with this young man who by the way – has not even had the decency to introduce himself yet."

"Walter, you've had your fun now leave us alone," she said.

"Yeah, yeah, don't worry. I'm not into threesomes. Besides, how could I possibly keep up with the likes of your latest conquest - Lance Hale II, isn't it?" I said while at the same time, and for no apparent reason, slipping the PR document into my jacket before they noticed what it was. "The Second, eh?" I said hoping they were not paying attention to the sheets of paper I was now having trouble stuffing inside my jacket. "Isn't that interesting. You see, I'm a second, too, oooh, get it – 'second', 'too' – why I've just engaged in word play!"

"Walter, please, you're drunk," the good lady Mayoress continued.

"And you're not? Why, I'd be celebrating too if I'd achieved what you two had today. Great job. And best of all – you got it on Channel 9 News! Do you get extra bonus points for that Lance or is that what tonight's all about? Say, has she done that helicopter thing yet with her tongue, whew boy, I gotta tell ya—"

"Walter, go now, please?!"

"No problem, ma'am. I am disappointed. You not only have my apartment and my car trashed, but then toss me aside for this city slicker who hopefully is not only Lance by name but lance by nature."

At this point, the Mayoress's partner raised himself from behind the couch and started to move toward me. He was wearing a brightly-colored pair of boxer shorts and a scowl.

"Easy, Sasquatch. I'm going. Nice shorts. Didn't realize satin boxers were in again. Do give me a call in the morning though, eh Aunt Stacey? There's so much to catch up on. And I do like to keep up with who's who in the petting zoo."

I got up early and prepared myself for the onslaught that was sure to greet me when I got to the office. I figured it was time to go on the offensive, however, since I knew that the Mayor, Mom and the Publisher were up to something. Thank god I'd been smart enough to hide the PR document. I had a feeling that would prove quite handy when I got to the paper.

❧

"Hey, Johnson – where you been? Get down to my mother's office. She needs to talk over a thing or two," called out Marty James at practically the same time I'd opened the main door to the newsroom. Talk about lying in wait.

I headed down to the Publisher's wing of the building. There were no lights on. Just the one emanating from her office. I could hear her talking to someone.

"He said what?" the Publisher said to the voice on the other end of the line. "Really? Don't worry. I'll find out what's going on," she said before hanging up without saying another word.

"Good morning, Ma'am," I said.

"Is it? Is it really?" she countered. "That was the Mayor."

"Oh?"

"Yes. It seems you two had a rather unusual 'meeting' last night," she said.

"Depends on what you call 'unusual'. If finding the Mayor bobbing for some guy's apples in her birthday suit in her office sounds 'unusual', then I guess it is. But I don't think it's the kind of thing that should go any further than this office, do you?"

"Don't get smart with me, Walter. Just leave it. And don't think I won't come down hard on you. How did we get scooped on the marina complex by a TV station of all things?"

"Yes, that was a surprise," I said now knowing she was following Lance's script nearly word for word.

"I"ll give you one last chance to redeem yourself, and it better be good this time," The Publisher said in her best scolding voice.

Bingo. I couldn't have asked for a better outcome. I now knew beyond a doubt that there was a direct link between the Mayor, the Publisher and probably my mother. The only downside to this revelation was that I still was no closer to figuring out just what the hell that connection was or where it was headed. Not even St. Vartan was helping me on this one. No, for the first time in a long time – I was well and truly on my lonesome. "Oh, it will. I just know it will," I lied.

"It involves the Almshouse," began the Publisher. "You'll be reporting to me on this one. It'll be strictly on a 'need to know' basis."

"Not even Marty will know?"

"Especially Martin," the Publisher said.

"How much time I got?"

"A week should do it. Here's some of the material. I'll arrange for you to meet with the main source tomorrow," she said.

"Great. And 'Mum's' the word," I said. By the time I left her office, I knew the story was crap. And interestingly, the 'main source' proved to be someone within the Mayor's office, so that fit in nicely. Christ, I hope Lance was getting extra for setting up innocent folk with alleged nefarious deeds.

The fact that I only had a week was interesting. The only connection I could make, (or should I say that Lance Hale II could make?), was the understanding that the Governor of Connecticut was due to announce the construction of two huge casino complexes to New Richmond's south any time now. I headed for the little boy's room and locked myself into one of the cubicles and opened up Lance Hale's document.

> *"As Indian tribes, particularly those long overlooked ones in the northeast have become flavor of the month, we believe it would be a perfect time to combine the areas' natural water heritage with its connection to the local indigenous tribes and more importantly, to the marvelous financial opportunities now available via gambling…*

The PR opus continued:

> *"It's proposed that we maximize full leverage of this once-in-a-lifetime opportunity by first announcing the soft launch of a marina on Foundation Day. We'll then follow this up with a couple of well-placed articles on unsavoury business practices threatening the town's untapped foreshore. Within days, via constant coverage in the local paper and by other neighboring media outlets, the good people of New Richmond will realize that they have yet to take full advantage of the great natural wonder on their doorstep – its own vast Great Lake! Once they've accepted the marina complex, we can then drop the blockbuster business deal - the floating casino to be called the 'Inkota Princess'."*

It was some of the worst writing I'd ever seen, but obviously Savage & Savage had gotten away with it before. And they were about to get away with it again. Maybe. Maybe not.

Now I know you know, dear reader, that I am not a very religious person, but lord knows something was happening to me lately that would make anyone think twice about the existence of a higher being. Forget about St. Vartan – I'm talking about someone or something that is REAL BIG. I still drank my fair share of holy fire water, but these spiritual feelings, ironically enough, were starting to hit me precisely because I was no longer hearing that voice. And now, unlike previously when I was under a lot of pressure, I didn't feel worried or the least bit concerned. I got the distinct impression that everything that was happening was part of some bigger plan in which I was but one of the miniscule icons being shuffled around the blueprint. I took some comfort in that feeling. Or, may be Uncle J.R. had been right when he used to tell me that 'Nothing ever happens for nothing'. As usual, I used to think it was just another one of his dumb-ass sayings, but not any more. I wished I'd paid a bit more attention to him. Shit, Bob Mitchum thought he was pretty cool. Bob 'Fucking' Mitchum!

It was another of dear ol' Uncle J.R.'s sayings that was pinballing its way around my addled brainpan more recently: 'If you can't beat 'em, arrange to have them beaten!' Indeed, I knew I couldn't beat the might and power of the town's three most powerful people, but if all fell exactly into place as had been laid out for me by some out-of-mind and body experience – then I certainly could not only arrange to take them on, but play a key role in bringing about their demise.

While the Publisher gave me seven days to turn in the story, I knew there was just a week left to my non-illustrious career as a journalist. At least in this shithole of a town. But I had an idea (or at least I thought it was my idea?!), on how to go out on top. The only possible complication was that I needed the help of a few others to get me there.

The first of these helpers presented himself in the way of the one and only member of New Richmond's finest, ringing me to find out more about the 'ebony and ivory nut-cases' they had pinned down in the local jail's only holding cell.

"What did you do to these two fruitcakes?" asked Sergeant Ron Schofield.

Sergeant Ron and I went back a long way. All the way back to Richmond Heights Elementary. He was known as 'Checkers', and not because of the way he moved pieces of black and white around a board game. Rather, because even by the age of 11, he boasted more fat than a bathtub full of Crisco. That's right, he was named after the Chub Man himself - Chubby Checker.

"Hey, long time no hear, Checkers. How ya been?"

"Cut the crap, Johnson. I just wanna know who and what these two guys are on about?"

"Hey, when you find out –let me know? Just do me a favor – don't let them out for at least another day or two – capice?"

"Oh, yeah. No problem, Kojak. When did I start workin for you?"

"That's the spirit, Checkers. Can you at least find out who put them up to it?"

"I can do better than that. I just don't know what it all means. Can you drop by later and take a look at their statements? These guys are singing so much they'll be confessing to killing J.F.K. and his brother any minute now."

"You're kidding, right?"

"I don't kid, Johnson. Even you have to remember that. I just want to know what the fuck they're on about."

"See you soon," I said and hung up the phone before he had a chance to change his mind. That was great news. And it only got better after dropping by the station and having an unofficial look at their statements. They not only dobbed in the Mayor, but the Publisher and my mother for hiring them to 'locate a particular copy of Marden's '*History of New Richmond*', which was in the hands of 'One Walter Johnson…'

I now had the definitive link bringing the three witches of New Richmond together. The only remaining piece of the puzzle was why?

Even with this clue, time wasn't just running out on me – it was running out at warp speed. There was only one thing for me to do: I dialled the number for 'The Final Edition' and asked Mel if she could set up a couple of boilermakers.

"This is early even for you," Mel said. "Why two boilermakers?"

"I need to do a lot of thinking and I always think better on a full stomach."

"Ready when you are," Mel said before hanging up.

Gotta love a woman who gives a guy what he wants when he wants – and needs – it. I downed the drinks within minutes and headed for the door.

"Hey, Walt. Your tab's getting a bit high," Mel said.

"Like how high?" I asked.

"Like Green Monster high," she said referring to the trademark towering left field wall at Fenway Park.

"C'mon, it ain't that bad."

"Man, you're gonna need a bank loan to pay it back soon," Mel replied.

"How about a Ty Cobb and Joe Dimaggio?" I replied, remembering I owed dear old Dad a call to see how he was going with J.R.'s baseball cards. And with Marrsha Brady if I dared to ask.

That was the next piece of good news. I caught Dad just before he was heading back to Boston to catch up with his latest 'lady love'.

"Dare I ask who it is?"

"You may, but I ain't gonna tell ya. You might jinx it."

"Fair enough. How about the cards. Any luck?"

"Oh, yeah, I took 'em to two different card shows – one in Worcester and the other on The Cape."

"And?"

"I got two dealers fighting each other for em."

"What kinda fight we talking here – Light, Middle or Heavyweight?"

"The last offer was $23,500 and going up," he said.

"That's Super Heavyweight! Great going, pops!"

"Hey, I'm not done yet. There's big show on in Nashua this weekend. I'll go and see if we can squeeze a bit more out of 'em."

"Great, Dad. Keep squeezing – both the cards and your lady love."

"Don't worry about that. I got lots to squeeze and I'm loving every frickin minute of it."

"So it is Marrsha, eh?!"

"Gotta go, son. See you soon," he said before hanging up.

I packed a few things and headed back to granddad's place. While everything was starting to fall into place, I couldn't afford to have it all fall down before I solved the final piece of the puzzle. And everything pointed to it being at the farm.

All was quiet for a change when I arrived. I headed straight for the cellar and pulled out the innocuous-looking hardcover book that had everyone in spasms. If only I could figure out why? I didn't have to wait long. Even though I'd only been able to get through the first 30 or so pages of the heavily-edited manuscript, I accidentally dropped the book on the dirt floor and when I picked it up – my gaze was drawn to a particularly badly scribbled section just above the page number 81.

"Many people have tried to discover the true meaning of the Menoshocutt word "Inkota'." My head began to race as I came across THAT word. *"It was not until I showed my flawed work to the town's most gracious grand dame – Miss Elizabeth Quincy Adams Winslow – that I discovered its true meaning."* Oh my gawd! *"She told me while taking tea yesterday afternoon that few words carried the power and passion for the local Indians that "Inkota' carried. She said it was part of the Menoshocutts' version of creation. While we believed the earth was created by one all-powerful God, their world was created by the efforts of three female deities – one which represented the sky; the second, the earth; and the third, the water. Together, these three all-powerful forces combined to give us life. Together they are known as the 'Inkota' or, providers of "The Way."*

In this irony of ironies, this direct ancestor of my mother now telling us why the region's three most powerful women had chosen such an odd name for their double-dealing company of mis-deeds, the next question now begged to be asked: How the heck did she know this? Who had told her? I'd always been led to believe that this woman – known rather unaffectionately within the family as that "Spinster Woman," had achieved little in her life – so little in fact that she had never even bothered to marry or bear children. It had been left up to her siblings to carry on the grand old 'Winslow' tradition of lying like rugs about the family's history.

And this is where things started to get truly spooky. While I madly tried to keep reading, my thoughts were interrupted by my grandfather inching his way down the steep cellar steps. He wasn't coming to see me. He didn't even know I was there. He was coming down to fetch some firewood, but not just any firewood, a neatly piled pack of fencing he'd dug some time earlier out of the floor.

"What're you doin, granddad?"

"Gotta make fire," he replied.

"Okay, I'll help you," I said and walked over to pick up the top two or three chunks of wood. My hand caught something sharp buried in the fat side of one of the fence palings. I pulled my hand away and stuck it in my mouth to stop the bleeding. When I picked up the chunk of wood, there stuck in it was a small, neatly carved piece of rock. It was not just any old piece of granite or flint, though. It was a fricking arrowhead! "Granddad, how many pieces of wood have you found here?"

"I dunno – I lost count long ago," he said nonchalantly.

"Okay, I think we're done here for today. I'll go get you some other wood," I said leading him back to the bottom of the stairs. I wasn't sure what was going on, but I was coming to think this was not just some bunch of discarded sheep fencing lying around. I decided to call Prof. Bryan Harvey at the University of Western Massachusetts to see if he could come take a look. And it was just as well. Because just as Prof. Harvey showed up – Flynn the Wonder Dog bolted out of the woods carrying a very large bone in her mouth.

"Granddad, what have I told you about serving up cow bones to the dog?"

"That is no cow bone," said The Chief who came out of nowhere and proceeded to kneel before the dog who graciously dropped the huge chuck of calcium in front of him.

"What is it, Chief?" I said as Prof. Harvey and I walked over to the prostrated octogenarian who I thought might have had a stroke.

I didn't know whether to laugh or cry. That is, until The Chief got up slowly from his knees holding the bone aloft. He gazed calmly at the heavens before turning toward me, kneeling again and offering the bone to me as some sort of peace offering.

"Hey Chief, enough already. I don't need any piece offering. Get it, 'piece', not 'peace' offering?"

Everyone became quiet. Even the dog didn't know what to do. "The Chief is right," Prof. Harvey began. "This is human remains and from what you've been telling me about what's in your cellar – I believe you have just uncovered New England archaeology's equivalent to King Tut's Tomb."

Chapter Forty Four

King Tut in Richmond Heights seemed like a stretch, but what was becoming clear was that whatever – or whoever – was in the cellar, just might give us a bit more breathing space before having to decide what to do with the illegal land claims case.

I headed back to town with the mighty manuscript well hidden in the trunk of the car. There was still a lot more to get through and hopefully, there were no more baddies left on the street to try and pinch it from me. Prof. Harvey said he'd be able to tell me more about the site by week's end. That was good enough for me. Meanwhile, I needed to keep up appearances at the newspaper and contact this great 'source' that Connie Wheeler-James gave me regarding the Almshouse. I felt like telling her there was no need for me to talk to anyone local. I might as well just interview Lance Hale who seemed to be the only other person coming up with copy – albeit highly fanciful and untrue. (Not that I was any better!).

I called the 'source' at Town Hall and told him to meet me at 'The Final Edition' for a beer. 'He' turned out to be a 'she' lawyer working in the Prosecutor's Office named Kelly Hart. She apologized for the deep voice, blaming it on the flu. That was fine by me. Apart from the sore throat, there was nothing remotely sickly about her. Even though she may have been on the wrong side of 40, she wore a short skirt that fit snugly against her thighs and buttocks. She had on a matching jacket that came to her mid-section and topped it off with a fluffy, white blouse that left little to the imagination.

"How do you want to do this?" she asked as the bartender placed two beers in front of me and a glass of chardy in front of Kelly.

"Are we talking about the story?" I asked.

"What else?" she said before realizing my none-too-subtle attempt at flirting.

"Yeah, the story but I gotta tell you, it's going to be hard to convince me that the Almshouse is going under," I said.

"Oh, you'll believe it alright," she said, pulling a bunch of documents out of her black brief bag. I began gazing over the papers like I knew what she was on about. Or even cared. I'd finished the beers and ordered another round when I felt someone's hand stroking the back of my head.

"Hi, Walter. Long time no see," said the Lady Mayor, slipping ever so bluntly between me and Miss Hart who was nearly knocked off her bar stool.

"Yes, and this time you even have clothes on," I said, which definitely knocked her off the stool.

"Now, now, Walter. You have such a vivid imagination," Mrs. Tucker-Morgan said before turning to her co-conspirator and telling her to take a hike. Politely, of course. Miss Hart nodded to us both, gathered up her papers and headed for the door.

"Fine looking woman," I said turning my gaze on the she-devil now perched precariously on the same bar stool. "Bit too old for you, isn't she?" said the Mayor.

"Hey, enough of my love life. Speaking of which, where's lover boy?"

"Now, Walter, please keep your voice down. Some people here don't understand your sense of humor."

"They wouldn't be alone. I'm not sure I get it. But seriously, where's Lance?"

"How do you know who he is?"

"Oh, that. It was nothing really. It seems he dropped by here a couple of times and shouted the bar a few rounds of drinks. Made quite a spectacle of himself and let everyone know who he was and where he was from. Very big time," I said.

Aunt Stacey nodded as if she knew what I was talking about. I was glad someone did. She downed her glass of wine as well as what was left of Miss Hart's before turning back to me: "Let's get something straight,

Walter. No more kidding around. You know what you have to do, right?"

"Oh, yes. I know what I have to do," I replied. "But just for the record – can you remind me?"

"Cut the shit, Walter. We're trying to do something good for this crap hole so you better not stuff it up again," she said.

"I appreciate what you and your, ahh, supporters are trying to do. I really do. No one wants to live in a stinking 'crap hole' forever, right? Why shouldn't we have what other great towns and cities of the world have? Electricity, running water, stale beer, free sex, etc, etc, etc. I think we're all reading from the same page on this if you know what I mean?"

Her eyes nearly bugged out of her head on the word 'page'. It caught her off guard, so much so that it was some time before she fumbled out a few words. "Yes, well, so long as we're all in this together. There will be plenty to go around."

"Oh, yes. I'm sure of that," I said. "I must be going. Gotta big story to write."

"Great. Let me know if you need any other information," said Aunt Stacey.

I nodded and headed for the back door. "Put it on her tab, will you?" I said to the bartender.

"And do go see your mother, Walter. She misses you," said the Mayor as if she meant it.

"Only if you promise to do the same for your two goons down at the police station. They need someone to tuck them in."

I went back to my apartment and tried to read more of Marsden's edited manuscript. There were thousands of more questions than answers at so many levels, beginning with what made him go back and scribble in the margins in the first place? The answer lay somewhere between pages 48 and 54. It seems the Civil War had come to an end and there was a great sense of new beginnings and change sweeping the country. There also was something else sweeping through Mr. Marsden – namely some sense of guilt for having pinched so much of the work of his idol and now departed compatriot – Henry David Thoreau. Marsden doesn't say how old he is, but he is obviously dying of something and he's trying desperately to make up for all the mistakes he'd made in his all-too-regrettable life.

"Dear readers, I am nothing more than a sham! Lo these many years, I have basked in the glory of a fellow traveller of the written word. My work has paled in comparison to even his lesser works, though I shall attempt to redress this regrettable situation through these scribbles in the margins," Mr. Marsden says at one point.

'I vow to expose the truth and nothing but the truth in these last few days and weeks that I live and breathe. I have found many compassionate assistants in this journey, including New Richmond's oldest and least understood resident – Miss Elizabeth Quincy Adams Winslow. For you see, she has read my work and found nothing but half-truths and out-right lies that must be cleared before she can move on to the next life."

Just when I thought I'd learned all that I could from these marginal markings, more – much more beckoned. Alas, it was not to be this night.

"Ohhh, mate – fancy a beer?" chimed my next door neighbor Ian.

"Not now, mate. Not now."

"Oii, my shout," he said.

"I appreciate it, mate. I really do. But I'm doing something important. Really important."

"Reading a book? Fucking hell, man. Get with it," he replied. "Alright, mate. Your loss. But tell me one thing: Are you and Lou still serious about doing what you said you'd do a while back?"

"Never been more serious in all my life," I replied.

"When?"

"The very next issue, my good man," I said.

"I will definitely shout you a beer for that even if I do think you're both puffin muffins," Ian said.

"Puffin muffins? Is that another Aussie term?"

"No way, mate. No way," he said. "Can I get you anything while I'm out?"

"Besides one ear and some common sense – not a thing," I replied. The door shut and I tried to get back to the book. I'd moved about five words when the phone rang. I thought about letting it ring, but thought better of it. "Hello?"

"Walter?"

"Yes. Who's this?"

"You know who it is, Walter."

"Hi Mom. Sorry I haven't called. You well?"

"Well? You want to know if I'm well? What do you care?"

"Oh c'mon now. You know I care about you, Mommie Dearest?"

"Í just want you to know I didn't mean for it to all end up like this."

"Like what? I don't follow," I said. "Have you been drinking?"

"Not nearly enough, Walter. I just want you to know that I didn't mean for all this to happen."

"All what to happen?"

"You know 'all what'," she said.

"Hey, do you want some company?"

"No, I don't want any company. I just wanted you to know," she replied.

"Hello? You still there?" I said to an empty line. She didn't sound depressed exactly. Certainly not suicidal. Almost sorry and/or resigned to whatever happened next. As if she gave me her blessing to let it all hang out – once and for all. I sure as hell didn't want to let her down. And I would have told her that if she was still on the line.

I'd never worked so hard at a newspaper in all my life. No more ducking out for phantom interviews for hours at a time when I was really just getting pissed. No more 'gotta run' when in fact, there was absolutely nowhere to run – or even to walk to. There was less than a week till F-Day (Freedom/Failure/Fucked Day – take your pick). And I had to not only 'research' a story I had little or no interest in, but gather every last shred of evidence I could muster and present it to some fairly high-powered people in a hurry. I even called on my mate 'Checkers' for help in getting in to see some high-powered cops in Boston while at the same time calling on dear old Aunt Stacey to open a door or three at the U.S. State's Attorney's Office. She was most helpful, but wondered if what I had cooking just might spoil the roast. That one trip to Boston was the only time I spent away from the paper for the last four days. I didn't even get to catch up with Dad and his latest love which was more of a disappointment for him, I must say, than for moi. I wasn't sure I could handle running into the Brady Bunch again.

I was truly burning the midnight oil at the paper, too, but fortunately my 'office' was still tucked away deep inside the Morgue where very few reporters ventured. Even my cell mate Wall Edwards was away – taking some long-planned holiday probably to the other side of the Big Puddle.

Every so often Marty or his sidekick Jack Saunders would stop by to see how the story was coming. I gave them glimpses of my work on the computer screen. It was quite good – even by my lofty B.S. standards. Even the Publisher called in occasionally – if not in person – by phone to see if there was any other info she could chase down for me. You know that something stinks when the Publisher is offering to get her hands dirty.

I was so caught up in the newspaper world, I hadn't even had time to think about the farm and how the 'dig' was going. I did take one call from Jenny who had stopped by and found granddad crying in a corner of his barn – convinced he was to be evicted any minute. I tried to explain to her as best I could that everything was going to be all right.

"Well, it's not, you piece of shit!" she yelled down the line before slamming the receiver down. It's always good when friends can share magic moments like this up close and personally.

It was after midnight when I got back to the apartment and I hadn't stopped by the bar for a few drinks. I was stone cold sober which was bizarre enough. I'd no sooner fell into a heap on the couch and tried reading some more of Marsden's book when the phone rang.

"Hello, Walt?"

"Yes," I said knowing full well it was Bryan Harvey.

"Sorry to be ringing so late, but it's just so damn exciting. I have to share it with someone."

"Share what?"

"I don't know where to start," said Prof. Harvey sounding more like a love-struck schoolboy than a highly-celebrated early American archaeologist.

"Let's try the beginning," I said.

"Okay – you know the fence palings in the cellar?"

"Yep," I replied.

"They are the remnants of the stockade surrounding the original Fort New Richmond."

"What original fort are you talking about? That's miles away from The Almshouse where the first fort was."

"That's just it. That was not the original fort. And that's what makes the other discovery all the more exciting."

"What other discovery?"

"I can't tell you over the phone. Can you be at the farm by 8 a.m.?"

"I can be there now if you like. Did you find King Tut?" I said.

"Bigger," was all the Professor said before hanging up in my ear.

Chapter Forty Five

I had to be back at the newspaper by 10 a.m. so I reached the farm not long after daybreak. There were four cars and a jeep already parked out front. They must have been other members of the good Professor's dig team. I was met at the top of the stairs by two young guys holding several pieces of fence paling the way one would carry something very precious like, well like, King Tut's mummy.

"Prof. Harvey near by?"

"Downstairs," one of the guys said making his way for the front door.

"You're here?" Bryan called out.

"I am and I'm starting to get a little worried about you, Professor. Don't you sleep?"

"How can I when I've just come across the biggest find in the history of New England archaeology?!"

"Is that all? What, no buried treasure?"

"Better than that," he said.

"So you said earlier. Okay, spill," I replied.

"Based on the number and position of the wooden palings, along with other findings now coming out of pits 1 and 4 in the cellar, I'm confident in declaring that this is the site of the long, lost original Fort New Richmond," Prof. Harvey began before continuing without so much as a breath. "It pre-dates the one on the grounds of the Almshouse by at least 20 years and dendrochronology samples from the wood will back this up."

"Dendrochronology? What's that – wooden toothpaste?"

"Tree-ring dating," he replied without acknowledging my weak attempt at humor. "But there's more. A lot more waiting for us outside."

"Lead the way," I said. "Where's everyone else? Like The Chief, my granddad and even my dog?"

"They're outside."

"Outside? Are they crazy? They'll all catch pneumonia," I said.

Even though the sun was shining brightly, it was still a very nippy morning in late spring. Flynn came running up to meet me, her nostrils blaring cold-induced smoke rings from a small break in the trees that marked the boundary between the farm and the Indian Reserve.

"Your dog will be duly credited with the discovery," Prof. Harvey said.

"The discovery of what?"

"Not what – whom," he said. But before the Professor could tell me who my dog had uncovered, The Chief appeared from the small clearing holding up my grandfather. When he saw that it was me, he let go of grandpa who nearly fell over and ran toward me – or perhaps 'ran' wasn't the right word – how about 'shuffled real quickly?'

"Chief, what is it?" I said.

He didn't say a word, preferring instead to kneel at my feet.

"Hey, big guy. It's no big deal. So I gave you a place to stay for a while. It's nothing, really."

He began chanting. I couldn't understand a word. Prof. Harvey took me aside. "We've found the long lost burial site of the legendary leader of the Menoshocutts," he said proudly.

"You mean that bone that Flynn had the other day was –"

"None other than Chief Wachuquin himself," the Prof. replied.

"How can you know that?"

"We're not 100% certain, but it won't be long before we can confirm it. You see, that bone, which was a femur, the longest bone in the body, was particularly large and we know from the records that the Chief stood at least six feet, five inches."

"Yeah, but surely there was more than one tall guy living back then? Why couldn't it have been a local farmer or soldier?"

"Because the bones were buried with arrowheads, some beads and several deerskin rugs. It's the site of a very important tribal leader and since we know that he had been killed near Fort New Richmond, we feel certain that all the pieces of the puzzle point to it being him."

"I'm feeling a bit faint. Can someone help get the Chief up while I sit down?"

The Chief quickly removed his top garment, and placed it on the ground where I was about to sit.

"Chief – relax. I'm okay," I said.

"You still do not know?"

"Know what?"

"You are the Chosen One. You are the Light!" he said.

"I apologize about The Chief, Professor. I don't know what he's been smoking, but this is all getting a bit weirder than weird," I said. I helped my grandfather down onto The Chief's coat. "You okay, granddad?"

"Me get overthrown?"

"Overthrown? Oh, you mean 'thrown out?' I don't think so. Not now, grandpa. Eh Professor?"

"Oh, absolutely. I will submit the papers to get this site declared a National Heritage Listing immediately. There will be no further action by either state or federal authorities taken here," said the Professor proudly.

"Hear that, Gramps? You're safe – forever!"

"Hooooooo-Hooooooo!" he yelled at the top of his lungs. Flynn began jumping on the two of us, licking and barking, barking and licking for all he was worth. And The Chief performed some sort of dance around us. Quite a sight. Quite a sight, indeed.

I left the group at the farm to continue their partying and excavation work. At the rate Prof. Harvey's team was uncovering vital bits of New England's earliest human history, it seemed remotely possible they would discover either the remains of the Lindbergh's baby or Noah's Ark – or both. In spite of all these great revelations – there still seemed to be so many loose ends regarding my family tree and just what the heck it all meant.

In spite of an overwhelming sense of calm that had come over me, the next couple of days would prove to be the most harrowing yet. While I longed to have a free day or three to pour over the remaining pages of Marsden's edited manuscript, I had to focus every part of my brain on the other job at hand – namely, bringing down the wicked witches of New Richmond – One, Two, Three.

"How's the Almshouse article coming?" said Marty James with his First Mate Jack Saunders beside him.

"Yeah, just about there. We'll nail it, no worries," I said.

"You'd better. We need the copy by mid-afternoon," Marty said.

"Tomorrow?"

"No, next year. Yes, tomorrow," Marty replied, heading once again for the door out of the Morgue. "We'll give you as much room as you want on the front page."

"Your mate Ian's got a beauty of a headline for it!" Saunders threw in as if for good measure.

"Can't wait," I said, not game enough to say all he needs now is the copy.

How marvelous. Reporters kill to hear their editors whisper sweet somethings like 'we're holding the whole front page for your story'. All I could think about was how quickly the week had flown by and how little I had to show for it. On top of all of these woes, was yet another teeny, tiny fly in the all-encompassing ointment. While computers were proving to be much quicker in getting copy turned around, they also presented users with the ability to store information on the machine. While that was great in terms of storing notes for upcoming stories, it was bad from the point of view of keeping prying eyes from viewing super-sensitive information. It also wasn't good for me to keep any notes lying around the office which meant I had to try and commit as much of the material as I could to memory. I also made a mental note to catch up with Lou before leaving for the night.

"How goes it?" said Lou Cassals merrily prancing into the Morgue like some school kid in heat.

"Great. Just great. Now I know what it's like on Death Row."

"No, you don't, silly," Lou began. "You're the fucking executioner – not the executed!"

"Only if we pull it off. So tell me one more time how we pull this caper off without getting ourselves clubbed to death by all and sundry?" I said.

"That'll cost you a few beers," Lou said.

"Easy. How about we meet back at my place around midnight?"

"Don't forget me," chimed in Ian joining us in the none-too-rueful Morgue. "Besides, I got you the headline already!"

"So I hear. Hey, you any good at writing copy?" I replied.

PoorHouse Meltdown Leads to Call for 'DisALMsament'

I had to admit, it wasn't a bad headline. I almost hated NOT to have a great story to go with it. In fact, the material that my superiors had supplied me with was so filled with holes, if it had been a slab of Swiss cheese, it would have long since crumbled into nothingness.

The 'inside' info was trying to make out like the guys at the top of the Almshouse had skimmed off thousands of dollars over the years to bankroll ski holidays in Aspen; pay for Italian sports cars; etc, etc. The only problem was there were no such vehicles registered to anyone remotely related to the Almshouse. Nor were there any signs of ski poles dipped in the alleged greed trough.

For once though, I didn't give a shit. I actually didn't have to prove this story. All I had to do was go with the flow and give them what they wanted. And that I could do with no problem at all. I just had to throw in some real juicy fictitious quotes – (My favorite was attributed to a 'source intimate to the investigation who said "the corrupt actions of

Almshouse officials made the Watergate plumbers look like a rank bunch of amateur tradesmen").

There was only one other thing that Lou, Ian and I had failed to consider. When news of the 'scandal' hit the newsroom, every other reporter either wanted in on the story or wanted to hang around and see how it looked when it was typeset. The one time I didn't want my illustrious 'colleagues' around and I couldn't get rid of them. Mason James in particular was so incensed by the supposed actions of Almshouse officials ('I knew they were dirty all along',) he told me at one point, indicating that his recent attempts at overcoming pie-in-the-sky conspiracies were still well and truly on the front of his one and only burner.

By night fall, most of the reporters had finally given up either because of Ian's kind offer to shout everyone drinks at the bar or because of Lou's ranting and raving about the story's lead. "Hey, Johnson – you call this a lead? Try again and give me something with enough guts to attract every stray cat in town!" he shouted at one point. That line scared the shit out of me, let alone any other half-self-respecting reporter. Even Marty James and Jack Saunders left after that one. They did say, however, they'd be back to check the Page One proof when it was ready. And this was where our plan had to be timed to perfection.

It was well past 7 p.m. By now, I was well on the way to alcoholic oblivion and/or already passed out. It hadn't helped that I had had little more than a couple hours sleep over the past few days. So, after the newsroom emptied – I pulled a few beers out of the bottom desk drawer, shut the door to the Morgue and blocked it with Wall Edwards' desk and began typing just another story. Eleven hundred words – give or take a few. Hell, I'd written hundreds of stories like this in my 10 years in the business. Hundreds of stories racking up thousands – even tens of thousands of words, pissing off everyone from the Admiral of the Navy to Katharine Fucking Graham. But all of these stories combined were not going to have the impact of the last 1100.

It went exactly like this:

Three Faces of Evil Arrested in New Richmond

State and federal authorities are investigating a string of fraudulent land deals involving the town's waterfront development complex and adjoining Native American land holdings by the so-called 'Three Faces of Evil' of New Richmond society.

In a statement released earlier by U.S. State's Attorney T. Fowler Wright - Mayor Eustace Tucker-Morgan, Mrs. Constance Wheeler-James, Publisher of 'The Record', and Mrs. Elizabeth Quincy Adams Winslow Bedrosian, a leading local philanthropist, have been named as "the ringleaders in a diabolical plot that carried out countless cases of wanton fraud and razed properties of rich and historical significance that as a direct consequence, destroyed the lives of many good and innocent townspeople."

Sources close to the investigation say that the charges to be laid on the three town leaders will not only deep-six the proposed grandiose designs for the waterfront marina complex, but involved reckless misappropriations of Federally-sanctioned Indian Land Claims dating back to the 18th century, forgery and 'willful attempts to dodge State and Federal Tax laws'. (See accompanying story for details).

"This is absolutely appalling behavior by the three people who represented the pillars of New Richmond's commercial, social and political societies and what truly concerns me is the possibility that there may be more to come," Mr. Wright said.

The complex case, which cuts across many state and federal jurisdictions, drew similar reaction from the Massachusetts

Attorney General's Office: "This case will
go down in history as not only one of the
most complex series of illegal property
deals, but also the most disgusting mis-use
of the 200-year-old legislation set up to
protect North American Indian tribes
regardless of whether they were in the
plains of North Dakota or the lakefront of
New Richmond. At its core, however, this
case is incredibly simple – It's all about
greed. Pure, unadulterated greed," said Mr.
Ernest Buckmaster, Massachusetts Attorney
General.

The homes of the three accused were raided
late Friday evening by members of a special
task force seeking to take them into police
custody as well as to seize vital documents
supporting the claims declared by the
various state and federal authorities.

"We had felt for some time that all was not
well with some of the land deals taking
place in New Richmond – particularly those
around the waterfront, but never in our
wildest dreams would we have believed that
any one of these women could have been
involved in such heinous criminal
activity," said Forrest Burgess, President
of the New Richmond Waterfront
Redevelopment Committee.

While investigators are loathe to say
exactly how the trio's treacherous plans
came unstuck, there were apparently a
series of events that eventually led to
their downfall, including forged signatures
used to illegally purchase parts of the
Menashocutts Land Claim which adjoins Lake
Menchogawogchegungamog.

"There is no room in our society for the
scurrilous actions carried out by this
culpable cabal. We will be going after them
on a series of serious counts at both the
state and federal levels and if successful,
would suggest that their families not

include them in any Christmas celebrations
until well into the 21st century," Mr.
Wright concluded.

And here is the text from the sidebar:

Illegal Indian Land Claims Priceless Prize

In a somewhat bizarre twist, the undoing of
this highly decorated trio has led to the
archaeological find of the century – the
New England equivalent to the discovery of
King Tut's Tomb.

Indeed, authorities said that in New
Richmond, few alarm bells went off until
irregularities began to emerge in the
supposed purchase of lands set aside for
the Menashocutts by a local farmer. In this
case, the farmer, who it now turns out was
the former father-in-law of Mrs. Elizabeth
Quincy Adams Winslow Bedrosian, believed
she was merely paying back outstanding
state tax bills on his behalf. In fact, the
shelf company that Mrs. Winslow-Bedrosian
had set up with her two cohorts – Inkota
Inc., had in fact paid back one outstanding
tax bill, but then claimed to purchase
hundreds of acres of adjoining land on the
farmer's behalf which it turns out belonged
to the Menashocutts.

Such purchases were deemed null and void by
the Nonintercourse Act of 1790 which had
been set up by the then federal government
to prevent any more Manhattan Island land
swindles in which 'naïve' Indian tribes
were led to believe that their parcels were
worth the whopping great sum of a few
pieces of chump change and a couple of
beads.

This particular land purchase in Richmond
Heights which backs onto 'The Big Puddle',
never received the appropriate federal
clearance, but went largely unnoticed until
two men on the Mayor's payroll were

recently involved in a bizarre car chase incident.

The men, whose names were being withheld pending further court action, were brought down by a particularly rambunctious ram and Richmond Heights' only constable following a wild car chase through many parts of the quiet township. The two men were allegedly tailing this reporter though it's still unclear why.

During the course of their lock-up, however, the two men provided authorities with details surrounding a series of other highly unusual recent land deals involving the three women, in particular, the ones involving the Menachocutts land bordering New Richmond and Richmond Heights. These purchases, it seems, were part of a grand plan to build a huge 'Las Vegas-like' casino complex in the adjoining woods while other gamblers gorged themselves on plates of sumptuous salmon pates, Maine lobsters and other seafood delicacies, aboard a reproduction Mississippi paddlewheeler on 'The Big Puddle' to be called the Inkota Princess.

"We thought the case ended when we turned over the forged checks allegedly signed by my grandfather to federal authorities," said Torkum Bedrosian II. "In fact, it led to the discovery in my grandfather's cellar of a pile of rotten timbers which it now turns out were part of the palisades surrounding the original Fort New Richmond."

This discovery, according to local archaeological Professor Bryan Harvey, proved providential as experts had believed for years that there may have been an earlier fort than the one found on the current site of the Almshouse, but were unable to prove it.

"This discovery, however, was trumped a day
later when Mr. Bedrosian's dog showed up
with a large femur bone that we believe
belonged to the greatest warrior in Western
Massachusetts history – Chief Wachuquin –
who united the will and spirit of several
neighboring tribes against the encroachment
of European settlers in the 1760s-1770s
until his untimely death at the hands of a
little known soldier," Prof. Harvey
explained.

"While still early days, we believe this
site will become a shrine to the life and
times of life on the wild western frontier
in the eighteenth century," he concluded.

❧

You're probably wondering how these two stories ever got printed. How could the Publisher, one of the so-called 'Three Faces of Evil', ever have allowed this story to disgrace the front page of her family's newspaper? Quite simple, really. You remember the discussion that Lou Cassals and I had had some time back about how either the Publisher or her son Marty needed to sign off the front page before it could go to print?

On most nights prior to publication, all copy had been submitted, edited and fitted to its rightful page by 8.30 p.m. That gave the typesetters and print guys a couple of hours to convert the raw material, photos, advertisements, etc., and set up the metallic plates for final sign off by the senior member of the James gang by 11 p.m. We also knew that while the Publisher herself generally took charge earlier in the week, it inevitably fell to her feeble son and heir to the evil throne to check the front page on Friday evenings. We also knew that following this 'final' sign-off, Marty liked to head across the street to the bar for a quiet ale. If any late-breaking story worthy of bumping the proposed Page One article came along, Lou was to contact Marty at the bar and get his okay before making the switch. Lou sort of followed the protocol last night. Knowing Marty's routine, we made sure our Aussie mate Ian was well ensconced at the bar and getting everyone, (including Marty) in some roaring singalongs so loud that when Lou made the phone call to get

Marty's okay, he was unable to hear anything other than our dear mate Ian singing '*Born to be Wild*' like it had never been sung before.

All I had to do was make sure that Story Number Two kept to the same word count – give or take a line or three so it would fit the available space. This took a bit of skill and a shit load of luck because now that we had computers, I could not take the chance that someone might find early drafts of the 'Three Faces' article on the system. This meant that I had to memorize my story and then 'transcribe' it as quickly as I could once Marty had left the building for the night. Not more than 45 minutes later, – I submitted the 'Three Faces' article to Lou who had no option but to stop the presses, which the print crew dutifully did and allowed us to place the new story over the old one.

To say the story caused a stir the next day was putting it mildly. Lou and I had decided to show up at the newspaper early the next day and see how management was reacting to the breaking news story.

I can recall Marty saying something about 'breaking', but it had more to do with certain bodily parts on both of our bodies rather than on any news story. Apparently Mrs. Wheeler-James was none too pleased either, but she was unable to drop by having been picked up for questioning, along with her two cohorts earlier in the morning. The investigators must have thought they'd struck pay-dirt when they realized the three women all lived next door to one another on the town's richest stretch of paved road!

By the time we left the building to the deafening applause of our colleagues, however, an equally boisterous scrum of people had gathered out front of the newspaper. It was comprised of reporters, both print and electronic varieties, and a number of townspeople, including Forrest Burgess, who seemed more interested in making sure the TV crews got footage of his restaurant.

While the management of New Richmond's only newspaper may have hated us, along with a defrocked Lady Mayoress and the world's poorest excuse for a mother, all was not bad for the latest members of the local rag to be thrown literally 'Off The Record'. People were screaming our praises from the streets, sidewalks and second-story windows. We were not unlike all-conquering heroes who either had just won the Great

War or returned from the first walk on the moon. We were now legends, not only among our immediate colleagues, but among the thousands of scribes who eke out a living across this vast nation with little or no say as to what truly goes into their articles. There were other supporters, too. Particularly those in the food and accommodation trade, because once again, New Richmond was on the map – albeit for all the wrong reasons - attracting people from near and far who required feeding, watering and recreation, though not necessarily in that order.

Yes, we could get as many free beers as we wanted. Free beers. How ironic. Because as members of the country's illustrious Fourth Estate, we'd been bathed in the belief that journalists were the bastions of Freedom of the Press. We were supposedly blessed with the ability to write without fear; without worry from any force seeking to blunt the truth. Alas, freedom of the press was never any freer than it had just been for us. Nor was it ever more quickly squashed than it was for us. But then again, how many reporters were able to claim that they got their own paper to uncover a vicious plot featuring their own boss and their own mother all in the same story?!

We knew it would be our last hurrah, but what a way to go. Lou hung around for a few days, spending most of them at the 'Final Edition' being toasted from near and far. He gave some of the best 'exclusive' interviews I've ever witnessed, though being called a two-bit pisspot by some sore loser from '*The Boston Globe*' seemed a bit harsh. He left by week's end for a job with Hugh Jackson at some fledgling weekly in a god-forsaken town along the Ohio River in southern Indiana. I know not where it was nor cared to find out. It's doubtful that Lewis and Clark could have found it. Hell, I doubt Lois and Clark Kent could have found it even with the aide of x-ray vision. But it didn't really matter. Lou Cassals was now immortal. For as long as black ink still flows through the veins of wannabe writers and reporters, there will always be one more rendition over a quiet ale or three for him to regale any and all who cared to listen about the night he set the truth free in a tiny New England town that gave it a chance for a new beginning.

Where Lou saw three colors – black and white – my kaleidoscope was still well and truly stuck on so many shades of gray. There were still so many questions; so many issues to sort out. About the only question that was easy to answer was why I didn't feel sorry for my mother's part in this sordid affair. Because she never ever felt sorry for anyone but herself. Still, I didn't feel good for having done it. She just happened to be in the way. I was still far from 'going home' – once and for all, though. Where to begin?

My first phone call was to 'Rabid' Rabinelle at Channel 9 in Worcester to tell her I had the classic follow-up to the 'Three Faces of Evil' piece. She was bullshit when she saw my story, because she knew that the good Lady Mayoress and the others had used her like a cheap streetwalker.

I assured her that that was not the case, but that if it made her feel any better, I was quite happy to feel her up. After picking myself up from the hardest left cross ever to travel down a telephone wire, I likewise assured her that there was still more, a lot more to this story - not the least of which was watching the venom spitting from the gob of Aunt Stacey's husband, the once high and mighty Wall Street lion himself - Jonathan Morgan - the very next morning when he faced the media pack outside of city hall.

"The charges claimed in this ridiculous news story are just that – ridiculous – and we will be answering each and every claim brought by any jurisdiction – state or federal," said the one-timed silvery-tongued devil who just for effect, took a copy of the paper with 'that' story on the front page, threw it to the ground and stepped on it.

"Do you represent the interests of all three women," several reporters asked simultaneously.

"I do and I will," he replied.

"What have you to say about the claim of illegally purchasing land from the Menashocutts reserve?"

"Nothing for now. All will be revealed in due course," said the guy who in his prime, would have had everyone wondering not only why any charges had been laid against his clients, but at the same time getting every viewer in TV land to confess to every petty crime they'd committed in their tiny, sordid little lives. Yes, he was really something, but not anymore. Where once his well-planned piece of theatre involving throwing the newspaper to the ground and grinding it into the pavement would have left onlookers breathless and baying for blood, it now looked tired and rather sad. The effects of all too many bottles of bourbon and god knows what other spirits had soaked the life out of him to the point where he could no longer control his own movements. Indeed, the copy of the newspaper which he held aloft was supposed to drop straight down in front of his right foot. Instead, it ended up a good two feet to the right so that when he went to step on it, he seemed to trip over a crack in the sidewalk. He looked to see if anyone had noticed this pathetic performance. I'm not sure what his gin-rummy, watery eyes beheld, but everyone within a mile of the media throng took note. It was now time for him to move on, but where once he would have parted that media scrum in Moses-like fashion, the journalists actually walked away before his ill-conceived newspaper stomping stunt had even finished. The limelight had long since past 'flickering' on the once invincible force known as Jonathan Morgan.

I watched this pitiable performance from the relative quiet of a park bench across the street from City Hall with MaryElena Rabinelle. "I hope that isn't the story you were talking about?" MaryElena said pointing toward the sad hulk of a human. "I'm hoping to move to Providence soon and it ain't gonna happen interviewing that drunken bum."

"Hey, have I ever let you down? Besides, why don't you put a little more pressure on me? Here I am unemployed and you're pumping me to get you up the next rung on the TV news ladder. Have a heart," I said.

"So what do we do?" she said obviously ignoring my plight.

"There's not much more to be reported on the law case. That'll be tied up in the courts for a while. The key now is the archaeological discoveries and how that will impact on the proposed new highway linking Western Massachusetts to New York State as well as to a very relieved old man," I said.

"C'mon Walt. You know I'm no good with soft, cuddly stuff. I like it hard and raw," she said before realizing how some guys may have taken these words in another meaning. "Don't even think about going there!" she added.

"Hey, believe me, my streetcar named desire left the station years ago. No, you'll see. It's a winner that should get you well beyond Providence," I said.

"Really?"

"Really. Should be good for Pittsfield or even Poughkeepsie," I replied.

I sensed another left hook coming and ducked beautifully instead into a solid right cross.

"You ever get tired of the news game, you should go into boxing. You got a future there, no doubt about it," I said checking to see if I had any enamel left on my front teeth.

"Where do we start?"

"In Richmond Heights."

"Where?"

"It's a little village just northeast of here."

"What's there?"

"A pile of splinters and a bone," I said. "And one helluva nice young guy that you are going to love."

"Do you want me to hit you again?"

"Not particularly. You obviously didn't see the other story in today's paper. It's just below the fold."

"You're giving me old news again?" she asked grabbing the paper and speed reading through the second story. "Is this the guy – Torkum Bedridden?"

"Yeah, that's the guy. You're gonna thank me when you meet him. Trust me. You will dine out on this one for the rest of your life!"

And with that we moved the moveable feast to Richmond Heights.

"So where's this great guy you've been telling me about?" said Rabid Rabinelle even before the car had stopped outside the farmhouse.

"All in good time," I said, bending over to greet my trusty four-legged friend who came bounding from the back of the house the minute the car door opened. There was no one else in sight, though there were plenty of people working somewhere. Christ, it looked as though Prof. Harvey had enlisted the better part of New England to help out on this most momentous dig.

"Where is everyone?" Rabid asked.

"Relax, will ya. What're you, on deadline?"

"Easy for you to say. You're unemployed," she replied with just a hint of a smile.

Just then The Chief appeared in the doorway, complete with deerskin jacket and full headdress.

"What's he doing here?" she asked.

"All will be revealed. All will be revealed," I said. "G'day Chief, where is everyone?"

The Chief slowly shuffled toward us; his head bowed as if the feathers in his Native headgear were each carved from stone. He was humming something. I prayed to god it wasn't some Springsteen tune, figuring that would've been a bit too much even for someone as hard core as the Rabid one.

Grandfather was next to appear in the doorway. Flynn ran over as if instinctively knowing the old man would need a guide to get him over to us. "Who's there?" he called.

"It's me grandpa – Torkum," I said turning MaryElena for whom the penny had finally dropped.

"I should've known," she said.

"Yep, that's moi – Torkum The Bedridden The Second," I said.

"You're really something, Walt, er, Torkum, oh whatever your name is," she said at which point the Chief fell to his knees and began chanting for all he was worth.

"Relax, Chief. You'll ruin your deerskin if you keep kneeling before me," I said.

"What's his problem?" MaryElena asked.

"He worships me. Can't you see that? And why wouldn't he?"

"Yeah, too bad it only works on old men, eh?" she replied.

"Just need to tinker with my cologne. Before you know it, the babes will be flocking here!"

And with that, the front door swung open again and out popped the babe least likely to flock to any man – particularly this one in particular.

"Hello, son. We need to talk."

"Hey, Mom, how good of you to come. What, didn't you like the prison food?"

"You mean to tell me that she's your mother?" MaryElena asked.

"Well, I'm not sure she'll admit to it, but apparently the DNA doesn't lie," I replied.

"I like this story," MaryElena said motioning to her trusty cameraman.

"No, no. This isn't the story. Trust me! This is nothing. Really!" I said.

"Nothing, my ass. Boy writes story about Mother. Mother, Publisher and Mayor go to jail. Do not pass Go. That's a story!" she replied.

"No, trust me. That isn't the story, dear," my mother cut in.

"Walter here has surely got a good one for you, though. A real winner. I couldn't be prouder of him, either," she said in a tone of voice I didn't think possible spouting from the lips of a She-Devil.

"I, I don't know what to say," I said.

"Then shut up and listen for once," my mother began. "I'm going to make this simple."

"What?" I asked.

"What this was really all about. The Chief, the farm, the wooden fence bits, everything. But don't take it from me. Take it from the source – Mr. Marsden," she said, handing me back the one and only copy of nearly everything ever written by the town's most notable nobody.

"For the record, Walter. I was only trying to protect you. Believe it or not. Because once you finally understand – you'll see that whatever happens to me, Eustace and Connie, will pale in comparison to what awaits you," she said while The Chief continued his moaning at my feet.

"Goodbye, Walter. Do keep in touch. I'm sure you'll know where to find me for the next few years," my mother said, but not before leaning over and kissing my cheek – a gesture I hadn't received from her – ever - as far as I could remember. And then, as if on cue, a taxi cab steamed down the dirt road and stopped in front of the house. My mother got in the back seat, shut the door and motioned the driver to move on. She was gone.

"Wow, that was some goodbye," MaryElena said. "Whatever did she mean?"

"No idea," I said. "No fucking idea."

Chapter Forty Six

"Walter, I think you better get down here," said Prof. Harvey bursting out of the front door.

"Not now, Professor. Why don't you take Ms. Rabinelle with you?"

MaryElena responded by giving me the coldest of stares.

"Trust me. You're gonna love what's been going on in the cellar," I said.

"I better and I'm not doing any digging," she replied.

With that the Professor, the reporter and her intrepid film crew were away, fighting their way around a cow or two carefully stationed outside the front door.

I gently rolled The Chief over onto his back and headed for the house to find a quiet spot to curl up and find out just what the heck this book held in store for me. I didn't have to wait long as the book seemed to magically open to the most important bit – at least regarding how it affected me. Before I could get to the scribbling from the town's most infamous scribe, a small piece of legal-pad yellow paper fell out. It was a note from my mother. She said that she had not been trying to steal the book. Rather, to locate it so she could put back a "few pages which would finally shed some light on things." It was classic 'Mom' in that it promised so much, yet delivered so little. I placed her note aside and began reading:

> *Oh woe is me. How derelict I have been in my natural duty to seek the truth…Alas, I spent all too many years of my wretched existence in search of fame and fortune at the expense of what truly matters – the truth!*

> *As I lay here with some unknown illness, unable to rise from my bed for more than a few moments without gasping for breath – I shall relate that which I have should have revealed many years ago when first I learned of it. I cannot say what possessed me to*

withhold these truths. Concern for another? No, not all. Pure fear of being exposed as a charlatan; a fraud would be closer to the truth.

The matter in question involved one of New Richmond's most revered figures – Abigail Adams Winslow, the only surviving daughter of one of the town's most notable – and wealthiest scions – Josiah Cotton Winslow.

I had dined many a night at their home, imbibing only the finest wines and spirits and gorging on the district's finest cuts of beef, deer and other delicacies. Was it for these tasty morsels that I turned my back on the truth? She summoned me to her bedside, as death drew near. She had no known relatives and for the life of me, could not imagine why she turned to me. It was, it would seem, that in my role as purveyor of the 'truth', that I might set her free by relaying her own secrets before she left this earthly plane, but I chose instead to conveniently forget what she said for fear of upsetting all that the town had stood for. Whatever that was.

It seemed that long before the current year of our lord, when Miss Adams was not more than 12 or 13, she, along with many other women and children, were kidnapped by Chief Wachuquin, the leader of the once powerful Menashocutts. For weeks, then months, they were given shelter and care from the savages, who cunningly always remained one step ahead of the 'white men's forces'.

At long last, the Indians were cornered and we were saved, though some of us, and me in particular, preferred our life among the red man where we were treated with kindness and respect, and yes, in my case, with love from the only man I ever cared for…

Cutting to the chase, it would seem that the 'spinster' had become pregnant to The Chief and was well and truly showing in the family way when her father and the posse caught up with the renegade Indian tribe. The young Winslow woman was immediately dispatched to Boston to live with relatives until the birth of her child, a boy, who she would never see again.

She did not return to New Richmond for several years and when she did, it was only to find that her father had executed The Chief and his remaining warriors without any concern for the law or legal proceeding. The killings were deemed to be 'god's will' and the Indians were buried in a mass pit near the front fence of the town's first fort.

The poor woman never recovered from these events and spent the rest of her life roaming the nearby forests and caring for whatever Indians she could, hoping beyond hope, that The Chief may not have been killed.

While she never found him again, she did make one interesting discovery – that the claims of her forefathers that they were direct descendants of the Mayflower Winslow clan were 'hollower than any carved out log'.

> *"My father had in fact left New Richmond early on because of some improper land dealings and re-invented himself while stationed near Boston. It was here where he learned of the Winslows and in so doing, changed his name from 'Winston' to "Winslow" so as to gain greater respect from the community."*

Holy shit. This was hotter than hot. No wonder my mother was such a mess. Even though the truth had been known for more than 100 years, it became buried again, deeper than the secrets of King Tut himself. But that was not the end of the discoveries pour moi. There was yet one last tit-bit of information that even Mr. Marsden could not have imagined how much it would mean to one person perusing it lo these many years later.

> *It seemed that for years, local settlers had interpreted the great warrior Wachuquin's name as meaning – "One Voice," as in, he the man who speaks for us all. Miss Winslow told me that this translation was not right. That in fact, the Chief had a most unfortunate defect that apparently happened at birth. He was born with only one ear which his people saw as a sign from above. This apparent loss was in fact a gift – a sign that he would hear only One Voice – that of the 'Greatest Spirit in the Sky'.*

The book fell suddenly to the floor. I didn't know what stunned me more. The fact that I was most likely the natural successor to the area's most powerful Indian warrior or the fact that I was related to both himself and his killer!

"WELCOME HOME, MY SON. I AM NOW AT PEACE – AT LAST!" came a voice that sounded very much like, St. Vartan, only without the static. The penny finally dropped. My occasional cerebral visitations hadn't been from a 1,500-year-old warrior, but from a 150-year-old model, who just wanted to go home with his ancestors.

"Hey, Walt. Where ya been? You weren't kidding, this is a great story," said MaryElena bursting into the living room where I was now totally spaced out.

"Huh?"

"Walter – the story. It's a winner! It just doesn't get any better than this," she said. "I got an old man whose house was set for demolition to build a new highway now being saved because it contained the earliest remnants of both the area's first European settlers and to the remains of its last great Chief," MaryElena beamed. "Tell me it doesn't get any better than this?"

"No, it certainly doesn't," I replied.

EPILOGUE

Call Me Walt. Or call me Torkum. Or, if you really want to get cute – call me Wachuquin The Last.

I swim in a very congested gene pool that seems even murkier now than ever before. I used to think I was related to one of this country's deepest bluebloods, but that seems to have been blown to bits. I may still be related to a couple of ex Presidents, but for now it seems more likely that I'm related to a one-eared Warrior Chief and to the mongrel of a man who gunned him down.

It doesn't get any better than that. Or does it? If I've learned anything from these last few months, it's simply this – people who make history are by and large past tense. Many of them are like the pictures on my dear old uncle's baseball cards, rarely more than two-dimensional, most certainly a little faded and well past their best condition.

There are exceptions to the rule – like a pristine 1951 rookie baseball card of Mickey Mantle by Bowman or a mint condition 1933 Babe Ruth printed by Goudey, but hey, apart from my dearly departed Uncle J.R., how many of us have a pile of them lying around?

The moral of this story is it's better to get to know the ones right under your nose. The ones who let you kick their tires, smell the whiskey on their breath and fill your heart with immortal thoughts like Hugh Jackson's call to me to 'Lead with the Cats' that shine the brightest. Hell, how lucky am I to claim in my pantheon of pantheons the following trio: An uncle who never knew how to not live life to the full; a crass crank of an editor who could take ordinary bits of information and spin them into pure gold; and a simple, short-sighted old man who had more understanding of the possibilities that a New World could deliver than all of the Mayflower's 102 passengers and their descendants combined.

Yes, gene pools can be confusing. For years, I'd thought my father's father was a killer. In fact, this was not the case. You see, not long after MaryElena left the farm that day and came out with her blockbuster story regarding the State's attempts to take away my granddad's property, my father returned with about $31,000 in cash from the proceeds of the sales of most of Uncle J.R.'s baseball card collection. It allowed us to pay back the outstanding taxes and left us enough to throw one helluva party.

The party featured many of my friends from the newspaper as well as relatives, including the two old farts who told me my grandfather had been a murderer those many years before.

"A murderer? Sarkis? No way," said the first old fart, before the second one began laughing so loud I thought he would break the glass in the windows.

"What's so fucking funny?"

"Whoever told you that Sarkis was a killer?" they asked me in unison.

"You did."

"Never, my boy," they replied. "You must have misunderstood us. The only thing we told you was how he had to leave the village out of shame because he could not even kill a goat. He was too nice even to kill a fly," they said.

"You mean all these years I thought he was a killer and he wasn't?"

"Wasn't what?" called out my father who now joined our little chat.

"Did you know about this?"

"What?" Dad asked.

"That granddad was not a killer?"

"Grandad? My father, a killer? I never thought that," Dad began. "Why did you?"

"Forget it, Pop. Let's get pissed," I said.

So that's the thing about gene pools. They're rarely smooth and calm. Rather, they're filled with troublesome bubbles and choppy swells designed to ruffle even the most unruffable soul. Take me, for instance. I not only didn't know which one of my relatives was not a killer, but that in one last quirk of fate, it was only through uncovering a long-lost murder that I discovered my own bizarre birthright.

It'll take a while for things to settle down. My mother and her two co-defendants are still awaiting trial, but the odds are they will be sent away for quite a while. My Dad has now happily traded in his HoJo mojo for a crack at a new life in Boston with his latest lady love – and it isn't Marrsha Brady. You guessed it – he's taken up with Mrs. Veronica Lincoln-Quaid. I know not what hold this rather rotund, balding short-order chef has on highly-cultured dames, but good luck to him.

I'm still trying to have one more chance with Jenny Lawton, but so far she's keeping her distance. That's okay. I'm in no hurry. In fact, I'm kind of glad I have some time to myself. Time to sort through all the rubble of the last few months, take stock and set a new course.

Then again, perhaps I could take a shot at Marrsha Brady or even MaryElena 'Rabid' Rabinelle. Better yet, why mess around with the amateurs when if I play my cards right, I could plan conjugal visits with the ex-Mayor of New Richmond!

The Chief, of course, has other ideas. He says I've now finally been given the sign and must stand up and take control of "my people," before quickly adding: "You must take heed of the True Spirit."

"I know - The Boss, right?" I ask.

"Right you are, my son! Right you are. We are born to run!" he says, breaking into a grin that was wider than the Mississippi.

As for 'The Record' well, not much changed there. Despite claims by some of my colleagues that it would shake, rattle and roll off this mortal coil, it in fact did no such thing. It did what any self-unsuspecting rag does when it takes a direct hit. It dusts itself off and lives to fight another day. And why? Because it's not a newsmaker. No, if anything it's a muckraker that feeds off the highs and lows of others and then shares them with a few thousand of their best friends. Within a few days, it was back to its best – and worst – making a meal out of any morsel with even the slightest sliver of grist for the non-stop rumor mills. Hell, Marty may one day give me a call and ask me to come back. And possibly, just possibly, I just might take him up on it.

For now though, I had ideas of starting my own story. Writing a book about my own history – for better or worse. I know not how it ends, but I damn well know how it begins:

"My father's father was not a murderer…"

About the author

Although trained as an anthropologist in his native New England, Mark Kestigian soon turned in his trusty trowel for a pen and paper and spent many years as a reporter for newspapers in Ohio and New England. He later became an occasional correspondent for *The New York Times* in bore-torn southeastern Connecticut in the early 1980s.

Since moving to Australia, Mark has published articles on topics ranging from technology and travel to eco-friendly urban developments, as well as co-writing two guidebooks on Australia for New York publishers.

In his spare time Mark enjoys pottering around in the backyard, playing the occasional round of golf and following the Carlton Blues. He's also a TV quiz show champion, but his proudest achievement is having a pet ox while growing up.

Mark lives in the Dandenong Ranges, about an hour's drive from Melbourne, with his wife Karen and their four-legged 'children' – Duke Ellington and Princess Tara.